THE MAMMOTH BOOK OF MORE

Historical Whodunnits

THE MAMMOTH BOOK OF MORE

Historical Whodunnits

Edited by Mike Ashley

CARROLL & GRAF PUBLISHERS
New York

Carroll and Graf Publishers
An imprint of Avalon Publishing Group, Inc.
161 William Street
16th Floor
New York
NY 10038–2607
www.carrollandgraf.com

First published in the UK by Robinson,
an imprint of Constable & Robinson Ltd 2001

First Carroll & Graf edition 2001

Reprinted 2001

ISBN 0–7867–0916–2

Printed and bound in the EU

Contents

Copyright and Acknowledgements

Cherith Baldry for "The Pilgrim's Tale"; Richard Butler and the Dorian Literary Agency for "The Last Legion"; Mat Coward for "And What Can They Show, or What Reasons Give?"; Carol Anne Davis for "On Wings of Love"; Jean Davidson and the Dorian Literary Agency for "A Lion Rampant"; Kate Ellis and A.M. Heath & Co. Ltd for "The Isle of Saints"; Paul Finch for "Flibbertigibbet"; Gail Frazer for "Heretical Murder"; Peter T. Garratt for "The Vasty Deep"; Philip Gooden for "King Hereafter"; Susanna Gregory and A.M. Heath & Co. Ltd for "The Death Toll"; Claire Griffen for "House of the Moon"; Edward D. Hoch for "A Moon for Columbus"; Michael Jecks for "The Amorous Armourer"; Michael Kurland for "Blind Justice"; Mary Reed and Eric Mayer for "And All That He Calls Family"; Rosemary Rowe and the Dorian Literary Agency for "A Payment to the Gods"; Keith Taylor for "Benefit of Clergy"; Marilyn Todd for "A Taste for Burning"; Peter Tremayne and A.M. Heath & Co. Ltd for "Death of an Icon"; Derek Wilson for "A Perfect Crime". "Poppy and the Poisoned Cake" © 1998 by Steven Saylor, first published in *Ellery Queen's Mystery Magazine*, December 1998, reprinted by permission of the author.

Introduction

Past Crimes

In the last ten to fifteen years the field of the historical mystery has grown from a small seed to a flourishing forest. It's wonderful to see a new genre establish itself like this in such a relatively short time. In my previous two anthologies in this series, the first volume of *The Mammoth Book of Historical Whodunits* and its companion *The Mammoth Book of Historical Detectives*, I put together a diverse selection of stories showing the type of material that had been written over the years, to show the pedigree of this field.

For this latest book, I have chosen to present all new material. Only one of the stories has previously appeared in print, and that in a magazine. None of these stories has been published in book form before, and all but one was written especially for this anthology.

The emphasis in this volume is on stories set in Roman and Celtic times and the Middle Ages. Stories span sixteen centuries from ancient Rome to the days of James I of England. In between you will encounter the last Roman crime in Britain, the days of the saints, Macbeth, the Crusades and the Knights Templar, Chaucer, the Peasant's Revolt, Columbus and even an Elizabethan serial killer.

The collection includes old friends and new. Steven Saylor, one of the new superstars of the genre, presents another adventure of Gordianus the Finder. Peter Tremayne provides another mystery for Sister Fidelma, whilst Mary Reed and Eric Mayer test the skills of John the Eunuch once again. All three of these detectives were with us in the first volume of *Historical Whodunnits* eight years ago. So too were the authors Margaret Frazer and Edward D. Hoch, who are here again. Joining them are a coterie of new authors who have established themselves in the historical mystery field in the intervening years, amongst them Rosemary Rowe, Michael Jecks, Susanna Gregory, Philip Gooden and Marilyn Todd.

In that first volume Ellis Peters said that the secret of the successful historical detective story was the ability to include a human and likeable detective in a background that is as real to today's readers as it was to those who lived in those times. In this volume I've brought together a wide range of detectives and investigators, not all of them likeable, but all of them living in real worlds and facing problems of their age. The way they tackle the crime and try to solve the mystery is what brings that past alive and allows us a tantalizing glimpse of distant ages. That in turn allows us to compare it with the modern world – and may be then wonder which is best.

Mike Ashley
April 2001

poppy and the poisoned Cake

Steven Saylor

*Steven Saylor (b. 1956) has become internationally es-
tablished for his Roma Sub Rosa series of mystery novels
set in the final days of the Roman Republic and featuring
Gordianus the Finder. The series runs Roman Blood
(1991), Arms of Nemesis (1992), Catilina's Riddle
(1994), The Venus Throw (1995), A Murder on the
Appian Way (1996), Rubicon (1999) and Last Seen in
Massilia (2000) plus a short story collection, The House
of the Vestals (1997). I have included previous Gordianus
stories in The Mammoth Book of Historical Detectives
and Classical Whodunnits and I'm delighted to start this
anthology with a new story, not previously published in
book form.*

"Young Cicero tells me that you can be discreet. Is that
true, Gordianus? Can you keep a confidence?"

Considering that the question was being put to me by the
magistrate in charge of maintaining Roman morals, I
weighed my answer carefully. "If Rome's finest orator says
a thing, who am I to contradict him?"

The censor snorted. "Your friend Cicero said you were
clever, too. Answer a question with a question, will you? I
suppose you picked that up from listening to him defend
thieves and murderers in the law courts."

Cicero was my occasional employer, but I had never
counted him as a friend, exactly. Would it be indiscreet to

say as much to the censor? I kept my mouth shut and nodded vaguely.

Lucius Gellius Poplicola – Poppy to his friends, as I would later find out – looked to be a robust seventy or so. In an age wracked by civil war, political assassinations, and slave rebellions, to reach such a rare and venerable age was proof of Fortune's favor. But Fortune must have stopped smiling on Poplicola – else why summon Gordianus the Finder?

The room in which we sat, in Poplicola's house on the Palatine Hill, was sparsely appointed, but the few furnishings were of the highest quality. The rug was Greek, with a simple geometric design in blue and yellow. The antique chairs and the matching tripod table were of ebony with silver hinges. The heavy drapery drawn over the doorway for privacy was of some plush green fabric shot through with golden threads. The walls were stained a somber red. The iron lamp in the middle of the room stood on three griffin's feet and breathed steady flames from three gaping griffin mouths. By its light, while waiting for Poplicola, I had perused the little yellow tags that dangled from the scrolls which filled the pigeonhole bookcase in the corner. The censor's library consisted entirely of serious works by philosophers and historians, without a lurid poet or frivolous playwright among them. Everything about the room bespoke a man of impeccable taste and high standards – just the sort of fellow whom public opinion would deem worthy of wearing the purple toga, a man qualified to keep the sacred rolls of citizenship and pass judgment on the moral conduct of senators.

"It was Cicero who recommended me, then?" In the ten years since I had met him, Cicero had sent quite a bit of business my way.

Poplicola nodded. "I told him I needed an agent to investigate . . . a private matter. A man from outside my own household, and yet someone I could rely upon to be thorough, truthful, and absolutely discreet. He seemed to think that you would do."

"I'm honored that Cicero would recommend me to a man of your exalted position and –"

"Discretion!" he insisted, cutting me off. "That matters most of all. Everything you discover while in my employ – *everything* – must be held in the strictest confidence. You will reveal your discoveries to me and to no one else."

From beneath his wrinkled brow he peered at me with an intensity that was unsettling. I nodded and said slowly, "So long as such discretion does not conflict with more sacred obligations to the gods, then yes, Censor, I promise you my absolute discretion."

"Upon your honour as a Roman? Upon the shades of your ancestors?"

I sighed. Why must these nobles always take themselves and their problems so seriously? Why must every transaction require the invocation of dead relatives? Poplicola's earth-shattering dilemma was probably nothing more than an errant wife or a bit of blackmail over a pretty slaveboy. I chafed at his demand for an oath and considered refusing; but the fact was that my daughter Diana had just been born, the household coffers were perilously depleted, and I needed work. I gave him my word, upon my honor and my ancestors.

He produced something from the folds of his purple toga and placed it on the little table between us. I saw it was a small silver bowl, and in the bowl there appeared to be a delicacy of some sort. I caught a whiff of almonds.

"What do you make of that?" he said.

"It appears to be a sweet cake," I ventured. I picked up the little bowl and sniffed. Almonds, yes; and something else . . .

"By Hercules, don't eat any of it!" He snatched the bowl from me. "I have reason to believe it's been poisoned." Poplicola shuddered. He suddenly looked much older.

"Poisoned?"

"The slave who brought me the cake this afternoon, here in my study – one of my oldest slaves, more than a servant, a companion really – well, the fellow always had a sweet tooth . . . like his master, that way. If he shaved off a bit of my delicacies every now and then, thinking I wouldn't notice, where was the harm in that? It was a bit of a game between us. I used to tease him; I'd say, 'The only thing that keeps me from growing fat is the fact that you serve my food!' Poor Chrestus . . .'' His face became ashen.

"I see. This Chrestus brought you the cake. And then?"

"I dismissed Chrestus and put the bowl aside while I finished reading a document. I came to the end, rolled up the scroll, and put it aside. I was just about to take a bite of the cake when another slave, my doorkeeper, ran into the room, terribly alarmed. He said that Chrestus was having a seizure. I went to him as quickly as I could. He was lying on the floor, convulsing. 'The cake!' he said. 'The cake!' And then he was dead. As quickly as that! The look on his face – horrible!''

Poplicola gazed at the little cake and curled his lip, as if an adder were coiled in the silver bowl. "My favourite,'' he said in a hollow voice. "Cinnamon and almonds, sweetened with honey and wine, with just a hint of aniseed. An old man's pleasure, one of the few I have left. Now I shall never be able to eat it again!''

And neither shall Chrestus, I thought. "Where did the cake come from?"

"There's a little alley just north of the Forum, with bakery shops on either side.''

"I know the street.''

"The place on the corner makes these cakes every other day. I have a standing order – a little treat I give myself. Chrestus goes down to fetch one for me, and I have it in the early afternoon.''

"And was it Chrestus who fetched the cake for you to-day?"

For a long moment he stared silently at the cake. "No.''

"Who, then?''

He hunched his thin shoulders up and pursed his lips. "My son, Lucius. He came by this afternoon. So the door-keeper tells me; I didn't see him myself. Lucius told the doorkeeper not to disturb me, that he couldn't stay; he'd only stopped by to drop off a sweet cake for me. Lucius knows of my habit of indulging in this particular sweet, you see, and some business in the Forum took him by the street of the bakers, and as my house was on his way to another errand, he brought me a cake. The doorkeeper fetched Chrestus, Lucius gave Chrestus the sweet cake wrapped up in a bit of parchment, and then Lucius left. A little later, Chrestus brought the cake to me . . ."

Now I understood why Poplicola had demanded an oath upon my ancestors. The matter was delicate indeed. "Do you suspect your son of tampering with the cake?"

Poplicola shook his head. "I don't know what to think."

"Is there any reason to suspect that he might wish to do you harm?"

"Of course not!" The denial was a little too vehement, a little too quick.

"What is it you want from me, Censor?"

"To find the truth of the matter! They call you Finder, don't they? Find out if the cake is poisoned. Find out who poisoned it. Find out how it came about that my son . . ."

"I understand, Censor. Tell me, who in your household knows of what happened today?"

"Only the doorkeeper."

"No one else?"

"No one. The rest of the household has been told that Chrestus collapsed from a heart attack. I've told no one else of Lucius's visit, or about the cake."

I nodded. "To begin, I shall need to see the dead man, and to question your doorkeeper."

"Of course. And the cake? Shall I feed a bit to some stray cat, to make sure . . ."

"I don't think that will be necessary, Censor." I picked up the little bowl and sniffed at the cake again. Most definitely, blended with the wholesome scent of baked almonds was the sharper odour of the substance called bitter-almond, one of the strongest of all poisons. Only a few drops would suffice to kill a man in minutes. How fiendishly clever, to sprinkle it onto a sweet almond-flavoured confection, from which a hungry man with a sweet tooth might take a bite without noticing the bitter taste until too late.

Poplicola took me to see the body. Chrestus looked to have been fit for his age. His hands were soft; his master had not overworked him. His waxy flesh had a pinkish flush, further evidence that the poison had been bitter-almond.

Poplicola summoned the doorkeeper, whom I questioned in his master's presence. He proved to be a tight-lipped fellow (as doorkeepers should be), and added nothing to what Poplicola had already told me.

Visibly shaken, Poplicola withdrew, with instructions to the doorkeeper to see me out. I was in the foyer, about to leave, when a woman crossed the atrium. She wore an elegant blue stola and her hair was fashionably arranged with combs and pins into a towering configuration that defied logic. Her hair was jet black, except for a narrow streak of white above her left temple that spiraled upward like a ribbon into the convoluted vortex. She glanced at me as she passed but registered no reaction. No doubt the censor received many visitors.

"Is that the censor's daughter?" I asked the doorkeeper.

"No."

I raised an eyebrow, but the tight-lipped slave did not elaborate. "His wife, then?"

"Yes. My mistress Palla."

"A striking woman." In the wake of her passing, a kind of aura seemed to linger in the empty atrium. Hers was a haughty beauty that gave little indication of her age. I suspected she must be older than she looked, but she could hardly have been past forty.

"Is Palla the mother of the censor's son, Lucius?"

"No."

"His stepmother, then?"

"Yes."

"I see." I nodded and took my leave.

I wanted to know more about Poplicola and his household, so that night I paid a visit to my patrician friend Lucius Claudius, who knows everything worth knowing about anyone who counts in the higher circles of Roman society. I intended to be discreet, honoring my oath to the censor, and so, after dinner, relaxing on our couches and sharing more wine, in a roundabout way I got onto the topic of elections and voting, and thence to the subject of census rolls. "I understand the recent census shows something like eight hundred thousand Roman citizens," I noted.

"Indeed!" Lucius Claudius popped his pudgy fingers into his mouth one by one, savoring the grease from the roasted quail. With his other hand he brushed a ringlet of frizzled red hair from his forehead. "If this keeps up, one of these days citizens shall outnumber slaves! The censors really should do something about restricting citizenship."

My friend's politics tend to be conservative; the Claudii are patricians, after all. I nodded thoughtfully. "Who are the censors nowadays, anyway?"

"Lentulus Clodianus . . ." he said, popping a final finger into his mouth, ". . . and old Lucius Gellius Poplicola."

"Poplicola," I murmured innocently. "Now why does that name sound familiar?"

"Really, Gordianus, where is your head? Poplicola was consul two years ago. Surely you recall that bit of unpleasantness with Spartacus? It was Poplicola's job as consul to take the field against the rebel slaves, who gave him a sound whipping – not once, but twice! The disgrace of it, farm slaves led by a rogue gladiator, thrashing trained legionnaires led by a Roman consul! People said it was because Poppy was just too old to lead an army. He's lucky it wasn't the end of his career! But here it is two years later, and Poppy's a censor. It's a big job. But safe – no military commands! Just right for a fellow like Poppy – been around for ever, honest as a stick."

"Just what do the censors do?"

"Census and censure, their two main duties. Keep the roll of voters, assign the voters to tribes, make sure the patrician tribes carry the most weight in the elections – that's the way of it. Well, we can hardly allow those 799,000 common citizens out there to have as much say in electing magistrates as the thousand of us whose families have been running this place since the days of Romulus and Remus; wouldn't make sense. That's the census part."

I nodded. "And censure?"

"The censors don't just say who's a citizen and who's not; they also say what a citizen should be. The privilege of citizenship implies certain moral standards, even in these dissolute days. If the censors put a black mark for immoral

conduct by a man's name in the rolls, it's serious business.
They can expel a fellow from the Senate. In fact . . ." He
leaned forward and lowered his voice to emphasize the
gravity of what he was about to say. "In fact, word has it
that the censors are about to publish a list of *over sixty men*
they're throwing out of the Senate for breach of moral
character – taking bribes, falsifying documents, embezzling.
Sixty! A veritable purge! You can imagine the mood in the
Senate House. Everyone suspicious of everyone else, all of us
wondering who's on the list."

"So Poplicola is not exactly the most popular man in the
Forum these days?"

"To put it mildly. Don't misunderstand, there's plenty of
support for the purge. I support it myself, wholeheartedly.
The Senate needs a thorough housecleaning! But Poppy's
about to make some serious enemies. Which is ironic, because he's always been such a peacemaker." Lucius laughed.
"Back when he was governor of Greece in his younger days,
they say Poppy called together all the bickering philosophers
in Athens and practically pleaded with them to come to some
sort of consensus about the nature of the universe. 'If we
cannot have harmony in the heavens, how can we hope for
anything but discord here on Earth?' " His mimicry of the
censor's reedy voice was uncanny.

"Census and censure," I murmured, sipping my wine. "I
don't suppose ordinary citizens have all that much to fear
from the censors."

"Oh, a black mark from the censor is trouble for any man.
Ties up voting rights, cancels state contracts, revokes li-
censes to keep a shop in the city. That could ruin a man,
drive him into poverty. And if a censor really wants to make
trouble for a fellow, he can call him before a special Senate
committee to investigate charges of immorality. Once that
sort of investigation starts, it never ends – just the idea is
enough to give even an honest man a heart attack! Oh yes, the
censorship is a powerful office. That's why it has to be filled
with men of absolutely irreproachable character, completely
untainted by scandal – like Poppy." Lucius Claudius suddenly frowned and wrinkled his fleshy brow. "Of course,

there's that terrible rumour I heard only this afternoon – so outrageous I dismissed it out of hand. Put it out of my mind so completely that I actually forgot about it until just now . . ."

"Rumour?"

"Probably nothing – a vicious bit of slander put about by one of Poppy's enemies . . ."

"Slander?"

"Oh, some nonsense about Poppy's son, Lucius, trying to poison the old man – using a sweet cake, if you can believe it!" I raised my eyebrows and tried to look surprised. "But these kinds of stories always get started, don't they, when a fellow as old as Poppy marries a woman young enough to be his daughter, and beautiful as well. Palla is her name. She and her stepson Lucius get along well – what of it? People see them out together now and again without Poppy, at a chariot race or a play, laughing and having a good time, and the next thing you know, these nasty rumours get started. Lucius, trying to poison his father so he can marry his stepmother – now that would be a scandal! And I'm sure there are those who'd like to think it's true, who'd love nothing better than to see Poppy pulled down into the muck right along with them."

The attempted poisoning had taken place that afternoon – and yet Lucius Claudius had already heard about it. How could the rumour have spread so swiftly? Who could have started it? Not Poplicola's son, surely, if he were the poisoner. But what if Poplicola's son were innocent of any wrongdoing? What if he had been somehow duped into passing the deadly cake by his father's enemies, who had then gone spreading the tale prematurely . . .

Or might the speed of the rumour have a simpler explanation? It could be that Poplicola's doorkeeper was not nearly so tight-lipped as his terse answers had led me to think. If the doorkeeper told another slave in the household about the poison cake, who then told a slave in a neighbor's house, who then told his master . . .

I tried to keep my face a blank, but Lucius Claudius saw the wheels spinning in my head. He narrowed his eyes.

"Gordianus – what are you up to? How did we get on to the subject of Poplicola, anyway? Do you know something about this rumor?"

I was trying to think of some way to honour my oath to the censor without lying to my friend, when I was saved by the arrival of Lucius Claudius's beloved Momo. The tiny Melitaean terrier scampered into the room, as white as a snowball and almost as round; lately she had grown as plump as her master. She scampered and yapped at Lucius's feet, too earthbound to leap on to the couch. Lucius summoned a slave, who lifted the dog up and placed it on his lap. "My darling, my sweet, my adorable little Momo!" he cooed, and in an instant seemed to forget all about Poplicola, to my relief. Bitter-almond is a difficult poison to obtain. I am told that it is extracted from the pits of common fruits, but the stuff is so lethal – a man can die simply from having it touch his skin, or inhaling its fumes – that most of the shady dealers in such goods refuse to handle it. The rare customer looking for bitter-almond is usually steered into purchasing something else for his purpose, "Just as good," the dealer will say, though few poisons are as quick and certain as bitter-almond.

My peculiar line of work has acquainted me with all sorts of people, from the highest of the high, like Poplicola, to the lowest of the low – like a certain unsavoury dealer in poisons and potions named Quintus Fugax. Fugax claimed to be immune to every poison known to man, and even boasted that on occasion he tested new ones on himself, just to see if they would make him sick. To be sure, no poison had yet killed him, but his fingers were stained permanently black, there was a constant twitch at the corner of his mouth, his skin was covered with strange splotches, his head was covered with scabs and bald spots, and one of his eyes was covered with a rheumy yellow film. If anyone in Rome was unafraid to deal in bitter-almond, it was Quintus Fugax.

I found him the next day at his usual haunt, a squalid little tavern on the riverfront. I told him I wanted to ask some general questions about certain poisons and how they acted, for my own edification. So long as I kept his wine cup full, he agreed to talk with me.

Several cups later, when I judged that his tongue was sufficiently loosened by the wine, I asked him if he knew anything about bitter-almond. He laughed. "It's the best! I always tell people so, and not just because I'm about the only dealer who handles it. But hardly anybody wants it. Bitter-almond carries a curse, some say. People are afraid it'll turn on them, and they'll end up the dead one. Could happen; stuff can practically kill you just by you looking at it."

"Not much call for bitter-almond, then?"

"Not much." He smiled. "But I did sell a bit of it, just yesterday."

I swirled my wine and pretended to study the dregs. "Really? Some fishmonger wanting to do in his wife, I suppose."

He grinned, showing more gaps than teeth. "You know I never talk about my customers."

I frowned. "Still, it can't have been anyone very important. I'd have heard if some senator or wealthy merchant died from sudden convulsions after eating a hearty meal."

Fugax barked out a laugh. "Ha! Try a piece of cake!"

I caught my breath and kept my eyes on the swirling dregs. "I beg your pardon?"

"Customer wanted to know if you could use bitter-almond in an almond sweet cake. I said, 'Just the thing!'"

"What was he, a cook? Or a cook's slave, I suppose. Your customers usually send a go-between, don't they? They never deal with you face-to-face."

"This one did."

"Really?"

"Said she couldn't trust any of her slaves to make such a sensitive purchase."

"*She?*"

He raised his eyebrows and covered his mouth, like a little boy caught tattling, then threw back his head and cackled. "Gave that much away, didn't I? But I can't say who she was, because I don't know. Not poor, though. Came and went in a covered litter, all blue like her stola. Made her bearers stop a couple of streets away so they couldn't see where she went and I wouldn't see where she came from, but I sneaked after her when she left. Watched her climb into that fancy litter – hair so tall she had to stoop to get in!''

I summoned up a laugh and nodded. "These crazy new hairstyles!''

His ravaged face suddenly took on a wistful look. "Hers was pretty, though. All shiny and black – with a white streak running through it, like a stripe on a cat! Pretty woman. But pity the poor man who's crossed her!''

I nodded. "Pity him indeed . . .''

The enviable corner spot on the street of the bakers was occupied by a family named Baebius; so declared a handsomely painted sign above the serving counter that fronted the street. A short young blonde, a bit on the far side of pleasingly plump but with a sunshiny smile, stepped up to serve me. "What'll you have today, citizen? Sweet or savoury?''

"Sweet, I think. A friend tells me you make the most delicious little almond cakes.''

"Oh, you're thinking of Papa's special. We're famous for it. Been selling it from this shop for three generations. But I'm afraid we don't have any today. We only make those every other day. However, I can sell you a wonderful cheese and honey torte – very rich.''

I pretended to hem and haw and finally nodded. "Yes, give me one of those. No, make it three – hungry mouths at home! But it's too bad you don't have the almond cakes. My friend raves about them. He was by here just yesterday, I think. A fellow named Lucius Gellius.''

"Oh yes, we know him. But it's not he who craves the almond cakes, it's his father, the censor. Old Poplicola buys one from every batch Papa bakes!''

"But his son Lucius *was* here yesterday?''

She nodded. "So he was. I sold him the sweet cake myself and wrapped it up in parchment for him to take to his father. For himself and the lady he bought a couple of little savoury custards. Would you care to try –''

"The lady?''

"The lady who was waiting for him in the blue litter.''

"Is she a regular customer, too?"

The girl shrugged. "I didn't actually see her; only got a glimpse as Lucius was handing her the custard, and then they were off towards the Forum. There, taste that and tell me it's not fit for the gods."

I bit into the cheese and honey torte and feigned an enthusiastic nod. At that moment, it could have been ambrosia and I would have taken no pleasure in it.

I made my report to Poplicola that afternoon. He was surprised that I could have concluded my investigation so swiftly, and insisted on knowing each step in my progress and every person I had talked to. He stood, turned his back to me, and stared at the sombre red wall as I explained how I came to suspect the use of bitter-almond; how I questioned one of the few men who dealt in that particular poison, plied him with wine, and obtained a description that was almost certainly of Palla; how the girl at the bakery shop not only confirmed that Lucius had purchased the cake the previous day, but saw him leave in a blue litter with a female companion.

"None of this amounts to absolute proof, I admit. But it seems reasonably evident that Palla purchased the bitter-almond in the morning, that Lucius was either with her at that time, and stayed in the litter, or else joined her later, and then the two of them went to the bakery shop, where Lucius purchased the cake. Then one or both of them together sprinkled the poison on to the cake –"

Poplicola hunched his gaunt shoulders and produced a stifled cry, a sound of such despair that I was stunned into silence. When he turned to face me, he appeared to have aged ten years in an instant.

"All this is circumstantial evidence," he said, "not legal proof."

I spoke slowly and carefully. "Legal proof is narrowly defined. To satisfy a court of law, all the slaves involved would be called upon to testify – the litter bearers, your doorkeeper, perhaps the personal attendants of Palla and Lucius. Slaves see everything, and they usually know more

than their masters think. They would be tortured, of course;
the testimony of slaves is inadmissible unless obtained by
torture. Acquiring that degree of proof is beyond my means,
Censor."

He shook his head. "Never mind. We both know the truth.
I knew it all along, of course. Lucius and Palla, behind my
back – but I never thought it would come to this!"

"What will you do, Censor?" It was within Poplicola's
legal rights, as *paterfamilias*, to put his son to death without a
trial or any other formality. He could strangle Lucius with
his own hands or have a slave do it for him, and no one would
question his right to do so, especially in the circumstances.
He could do the same thing to his wife.

Poplicola made no answer. He had turned to face the wall
again, and stood so stiff and motionless that I feared for him.
"Censor . . .?"

"What will I do?" he snapped. "Don't be impertinent,
Finder! I hired you to find out a thing. You did so, and that's
the end of your concern. You'll leave here with some gold in
your purse, never fear."

"Censor, I meant no –"

"You swore an oath, on your ancestors, to speak of this
affair to no one but me. I shall hold you to it. If you're any
sort of Roman –"

"There's no need to remind me, Censor," I said sharply.
"I don't make oaths lightly."

He reached into a pouch within his purple toga, counted
out some coins, laid them on the little table before me, and
left the room without saying another word.

I was left to show myself out. On my way to the foyer,
addled by anger, I took a wrong turn and didn't realize it
until I found myself in a large garden surrounded by a
peristyle. I cursed and turned to retrace my steps, then
glimpsed the couple who stood beneath the colonnade at
the far corner of the garden, their heads together as if
engaged in some grave conversation. The woman was Palla.
Her arms were crossed and her head was held high. The
man, from his manner towards her, I would have taken to be
her husband had I not known better. Lucius Gellius looked

very much like a younger replica of his father, even to the chilly stare he gave me as I hastily withdrew.

In the days that followed, I kept my ears perked for any news of developments at the house of Poplicola, but there was only silence. Was the old man plotting some horrible revenge on his son and wife? Were they still plotting against him? Or had the three of them somehow come together, with confessions of guilt and forgiveness all around? I hardly saw how such a reconciliation could be possible after such a total breach of trust.

Then one morning I received a note from my friend Lucius Claudius:

> Dear Friend, Dinner Companion, and Fellow Connoisseur of Gossip,
>
> We never quite finished our discussion about Poplicola the other day, did we? The latest gossip (horrible stuff): On the very eve of the great purge in the Senate, one hears that certain members are planning to mount a prosecution against the censor's son, Lucius Gellius, accusing him of *sleeping with his stepmother* and *plotting to kill Poppy*. Such a trial will stir up a huge scandal – what will people think of a magistrate in charge of morals who can't stop his own son and wife from fornicating and scheming to do him in? Opponents (and likely targets) of the purge will say, "Clean up your own house, Poplicola, before you presume to clean ours!"
>
> Who knows how such a trial might turn out? The whole family will be dragged through the mud – if there's any dirt on any of them, the prosecutors will dig it up. And if Lucius is found guilty (I still can't believe it), they won't allow him exile – he'll be put to death along with Palla, and to save face Poplicola will have to play stern *paterfamilias* and watch while it's done! That would be the death of Poppy, I fear. Certainly, it would be the end of his political career. He'd be utterly humiliated, his moral authority a joke. He couldn't

possibly continue as censor. No purge of the Senate, then, and politics can go on as usual! What an age we live in.

Ah well, come dine with me tonight. I shall be having fresh pheasant, and Cook promises to do something divine with the sauce . . .

The pheasant that night was succulent. The sauce had an intriguing insinuation of mint that lingered teasingly on the tongue. But the food was not what I had come for.

Eventually we got around to the subject of the censor and his woes.

"There's to be a trial, then," I said.

"Actually . . . no," said Lucius Claudius.

"But your note this morning –"

"Invalidated by fresh gossip this afternoon."

"And?"

Lucius leaned back on his couch, stroked Momo, and looked at me shrewdly. "I don't suppose, Gordianus, that you know more about this affair than you're letting on?"

I looked him in the eye. "Nothing that I could discuss, even with you, my friend, without violating an oath."

He nodded. "I thought it must be something like that. Even so, I don't suppose you could let me know, simply yes or no, whether Lucius Gellius and Palla really – Gordianus, you look as if the pheasant suddenly turned on you! Well, let no one say that I ever gave a dinner guest indigestion from pressing an improper question. I shall simply have to live not knowing. Though in that case, why I should tell *you* the latest news from the Forum, I'm sure I don't know."

He pouted and fussed over Momo. I sipped my wine. Lucius began to fidget. Eventually his urge to share the latest gossip got the better of him. I tried not to smile.

"Very well, since you must know: Poppy, acting in his capacity as censor, has convoked a special Senate committee to investigate his own son on a charge of gross immorality – namely this rumour about adultery and attempted parricide. The committee will take up the investigation at once, and Poppy himself will preside over it."

"But how will this affect the upcoming trial?"

"There won't be a trial. The investigation supersedes it. It's rather clever of Poppy, I suppose, and rather brave. This way he heads off his enemies, who would have made a public trial into a spectacle. Instead, he'll see to the question of his son's guilt or innocence himself, behind closed doors. The Senate committee will make the final vote, but Poppy will oversee the proceedings. Of course, the whole thing could spin out of his control. If the investigating committee finds Lucius Gellius guilty, the scandal will still be the ruin of Poppy." He shook his head. "Surely that won't happen. For Poppy to take charge of the matter himself, that must mean that his son is innocent, and Poppy knows it – doesn't it?" Lucius raised an eyebrow and peered at me expectantly.

"I'm not sure what it means," I said, and meant it.

The investigation into the moral conduct of Lucius Gellius lasted two days, and took place behind the closed doors of the Senate House, where none but scribes and witnesses and the senators themselves were allowed. Fortunately for me, Lucius Claudius was among the senators on the investigating committee, and when the investigation was done he invited me once again to dine with him.

He greeted me at the door himself, and even before he spoke I could tell from his round, beaming face that he was pleased with the outcome.

"The committee reached a conclusion?" I said.

"Yes, and what a relief!"

"Lucius Gellius was cleared of the charges?" I tried not to sound sceptical.

"Completely! The whole business was an absurd fabrication! Nothing to it but vicious rumors and unfounded suspicions."

I thought of the dead slave, Chrestus. "There was no evidence at all of Lucius Gellius's guilt?"

"No such evidence was presented. Oh, so-and-so once saw Palla and Lucius Gellius sitting with their legs pressed together at the Circus Maximus, and another so-and-so saw them holding hands in a marketplace one day, and someone else claims to have seen them kiss beneath some trees on the Palatine Hill. Nothing but hearsay and rubbish. Palla and Lucius Gellius were called upon to defend themselves, and they both swore they had done nothing improper. Poplicola himself vouched for them."

"No slaves were called to testify?"

"This was an investigation, Gordianus, not a trial. We had no authority to extract testimony under torture."

"And were there no other witnesses? No depositions? Nothing regarding the poisoned cake that was rumored?"

"No. If there *had* been anyone capable of producing truly damning evidence, they'd have been found, surely; there were plenty of senators on the committee hostile to Poppy, and believe me, since the rumors first began, they've been scouring the city looking for evidence. It simply wasn't there."

I thought of the poison dealer, and of the blond girl who had waited on me at the bakery shop. I had tracked them down with little enough trouble; Poplicola's enemies would have started out with less to go on, but surely they had dispatched their own finders to search out the truth. Why had the girl not been called to testify, at least? Had no one made even the simple connection between the rumour of the poisoned cake and the bakery shop which produced Poplicola's favourite treat? Could the forces against the censor have been so inept?

Lucius laughed. "And to think of the meals I left untouched, fretting over Poppy! Well, now that he and his household have been vindicated, he can get on with his work as censor. Tomorrow Poppy will post his list of senators who've earned a black mark for immoral conduct. Good riddance, I say. More elbow room for the rest of us in the Senate chambers!" He sighed and shook his head. "Really, all that grief, and the whole thing was a farce."

Yes, I thought warily, so it had ended up – a farce. But what role had I played in it?

The next day I went to the street of the bakers, thinking finally to taste for myself one of the famous almond sweet cakes baked by the Baebius family – and also to find out if, indeed, no one from the Senate committee had called upon the blond girl.

I strolled up the narrow, winding little street and arrived at the corner with a shock. Instead of the blond girl's smiling face behind the serving counter, I saw a boarded-up storefront. The sign bearing the family name, there for three generations, had been obliterated with crude daubs of paint.

A shopkeeper down the street saw me gaping and called to me from behind his counter.

"Looking for the Baebii?"

"Yes."

"Gone."

"Where?"

"No idea."

"When?"

He shrugged. "A while back. Just up and left overnight, the whole lot of them. Baebius, his wife and daughter, the slaves – here one day, all gone the next. Poof! Like actors falling through a trapdoor on a stage."

"But why?"

He gestured that I should step closer, and lowered his voice. "I suspect that Baebius must have got himself into serious trouble with the authorities."

"What authorities?"

"The Senate itself!"

"Why do you say that?"

"Just a day or two after he vanished, some pretty rough-looking strangers came snooping up and down the block, asking for Baebius and wanting to know where he'd gone. They even offered money, but nobody could tell them. And then, a few days after that, here come more strangers asking questions, only these were better dressed and carried fancy-looking scrolls; claimed they were conducting some sort of official investigation, and had 'senatorial authority.' Not that it mattered; people around here still didn't know what had become of Baebius. It's a mystery, isn't it?"

"Yes . . ."

"I figure Baebius must have done something pretty bad, to get out of town that sudden and not leave a trace behind." He shook his head. "Sad, though; his family had been in that shop a long time. And you'd think he might have given me his recipe for those almond cakes before he disappeared! People come by here day and night asking for those cakes. Say, could I interest you in something sweet? These honey-glazed buns are fresh out of the oven. Just smell that aroma . . ."

Is it better to visit a poison dealer on a full stomach or an empty one? Empty, I decided, and so I declined the baker's bun and made my way across the Forum and the cattle market to the riverfront, and thence to the seedy little tavern frequented by Quintus Fugax.

The interior seemed pitch-dark after the bright sunshine. I had to squint as I stumbled from bench to bench, searching among the derelicts. Only the most hardened drinkers were in such a place at that time of day. The place stank of spilled wine and river rot.

"Looking for someone?" asked the tavern keeper.

"A fellow called Fugax."

"The scarecrow with the rheumy eye and the bad breath?"

"That's him."

"You're out of luck, then, but not as out of luck as your friend."

"What do you mean?"

"They dragged him out of the river a couple of days ago."

"What?"

"Drowned. Poor sod must have fallen in; not my fault if a man leaves here too drunk to walk straight. Or maybe . . ." He gave me a significant look. "Maybe somebody pushed him in."

"Why do you say that?"

"Fugax had been strutting around here lately, claiming he was about to come into a big sum of money. Crazy fool! Saying a thing like that in this neighbourhood is asking for trouble."

"Where was he going to get this money?"

"That's what I wondered. I asked him, 'What, are you planning to sell your garden villa on the Tiber?' He laughed and said he had something to sell, all right – information, important information that powerful people would pay a lot for; pay to get it, or pay to keep others from getting it. Not likely, I thought! 'What could a river rat like you know that anybody would give a fig to find out?' He just laughed. The fellow was half crazy, you know. But I figure maybe somebody heard him bragging, tried to rob him, got angry when they didn't find much, and threw him in the river. The dock workers that found him say it looked like he might have hit his head on something – hard to tell with all those scabs and rashes. Did you know him well?"

I sighed. "Well enough not to mourn too much over his death."

The tavern keeper looked at me oddly. "You need something to drink, citizen."

I had declined the baker's bun, but I accepted the tavern keeper's wine.

The doorkeeper at Poplicola's house tersely informed me that his master was not receiving visitors. I pushed past him and told him I would wait in the red study. I waited for quite a while, long enough to peruse a few of the scrolls in Poplicola's little library: Aristotle on ethics, Plato on the examined life. There was a movement at the green curtain drawn over the doorway. It was not Poplicola who entered, but Palla.

She was shorter than I had thought; her elaborate turret of hair gave an illusion of height. But she was actually more beautiful than I had realized. By the reflected light of the red walls her skin took on a smooth, creamy luster. The bland youthfulness of her face was at odds with the worldliness in her eyes. Seeing her so close, it was harder than ever to calculate her age.

"You must be Gordianus," she said.

"Yes."

"My husband is physically and emotionally exhausted by the events of the last few days. He can't possibly see you."

"I think he should."

"Has he not paid you yet?"

I gritted my teeth. "I'm not an instrument to be used and then disposed of. I helped him discover the truth. I brought him certain information. Now I find that an innocent family has been driven into hiding, and another man is dead, very likely murdered to keep him quiet."

"If you're talking about that wretch Fugax, surely the whole city is better off being rid of such a creature."

"What do you know about his death?"

She made no answer.

"I insist that your husband see me," I said.

She looked at me steadily. "Anything you might wish to say to Poppy, you may say to me. We have no secrets from each other – not any more. Everything has come out into the open between us."

"And your stepson?"

"Father and son are reconciled."

"The three of you have worked it all out?"

"Yes. But that's really none of your business, Finder. As you say, you were hired to find out a thing, and you did. There's an end of it."

"An end of Chrestus, and of Fugax, you mean. And who knows what's become of the baker and his family."

She drew a deep breath and gave me a bemused look. "The slave Chrestus belonged to my husband. His death was an injury to my husband's property. Chrestus was old and slow, he pilfered from his master's food and might not have survived another winter; his market value was nil. It's for Poppy and Poppy alone to seek recompense for the loss, and if he chooses to overlook it, then neither you nor anybody else has any business poking further into the matter."

She crossed her arms and paced slowly across the room. "As for Fugax, as I say, his death is no loss to anyone. A public service, I should think! When the trial began to loom, and then the investigation, he tried to blackmail us. He was a stupid, vile, treacherous little man, and now he's dead. That, too, is none of your business."

She reached the far corner and turned around. "As for the baker and his family, they were paid a more than adequate compensation for their trouble."

"The man's family had been in that shop for generations! I can't believe he left of his own free will."

She stiffened her jaw. " 'True, Baebius was not completely cooperative, at first. A certain amount of pressure was required to make him see reason."

"Pressure?"

"A black mark from a censor could have made a great deal of trouble for Baebius. Once that was explained to him, Baebius saw that it would be best if he and his family left Rome altogether and set up shop elsewhere. I'm sure his almond cakes will be just as popular in Spain as they were here in Rome. Poppy shall miss them, alas." She spoke without a shred of irony.

"And what about me?"

"You, Gordianus?"

"I knew more than anyone."

"Yes, that's true. To be candid, I thought we should do something about you; so did my stepson. But Poppy said that you had sworn an oath of secrecy upon your ancestors, that you gave him your word, Roman to Roman. That sort of thing counts for a great deal with Poppy. He insisted that we leave you alone. And he was right; you kept silent. He expects you to remain silent. I'm sure you won't let him down."

She flashed a serene smile, without the least hint of remorse. It struck me that Palla resembled a bit of poisoned cake herself. "So you see," she said, "it's all worked out for the best, for everyone concerned."

Legally and politically, the affair of Poplicola and the poisoned cake was at an end. The court of public opinion, however, would continue to try and retry the case for years to come.

There were those who insisted that the Senate investigation had been rigged by Poplicola himself; that vital witnesses had been intimidated, driven off, even killed; that the censor was morally bankrupt, unfit for his office, and that his happy household was a sham.

Others defended Poplicola, saying that all the talk against

him originated with a few morally depraved, bitter ex-senators. There were even those who argued that the episode was proof of Poplicola's wisdom and profound sense of judgment. Upon hearing such shocking charges against his son and wife, many a man would have rushed to avenge himself on them, taking their punishment into his own hands; but Poplicola had exercised almost superhuman restraint, called for an official inquiry, and ultimately saw his loved ones vindicated. For his patience and cool-headed perseverance, Poplicola was held up as a model of Roman sagacity, and his loyal wife Palla was admired as a woman who held her head high even when enduring the cruellest slanders.

As for his son, Lucius Gellius's political career advanced more or less unimpeded by the scandal. He became more active than ever in the courts and in the Senate House, and openly expressed his ambition to be censor someday, following in his father's footsteps. Only rarely did his unproved crimes come back to haunt him, as on the occasion when he sparred with Cicero in a rancorous debate and threatened to give the great orator a piece of his mind – to which Cicero replied, "Better that, Lucius Gellius, than a piece of your cake!"

Blind Justice

Michael Kurland

Michael Kurland (b. 1938) has been writing for nearly forty years and has established himself in the fields of fantasy and science fiction as well as mystery and horror. His other mystery novels include A Plague of Spies *(1969), which received an Edgar Allan Poe Scroll from the Mystery Writers of America,* Too Soon Dead *(1997) and* The Girls in the High-Heeled Shoes *(1998). He has also written novels featuring Sherlock Holmes's arch-adversary, Moriarty, in* The Infernal Device *(1979),* Death by Gaslight *(1982) and* The Great Game *(2001) as well as continuing Randall Garrett's series about the wonderful magician-cum-detective, Lord Darcy, in* Ten Little Wizards *(1988) and* A Study in Sorcery *(1989). As if that is not enough he has also written a forensic handbook,* How to Solve a Murder *(1995) and* The Complete Idiot's Guide to Unsolved Mysteries *(2000).*

In the following story we meet Marcus Fabius Quintilianus (AD c35–95). He was one of the most distinguished and respected rhetoricians of Imperial Rome. His Institutiones Oratoriae *(Education of an Orator) gave such good advice on the principles of educating children that sections of it are quoted, sometimes unknowingly, to this day. The story told here is based on a possibly apocryphal description of one of his cases.*

My name is Plautus Maximilianus Aureus. I shall soon be twenty-two years old, and I have accomplished nothing in my life. When Alexander the Great was my age, he had conquered all Persia. When Cicero was my age, he had tried and won his first cases before a Roman jury. But I – I have a stammer and a slight limp from a childhood illness that twisted my spine and left me just crippled enough to be useless in battle and unattractive to women. I am commonly known as "Max the Scribbler", or sometimes just "Scribbler" for the way I write down everything said by my patron and mentor, the great teacher, jurist and orator Marcus Fabius Quintilianus. I carry about a great supply of wax tablets in a canvas sack for that purpose.

The instance I am relating occurred but a few months ago, in the spring of the second year of the reign of the Emperor Vespasian. It was then that, with many misgivings, Quintilian agreed to defend a youth named Rufus Abracius against the charge that he had murdered his own father. This was not a popular case to take on, as you can imagine: the grumbling in the Forum was that banishment was insufficient and death, unless it were a particularly lingering and painful death, was too lenient a punishment for such a crime. The fact that the accused lad was blind made the crime somehow even worse, as was the fact that his own stepmother was his accuser, and it was she who was bringing the case to trial.

The commission was brought to Quintilian by his friend Titus, the shipowner, who had known Quintilian since they were boys together in the sunny hillsides of Spain. I assume Spain has sunny hillsides, why shouldn't it? The two of them sat together on the bench under the single fig tree growing in the courtyard of Quintilian's villa, which is on the outskirts of Rome by the Via Sculpa. The kitchen girl brought out a pitcher of heated wine and three goblets, and the two old friends talked over the events of the week; Quintilian waiting patiently for Titus to bring up whatever had brought him along the dusty road in his sedan chair so early in the day. I sat on a stool by Quintilian's feet, ready with tablet and stylus in case Quintilian said anything worthy of recording.

"Rufus Abracius needs an advocate," Titus said, after hemming and hawing through his first goblet of wine and refilling the vessel.

"The lad accused of killing his own father?"

Titus nodded. "I'm afraid there'll be little glory in this for you," he said, an understatement if I've ever heard one, "but at least you'll get paid. I'll guarantee your fee."

Quintilian scowled into his goblet. "This is not a good time," he said. "I am devoting much of my energy to preparing notes for a book on the teaching of rhetoric and oratory to the young."

"In addition," I added from my place on a small stool at the foot of the bench, "to actually teaching rhetoric to eleven youths and three advanced students. That takes up much of the week."

They both turned to glower at me. "They would come to the trial and watch and listen," Quintilian said. "They would learn much from seeing for themselves how it should be done."

"Watching the master in action is worth many hours of classroom instruction," Titus agreed firmly.

"Silly me," I said. "I abase myself."

Quintilian turned to Titus. "Tell me about it," he said.

Rufus Abracius, as Titus told Quintilian, was the son of Marcus Vexianus Abracius, a grain merchant, who had shipped many cargoes from the wheat fields of Egypt in tub-hulled vessels owned by Titus. There had been no bad blood between father and son until the father had remarried. Indeed, some five years before, Rufus had saved his father's life in a fire, and had been blinded when he went back in an unsuccessful attempt to rescue his mother.

According to Titus, Rufus had erected a shrine to his dead mother in a corner of his room and spent most of every day lying on his bed, weeping. Although such abject mourning was certainly unmanly, it was at least understandable, as the boy had been very close to his mother and blamed himself for her death.

The rift between Rufus and his father had grown since the father took Lucella Collesta, a dark-haired Syracusan beauty a full two decades younger than himself, to be his new wife. The lad refused to attend the wedding and, although outwardly civil to his stepmother, had as little to do with her or his father as possible from that moment onwards; going so far as to move to a room in a distant part of the house beyond the kitchens. Two servants' rooms were combined to provide him with his new quarters.

On the second day of Parentalia in February – the solemn festival for honouring dead parents – Rufus had walked more than a mile out of the city along the Via Appia to the family mausoleum where his mother's ashes lay. He had chosen to go by himself and had scorned the use of a sedan chair or the company of his body slave, although it was a chill and drizzly day and the road was rough and dangerous, even for the sighted. He had spent the night at the mausoleum, wrapped in his woollen cloak, with his head resting on a convenient slab of marble.

When he returned, his stepmother had discovered a vial of poison in his shoulder bag. Whether he intended to take his own life, or attempt the life of either his father or stepmother cannot be known. The vial was taken away from him, and after that he seldom left his room.

Titus refilled his cup. "As to the murder itself," he went on, "Marcus was stabbed right through the heart while he slept, one clean blow, and his son's bloody hand prints were discovered on the wall of the corridor –"

"That's very interesting," Quintilian interrupted. "Stabbed with what?" Then he raised his hand. "Wait, don't go on. If I am to take this case I must at least gather the facts second-hand and not third-hand. We must go to the home of Marcus Vexianus Abracius and see for ourselves what there is to be seen and listen to what there is to be told."

"Then you'll take the case?" Titus asked.

"First tell me why you're so willing to defend the lad," Quintilian said. "If we lose the case Rufus cannot inherit and will be penniless. Why are you willing to support him to the extent of guaranteeing my exorbitant fee?"

Titus thought about it for a minute and then shrugged. "I

like the lad," he said. "Black as the case against him seems, I cannot believe he killed his own father. It's not in his character, as I know it, to do so."

"Then I will look into it," Quintilian told him. "Whether or not I'll appear in court for the lad depends on what I find."

The next day we journeyed across Rome to the home of Rufus and his stepmother, Quintilian walking briskly the whole way and I scurrying along behind as best I could. Over Quirinal Hill and Viminal Hill we went without pausing. Even the two slaves we brought along as bodyguards, great, hulking Celts from the Islands of the Mists, had trouble keeping up with him. There was a brief respite before we climbed Esquiline Hill, but only because a senator recognized Quintilian and bade him stop and answer a brief question regarding the proper raising of the senator's young nephews. Quintilian loved to walk in all weathers, claiming he could think better as he strode along. For my part, I had all I could do to breathe, and had little energy left for thinking at all.

When we arrived at the home of the deceased Marcus Vexianus Abracius, the bier that had held his body still stood in the atrium, although Marcus himself had been cremated several days before and his ashes now rested with those of his first wife in the family mausoleum outside the gates of the city. It was during the procession to the funeral pyre that the grieving widow, while rending various garments in her agony, had declared her intention of having the son tried for murdering his father.

Quintilian began by interviewing Rufus in his windowless room beyond the kitchen, where the lad would remain, with a pair of guards at the door, until the trial. Quintilian sent a slave for a burning rush to light the two oil lamps in the room, since Rufus, naturally enough, was sitting in the dark.

The room was starkly furnished: nothing but a simple pallet, a stool, a chest for clothing, and a small altar in the corner holding a miniature portrait of a strikingly good-looking woman and some items of jewellery. The boy was about nineteen and handsome enough except for some small scars about his ears and neck. It wasn't until he turned his face towards you that you got an eerie feeling of strange thoughts at work behind those white, sightless eyes. Or at least I did.

"You must cooperate with me and tell me the truth if I am to defend you," Quintilian told the lad.

"It hardly matters," Rufus answered listlessly, sitting cross-legged on his pallet by the back wall. "Whether I live or die is of little importance."

"Did you kill your father?"

"Of course not!" Rufus turned his sightless eyes toward Quintilian. "I would not do such a thing. I honour – honoured – my father."

"But you loved your mother?"

"I did." He turned his face towards the small altar in the corner. "I do."

"You disapproved of your father's remarriage?"

"He did not seek my approval, nor would it have been my place to give it. He is paterfamilias – head of the family. I was his son."

"Yet parricide is not unheard of in Rome," Quintilian mused. "That's why there is a name for it. Under Roman law children are unable to marry or conduct business without their father's consent as long as he is alive, no matter what their age. Sons with a cruel or overbearing father, or merely anxious for their inheritance can be severely tempted to perform rash acts. It is among the most severely punished of crimes, yet it is not even uncommon."

"I have no interest in marrying," Rufus said, "and I conduct no business."

"You dislike your stepmother?"

The lad shrugged. "I neither like nor dislike Madam."

"What can you tell me of the night of the murder?"

"I slept through the night. I was awakened by rough hands grabbing at my body and Madam's voice in the background yelling curses and imprecations. I do not know what happened or who was to blame."

"Have you any conjectures?"

"None. My father was well liked. He did not involve himself with politics. Most murders, I believe, are political."

"Most murders are for gain," Quintilian told him. "Did anyone stand to gain from your father's death?"

Rufus thought for a moment and then shook his head. "I inherit," he said. "But father always gave me anything I asked for, so I had no need to kill him. Likewise, my stepmother gets the widow's portion, but father never denied her requests. So, if anything, she loses by his death, since I inherit most of the estate and she cannot expect me to be so generous."

"Well thought out," Quintilian commended. "Then it is a mystery, isn't it? We must continue our examination. I will get back to you."

"As you will," the lad agreed listlessly.

We left the room and walked down the narrow corridor which bypassed the kitchen and led directly to the inner courtyard, with one door towards the end giving into the father's bedroom. The bloody prints of the young man's hand – well, of someone's hand – could be seen on the wall by the flickering light of the oil lamp. "Who uses this corridor?" Quintilian asked the young household slave who was lighting our way.

"Nobody," she told him. "The young master used to use it to go sit in the courtyard and have the old Greek read to him. But now he doesn't leave his room."

"Even before he was confined to his room by the guards, he stayed there?"

"Oh, yes. He didn't leave that room for anything. Except every evening he went down this very corridor to ask his father how the day went and whether he needed anything. His father would always say the day went well, and no, thank you, and the young master would go back to his room. He stayed in the dark. Sometimes we'd hear him talking."

"Talking?"

"Reciting, like. '*Tempus erat quo prima –*'"

"Oh, yes. Virgil. From *The Aeneid*." Quintilian recited in his sonorous voice: " 'It was the hour when the first sleep of suffering mortality begins, and, by the grace of heaven, steals on its sweetest errand of mercy.' Schoolboy memorization, but some of it may be comforting to him."

"That damn poem!" came a woman's voice from behind the door to the master bedroom. The door swung open and a woman stood, one hand on her hip, the other leaning against the door, glaring at us. She was young, with long black hair and a heavily made-up face in the Greek fashion: dark-rimmed eyes and rouged cheeks, and heavy gold earrings. Too much for my taste, but beautiful nonetheless. She stared at us for a long minute, and then demanded, "Who are you?"

"Marcus Fabius Quintilianus," Quintilian told her. "And this is my associate, Plautus Maximilianus Aureus. You must be Lucella Abracius, widow of Marcus."

"I must," she agreed. Then she shuddered. "Widow. I hate that word."

He took her hand. "Madam, I regret interrupting your grief, but there are a few questions I must ask you."

"Of course," she said.

He did not release her hand immediately, and she did not seem eager for him to. She squeezed his hand and then put her palm up so that she was, ever so slightly, clutching his thumb. It was an erotic gesture, and she was clearly a woman who was created for erotic gestures. She couldn't help it, it was her nature. Even I felt – well, no matter what I felt.

Quintilian looked at her hand, as though suddenly becoming aware that he had been holding it, and then released it. "You have accused your stepson of murdering your husband," he said. "Do you have direct knowledge that he did so? Did you see him commit the murder?"

"No," she said. "Though I slept at my husband's side, I slept through whatever happened." She shuddered again and backed into the room, dropping on to the bed. "You'd think that the gods would have awakened me so that I could have put my own body between Marcus and the downthrust sword."

"Then it was a sword that killed him?"

"Yes: a military short sword. It was still in his body."

"Was it from the house?"

"I don't think so. I'd never seen it before."

Quintilian entered the room after her and looked around. There were two doors, one to the corridor we had just quit and one to the courtyard. A large window, its shutters swung open, provided light and air. "I know it will be difficult for you, but if you could tell me just what happened that day, it would help."

She sat up, her posture changing from one of invitation to one of defiance. "Help him, you mean," she said. "I know who you are and what you are doing here."

"Of course you do," Quintilian told her.

She paused for a second and then shook her head. "But I suppose . . . if you could find a way to show that the boy *didn't* do it, you would please the shade of my dead husband. He always liked the boy, may the gods forgive him!"

"Just tell me what happened," Quintilian insisted softly.

"Someone – and if it wasn't the boy I don't see who it could have been – came into the room while we slept and drove the sword through my husband's heart."

"He didn't cry out or make a sound?"

"I'm a heavy sleeper, but not that heavy. I heard nothing."

"There was no sign of a struggle?"

"None."

"And then?"

"And then I awoke and rose and opened the shutters. And by the morning light coming in the window I saw my husband lying dead in the bed beside where I had slept. I screamed and ran into the corridor."

"In this very bed?"

She shook her head. "I had the bed destroyed on which the murder took place. There was too much blood."

"So you ran into the corridor?"

"And I saw there, by the light through the open door, a bloody print of a hand on the wall. So I suppose I screamed again, and kept screaming until a couple of the slaves came. Big, brawny men who work in the garden. They had been guarding the front door that night. I had them fetch a light and we followed the hand prints back down the corridor to Rufus's room. Then I called the city guard."

"And you think your stepson committed this deed – murdered his father?" Quintilian asked.

The woman stared at him blankly. "What else is there to think?" she replied.

"And you're determined to prosecute him for murder?"

"What else is there to do?"

"What indeed?" Quintilian took an oil lamp from the table and went back into the corridor to look at the hand prints. He had the slave girl hold her lamp on one side of each hand print while he held his on the other, and he peered closely at each one, making his way slowly back down the corridor. There were seven of them along the right-hand wall, where someone might have put his hand on the wall for support as he blindly staggered back to his room. Seven very well delineated prints of the same right hand – all clear and heavy with blood and pointing inexorably towards the blind boy's room.

At one point Quintilian spotted something on the floor and bent down to examine it.

"What have you found?" I asked.

He stood up. "Wax," he said. "Candle wax. Just a few drops. Mixed with a bit of blood, so they're recent, unless someone else has been bleeding in the corridor." He turned to the girl. "May I assume that these bloody hand prints are the only traces of blood that you've found in the corridor?"

"Oh, yes, sir," she told him.

"At any time?"

"As far as I know, sir. Since I've been here, and that would be two years come the feast day of Flora this April."

"Thank you, girl. You may lead us to the gate, now."

And with that we went home. Titus came by the next day to see whether Quintilian would take the assignment. "I will venture it," Quintilian told him, "but with no guarantee of success."

"You don't believe the lad is innocent?"

"Only the gods can determine true innocence or guilt," Quintilian told him. "What matters to a Roman jury is the force of argument and how well presented it is. It's just as important to keep fifty-one Roman jurors awake as it is to convince them. I will endeavour to keep them awake."

"But what do you think? Do you believe the lad is innocent?"

Quintilian patted him on the shoulder. "What I think hardly matters. The jury decides who's innocent and who's guilty. The beautiful Lucella has engaged Blasus Parenas as prosecutor, and Blasus has a slippery and well oiled tongue. After he has finished greasing the jury with his well chosen words we'll be lucky if I'm allowed to speak at all. They may all leap to their feet and acclaim the guilt of my client in a unanimous burst of enthusiasm."

"You must have bad dreams," Titus told him.

"When I'm trying a case I don't permit myself to dream."

"But is the lad guilty or isn't he? Surely you have an opinion."

"Oh. Your instincts were right. Rufus Abracius did not kill his father."

"But the bloody hand prints?"

"Exactly. The bloody hand prints."

And that was all Titus could get out of him. I, of course, did not try, curious as I was to know what my mentor had discerned, and what he thought of the case. He would merely tell me to observe and to learn. I observed, but I did not see what he saw. I learned, but he learned more. How was I ever going to be able to emulate the master when from moment to moment I had no idea of what the master was doing?

The trial commenced three weeks later. Blasus Parenas was as good as Quintilian predicted. A handsome man with long, brown hair, he wore his toga creased into precise pleats, with the end carefully folded over his arm. He called Lucella, the stepmother, as his first witness. She had arrived in a litter carried by eight porters and preceded by a centurion in full dress uniform. She showed more leg than was proper and told the jurors how she missed her husband more every day, and how sweet and good he had been, and if Rufus didn't kill him, who could have?

Quintilian's cross-examination was brief. "Have you ever heard Rufus Abracius say anything against his father, or speak to his father in anger?"

"Well," the good Lucella said, trying to look as though her teeth were being pulled against her will, "since you asked – I have heard him mutter imprecations under his breath. I believe he never forgave his father for marrying me."

"Thank you," Quintilian said, sitting down. I looked at him with some astonishment. He never before, to my knowledge, had led a witness into giving questions harmful to his client. But he looked satisfied, and I said nothing.

Blasus then called the two gardeners who had watched the front door that night, and received agreement that they didn't have to be questioned under torture. (The custom is dropping out of favour anyway. The Emperor himself has said that a slave under torture will say whatever the torturers want to hear, and therefore his testimony is useless.) They affirmed that no one could have got through the door without their knowing it, and that no one at all, friend or stranger, came in that night. They were also the two who rushed to Lucilla's aid when she began screaming that morning. They testified to seeing the bloody hand prints and following them to Rufus's chamber.

Quintilian rose in cross-examination when the second one was done. "The hand prints were easy to follow?"

"Yes, sir."

"Good. Bold, strong hand prints, were they?"

"Yes sir?"

"And the boy, Rufus, what was he doing when you entered his room?"

"He were asleep, your honour."

"So you had to wake him up to tell him what he did?"

"Yes, sir."

"There was blood all over him, of course."

"No, your honour. I didn't see no blood."

"Thank you. That's all."

Dr Heraclates, who had been treating Rufus for the past year, was the next witness. "The lad is suffering from melancholia," he said, "brought on by the death of his mother."

"But his mother died two years ago," Blasus pointed out. "Surely Rufus should have got over that by now."

"Normally yes, I would say," Dr Heraclates said, his white Greek beard bobbing as he spoke. "But the lad and his mother were very close,"

"Ah!" Blasus adjusted his toga with his thumb and forefinger, getting the crease *just so* as he turned to face the jury. "You mean to say," he asked, his hands behind his back, his face bland, "that Rufus Abracius had an unnatural" – he drawled out the word "unnatural" – "affection for his mother?"

"Well, very strong, yes."

"Unnatural?"

"I wouldn't go that far."

"You don't need to, Doctor," Blasus said, with a wave of his arm leaving it for the jury's imagination to go at least that far.

Then Serpo, Rufus's own body slave, was called. Quintilian, who had been dozing, or pretending to doze, suddenly jumped to his feet. "Come now!" he thundered. "A slave cannot be called to testify against his own master. Surely my learned opponent knows that. The chairman of the court knows that. Everybody in this room" – and he waved his hand to take in the entire fifty-one jurors and the hundred or so onlookers – "knows that!"

Blasus Parenas turned to Senator Claudius Aquillus, the chairman of the court, an elderly man with a hawk nose, piercing blue eyes, and a brain like a lawbook of Roman custom and precedent, for a ruling. "Your honour?"

"He's right, Citizen Parenas," Chairman Claudius said. "Why should this slave be exempt from the established custom?"

"Technically, your honour, the slave was not Rufus's property at the time in question; Rufus's father was still alive, and so everything of which Rufus was possessed, including his slave, was, in law, his father's property. He should not be allowed a legal defence for the crime of murdering his father that is only made possible because he murdered his father."

"Ah, but that's what you must prove!" Quintilian said. "Can you seek to prove that my client murdered his father by

bringing in evidence that is only admissible provided that he
did murder his father?"

"Interesting," Claudius said, looking from one advocate to
the other. He leaned back and pondered, closing his eyes.

After a minute he opened them to look at Blasus Parenas.
"I believe that this time you've won your point, counsellor,
by a hair. Go on with questioning the slave."

Quintilian leaned back on the bench and smiled benignly.
"There's nothing old Claudius loves so much as a point of
law," he murmured to me. "I thought Blasus would have to
work a little harder to get that in. Still it might throw him off
his stride."

"Is this slave's testimony damaging to our client?" I asked
him in an undertone.

"I don't see how," Quintilian murmured. "But Blasus
doesn't know that. Even now he's wondering what question I
fear his asking the little slave."

And so it proved. Serpo said all he could say that was of
interest in the first three sentences: He'd been body slave to
Rufus since the lad was twelve. It was he who had warned the
stepmother about the poison, since he'd followed Rufus to
the Mausoleum that day and watched him clutch the small
vial to his chest and occasionally raise it to his lips, and then
shake his head and put it away. He had on occasion heard
Rufus muttering curses that might have been directed towards his father.

Quintilian stood up and interrupted. "Those curses, you
didn't hear them clearly?"

"No, sir."

"Could have been against his father?"

"Yes, sir."

"Could have been against the gods who blinded him and
killed his mother?"

"Yes, I suppose so, sir."

"Could have been against himself, for being so accursed as
to fail to rescue his mother?"

"Well, yes, I suppose so."

"Could have been against the green team for losing in the
chariot races that day?"

"Well –" Serpo shifted uncomfortably as the jurors chuckled.

Quintilian sat back down, and Blasus artfully ignored him and went on. He gnawed at every possible relationship that Serpo might have been privy to, convinced that there was meat in there somewhere. He came up without even a radish.

Quintilian stood again and asked, "That sword we've heard about; did you ever see young Rufus Abracius with a sword?"

"No, sir."

"Did his father have any swords that you know about?"

"No, sir."

"No, indeed, and what would he be doing with a sword?" Quintilian asked rhetorically, and sat down.

"We'll get to the sword soon enough," Blasus said dramatically, signalling for his next witness to come forward. This was the city guard who had come in response to the call for help from within the house. He described the scene he found there: the head of the family dead in his bed with a sword thrust deep into his chest, the weeping widow, the dazed and silent blind boy, the bloody hand prints in the corridor leading from the murder room to the boy's room.

"And what sort of sword was it that did the deed?" Blasus demanded.

"A regulation legionnaire's gladius. The short sword that is used by all the legions."

"And do you have that sword with you?"

"I do." The guard unrolled a bolt of red fabric he was carrying and revealed a plain, iron, double-edged sword, of the sort used by the regular infantry. The fore part of the blade was still crusted with the dried blood of Marcus Vexianus Abracius, and several of the jurors or audience members gasped at the sight. They had, most of them, performed military service for the State, and had seen men die before their eyes, and probably killed a few themselves. But there is a difference between battle and murder: one is sanctified by the gods, the other is a foul and cowardly act.

Blasus Parenas passed the sword around the jury and,

eventually, even to the spectators. Finally, with a great sweeping gesture that fluttered his toga, he handed it to Quintilian. Then he turned back to the jury and, pacing from side to side in front of them with a deliberate gait, began his summation.

In the best tradition of the Roman prosecutor, Parenas went on for hours, and he had no trouble keeping the jurors awake. He began by drawing a word-portrait of the murdered Marcus: what a fine husband and father he had been, what a prince of an employer, what a noble Roman, with all the virtues that Rome looks for in her citizens. And then on to the most important thing in a murder trial: motive. Unless the speaker can convince the jury that the defendant *wanted* to kill the victim, it's hard to convince them that he *did* kill the victim. And oh how Rufus wanted to kill his father, according to Blasus: "And then a worm grew slowly inside him: the worm of hate. He hated his father as the cause of his blindness; he hated his father because, in saving him first from the fire, he failed to save his beloved mother. Perhaps too beloved, but we'll let that pass."

Blasus trotted out all the usual reasons why a son might murder his father, and added a few of his own: Rufus was angry that his father remarried, thus dishonouring his mother's memory. Rufus was secretly in love with his stepmother and jealous of his father. Marcus Vexianus Abracius had been a rich and successful man; Rufus was jealous of the success, and wanted to inherit his father's money and be free of his father's stifling influence. Free to do what, Blasus didn't say.

"And all these," Blasus intoned, "finally came together in the disturbed mind of this poor boy one night a month ago when he took the sword that he had been hiding – possibly under his bed so he could reach down and feel the strength of the blade, the sharpness of the edge – and determined to strike, strike, strike! And cut down his father while the man slept – slept peacefully, expecting no harm, next to his loving wife."

Now we were getting to it: the murder itself. The coughing and fidgeting among the jurors ceased, and they listened intently.

"Picture the scene," Blasus told them. "In the dead of night, the only time when a blind man can successfully hope to commit such a dastardly crime, Marcus's son leaves his room and creeps down the hall, sword in hand. He enters the bedroom where his father and stepmother are sleeping and – with one well aimed thrust – stabs his father through the heart!" Here Blasus mimed a well aimed thrust, and some in the audience shivered.

"And then young Rufus staggers back to his room, blindly leaving behind him the blood-red hand print of a murderer – not once but seven times – along the wall of the corridor."

Blasus raised his hands to the heavens. "Perhaps it was the gods that caused him to leave behind these bloody markers." Blasus dropped his hands sadly to his sides. "Perhaps, after his dreadful deed, the lad wanted to be caught. Who can say? But no one can deny his guilt – it is marked by his own hand on the corridor wall – and marked, and marked, and marked, and marked." And Blasus sat down.

After a suitable pause Quintilian rose and faced the jury. "Honourable Romans," he began, "I stand before you, charged with the task of defending a young blind boy of impeccable character who has been accused of murder – and the most foul murder imaginable at that: the murder of his own father.

"I have heard speculation as to how I am going to plead this unfortunate lad's case." Quintilian raised his right hand, palm upraised, in supplication to the jurors. "I could beg for the court's mercy because the boy is blind and an orphan. I could attempt to convince you that he was driven mad with grief, and is therefore not responsible for his actions. I could speak to you of his heroism in saving his father from a terrible fire, and losing his eyesight in the attempt to save his mother. I could somehow try to justify this horrible crime." He lowered his hand.

"But there is no justification for such a horrible crime. And, thanks to the gods who have opened my eyes to the truth, I do not have to attempt such a hopeless task. The fact is, as I will prove to you by the evidence we have already heard and about which there is no dispute, Rufus Abracius is innocent of the charge." Quintilian moved over to stand next to his client, and put his hand on the boy's shoulder. "He did not murder his father."

There was a murmur from the jurors. The chairman of the court turned to glare them into silence, and then nodded at Quintilian to continue.

Quintilian gave the jurors a word-picture of the life of Marcus Vexianus Abracius, his first wife and their son in the days before the fire, showing what a close and loving family they were. Then he spoke of Rufus's double tragedy of losing his mother and his eyesight. "Even though it was not his fault," Quintilian told them, "the guilt and remorse he felt overwhelmed him. Yes, he loved his mother, just as you and I love our mothers. We have no need to look to Oedipus for an explanation." He looked slowly around at the jurors. "Consider this my friends: How would you like to be on trial for something – anything, it doesn't matter what – and have some unctuous prosecutor tell the jury that your love for your mother was 'unnatural'? Bah! We will speak no more about it."

Quintilian then verbally took the jurors along to watch sympathetically as Rufus retired to his room after the fire, to spend his days in darkness and in pain. Slowly he brought them along when Rufus suffered the new shock of his father's remarriage. "Rufus was still clinging to the ghost of his mother," he told them, "when his father gave it up for a new love." Rufus moved his bedroom further away from his father's so he would not have to listen to the endearments his father whispered to someone who was not his mother. But he didn't resent his father's new happiness, he merely didn't want to have to deal with it. "A deceased wife," Quintilian said, "no matter how well loved, will make way in the mind for a new wife; replaced but not supplanted, the new love separate from the old. But a mother cannot be replaced."

After a short pause, Quintilian continued, "There is the vial of poison we have heard about. You all heard Serpo's description of Rufus's actions at his mother's tomb. Can any of you doubt that what was on his mind was suicide? Not the actions of an untroubled mind, perhaps, but hardly the equivalent of murder. We will speak no more about it."

Now Quintilian reached down and picked up the sword Blasus had passed to him earlier and held it flat out before the jurors. "We have been told this is the murder weapon, my friends. A good, honest Roman gladius. Perhaps it is, perhaps it isn't. But if so, and if Rufus is the murderer, then where did he hide it before the murder? For he must have had it for a long time; he hadn't been away from his room, other than briefly, for months. And those times he did leave his room, his faithful body slave Serpo went with him. Even when he didn't want Serpo along, even when he didn't know Serpo was following him, Serpo was there. But Serpo never saw Rufus with a sword. Did you, Serpo?" he looked out into the audience, where Serpo might be standing, and then looked back. "And so blind Rufus must have hidden the sword, and he must have hidden it well."

Quintilian suddenly raised both the sword above his head with both hands. "Close your eyes!" he commanded. "All of you, close your eyes. Now you are blind – only for the moment, fortunately. Now you must go to some place in your house, with family, servants and slaves all about, and hide a sword. Make sure no one sees you, even though you're blind and cannot tell who might be watching. Where will you put it? Under your bed, as Blasus would have it? And will the slave who makes up your bed not see it? And remember, at some future time you're going to have to come to this hiding place, wherever it is, and remove the weapon, in stealth and silence and unobserved. But are you unobserved? Can you be sure?"

Quintilian lowered the sword. I made a slight noise as I reached for a fresh tablet to continue taking down his words, and he looked crossly at me. Then he returned his gaze to the jurors. "Let us look at the story of this crime as presented by my good friend Blasus Parenas," he told them. "He would have it that young Rufus rose from his bed in the middle of the night and retrieved the gladius from whatever secret location he had placed it, unobserved. Then he crept down the corridor and opened the door to his father's room. Had his father been awake and cried, 'Why Rufus, what are you doing with that sword?' what would he have replied, do you suppose?

"And then perhaps the strangest act of all. Blind Rufus goes to his father's side and, with one unerring thrust, drives the point of the sword cleanly between the second and third rib and into his father's heart. There were no hesitation marks on the body, no secondary cuts, just the one clean thrust. How many among you, sighted men, trained soldiers many of you, could have done as well? Indeed this Rufus is a paragon."

Quintilian lowered his voice dramatically and leaned forward. "No, I was mistaken, there was one thing stranger – so strange indeed as to have been impossible. The bloody hand prints – the hand prints that were meant to convince all of my clients guilt, to secure his conviction before this court – could not have been created as we are supposed to believe they were created.

"The noble Blasus has left a picture in our minds of Rufus, fresh from murdering his father, staggering back to his room and leaving a bloody hand print here, and a bloody hand print there, seven in all, as the unwitting signature of his guilt. But this was a corridor that Rufus was intimately familiar with; he walked it daily. He had no need to feel his way along." Quintilian pointed a lecturing finger at the jurors. "Consider: would a man who, although blind, could thrust a sword cleanly between two ribs and into the heart have to feel his way along a familiar corridor?

"But, unlikely as it might be, I suppose it is possible. And I promised you a sight of the impossible. Well, you shall have it. Each of those prints on the corridor wall, as you have heard them described, as I myself have seen them, is from a hand freshly dipped in blood. It is a complete, whole, and damning print. But it does not damn Rufus Abracius. It is impossible for young Rufus to have made those prints. Blood does not behave that way."

Quintilian paused and looked over his audience. "Many of you are familiar, perhaps all too familiar, with the behaviour of fresh blood. It would not stay on the hand to be impressed, time after time, to form a detailed image. The first one" – he pressed his hand against an imaginary wall – "would be clear. And perhaps the second. But by the third" – again his hand went up and pressed the air, and the jurors watched carefully – "there would be less blood, and the print would be less distinct. And by the fourth, and fifth, and sixth, the print would diminish and diminish and diminish, until by the seventh it would be scarcely visible at all."

He lowered his hand. "No, my friends, those prints were made by someone who was unfamiliar with the action of blood. Someone who wanted Rufus to get the blame for her acts." He turned to face the widow Lucilla. "Yes, madam, I speak of you. For you murdered your own husband, and contrived for his son – his poor blind son – to get the blame. No one else could have, and no one else had the motive. Who helped you? Who procured the sword? Was it that handsome centurion who sits by your side? Has he been your lover while you were married to Marcus Vexianus Abracius, a tiresome old man twenty years your senior?"

The centurion leaped to his feet, his face red, and clutched the hilt of his sword. Then he looked around and gulped and sat back down.

"Your motive, madam? Your stepson told me without knowing he did. When your husband dies you get only the widow's portion, and Rufus gets the rest – unless Rufus is found guilty of his father's murder and exiled or executed. Then he cannot inherit, and you get it all. So you had a double scheme all along: murder the father and blame the son."

Lucilla stared stolidly at him across the rows of spectators and said nothing.

"And the sword, madam. Was he really killed with that sword? Or was it picked as a man's weapon, one that would not cause anyone to think of you? Did you kill him with a knife first? I rather think you did: a long, slender knife. And then you thrust the sword in the gaping wound; enlarging it so you could get enough blood to make those damning hand prints. And they are damning, madam, they truly are. For they are the prints of a small hand – the hand of Rufus, or the hand of Lucilla. And, as they were made on purpose to point to Rufus, we must assume they were made by Lucilla. What do you say, madam?"

She said nothing.

Quintilian turned back to the jurors. "It is not my task here to prove this lady's guilt, only to establish my client's innocence. And I believe I have done that."

And the voting bore him out. When the ballots were removed from the jar and counted, there were forty-six for innocent and only five for guilty.

The next day Titus came by to congratulate Quintilian and to see to his fee. "Rufus will pay you when the estate is settled," he told him. "He has evicted that woman, but hasn't decided whether to prosecute her or not. Apparently the centurion, a young man from the northern provinces, was indeed her lover, although he has admitted nothing."

"I assumed as much," Quintilian said.

"How did you figure it out?"

"Yes," I added, "how?"

"Once I knew the lady was guilty, the pieces fell easily into place," he told us.

"And how did you know that?" Titus asked.

"The hand prints were of *her* hand," Quintilian said. "When I looked closely at them I saw a slight curve in the print of the thumb. The lady had a scar on her thumb that matched the curve."

"You did not mention that at the trial."

"Of course not. Jurors don't like technical evidence, they will disagree with it as a matter of course. What they are swayed by is oratory: fine words strung together in telling sentences. That's what I teach, not peering at walls!"

"Oh," Titus said.

"You are the master," I told him, "you really are."

"You may write this case up," Quintilian told me. "I can use it as an example in my text book."

"Yes, sir," I said.

"But remember to stress the importance of the rhetoric," he said. "Not those little deductive details. They are not important."

"Of course, sir," I agreed.

A Payment to the Gods

Rosemary Rowe

In Classical Whodunnits, *I was pleased to introduce the
character of Libertus the Pavement-Maker in the story
"Mosaic". Since then Rosemary Rowe has developed the
character in a series of novels –* The Germanicus Mosaic
(1999), A Pattern of Blood *(2000) and* Murder in the
Forum *(2001). So I'm even more pleased to introduce a
new Libertus short story set in Glevum (Gloucester) at the
end of the second century AD.*

*Rosemary Rowe is the maiden name of the author
Rosemary Aitken, a highly qualified academic who has
written over a dozen bestselling textbooks on English
language and communication. There's some rather subtle
communication that takes place in the following story.*

"Why! Libertus the pavement-maker! Come in!
Come in!" My patron, Marcus Aurelius Septimus
greeted me with much assumed surprise – as if I had not in
fact dropped what I was doing in my mosaic workshop and
scuttled half-way across Glevum to be here at his express
command. He turned to the oiled and well fed citizen
reclining on the couch beside him. "Why, this is the very
fellow I was telling you about. Get up, Libertus . . ." this
because I had dropped to one knee before him, as custom
demanded . . . "You know Graupius Lividius, perhaps?"

I did not know Lividius, though I had heard of him. Rich,
much travelled and famously superstitious, he was said to be

a generous patron of the temple (indeed, all his daughters had been dedicated to temple service from birth) and was reputed to offer a personal sacrifice in every town he entered. Men joked that he was afraid of offending the gods, for fear of losing the considerable fortune he had amassed exporting his fine fleeces all over the Empire. Perhaps he did owe his success to divine intervention. Certainly, "the luck of Lividius" had become a local byword, and one look at his stolid, well fed face was enough to suggest that – though he might possess a certain market cunning – he had not become wealthy through the power of his intellect.

"I have not had that honour," I muttered, preparing to drop to the tiled pavement again. I am no longer a young man, and all this formal courtesy is hard on aging knees, but I was grateful to Marcus all the same. It was clear now why he had summoned me. If he had been speaking of me to Lividius, it could only be to recommend my services, and for the sake of gaining a rich commission I would have done more than bob up and down a few times on a hard surface.

But I was spared even that necessity. Graupus Lividius stretched out a restraining hand. "No, no, citizen, do not kneel to me, I was warned by a rune-reader once that undeserved flattery from a stranger would augur ill-luck."

Marcus met my eyes across the table. That rune-reader knew his business, the look said. One day or another his prediction would assuredly come true – and even if it did not, Lividius would attribute this to his own vigilance. I wondered how many sesterces that little piece of advice had cost him.

"Graupius Lividius wishes to commission a pavement," Marcus told me. "He has received good news, and this will fulfil a promise to the gods."

"Good news indeed," Lividius said, eagerly. "The answer to years of prayers, petitions and sacrifices. Monnia, my wife, has given me a son. After two marriages, five daughters – at last a son."

I nodded. "Good news indeed."

It was. Every citizen hoped for a son to carry on the family name, and inherit his father's wealth. A daughter (if she had

not been first given as a temple slave!) of course might have
inherited, but a woman will always be the legal ward of her
husband or of someone in authority, and where great estates
were concerned that is always a liability: it inevitably occasions disputes – in which case there is a lawsuit and half the
fortune ends up in the official coffers. Many son-less citizens
legally adopt a male heir, specifically to avoid such difficulties. My pavement at least would be in honour of a genuine
blessing. "When did this auspicious event take place?"

Lividius put down the wine goblet he had been cradling,
and beamed, proudly. "I received word of it three days ago. I
was returning from Rome, and messengers were sent to greet
me. I have ridden on ahead of the party, and shall arrive
home at my country house tonight."

Again I glanced at Marcus. A man journeying to Rome
might be away for months. I wondered whether the gods
(and Monnia) had after all been jesting with Lividius.
Marcus, though, was shaking his head discreetly, and Lividius's next words disabused me.

"I have been away more than three moons already. I was
sorry to leave my wife at such a time, but the Emperor
wanted fleeces, and of course I could not deny him. I thought
to be back before the birth took place, but it was not to be.
Perhaps her calculations were astray."

I must have a suspicious mind. I was beginning to wonder
how long Lividius and his wife had been married, and if –
after all – it might turn out to be some other man's child he
was fostering, but again his words surprised me. "We had
hoped, you know, before this – last year, when we were first
married. But she fell and lost the child. She was very ill
herself. This time, I was determined to take good care of her.
I have lost two wives in childbirth before. So she had her
own cousin to attend her – more than a midwife, a sort of
female *medica* – right from the start, as soon as ever we knew
she was with child again. And I had the city wise-women
bathe her stomach in a decoction of sacred herbs every night,
right until the birth, to ensure the desired outcome."

He stopped, as though his very words might bring ill-luck,
and emptied the few drops in his goblet into the Vestal fire,

as if to propitiate the fates. "And, the gods be praised, it all worked splendidly. She was brought to bed perhaps five days ago. My brother sent a letter to inform me of the event – since, of course, Monnia has never learned to write. A lusty child he said – active in spite of all the swaddling – and bawling its lungs out when he saw it. Of course the omens were always good." He leaned forward conspiratorially, "I had augurers attend us every night, before we attempted to achieve conception, to decide which was the most auspicious moment."

This unexpected picture of Lividius's married life brought a smile to Marcus's lips, but I had spent ten years in servitude, and I knew how to disguise unseemly amusement. However, the recital had put to rest any doubts I might have had. I sent up a mental apology to the unknown Monnia. "You must be anxious to see your son," I said.

He smiled again, but this time there was anxiety in the darting eyes. "It was important that I should arrange this pavement first. I vowed it to the temple. The priest himself suggested it. He was reading the entrails of a sacrifice I made – before I went to Rome – and he told me then that, if it was a boy, I must make a due and ample sacrifice, before I ever took the child up. Otherwise there would be much unhappiness, he said. He suggested 1,000 sesterces, a sacrificial lamb and a small decorative pavement for the temple. About so big . . ." he gestured with his hands.

I nodded. Before he "took up the child" literally, Lividius meant: the simple civic ceremony where a father seeing his child for the first time, "took it up" from the floor in front of witnesses – usually a priest – and by so doing acknowledged it as his. This priest, obviously, had seen an opportunity to gain something for his deity in the process. And, of course, rather a pleasant roast dinner into the bargain. The meat from sacrifical animals is often distributed to the poor on public occasions, but at more private ceremonies it is the *sacerdotus* who usually consumes it – on behalf of the god, naturally. "I should be honoured to accept the commission," I said, as gravely as I could.

A price must be agreed (of course) under Roman law, to

make the contract binding, and Lividius's offer almost made me whistle. I accepted it with unseemly haste, and the bargain was formally concluded. It seemed to lift a load from Lividius's mind – and (I don't mind admitting) from mine also. The sum involved would keep me in candles and oil for many moons to come.

"Do you have a motif in mind? For the mosaic?" I asked.

Lividius looked at me blankly. "Motif? I . . . I don't know, citizen. Whatever you think appropriate."

Arranging for the pavement had been a priority, clearly, and once he had done that the details of the design were unimportant to him. On the other hand, they were of the utmost moment to me. If my choice displeased him, he might disown the whole contract.

"Some symbol of your household," I pleaded, "Personal to yourself? Or to your wife?"

It was Marcus who came unexpectedly to my aid. "Lividius has asked me to escort him home, to act as witness to the 'taking up'." So that was why Lividius had called on him! It made sense. As the Provincial Governor's personal representative, my patron was one of the most senior magistrates in the country, and in that capacity often acted as celebrant for the imperial religion in civic matters. For a small fee of course. And Marcus had taken the opportunity to put in a word on my behalf.

He did it again. "We shall be travelling in my official carriage," Marcus went on. "If you wished to accompany us, you could act as witness to the ceremony – and at the same time look for inspiration. Something in the villa, I am sure, will strike your artist's eye."

Rather to my surprise, Lividius accepted the idea – almost with relief. "It would seem a most suitable arrangement. If you have nothing more pressing to do this afternoon, citizen?"

I forbore to mention that any plans that I might have had for the afternoon – such as literally minding my own business – had already been superseded when Marcus sent for me. But this was a very lucrative commission. I murmured my agreement, and in a very short space of time found myself sitting between them in a cramped official carriage, trotting southwards from the city, with a pair of slaves in a cart behind, and a couple of Marcus's guard as outriders. Lividius's own servant had been sent on ahead to warn the household of their master's approach.

They were waiting to greet him as we arrived – the whole household of slaves lined up in the entrance as we turned off from the lane. The gatekeeper half-prostrated himself as he opened the gate, and a pair of page-boys ran before us strewing rose petals in our path, while the waiting servants set up a chorus of "Welcome, welcome, the *genus pater-familias.*"

This was, of course, no more than a simple statement of Roman religious "truth". The master of the household was the "genus" of his own hearth, and a statue of him was always included among the household gods. Yet the slaves knew their man. The new father's face flushed with pleasure and he began to look more and more like a *paterfamilias* as we neared the front door. One could almost see the man expanding with self-importance. That would be worth a few quadrans in gifts to the servants later.

The carriage drew to a halt and a dozen hands reached to help us down. Platters of delicacies arrived, as if by magic – sugared plums, and cheese and honeyed cakes. Lividius brushed them all aside. "Time for that later, where is my lady wife?"

She was in the courtyard garden, we were told. It was the first time she had left her bed since the confinement – such a lusty infant had taken its toll of her – but as soon as she had heard of her lord's return she had insisted on rising and getting dressed to meet him. She was . . . but Lividius had already swept them aside with a gesture and was striding through the atrium and out through the passage to the courtyard garden beyond.

We followed.

She was no more than fifteen years herself, if her looks were any guide. She was sitting under a statue of Fortuna, and was dressed in a pale tunic and stola, with a woven blanket around her kees. She looked pale and shaken, as if this getting-up had been too much for her, and her smile for Lividius had a desperate fixity. She half-rose as we approached. "Husband! You have come. This is an unexpected joy – we did not look for you so soon!" She would have said more, have come to meet him perhaps, but the woman standing at her side restrained her.

"Good Monnia, do not over exert yourself." She was beautiful, dark, with a lively intelligent face and a fearless bearing which – to my Celtic taste – made the little-girl blonde prettiness of Monnia seem vapid in comparison. This, clearly, was the female "doctor" Lividius had told us of. She was speaking now. "Most honoured citizen, can you not speak to Monnia? She should be resting – it was a long labour and she has lost much blood. But she insisted that she must rise and come to you. To beg you the indulgence of a resident wet-nurse, though I swore to her that you would grant her supplication instantly."

Lividius preened. But he still said sharply, "Of course I shall do so, Claudia, if you ask it. But have we no wet-nurse in the household? No female slave who has given birth? It would be a pity to waste the opportunity." He spoke dispassionately. The children of slaves were often exposed immediately, to save their owners the cost of raising them, and hiring the woman as a wet-nurse could be a valuable resource.

The girl he had called Claudia looked grave. "For your son, citizen? Suckled by a common slave girl? That scarcely seems fitting. Besides, there is no such female here. That is why I have recommended this girl – Sylvia, come – let the citizen see you."

A buxom woman emerged from behind the arbour. Her ample form, only half-hidden by her tunic and shawl, suggested that she was abundantly equipped to undertake the task for which Claudia had recommended her. She smiled, a fat good-natured grin, dropped a quick curtsey and scampered back to the shelter of the arbour.

"She had a child herself not long ago, and she has raised a lusty family," Claudia went on. "She has enough milk to feed a dozen infants. She has worked for me before: clean, honest, no disease. She has been feeding your boy since he was a few hours old, and he is thriving on it. But she must come and go here, constantly. If you would consent to finding her a room?" Claudia smiled, "As soon as might be possible, citizen. Your son is often hungry, and your wife . . ."

Lividius waved a lofty hand. "I should not expect my wife to feed the child. Well, I agree. As who would not? She shall have her room, here in the villa, near the child. Tonight, if she wishes it." He nodded at the woman, who picked up her basket and hurried off. "Come Monnia, these gentlemen have come to act as witnesses. Where is the child?"

"He is asleep, citizen, in his cradle. Just in his mother's bedroom, in the shade. It is not good for a new child to be brought out into the draughts and chills of the courtyard, even on a sunny day." She nodded towards one of the rooms which led of the verandah around the court. "Monnia and I will fetch him for you now."

"Well, see that you wrap him warmly when you do," Lividius said sharply, obviously alarmed by all this talk of chills.

Claudia laughed, "He will have to be naked for the ceremony!" and taking Monnia gently by the elbow, she led the way slowly towards the mother's room.

The scream that followed made the columns ring. Everyone stared towards the door. Monnia rushed out into the courtyard, looking paler than ever and gesturing wildly, but her voice seemed to have failed her entirely. It was Claudia, following her and clinging to the doorpost for support, who managed to articulate the words. "The boy! The child! Oh, Citizen Lividius, the child has gone!"

"Gone?" We gasped in unison. Marcus added, "How could he have gone?"

Claudia shook her head. "I cannot answer that, Excellence. The child was there, only moments ago. Sylvia has just been feeding him. See – the cradle is still warm from his body. But the child is not there."

"Was he not attended?" Lividius demanded.

"Always, most honoured citizen, until tonight. But then,

with your unforeseen arrival . . . the household was concerned with your return. All the servants, and ourselves as
well . . . But we were here, in the courtyard all the time, and
there is no other exit from the room – except into your
chambers, citizen, and that also gives out into the court."

She broke off, shaking, while tears began to course un-
checked down Monnia's face.

"Gone!" Lividius said, and he looked as shocked and
stricken as his wife. "Let me see there!" He strode into
the bed-chamber. We followed, all of us – slaves, visitors,
women – as he crossed to the cradle and thrust back the linen
blanket as if he half-expected to find the child lurking there.

There was no sign of his son, but there was something in
the cradle. A crude wax-tablet, such as tradesmen use, and
on it had been scratched – in poor Latin and in poorer script
– "CDENIIPROFILIOTUO" – "100 denarii for your son".

I looked at Marcus and he looked at me. I had been
inclined, until that moment, to regard this as some internal
matter in the household – some servant exceeding his duty or
playing some cruel trick upon his mistress, perhaps. This put
an altogether different complexion on the matter.

Lividius had turned pale. "They have stolen him, for
money."

"You know who might have done this thing?" I was,
perhaps, speaking out of turn, but Marcus's glance had
given me authority – I had often assisted him in inquiries
before[1] and his look had said, as plainly as if it had been
written on the wax. "*Find out, Libertus, before we are here all
night.*"

Lividius shook his head in bewilderment. "No," he said,
"A man of my wealth often has enemies – but this? A poor
defenceless child. No, Libertus, I do not know who – and I
do not understand *how*, either! The child was here one
minute, and the next minute he was not – and the were
witnesses in the court the whole time. It is impossible!"

"Yes," I said, slowly. "It does seem so, certainly. Perhaps
the child is in the villa still?"

1 see *The Germanicus Mosaic, A Pattern of Blood*, and *Murder in the Forum*
for accounts of these inquiries.

"Then search!" Lividius bellowed. "And warn the gate-keepers. No one is to enter or to leave until the child is found." Immediately a dozen slaves were scampering in all directions. Monnia began to falter after them.

"Monnia!" Lividius cried. "You are not strong enough . . ." but it was clearly hopeless. His wife turned such huge and frightened eyes on his that he shrugged his shoulders in resignation.

"I will attend her," Claudia said, and the two women left together.

Lividius turned to Marcus. "Well, we shall search the villa – though we may be too late. Whoever stole the child could be a mile away by now. The back entrance, through the farm, is not well guarded. And the child should not be out in the air, so Claudia says. Please Jove that nothing happens to it." He shivered. "I should have made a bigger sacrifice at the temple before I left Glevum, but I was in haste. This is the hand of the gods, I feel it." He looked wildly about him, and then dashed out to join in the search.

Marcus raised an eyebrow. "The hand of the gods, Libertus? You do not believe that."

I did not believe it, but I do not speak lightly against the immortals. "The hands of the gods, I think," I said, carefully, "would write better grammar."

Marcus nodded. "But it is strange, is it not? The child disappearing so completely. And then – the message – it almost seems . . . supernatural."

"Yes," I said. "The message. That is the strangest thing of all."

"Because of how it appeared?"

"Because of what it said. Or didn't say." It was tempting to go on teasing Marcus, but he was looking perplexed – which never pleased him – so I went on. "One hundred denarii to whom? And where? Lividius says he does not know. How, then, is he supposed to pay? And why 100 denarii? It is a large sum, certainly – but not a fortune. Far less, for instance, than the cost of what that priest demanded as a 'due and ample sacrifice'. Surely a child-thief could have asked far more."

Marcus's face cleared, "So you think . . . what? That
Lividius knows more than he admits?"

"I think . . ." I began, choosing my words carefully. I did
not know what I thought – beyond an uncomfortable feeling
that all was not what it seemed – but I was spared the
necessity of saying so by the reappearance of Lividius at
the head of his contingent of slaves. They had searched, he
reported, everywhere – the public rooms, the gardens, the
outhouses – even the ornamental pool, and the farm-labour
slaves were even now searching the farm – combing the
haystacks, the stables, byres and stres. And a pair of riders
had been sent to scour the paths and lanes around.

"Yet no one working in the fields behind the house or the
gardens in front of it has seen anyone nearby, on horseback
or on foot, since we arrived ourselves." He shook his head.
"This is an enchantment, witchcraft, Marcus. Some malice
of the gods." He was punching one fat fist with the other, in a
kind of frenzied frustration.

"A strange enchantment," I said, quietly, "that asks a
ransom."

He looked at me morosely. "What other explanation is
there? The infant was here when we arrived, and now he is
not here – and the gatekeeper swears that no one has gone in
or out of the gate since we did."

That stopped me. "No one?"

"No one." He stared at me.

"That woman," I said, "Sylvia! Why am I such a fool? She
was about to leave the villa. And she had a basket with her – a
big straw thing she slung upon her back. I saw her with it.
Where is she now?"

A young slave girl stepped forward, her face ashen. "Citizen, there is no mystery in this. Sylvia is in the slave
quarters as we speak. I saw her there when we were searching. She goes there always, when she has fed the child, to
wash her breasts – by Claudia's orders. There is always
perfumed water set for her. Claudia is with her now."

"And Monnia?"

"Resting, as I saw her," a small page-boy said. "In
Claudia's quarters. Claudia urged that she should lie upon

the bed, and there were . . . gentlemen" (he gestured, blushing, towards myself and Marcus) "in here."

My patron looked at me. It was true, of course, we had usurped her bedroom. "Well, Libertus? What say you now?"

"I say that I would like to see this Sylvia – and quickly too."

Lividius nodded, and the small maidservant led the way across the courtyard to the crowded barn where the slaves had their beds. It was divided into rough sections by coarse, ragged sacking curtains, sagging from the beams. From one of these makeshift cubicles there came the sound of hushed voices and of splashing water.

"So you will come tonight? As soon as can be? Lividius has given his consent . . ."

I might have stayed to hear more, but Lividius, who had followed me, with his retinue (the first time, doubtless, he had ventured into this area of his domain) strode past me and wrenched aside the curtain.

Sylvia was there, rinsing her swollen breasts in a copper pan – in which, as everyone could see, dried heads of lavender were floating. Her heavy basket was lying on the straw which formed the bed. She turned at our approach and snatched up her cloak around her.

"The basket!" Lividius roared, ignoring her nakedness. "What have you in the basket? Seize it, slaves! Libertus thinks the child is hidden there." At his voice, as if to prove the point, a feeble whimper issued from the basket. "Great Jove!" Llvidius said. "He was right." He whirled on Sylvia, who cowered away from him. "You have stolen my son. I shall have you whipped. If there is any harm to him, I shall have you killed."

Slyvia dropped to her knees, imploringly, but it was Claudia who broke the silence – with an unhappy laugh.

"There is a child, citizen. That is true. But – I much regret – it is not your son."

Lividius frowned.

"No," Claudia said, "No – citizen, hear me out, I beg of you. This is my fault. I befriended this poor woman. Her husband is dead, and she has a child – she needed work, and I recommended her here, as wet-nurse. This you know. But she could not leave the child unattended – and sometimes she could find no one to sit with it. I persuaded her that it was safe to bring it here There was no harm, citizen, and the woman is innocent. Blame me, if anyone." She looked from Llvidius to me, and there was a high spot of colour in her cheeks. A formidable woman, and an attractive one.

All eyes were on Lividius, but he was not susceptible to this kind of beauty. "You are telling me, woman, that this . . . creature . . . has been smuggling an infant in and out of my house for days? And then my son mysteriously disappears? You expect me to believe this nonsense?"

"Not smuggled, no citizen. Until today she has brought it openly when she must. But when you arrived so unexpectedly – she feared you would be angry at her presumption. I gave her something – to make it sleep. It is not wise with infants, but it was the best we could contrive. And then someone played this foolish trick – and see what a dreadful position it has put us in."

I had not been expecting this, I confess. I said, "There is, I suppose, some way that you can prove this tale? Who has ever seen her with this child? Except yourself, of course?"

Claudia looked at the assembled slaves. "Why, many people, citizen. The gatekeeper for one, and other servants too."

There was a little murmur of agreement – the maidservant who had shown us the way said shyly, "I have seen Sylvia's child often, citizens. I asked to dandle the child one day, while Sylvia was feeding the boy – but Claudia bid me let it sleep lest it disturb the household."

What the girl had said struck me forcibly. "So you have seen both of the infants together, at one time? You are quite sure of this?" If this were true, my suspicions were unfounded.

The child turned big, liquid eyes on me. "Quite certain, citizen. Sylvia was suckling one, and the other was lying in the basket. And I had seen Sylvia's child before – when she came to the villa even before Monnia's child was born. A small baby, it seemed, compared to Monnia's when it came –

though I saw him only an hour or two after he was born. And only yesterday . . ."

So another of my theories lay in ruins. I would have asked the girl more, but Lividius had lost patience with my enquiries. "Lies, lies, all lies!" he exclaimed. "The child in the basket must be mine, and this wretched woman hoped to wrest money from me for its safe return. Well, she shall have her reward – though not the kind she hoped for! Take her away – and take my son back to its mother."

Claudia prevented him. "Citizen, believe me, this is not your child."

"How can you prove that?" Lividius sneered. "As I have never seen the child?"

"No citizen, believe me . . ." Claudia moved to the basket and lifted back the covers as she spoke – "there is other proof, more pressing than my word."

And then, of course, I saw. I looked at Claudia. "You mean . . .?"

She met my eyes. "Of course." She lifted from the basket a small, whimpering child, and unwrapped its limbs and body from the bandages which wrapped it, so as to preserve its strength and encourage its limbs to grow straight. I am no expert on babies, but even I could see that this was nobody's son.

I felt a little foolish. Everyone's eyes were now on me – accusingly, as if I had brought them to this embarrassment. "Excuse an old man, Claudia," I said. "I see that I was mistaken. Pray, wrap the girl-child up again. As you have already said, it is not fitting for an infant to be exposed to cold airs."

"Then," Marcus said, "We are no further forward. The child is missing, stolen by some person unknown – demanding money for his safe return. Strange, as Libertus said, that they left no instruction where to send the coins."

Lividius seemed to feel the need for action. "Well, we will continue the search. And this women – Sylvia – can go: we will not need her services again."

I saw Claudia stiffen. "But, Lividius," she said urgently. "Don't you see? Your child must be safe. If he were dead, he would be worthless to his captors, whoever they are. Perhaps they will try to contact you again. I'm sure they will and soon." Her voice was urgent.

"It is that priest," Marcus said. "I would lay money on it. Seeing another way to seize money for his temple."

As if in answer to the blasphemy, the first few drops of rain began to fall on the courtyard. "An omen!" Lividius said. "For speaking ill of the temple."

I looked at the rain, and at Claudia, at Sylvia, and at the child sleeping again in the basket. The temple! Of course! "I think, perhaps," I said slowly, "that I understand."

Claudia looked at me anxiously, then glanced away. That confirmed it. I was correct, I was sure.

"It seems that you were right, Lividius, all along" I said. "This omen cannot be an accident. This was some ordeal sent you from the gods – a test of your loyalty to them. That 100 denarii – it is clear to me now. It is to be an offering to the gods. You must take it to the temple, straightaway. Yourself, in person. Meanwhile, have sacrifices offered here at every household shrine. But you have read the legends – you must trust the gods! Make everything here ready for your son's return. Do you not think so, Claudia?"

She met my eyes, and coloured. "Citizen, I do."

Marcus was looking at me as if I had taken leave of my senses, but I signalled to him with my eyes. "Then I will accompany Lividius to the temple," he said, judging my message rightly. *And I will deal with you later*, his tone added.

Even then it took ten minutes for Lividius to collect his 100 denarii and get himself into the carriage. I waited until the wheels had faded from our hearing before I went back into the triclinium and confronted Monnia.

"Why did you do it, Monnia?"

She seemed about to protest, but changed her mind. She looked at me plaintively. "How did you know?"

"When something is impossible," I said. "That may be because it is not true. We had a cradle – still warm – we had a baby in the house. It seemed to me there was only one solution. That was the baby from the cradle. The missing child could not be found because no child was missing. I presume that Sylvia's child is a boy?"

She nodded. "We agreed from the beginning. All the omens, you see – they'd said it was a boy. And I began to think, suppose that it is not? And then Sylvia had a son – a healthy boy. And her husband was dead – Claudia had used her before as a wet-nurse, and it seemed . . . well, fated almost. If my child was a boy – no harm was done. It was Claudia's plan. If it were a girl – then – I would take Sylvia's child and she mine. She would come to live in the villa, and bring the girl-child with her as her own. It was so simple. But, when it came to it, I could not bear to part with my child. I kept putting it off. And then, Lividius returned. Much sooner than we expected. The servant suddenly came and said he would be there within the hour. I sent for Sylvia. She was to take my child in her basket and come back with her own."

"And then," I suggested, "Lividius came too soon?"

"Sylvia had hardly reached us when he came. When I heard the carriage come I could not think. Claudia saw to it. She took my child from its cradle and gave it to Sylvia. They could hunt the boy now, she said, and never find him. And then, next morning, there the child would be. At the temple, perhaps, or in a cradle by the nymphaeum. Lividius is a superstitious man – he would think it marvellous. That was the plan, the best we could contrive between us at the time."

"Who knew of it?"

"Only we three. Claudia attended me at the birth – only she knew the sex of the child. And it was a lusty baby – Lividius's brother took it for a boy."

"Yes," I said. "It took some time for me to realize that it would have been swaddled when he saw it. But why did you not bring Sylvia to the house at once?"

"I dared not do so. Quite apart from my husband's displeasure, the servants would have got to know the child, if it lived in the servant's quarters, and noticed any substitution at once. As it was, the little maidservant was showing an unhealthy interest in him. I could only allow my own child to be glimpsed by the servants when it was swaddled and asleep. Fortunately, babies change very fast. Claudia had to keep the maids away and tend to me herself, claiming that I was ill. Though today I was glad enough of her subterfuge – I was half-fainting with alarm."

"And the note?"

Monnia flushed. "That was my idea. I thought that it would draw attention away from us. Lividius knows I cannot write, and Claudia has a distinctive hand. I made Sylvia do it – she taught herself her letters by reading the inscriptions on the graves by the road. I never thought of suggesting where to pay the money."

"And you were not afraid, ever, that Sylvia would betray you?"

Monnia looked at me. "Claudia is my cousin," she said simply, "And Sylvia is her niece – but now all our other family is dead of the plague. Sylvia would starve without Claudia. As she would starve without me." She sighed. "So what will you do now? Tell Lividius? He will divorce me. I suppose you think he had reason, since I deceived him. There will be disgrace. I know what the magistrates will say. What kind of wife would sacrifice her child for ever, just to satisfy her husband's desire for a son?"

"But," I said softly, "that is not what you did, is it?"

"So you *do* understand?"

"I think so. You wanted to give your husband a son, in order NOT to sacrifice your child for ever."

She nodded.

"Yes, I know. It was a mention of the temple that made me see the truth. What did Lividius ever do with girls? He gave them to the temple at birth, and their mothers never saw them again."

Monnia nodded again. "But if Sylvia was to be my wet-nurse, I should keep the child near me. I should have asked Lividius to buy her as my pet when she was old enough. I know my husband. He would be so pleased to have his son, he would have done anything for me. But – I suppose you must tell him, if you must."

I shook my head. "I am here to design a pavement. For his son, supposing he can be found. Although I imagine, don't you, that when Lividius returns, the boy will be miraculously back in his cradle? A simple mosaic, I think – don't you agree – with perhaps a swaddled child as a central motif?"

The Last Legion

Richard Butler

Born and educated in England, Richard Butler's move to Australia in 1963 to take up a teaching appointment was replete with incident. The ship caught fire and soon after his arrival he was involved in a light aircraft crash in Tasmania's rugged south-west. He moved to Victoria where, following the publication of his fourth novel, The Buffalo Hook *(1974), he gave up teaching for a dual career as a writer and actor. So far he has published a play for television, two radio plays, nineteen novels, and four stories in the Mammoth series. He lives near Melbourne, working as a writer and script consultant, and presenting a weekly local radio programme.*

In the following story he takes us to the final days of the Romans in Britain and perhaps the last crime they had to solve! Richard also remarked that the language of soldiers has been much the same throughout history, so he has used colloquial English to represent the speech of the Roman legionaries.

"So you're not coming with us, Spiro?"

"No, I'm not. We were given a choice, weren't we? Go or stay. I'm a Briton. I was born here; I joined up here when they wanted local recruits and I've done five of my twenty-five here. What's Rome to me, that I should go poncing off to defend it? It's not even as if there were games and chariot races, like in the old days. Half empty, from what they say. It's different for you, Marcellus. You're a Roman. Parents in Ostia, aren't they?"

"And my sisters. If that barbarian bastard Alaric and his Visigoths are coming down from the north, I want to be there to protect them."

"Course you do, mate, course you do. Mind you, I doubt if our lot will exactly put the frighteners on the Visigoths, unless they die laughing. The rearguard, left behind to pack up, that's all we are. The odds and sods from the 2nd, 19th and 40th who've already left. Blokes who'd gone sick or AWOL."

The two legionaries of the 2nd centuria of the 3rd cohort of the 15th Legion* – *Legio XV Britannia Felix* – were sitting with their *bracae*, their woollen calf-length trousers, round their ankles in the latrine of the fortified camp at Rutupiae on the south-east coast of Britain. On this warm June morning, it was a cool and comfortable place. Beneath wooden benches, arranged in a U-shape and with holes two *pedes* apart, was a deep stone channel through which water, piped from a nearby stream, flowed in, round the U and out again, taking the waste with it. Another smaller channel at the soldier's feet carried clean running water to wash the sponge on a stick with which he cleaned himself. A tiled roof above the benches kept off the rain and sun but in the middle the building was open to the sky. There was no foul odour, no flies.

"All the same, I have to go," Marcellus said. "Just as you've got to stay with your woman. Or," he added with a grin, "women". Spiro's full name was Silanus Gaius Escobinius but his nickname was short for *suspirium puellarum* – "the one the girls sigh for" – because of his incredible success with them.

"Just the one at present." Spiro, twenty-six, good-looking, black-bearded and, at 70 *unciae*, just over the minimum height for the Legion, grinned back. "My Gwynedd."

* In its prime, a Roman legion consisted of ten cohorts, each commanded by a prefect (*praefectus*). A cohort was made up of six centuriae each under a centurion. However, by the beginning of the fifth century, at which time this story is set, the Army, like everything else Roman, was in a state of flux and its organization varied considerably.

"I suppose you realize it's not exactly going to be a public holiday here once *Britannia Felix* leaves and the Painted Men come roaring over the Wall looking for blood and plunder and women?"

"Aw, the Picts are a long way off. It's the Angli and Saxones we'll have to contend with here in the south. And the Alemanni and Marcomanni and anybody else who feels like a nice sea voyage with a spot of rape and pillage thrown in." For a moment they were silent, thinking of the unknown future, while the water in the channel below gurgled soothingly. "Mind you, I don't know why the barbarians bother to come here. Poor crops, wine like piss and prices going up like sparks in a fire. God only knows how Rome let it get like this."

Marcellus sighed. "The fact is, we've been going downhill for a long time and the barbarians have got stronger and more organized. As for the Saxones and Angli, they're down to your people, Spiro. Once the townsfolk heard we were leaving, they decided to invite them in as mercenaries to fight the Picts." Marcellus grunted cynically. "It was pretty stupid – like asking a wolf to guard your larder. Once they'd got their foot in the door that was it."

"I suppose so, but they didn't have much –."

He was interrupted by a shout. "Silanus Gaius Escobinius!"

"Oh God protect us! It's Roscius the Rat. Whatever he wants, it means trouble."

Marcellus said, "Shut up! If we lie low he might go away." Roscius Marius Commodus was a *librarius cohortis*, an orderly room clerk. Toadying, treacherous and corrupt, he was one to be avoided at all costs.

No dodging him on this occasion, however. He came into the latrine at the double, panting, his pimply face blotched with the unaccustomed exertion. Spiro said, "Hallo, if it isn't me old mate Ratty! What's the hurry, darlin'? Been at the prunes again, have we, then? Tucking into the beans at breakfast? I heard that the pigs threw up when they smelt those beans –."

"I'll report you, Silanus Gaius Escobinius! You should be helping to load the carts!"

"Ah, but I got this call of nature, see, Ratty? Prunes, it must have been. Or the beans." He picked up his sponge-stick and waggled it at the spindly clerk.

Roscius glowered at Spiro. "You insolent British barbarian! I'll teach you a lesson before I leave this horrible hole! Meanwhile you are to report to the Commanding Officer immediately! In the *Praesidium*!"

"The Prefect's quarters?" Spiro's heart ceased to function briefly, then picked up at twice its normal speed. "Not at HQ?"

"Are you deaf? The *Praesidium*! And be quick about it!" The Rat turned and left.

"*Medius fidius*, Spiro! You've gone as white as the Emperor's toga! What have you been up to? Sneaking off to the shrine of Mithras again? You know it's forbidden for a Christian to worship any other gods –."

"Worse than that." Spiro was using his sponge, wincing as usual at the cold water. "I had it off with the Prefect's wife, see –."

"What? The Lady Serenilla? Jesus Christ and Jupiter, Spiro! You must be mad!"

"Had no choice, did I? I was replacing some tiles in their bathroom. The CO was away at a meeting with the Prefect of the 6th Cohort. She comes in, whips her togs off and orders me to hop in with her. When I hesitated –."

"And who wouldn't? Why didn't you refuse, idiot?"

"Do me a favour! How could I? She said if I disobeyed, she'd scream the place down and accuse me of attempted rape. Talk about Scylla and bloody Charybdis! Said she wanted a child and her husband couldn't give her one." He washed his sponge. "Funny if I had a son in the Roman upper crust, eh?"

"If the Prefect's found out, he'll have you torn apart by horses!"

"D'you think I don't know that?" He pulled up his *bracae*. "Ah well. We who are about to die salute you!" He gave a forlorn wave. "If you see Gwynedd, tell her I might not be home for supper." He went out.

★   ★   ★

Along the ruler-straight Via Praetoria, dodging the rumbling carts that were carrying everything from paintings to pots and pans down to the ships. Along the Via Principalis to the luxurious *Praetorium* that took up one tenth of the camp. He stood at the side door set in the painted red and white wall. A legionary could not expect to enter the CO's quarters through the front. He straightened his grubby tunic, combed his beard with his fingers. He had calmed down somewhat. *Surely if they'd wanted to arrest me, they'd have sent a squad, not Roscius the Rat?* He drew a deep breath and knocked.

The door flew open instantly – the slave must have been watching though the peephole. "Legionarius –." He cleared his throat. "Legionarius Silanus Gaius Escobinius, reporting to the Prefect," he said, keeping his voice steady. The slave beckoned and led the way.

Across the stable yard. Into the waiting area, its floor a mosaic of flowers and birds. Down marble steps and along a tiled corridor that ran beside the columned atrium, filled with sunlight. Three steps up. The bathroom was round to the right, he recalled with a shudder. The slave tapped on a door at his left, went in and bowed. "Legionarius Silanus Gaius Escobinius!" Spiro went into the *tablinum* – the Prefect's study, with its table and stool, its shelves with cylindrical leather boxes holding scrolls. He raised his right arm in salute.

Quinctilius Fabius Cornelius Silvanus, the elderly, aristocratic Prefect of the 3rd Cohort, sat behind his table dressed in an immaculately folded toga, his clean-shaven, olive-skinned face set in a frown. No fighting man, he had been sent out from Rome to administer the dismantling of the fortress at Rutupiae and see the cohort safely home.

Beside the table stood Julius Gregorius Draccus, centurion of the 2nd centuria, a colossus in plated body armour, standing 8 *pedes* from the soles of his hobnailed boots to the crimson crest on his gleaming helmet. Born in the slums of Rome, he was a grey-bearded veteran who, like all centurions, had risen from the ranks and now had thirty years' service to his credit. Tough as teak, with a craggy, beetle-browed face that looked as if it had been cast in bronze, his boast was that he could out-march, out-drink and out-fight any man in the centuria. He'd done it, too, competing with men half his age. He glared at Spiro. "Escobinius!" he rasped. "You're out of uniform! How dare you report improperly dressed?"

"Aw, Centurion, I was told to report immediately –."

"Never mind that!" The Prefect rapped the table. "Silanus Gaius Escobinius, you are called here because of a murder that took place last night in the *Principia*."

Murder? "Wasn't me, sir." *MURDER?* "Never went near HQ last night –."

"Be silent!" snarled the Centurion.

"You are not accused," the Prefect said. "Someone broke into the *aedis*, robbed the treasure-chest and murdered Marcus Sextus Curtius, the *signifer*."

Jesus and Jupiter! The *aedis*, the chapel, was the most important room in the HQ building. There were stored, under double guard, the Emperor's statue, the cohort's standards and its battle flags. Beneath a stone slab was kept the great iron-bound wooden chest that contained the unit's funds – pay for the troops, cash to buy horses, fodder, food and any other running expenses. It also held the legionaries' savings deducted from their pay, out of which they bought their clothing and weapons. It was all managed by the standard-bearer, the *signifer*, who was also the cohort's banker. *But what's this got to do with me?*

The Prefect pointed a finger at Spiro. "The Centurion has recommended that you should be given the task of finding the murderer –."

"What? Me?"

"– And thus recovering the money."

They were both looking at him. There was a silence. He said, his brain in a daze, "Sir, I'm right chuffed – pleased, that is – to be given this task. And honoured, of course. But, well, I dunno as I deserve it."

"Nonsense," snapped the Prefect. "The Centurion has told me how you cured our horses of the disease that threatened to kill them all. He's told me about you and my wife –."

"Aagh!"

"What?"

"Sorry, sir. Touch of wind, sir."

"Were you not heard to predict one night in the inn that she, who had been barren, would conceive? Which indeed has come to pass. It's well known that you Britons possess magic powers. I command you to use them."

"Sir, what about the guards in the *aedis*?" Spiro asked. "Why didn't they sound the alarm?" In case of an emergency they couldn't handle, the guards could pull a rope and ring a bell on the roof.

"They were snoring like hogs," the CO said contemptuously.

Draccus growled. "I have yet to decide how they will die."

"Here." The Prefect pushed across the table a wooden tablet with a message written in wax. "This is my authority for you to question anyone and go anywhere. That is all." He waved a hand in dismissal.

The Centurion and Spiro saluted. Outside, Spiro said, "Sir, I'm not up to this."

Draccus growled, "You'd better be, laddie."

"I cured the horses with an ordinary draught. As for the Prefect's wife –." He stopped.

"Well?"

"A lucky guess," he said quickly. "How am I going to –?"

"That's enough!" The Centurion turned to face him. "Now you listen to me, Silanus Gaius Escobinius. The Prefect's given you an order and you're bloody well going to obey it. If you refuse, it's mutiny and field punishment. Like being tied to a tree in the forest and left for the wolves. Or buried alive –."

"I'll do it! I'll do it!" Spiro said quickly.

"Good lad! Thought you would." Draccus showed his teeth in the snarl that was the closest he got to a smile. "But you'll have to work fast. You've only got a few days. As soon as the ships are loaded, we'll sail with the next favourable wind. Come with me." He strode off to the *Principia*, which was next door to the CO's quarters. "You can start with a look at the *aedis*."

There were the usual two guards outside the *Principia* but two more were posted just inside. All were armed with sword, dagger and javelin. They saluted as Draccus tramped through the archway and across the courtyard, where legionaries stood in little clusters, talking. They saluted and fell silent as the Centurion passed. In the colonnaded *basilica* the sentries were doubled again, the two in front of the *aedis* looking particularly alert. Draccus snapped, "Nobody's been inside this morning?"

"No, Centurion," one said. "Apart from the burial party."

"Blood and brains cleaned up, I hope? Floor polished?"

"Aye, Centurion."

"Brains?" Spiro asked.

"Head bashed in."

They went up four steps into the *aedis*. The statue of Honorius Flavius, Emperor of the West, eyed them knowingly, as if to say, "Oh, yes, I saw who did it but I'm not saying a word." Behind him in their racks were the cohort's eagle standards, one for each of the six centuriae. Ten *pedes* long, they bore the badges of the unit's success in battle. At the top of each was a plaque embossed with *Legio XV Britannia Felix*, the number of the centuria and a bronze lourel wreath surmounted by an eagle, its wings spread. At the Emperor's feet the stone slab stood open, revealing the empty treasure-chest. The tasselled bell-rope hung in a corner.

Spiro said, "Who found him?"

"The relief guards. They also found the street gate open."

"Ah!" Spiro nodded. It was always barred by the guards from sunset to dawn.

"One of them reported to me immediately. Had the sense not to sound the alarm."

"How much was taken?"

"All the bags of gold coin. The copper and silver were left behind."

"Not worth carrying away, I suppose." Spiro looked around. "Aha!" He pointed at the rack. "Look there, sir!"

Wedged behind the hafts of the standards and hardly

visible was a small jute sack encrusted with dried blood. "The weapon the murderer used!" Spiro said.

"*Mehercule*, I believe you're right" Draccus said. He strode across to the rack, picked up the heavy bag and clinked it. "You've got good eyes, Silanus Gaius Escobinius. One of the bags of copper *denarii*. You could certainly smash a man's skull with this. But a strange choice of weapon, eh?"

"I was just going to say that, Centurion. You'd think the murderer would have used his sword."

"You would indeed." Draccus fingered the short sword on his left hip. "Quick thrust and that would be it."

"Unless," Spiro said excitedly, "he had no sword!"

"Wasn't a soldier, you mean?" The Centurion stared at him "That's brilliant! I believe you do have magic powers! Someone from the village, eh?"

"Of course! Let's say he and the *signifer* were in league. They found the guards asleep, came in here and opened the slab. But then the accomplice decided to have all the gold for himself so he grabbed the bag of copper coin, killed the *signifer* and made off."

"That's very good, Spiro," Draccus said. "You're halfway there already. I knew you'd do it. Go into the village and see what you can find out."

"Thank you, sir." Spiro watched him stride away, noting that he was now using his nickname. But his excitement was cooling off. *No, that won't work – it's too easy. Marcus Sextus Curtius, the signifer, was well known to be an honest man – wouldn't have been trusted with the money, otherwise. And how could they count on the guards being asleep? No, too many holes in that theory.*

He went out into the *basilica* and round to the cells. A guard said, "And where do you think you're going, mate?"

"To talk to the prisoners."

"Oh, no, you're not. Piss off before I report you!" Silently, Spiro dangled his authority under the guard's nose. "What's this, then?"

"Can't you read?"

"Not much. Well, not at all, in fact."

"This is a written order from the Prefect saying that

anybody who gets in my way will be down for javelin practice tomorrow morning."

"That's all right, then. I don't mind javelin practice."

"You would if you were the target."

"Ah! Right!" He stood aside and drew the bolt on the door.

The smell was horrible. No latrine for prisoners – just a hole in the floor. Spiro peered at the two legionaries, who were huddled in a corner. They stared at him in terror, relaxing somewhat when they saw he was unarmed. He went inside and the guard slammed and bolted the door behind him. "What happened?" he asked. "And remember, your only chance is to tell the truth."

"We tried to tell the Centurion," one of them said. "But he wouldn't listen. It was all down to this redhead, see? She –."

"What redhead?"

"Dunno, but she was a real looker and no error," said the first guard. "Wearing a short tunic. Lovely legs, she had, all the way to the ground. Hair down her back the colour of copper. Had this amphora of wine, see? And a cup. Just appeared from nowhere."

"Nobody about at that hour, o'course," the other said. "She said we looked bored. Needed cheering up. Poured wine for us both."

"Bloody fools we were. Next thing we knew, the Centurion was kicking the shit out of us and there was the *signifer's* corpse lying beside the hole." He looked beseechingly at Spiro. "Can't you put in a word for us, sir? I got a clean sheet up to now –."

"Me, too, sir," the other said eagerly. "Do what you can for us, eh?"

"Don't call me sir. I'm just a ranker like you, mates." *Poor devils!* "I'll speak to the Centurion but I wouldn't put money on it. Would you be able to identify the girl?"

"Would I ever!" said the first one. "Hair like that? You wouldn't forget her in a hurry."

"Just gimme a look at her legs," the other said.

"I'll do what I can." *If they can identify the woman, they may get off with a whipping. Because, once we've got her, Draccus will make her give us the name of her accomplice. Torture her, if necessary. Perhaps this won't be too difficult, after all!* He turned left towards the south gate, the one that led to the *vicus*, singing to himself, "Oh, the girls of Londinium are beautiful to see/ But if you don't watch it you'll tum-tum-diddly-dee . . ."

The *vicus*, the camp-followers' settlement, consisted of a paved street lined with wooden buildings with shingled roofs. Most were shops with an open end that could be closed at night with wooden slats. A stone counter stood in front. They provided almost anything the legionaries could want, from honey cakes and helmets to salted fish and sandals. The street was a bedlam of noise, crowded with rowdy soldiers, bellowing cattle being driven to the wharf, porters yelling for the right of way and laden carts with cursing drivers. Spiro made for the *caupona*, the largest building in the village.

It had six bedchambers, baths with hot and cold rooms, and a big dining room serving excellent meals. Magus, the innkeeper, did a roaring trade with the camp, the inn being the only place to go when a legionary was off duty. He could drink there with his comrades, eat, roll dice or hire a slave girl for a small charge and have a bath. The girls assisted the customers by cleaning their bodies with perfumed oil and a *strigil*, a wooden scraper. Or, for an extra payment, they could assist in other ways . . .

Magus the *Caupo*, a short, paunchy but powerfully built Briton, stood behind the bar stroking his curly grizzled beard while a couple of pretty slave girls, one dark-haired, the other fair, served his midday clientele. He looked worried, and didn't greet Spiro with his usual crafty grin. "What d'you want, Spiro?" His tone was surly. "If it's credit, you can bugger off. Cash only from now on, it is."

"It's information I'm after. Where were you last night?"

"Who wants to know?"

"The Prefect." He took out his wax tablet.

The Caupo glanced at it. "On his staff, then, are you? He can't be very choosy, you in that mucky tunic."

"Just answer the question, Magus."

"All right, all right. Well, if you must know, I was in my own bed." He pointed to the dark-haired slave girl. "With Florentina there. Ask her."

"What use is that? She'll say anything you want."

"Suit yourself. I can't provide witnesses – don't go in for bloody orgies." Magus scratched his balding head. "Anyway, I got problems of my own."

"There was a murder up at the camp last night. I've been ordered to find out who did it."

"*Signifer* of the 2nd centuria, eh?"

"How d'you know?"

"I run an inn, mate. Everybody talks in an inn. Like how your *tubicen* had a row with the *signifer* over a girl."

"The trumpeter, eh? What girl?"

"How should I know? As far as I'm concerned, girls are all alike. All with the same equipment. All I know is that somebody told me the standard bearer and the trumpeter of the 2nd were in a fist fight in the bath house the other night."

"Anything else?"

"You want to know about the centurions' gambling school?"

"Which centurions?"

"Ha! It's pretty ignorant you are. Nearly all of 'em. They roll dice in the quarters of Marcus Annaeus Valerius, your *ordo princeps*, the Chief Centurion. You might also be interested in the fact that I looked out of my window in the small hours and saw three legionaries digging a hole in the meadow behind my inn."

"What did you do?"

"Shouted. They cleared off."

"Did you see what was in the hole?"

"I looked this morning. Just air. Right size for a grave, though."

"A grave, eh?" The fair-haired girl gave him a smile as she went past to the kitchen. He watched the way her hips moved in the brief tunic.

"Looks good, eh?" Magus said. "Looked even better

before she cut her golden curls off. But don't even think about it. Cold as a carp, she is. I've tried."

"Depends how you warm her up, Magus. You got a redhead working here?"

"It's redheads you fancy, is it? And you a married man? Well, you're out of luck. I haven't got one." As Spiro turned to leave, Magus grabbed his arm. "Wait a minute, mate. Have a cup of wine. No charge." He nodded to the dark-haired girl.

"With you, there's always a charge, Magus, one way or the other. What is it you want?"

"If you're so well in with the Prefect, can you put in a word for me?"

"Me?" Spiro laughed. "You must be joking." The girl brought the amphora and poured wine for him.

"You're working for him, aren't you? I'll make it worth your while."

Spiro took a drink. "What's it about, then?"

"I told you I got a problem, didn't I?" He put his elbows on the bar. "It's this. When the 15th leaves, what happens to me? No more ships. No wine and food coming in. No customers. I'll be finished."

"So where do I come in?"

"I want you to ask the Prefect if I can buy a passage on one of the ships."

"Go to Rome, you mean?"

"That's right," the Caupo said eagerly. "I could start again, buy a tavern –."

"It's no good me asking the Prefect anything, Magus. I don't have his ear." Spiro finished his wine. "In any case, Alaric and his Visigoths'll be in Rome within a year or two, slitting all the innkeepers' throats. You'll be better off here, believe me, with the Angli and the Saxones. You may even be able to flog them your watered ale. Thanks for the drink, though." He went out into the noise of the crowded street.

Plenty to work on there. The trumpeter fighting with the signifer, eh? Centurions' gambling school – somebody getting into debt, perhaps? And the men digging a grave? For the signifer? How would they get the corpse out of the camp?

And let's not forget Magus himself. "I could start again in Rome," he'd said. *You'd need money for that. A lot of money.*

In front of a baker's, he saw the blonde girl in the crowd waiting to be served. He stood behind her. *No harm in being civil, eh?* "Well, hello, pretty one," he said. "We meet again, it seems."

She turned, smiled at him. "You were in the *caupona*." *Oh, definitely no harm in being civil!* Blonde hair cut short like a boy, green eyes and white teeth, her long and very shapely legs tanned and nicely displayed by the short tunic.

He said, chatting her up, joking, "Buying bread, eh? Doesn't Magus feed you?"

"He feed me, *ja*. I buy the bread, but for the inn, not me." She had a husky voice and an appealing accent.

"What's your name?"

"Gerda. I am Saxone."

"How did you get here?"

"My man was chief. We came with others to find land. But there was fighting. My man killed, I captured. Sold."

"Next!" shouted the baker. She bought a dozen loaves then tried to tuck them under her arms.

But she hadn't enough arms. "You should have brought a sack. Here, give me a few," Spiro said.

"Ne, you are kind but I can –"

"Oh, come on." He took half a dozen loaves. "We're only going round the corner." They set off. Outside the inn he said, "I'd like to spend some time with you. In the baths."

"That would be good, *ja*. But you pay Magus. I belong to him." She went inside, dumped her load then came out to take his. "I thank you for help me." She gave him a warm smile and touched his arm briefly. "Until we meet again."

Cold as a carp, is she? Well, we'll see about that. I'll melt her down . . . He turned to find his wife facing him, her arms folded, her dark blue eyes flashing. "Well! Well!" Gwynedd snapped. "Baker's errand boy now, are we, Silanus Gaius?"

Oh, Jesus and Jupiter! She only calls me that when she's really pissed off! The foolish grin on his face vanished. "Gwynedd, my dearest!" he said, his voice a squeak. "This is a surprise!"

"It is indeed! Isn't it loading carts you're supposed to be, up at the camp?"

"Yes, well, I was –."

"But here you are, dodging into the inn with a slave girl stroking your arm. And then straight into the baths, is it?"

"No, no, I wasn't –."

She came closer and sniffed. "And you've been drinking!"

"Only one, my dear," he said feebly. "Magus gave me –."

"It's no use blaming that wretch of an innkeeper! Just tell me why you are in the village in the middle of the day. Apart from drinking and chasing girls, that is."

"I'm on special duty for the Prefect."

"Ha! Ha!" She snorted derisively. "Special duty for that trollop, more like. Is that the best you can do?"

He produced his written authority. She studied it, frowned and stared at him. "You'd better come home and tell me about it." She turned with a swirl of her blue gown and began pushing through the crowd.

She lived with her mother in a small wooden house in a side street, adding to Spiro's pay by making up and selling herbal remedies from the old woman's vast collection. It was one of these that had saved the cohort's horses. She lifted the latch and he followed her inside. Her mother was pounding some concoction in a mortar, her hair dishevelled and her wrinkled face red with effort. She gave Spiro a basilisk glare – he wasn't her ideal son-in-law, by any means – and shrieked, "What are you doing here in the middle of the day, you idler?" She was stone deaf, which was just as well considering the ululation and bed-rattling that went on when her daughter was in bed with Spiro in the only other room.

Spiro smiled sourly at her and said with heavy irony, "I'm delighted to see you, too, Ma."

"To see me? Who's coming to see me?"

"A large Pict with an axe, I hope."

Gwynedd said severely, "That's quite enough of that, husband. What's this special duty you've been given?"

"There's been a murder in the *Principia*." He told her what had happened. "I have to find out who did it."

"What idiot gave you that job?"

"The Prefect. Centurion Draccus suggested it. They think I possess magic powers."

"They must be moonstruck, both of them. You'll never do it." She put bread and cheese on the table and poured home-brewed ale for him from a jug.

"I thought so too, at first." He munched cheese from one hand, bread from the other. "But I've got a few ideas." He told her about the red-haired girl who had drugged the guards; about the *tubicen*'s quarrel with the *signifer*, about the legionaries digging a grave and about Magus wanting to go to Rome. "Have you sold any sleeping potions lately?"

"No –."

The old lady shouted suddenly, "I want to know who's coming to see me! I might need a new shawl!"

"Now see what you've done?" Gwynedd said. She shook her head at her mother and mouthed, "*No one is coming.*" To Spiro: "Wait! Yes, I did. To Magus. I sold him powdered poppy seeds. He said he'd been unable to sleep."

"To Magus?"

She nodded. "But it was a while ago. What are you going to do next?"

"Find the red-haired girl." He drank his ale.

"Yes, I thought you might start there." Her voice sharpened. "Pretty, I suppose she is?"

He shrugged, feigning indifference. "The soldiers said so."

"I haven't seen any red-haired girls in the *vicus*."

He said, his mouth full, "She may be from up the coast. Londinium, even."

"What will you do if you find her? After you've got her on her back, that is?"

"Gwynedd, how can you be so unkind? You know you're the only girl for me. If I find her I plan to parade her in front of the soldiers. See if they can identify her. Then get the name of her accomplice. It's Magus, I know it."

"Who let her into the *Principia*?"

"What?" He took another piece of bread. "Let her in? How should I know?"

"You'd better find out, husband. The gate's barred at night, isn't it?"

"The relief guard found the gate open –."

"But the guards would have closed it at sunset. So she couldn't have found it open, could she? Somebody must have let her in. Unless she climbed the wall balancing a jug of wine on her head."

"Aye, somebody must," he said, chewing thoughtfully. "Curse it! That lets Magus out. It must have been a soldier after all. One of the guards. They were the only ones in there."

"Whatever would the guards let her in for? Just for a drink, knowing they'd be sentenced to death if they were caught?"

"Well, if you put it like that – perhaps they didn't." He drank his ale and stood up. "I'd better go and have another word with them. Thanks for the grub, my love. See you at supper."

She glanced at her mother, who was carrying on a pitiful conversation with herself about poor old women who'd slaved all their lives for their daughters not being allowed to receive visitors. "I want to talk to you tonight, Spiro. I've something important to tell you. And we must decide what we're going to do."

"Do?"

"After the Legion's gone and the barbarians arrive."

"Simple. We'll just prop your Ma up outside the door. They'll take one look and run a mile."

She tried to look severe and grinned instead. "Be off with you, you creature." She gave him a push. He kissed her and she responded with enthusiasm. All's well, he thought as he went up the street.

He went into the HQ building and round to the cells. The same guard was there but the door of the soldiers' cell was unbarred. He said, already knowing the answer, "Where are they?"

The guard smirked and drew a finger across his throat. "On parade in the Infernal Regions, I should think. Centurion Draccus sent two legionaries soon after you left. Nothing fancy – throats cut. Reckon they got off light."

Draccus was in the *basilica*, studying a roster-board. "Well? How far have you got, Spiro?"

"I'd been hoping to get the prisoners to identify the red-haired girl who drugged them. But they're dead and she's disappeared."

"I don't think you'd have got far with that." Draccus's plate armour clinked as he shrugged. "How do we know there *was* a girl? Only their word for it. No, you'll have to do better than that, my lad, and be quick about it. The Prefect's been advised by the ships' captains that there's bad weather coming. We have to sail in two days' time at the latest or be stuck here for weeks. So two days is all you've got." He strode into the Orderly Room.

Two days? Well, that's that, Spiro thought. *What can I do in two days? But did it really matter? In two days the 15th would be heading for Gaul.* He stood looking at the orders on the board. Minutes later the centuria's trumpeter came out into the *basilica* in full parade dress.

"Lucius Menenius Lanatus!" Spiro said. "Can I have a word?" He was clutching at straws but what else was there?

"What about?" The *tubicen* was small and stout, with puffed-out cheeks as if he was forever blowing an invisible trumpet. Normally garrulous and friendly, he seemed strangely unwilling to stop and chat. "I'm in a hurry."

"Won't take a minute. I believe you had a fight with the *signifer*, Marcus Sextus Curtius, the other night?"

"Ah!" He looked sheepish. "Magus has been talking, eh? Well, I did, but there was nothing in it. We were both pretty far gone and each of us wanted the same girl to scrape his back."

"Where were you last night?"

He fiddled with his belt, looking even more embarrassed. "Well, as a matter of fact, I was on one of the ships down at the wharf."

"Doing what?" *Why doesn't he query my right to ask questions, as the others have done?*

"I'd become – er, friendly with one of the sailors. We had a few drinks on board. I ended up spending the night."

"When did you leave?"

"Soon after the sun was up." He shrugged. "You can find out easily enough. They keep a watch" He hesitated, refusing to meet Spiro's eye. "You're investigating the murder and the theft of the unit's funds, aren't you?"

"Yes. How do you know?"

"I've been in the Orderly Room. I overheard Roscius the Rat talking to Centurion Draccus. They thought they were alone but I was in the store room at the back." He hesitated again and looked around furtively. "I'm afraid you're in trouble, Spiro."

"Me? What for?"

"Come over here." He led the way to the platform at the far end of the *basilica* from which the Prefect addressed his centurions at morning report. "Do you know anything about politics?"

"Politics? No. Why should I?" Spiro was apprehensive and bewildered. "What are you getting at?"

He dropped his voice. "The Silvanus family is out of favour in Rome – suspected of conspiracy. That's why the Prefect was sent out here – to get him out of the way. So can you imagine what will happen if he goes back and says he's lost the cohort's treasure-chest? There'll be a Senate inquiry and he'll be told to take poison."

"Well, that's hard luck for the old boy but what's it got to do with me?"

"Quite a lot, I'm afraid." He paused as a soldier went past. "I shouldn't be telling you this, Spiro. But it seems Roscius suggested that the CO should find what he called a sacrificial goat. He put your name forward."

"Me? The bastard! I know the Rat hates me but he can't do that! I didn't do it –"

"I know that and you know that. But you know how the Army works. Whatever's in the record is the truth. And Roscius said that the record will show that, after due investigation, the murderer was found to be one Silanus Gaius Escobinius, who unfortunately died under torture before he could reveal where he'd hidden the gold. He boasted that the CO commended him. Thought it was a good idea."

"Jesus and Jupiter!" Spiro stared at him in horror. "What did Draccus say?"

"He just grunted. But you know him. If he was ordered to jump off a cliff he'd do it."

"But why me?"

"Roscius said you'd be a good choice because you're a Briton with no family in Rome. Nobody to ask questions." He looked round again. "So my advice is – make a run for it. Go north until we've gone."

"I can't." Spiro tugged at his beard in frustration. "It'd be just what they want – a confession of guilt. And you know what the Army does to discourage deserters. It punishes their families. They'd take Gwynedd back to Rome as a slave."

"Take her with you, then."

"There's her mother. The old girl can't travel and Gwynedd wouldn't leave her."

"Then I'd say you're down to the power of prayer, mate. And don't forget – we never had this conversation."

Two days! Spiro thought, trying not to panic. A curse on Roscius Marius Commodus, on the Prefect and on that double-dealing Centurion as well. *How can they do this? Quite easily, if it's a matter of the Prefect's neck or mine. But what in God's name am I going to do?*

Filled with bitter foreboding, he went towards the barracks and his *contubernium*, the quarters he shared with seven other men when he spent a night in camp. Each centuria had its own barrack block, consisting of ten *contubernia*, with a large, well equipped annexe at the end for the centurion. Each *contubernium* had two rooms, one fitted with bunks, the other used for cooking and the storage of shields, weapons and clothing.

His friend Marcellus was frying a fish on the stove. "Spiro returns!" he said. "So they didn't execute you after all!"

"Don't tempt fate," Spiro said gloomily. He was rummaging in his locker for a clean tunic. "I was put on special duty instead – finding who murdered the *signifer*. The old man thinks I possess magic powers."

"Magic powers for dodging the heavy work tomorrow,

more like." The oil sizzled as Marcellus flipped his fish over. "You've wangled a really cushy job, I'd say."

"If you want it, it's yours. I wouldn't recommend it, though. Because, if I don't have any answers for the CO by the time the Legion sails, I'm in dead trouble – literally."

"You mean, if you fail, they'll –?" When Spiro nodded: "*Mehercule!* That's bad. It means you've only got today – what's left of it – and tomorrow. Anything I can do?"

"Wish there was."

"Made any progress?"

"Not much, apart from three soldiers Magus saw digging a grave behind his inn early this morning."

Marcellus shook his head. "Then you've got nothing, mate. They've been caught and locked up. Three legionaries who'd opted to stay behind. They'd been at the stores. They were planning to bury the loot and dig it up after we'd had left."

"Well, thanks very much," Spiro said bitterly. "Now Magus is all I've got left."

"Well, he's a likely suspect. Want a bit of fish?"

"No, thanks. I'm having supper with Gwynedd."

"And her charming Mum, eh?" Marcellus gave him a sly look as he dumped his fish on a wooden platter and broke a piece off a loaf. "Somebody once said that girls always turn out to be like their mothers in the end."

"You're a real ray of sunshine, Marcellus."

But when he arrived there was only Gwynedd at home, her eyes sparkling, her raven hair brushed until it gleamed. "Mother's gone to supper with the wheelwright's family." There was a delicious aroma of roast pork. "Sit down. I've something to tell you, my husband." She gave him a kiss and poured a mug of wine for him.

"Ah, yes?" he said. His mind was elsewhere, thinking about the only suspect he had left. Magus. *How could he have got into the Principia at night?*

She sat beside him and put a hand on his arm. "What would you say if I told you that you are about to become a father?"

"Gwynedd! That's wonderful news!" he said flatly. *But will I ever see the baby?*

She frowned at his tone. "You're pleased, my husband?"

"Of course I am!" He pulled her to him and kissed her. *I can't spoil the moment by telling her what's in store for me.* "Overjoyed!"

"I hope I don't lose my looks. Some women grow fat. There was a girl in the village who lost all her hair. She had to wear a wig."

"A wig? Where on earth would she have got it from?"

"Old Mother Martha makes them. She buys hair from the families of dead women."

Spiro nodded. "Wigs are all the rage in Rome, I believe. They all want to have fair hair like the barbarians so they won't be singled out. They say even the Emperor wears one –." He broke off. Something had flashed in his mind like a lamp being lit in a dark room.

Magus had said, "Looked even better before she cut her golden curls off."

"You see I've bought a jug of wine to have with the roast pork?" she said happily. "We're celebrating!"

"That's nice. A jug of wig," he said abstractedly. "Wine, I mean."

She looked at him questioningly. "You don't sound as if you're listening to me."

"Oh, but I am! I'm just overwhelmed," he said. *Lovely legs, the guards had said. Hair down her back the colour of copper. It all fits!*

He put it out of his mind for Gwynedd's sake while they ate their pork and drank the wine and talked about the child, which was sure to be a boy, she knew. "But how can we keep him safe when the barbarians arrive?"

"We'll move into the fortress," he said. *If I'm still alive.* "They'll be too busy plundering the village to bother about the camp – they know there'll be nothing left for them there."

They left the lamp lit for the old lady and went to bed. After their lovemaking, he lay awake thinking about fatherhood and wigs and time slipping past like sand through the hour-glass. Then came the door-banging entrance of Gwynedd's mother, followed by a series of grunts and crashes as she prepared for bed in her customary corner near the fireplace. When that had settled down to a steady drum-roll of snores, he slid out of bed without disturbing his wife. He put on his *bracae* and tunic then, boots in hand, padded to the front door. In the street, he put his boots on and headed for the inn. Magus would keep it open, he knew, as long as there were customers with money to spend.

It was a calm night with a half moon drifting lazily through thin wisps of cloud. The scent of the sea mingled with the sharper smells of horse dung and wood-smoke. The streets were empty now and silent apart from shouts and raucous singing from the inn that he could hear as he turned the corner.

And saw the figure slinking from shadow to shadow.

A figure that moved in a way he recognised. A female, hip-swinging walk. *Gerda!* He pressed himself against a shuttered shop front and let her pass. He turned and followed.

Straight up the street to the camp's southern gatehouse, which was always open and guarded only if there was danger of attack. Straight into the camp, past the darkened *Praetorium* and the barred *Principia* and left towards . . .

His barrack block!

He caught up with her outside it. She gasped as he grabbed her shoulder and spun her round. "What are you doing here?" he snapped.

The moon came from behind a cloud and gleamed on her sleek golden hair. She said, "I look for you."

"And I suppose you were going to search all the barrack blocks until you found me? Ha! You expect me to believe that?"

"I would find you somehow." She came close to him. "I want you to love me." She put her arms round his neck and he felt the warm firmness of her body against him.

"No," he said, but without much conviction. "I have to –." Her mouth silenced him. He put his arms round her, enjoyed it for a minute then tore himself away. It wasn't easy.

"And what the hell d'you think you're doing, Spiro?" growled a familiar voice behind him.

"Centurion!" he said. "I think I have the murderer."

"You have? Good!" Draccus looked enormous in the moonlight, even out of uniform and in his tunic and sandals. "Get rid of her. We'll go into my quarters. You can tell me about it."

"Sir, she'll have to come. She's part of it, I know."

"Bring her, then."

The Centurion's quarters were smaller than the Prefect's but almost as luxurious. Oil lamps cast a soft light on walls that were painted pale blue; one was intricately pattered with suns, moons and stars. The white ceiling was decorated with a frieze of war chariots driven by Nubians beneath a sky in which flimsily clad females floated, casting down flower petals. Through an open door Spiro could see crimson couches arranged in a dining room with a kitchen opening off it. The floor was covered with soft woven matting; as he went inside, he felt boards beneath it at one point. "Now" Draccus sat down on a stool and pointed at another. "What have you discovered?"

Gwynedd woke to her mother's voice. "Who's that?" the old lady quavered.

"What is it, Ma?" Gwynedd, naked, put on her robe. She went into the other room.

"Somebody's in here."

The room was lit by the half moon. "There's nobody," Gwynedd said. *But where's my husband?* She opened the door in time to see him disappearing up the street. "Go to sleep, Ma." Before the old lady could start asking questions, she followed, silent on her bare feet.

And saw him turn at the corner to follow a girl. *By heaven! It's the blonde, long-legged harlot from the inn! And on the very evening I tell him about the child! This is disgusting! I'll kill the villain!* She opened her mouth to shout abuse at him. Then paused, curious. *Where's he off to, the lecher?* She set off in pursuit.

Past the darkened *Praetorium* and the barred *Principia* to the barracks. She stood in the shadow, clenching her fists with fury as she saw them embrace. Then the tall figure of the Centurion appeared. She heard his harsh voice: "We'll go to my quarters. You can tell me about it . . . Bring her, then.''

A door opened and closed.

Tell him about what? And why go to his quarters with the slave? Intrigued, she flitted across to the barrack block and along it to the partly shuttered window of the Centurion's quarters. She heard her husband's voice . . .

"The guards told the truth, Centurion. There *was* a red-haired girl. And here she is!''

"Are you drunk?'' Draccus asked. "She's blonde.''

"A wig," Spiro said. "She wore a wig.''

"No!'' Gerda said.

"I can easily prove it by asking Old Mother Martha. You turned up at the Principia in a red wig, carrying an amphora of wine containing a drug you'd stolen from the inn.''

"Interesting," Draccus said. "Who let her in?''

"I don't know." Spiro shook his head. "But we can get it out of her by torture. Hot irons. Thumbscrews –.'' He hoped she'd confess. The thought of torture made him feel sick.

"Oh, no." She didn't look in the least afraid. "You will not do that.'' She turned to Draccus. "Will you?''

"Why not?'' Spiro asked with assumed callousness. "You took part in a murder. What do you say, Centurion?''

He paused, staring at her. "You can leave her to me, Spiro.'' He stood up, went into his bedchamber and came back holding his dagger. "I'll get the truth out of her.''

"No!'' Gerda looked at him, then at the dagger. The colour drained out of her face. She seized Spiro's arm. "Don't leave me with him!''

Draccus gestured to Spiro. "You've done very well, Spiro. Now, dismiss!''

"Don't go! I beg you!'' Gerda clung to him. "Don't you see? He's going to kill me! He'll silence me as he silenced those –.''

"Enough!'' Draccus thundered.

"Sir –," Spiro looked at the girl's terrified face. *If she's acting, she could make a fortune on stage in Londinium.* "What is she trying to say?''

"I'm telling you he had the guards killed —"

"Of course I did," Draccus snapped. "For sleeping on duty after they let her in."

"But, sir," Spiro said hesitantly "the guards wouldn't have let her in. Not only because it was against orders but also because, for all they knew, she might have been a decoy to get the gate open and let in a horde of barbarians." He turned to Gerda. "Who let you into the Principia?"

She hesitated.

Then pointed silently at Centurion Draccus.

"Me?" Draccus laughed. "Why not the Prefect? She's mad."

Spiro said, "Why did you come here tonight?"

"To spend the night with him. He is — was — my lover." She turned to Draccus. "Can you deny it?"

Spiro looked at him and said slowly, "My God! It's true! She came straight to this barrack block. Your quarters were the only ones she knew." To Gerda. "But if you love him why are you telling me this?"

"Love him? An old man?" she said contemptuously. "I hate all Romans! I want gold and my freedom, that is all."

"So he told you to wear the wig and bring drugged wine. He did somewhere after the gate was closed." Spiro could hardly believe what he was saying. "Then he let you in to drug the guards. But why did he need you when he could easily have dealt with the guards himself?"

"Not without a fight," she said, "in which one of them could have got to the alarm."

"Of course. So, when they were well away, you and he raised the slab. It was then that the *signifer* arrived, wasn't it? He'd found the gate open and wanted to know why. When he saw the Centurion helping himself to the money he jumped at the alarm cord. He", pointing to Draccus, "hit him with the bag of copper coin he had in his hand." He turned to the impassive Centurion, who was tapping his left hand with the dagger blade. "But what was it all for? You couldn't take the gold to Rome."

"He wasn't going to Rome," the girl said. "He planned to desert with me and the gold when the Legion left. I was to take him to my people, the Saxones, when they arrived." She smiled thinly. "I had been the wife of a chief. They would obey me when I told them to cut his throat. Then the gold would have been mine."

There was a silence until Draccus said grimly, "You treacherous whore! You have just committed suicide. And you, Spiro, you've been too clever for your own good." He stood up, the dagger in his hand.

Spiro said, backing to the door, "Why did you recommend me to the Prefect?"

"Because I thought you were a stupid Briton who'd be bound to fail. And don't try the door." He took the dagger by the point. "I can throw this before you lift the –."

There was a shrill cry from outside. "Sound the alarm! The barbarians are attacking! Sound the alarm!" The girl darted into Draccus's bedchamber and slammed the door. A moment later the alarm bell began to toll. In a bedlam of shouts and orders the legionaries poured from the barracks.

The Centurion stood, indecisive. Spiro picked up a stool by the legs. Facing Draccus, he felt behind him and lifted the latch. The Centurion's arm went back. The dagger hissed through the air. Spiro raised the stool. The blade struck the seat with a clunk. Spiro pulled it out and stood like a gladiator, knife in one hand, stool like a shield in the other.

Draccus kicked open the door of his bedroom, went in. There was a scream, cut off abruptly. He came out, his two-edged short sword dripping blood. "Now. Spiro!" He dropped into a crouch. "Do you know how many men I've killed?" He circled, trying for an opening, grinning. "Let's see if you can be the first man in the centuria to defeat me."

He straightened up as, behind Spiro, the door flew open. Quinctilius Fabius Cornelius Silvanus, *Praefectus* of the 3rd. Cohort, strode in, wearing a hastily folded toga, his sparse hair rumpled. Behind him were two legionaries. And, to Spiro's amazement . . . Gwynedd.

"What is the meaning of this?" Clearly, the Prefect did not appreciate being awakened abruptly in the middle of the night. "Put down your weapons!"

Draccus put down his bloodstained sword and saluted. "Sir, this legionary has just confessed to the murder of the *signifer*, Marcus Sextus Curtius –."

"That's a lie!" Gwynedd snapped. "My husband, Silanus Gaius Escobinius, has revealed that Centurion Draccus is the murderer –."

"And also the killer of a slave girl whose corpse is in the next room," Spiro added. "At least, I think she's dead."

One of the soldiers strode into the bedchamber. He nodded as he came out. "Couldn't be more dead, sir. Been beheaded."

"You killed her, Centurion? Why?"

"She was in league with Escobinius, sir," Draccus said. "They both attacked me."

"More lies," Gwynedd said scornfully. "I heard what happened. I was outside the window."

Draccus grinned. "Sir, she's bound to support her husband, isn't she? He hid in the *Principia* and let the slave girl in. She drugged the guards. While they were robbing the treasure-chest, the *signifer* appeared so they killed him."

The Prefect said to Spiro, "Can you disprove that?"

"Of course he can't. It's his word against mine." Draccus stared contemptuously at Spiro. "And whose word is of greater worth, sir? That of a Roman officer or a British legionary?"

"True." The Prefect turned to the guards. "Take this man –."

"One moment, sir, please!" Spiro was gambling for his life. "I know where the gold is!"

"You confess?" The Prefect asked. "You hid the gold?"

"No, sir. Centurion Draccus did."

"Where?"

Spiro prayed that he was right. He walked across the room. He stamped his foot on the place where he had felt wooden boards under the matting. "Here, sir," he said.

The Prefect and the soldiers followed him. The Prefect pointed. One of them drew his sword and slashed. The matting split apart. The soldier lifted one of the boards.

Beneath was a pile of small jute sacks.

The Prefect swung round. "Centurion, how can you explain this?"

Draccus said nothing. He picked up his sword, presented the point to his chest and fell. He uttered a groan, his legs kicked, then he went still.

On the morning after next, Spiro and Gwynedd stood on the wharf watching the ships' sails filling with the stiff north-westerly breeze. "I can't believe that they've all gone," he said. "Marcellus, all my mates in the 2nd centuria, the trumpeter – even Roscius the Rat. Gone, never to return. It's going to be a different world, sweetheart."

"I know. It doesn't seem possible. No *pax Romana* – no Roman peace. No Roman law. No more fine roads. And after how many years?"

"I dunno. Few hundred, I suppose. And now we're on our own." The transports were hull-down now, their sails white against the overcast. Spiro raised an arm. "Hail and farewell, comrades," he said, a choke in his voice.

He turned and walked slowly back to the fortress camp of Rutupiae, his arm round his wife's shoulders. "The child," he said. "You're sure it's to be a boy?"

"Certain sure. And he is to be a great king."

"Is that so? And what are we going to call him, this king?"

She looked up at Spiro, smiling. "Arthur," she said.

And All That He Calls Family

Mary Reed and Eric Mayer

The first volume of The Mammoth Book of Historical Whodunnits *introduced the character of John the Eunuch in "A Byzantine Mystery". Since then I have published other investigations of his, "A Mithraic Mystery" in* The Mammoth Book of Historical Detectives *and "Beauty More Stealthy" in* Classical Whodunnits, *and he has also featured in two novels to date*: One for Sorrow *(1999) and* Two for Joy *(2000). The stories are set during the reign of the Byzantine Emperor, Justinian (AD 527–65). Mary Reed and Eric Mayer are a husband-and-wife writing team who, when they are not writing about John the Eunuch have produced another series featuring the Mongolian Police Inspector Dorj.*

"I t was a difficult pregnancy and a harrowing birth. Anthea is fortunate indeed to have survived." Hypatia dropped another handful of figs into the pot steaming on the kitchen brazier. "If only Damian had lived long enough to see his son!"

"The late master will meet Solon much too soon if the child remains so sickly." Helen had forsaken her culinary duties to slump in exhaustion on a low stool at the kitchen table. The plump cook had served in Damian's household for many years, having arrived long before Anthea was purchased to attend the old mistress, and even longer before Hypatia had laboured briefly in the estate gardens. "Your employer was most kind, allowing you to stay with us this past week or so," she concluded.

"The Lord Chamberlain knew Damian well," Hypatia smiled. "And he wished me to assist as much as possible."

"Without your aid and Rhea's potions, of course, I don't know how we would have managed," Helen sighed.

Hypatia, knowledgeable in herbal matters, remarked that she was impressed that a woman of such obvious learning as Rhea would be content to live in the nearby village.

"But you've worked much harder than anyone, Helen," she went on, vigorously stirring the syrup. "Making nourishing meals to tempt an expectant mother's appetite is penance enough, but when she's ill besides it's even harder to please. And all the cooking to be done in this terrible heat besides."

The kitchen window stood wide open but afforded no relief from the oppressive weather that had clung, honeylike, to the countryside for the past two months. The aroma from the fig syrup boiling on the brazier hung cloyingly in the air, with no breeze to stir it into the wilting herb garden, whose riot of spindly coriander and coltsfoot, dill, thyme and oregano were coated with a fine layer of dust.

Helen pushed a straying strand of white hair away from her scarlet, perspiring face. "Yet if the mistress had spent the last few weeks in the city, it would have been even more of an ordeal. I've rarely seen a woman be so ill and yet not lose her child."

"When I left Constantinople there was some talk of the cisterns getting low," Hypatia remarked. "But I suppose it was more a case of Anthea wanting to get away from all the clamour and dirt."

"Ah, well, you might think so," The cook pitched her voice lower, looking around as if to ensure no one lurked at door or window to overhear her indiscreet tattle. "But the truth is that the mistress wished to be near her husband when she gave birth."

Hypatia's dark eyes conveyed her surprise at the statement. Damian had died some months before Anthea had borne his son. "Pregnant women often get odd fancies, and not just about their food," she finally ventured.

"Indeed they do. Although I must say that I would not have buried my husband practically under my bedroom window. His parents were not interred here, why isn't he with them?"

Before Hypatia could respond, a shriek broke the heavy stillness of the garden.

Helen paled and half rose from her seat as Hypatia looked hastily out. A man she recognized as Jason, one of the house servants, was racing across the herb garden, heedless of the heat and the drought-stricken plants he was trampling underfoot.

He burst into the stifling kitchen. "Look what I just dredged up out the well," he shouted.

Helen gave a cry of disgust as she saw what he threw down on the table. It was a small, dark roll of metal, dripping wet.

A curse tablet.

John the Eunuch, Lord Chamberlain to the Emperor Justinian, sang softly to the infant he was awkwardly holding. Having accomplished this unaccustomed task, he thankfully handed the child back to the woman sitting on the couch opposite him.

"It is as well Solon does not understand Greek yet," Anthea smiled wanly. "I am not certain that your military song was fit for the ears of a child of such a tender age!"

"I am ignorant of such things," John admitted with a smile, "but despite its sentiments the song seemed a fitting lullaby for a sturdy son, especially one carrying such a weighty name."

Anthea bit her lip, obviously distressed. Despite John's courtesy, it was clear that Solon was anything but sturdy. The infant was thin and fretful, his skin sallow.

His mother, round-faced and pale, was dressed in white silk robes, her fair hair confined by a pearled net. She was softly pretty, John thought. Had that been enough reason for Damian to choose her – a slave – for his wife?

John recalled the earnest but bewildered young aristocrat

who had often sought his advice, most recently a week or two before his untimely death. Newly appointed to oversee the planning for one or another of Justinian's endless city improvement projects, Damian had somehow contrived to run afoul of a high legal personage in the quaestor's office. John would have been able to help him, had there been more time. Now, the best he could do was assist the man's family.

"Hypatia has been of great assistance to me," Anthea was saying. "I've enjoyed renewing my acquaintance with her, brief though our original friendship was. Our respective circumstances have certainly changed greatly since we first met. But to get to the matter in hand, tell me, Lord Chamberlain, what are your thoughts concerning this disgusting tablet?"

"I've heard of them being buried by the superstitious in the Hippodrome years ago," John told her. "Apparently it was believed they would thereby influence the racing, although personally I suspect that the necessary bribes to gain access to the track in order to conceal them at the turning post would far outweigh any possible winnings. But this is the first time I've seen one on a private estate." He paused tactfully. "I've taken it into my charge."

"Feel free to question everyone, of course. The sooner this is resolved, the better."

"Do any of the servants understand Latin?"

She looked perplexed. "No, just Greek. The only people in this household with any knowledge of Latin are myself – my late husband provided instruction – and my brother-in-law Burrhus. Why do you ask?"

"Because the curse is inscribed in Latin," John explained, "and these tablets are usually written in Greek. It is the custom."

Burrhus was outraged by John's questioning.

"Of course I know Latin," he said icily. "I'm an advocate. Do you then plan to accuse me of causing my brother's death as well as my nephew's illness?"

He was a big man, verging on corpulent. Sweating from the sticky heat, he had pushed up the sleeves of his heavy dalmatic to reveal brawny arms resembling those of a baker's assistant. John had found Burrhus in his wing of the rambling villa, sitting in the humid shade of a peristyle surrounding a courtyard displaying a number of desiccated shrubs.

"I'm not accusing anyone of any crime, let alone murder," John replied sharply. "Damian died of a fever in Constantinople, far from this curse tablet about which your sister-in-law is so concerned."

"As if a thin piece of lead inscribed with some wordy nonsense could harm anybody," Burrhus said impatiently. "Now if it had been a proclamation from the emperor, that would be different." He gave an unpleasant laugh.

"You and Anthea are on friendly terms?" John enquired.

Burrhus gave him the sort of appraising look he would have levelled at a legal opponent in court. "What makes you ask such a question?"

John shrugged. "It's natural enough. After all, you are sharing an estate with her."

The other man sighed. "Do not deduce too much from the domestic arrangements, Lord Chamberlain. Naturally I shall strive to do my duty towards my deceased brother, which is to say I will continue to do my best in the interests of his son and, of course, his son's mother, despite the irregularity of their union."

John said he understood that, under the law, a free born man may marry a freed woman.

"Unless he is a senator or the child of a senator," the other confirmed. "But as the esteemed Modestinus put it, in marriage, in addition to that which is legally permissible what must also always be considered is that which men call decent. I fear, given the state of the law today, his sentiment is mere philosophy, for it's my opinion that although a slave may be manumitted and tutored and clothed in fine silks, yet still she remains a slave."

John gave a thin smile.

"Everyone at court knows your history, Lord Chamberlain," Burrhus continued, unabashed. "You too were once a slave. But your circumstances are different, for if a man is free born he does not lose *ingenuus*, as the law terms it, if he was forced into slavery. And you, I dare say, do not believe, as slaves do, in foolishness such as this tablet."

"No," John admitted, "but I do believe that whoever is responsible for it may decide to take more direct action to accomplish what a mere curse cannot."

"But what can we do? Dismiss all the servants? And there are other possibilities to consider. A business rival might have bribed one of the estate workers to drop the wretched thing into the well, for example."

John asked Burrhus if he could think of anyone who harboured resentment against the family.

"I have no reason to suspect anyone," the other replied. "And Anthea was already ill when she arrived here from Constantinople. I personally employed the village herbalist, Rhea, to treat her." He halted abruptly, as if suddenly aware that what he had said might provide a weapon to be wielded against him.

"Rhea is most dependable, Lord Chamberlain," he went on hastily. "She was employed for some years by a legal colleague of mine before retiring to the countryside. She's cared for our family and many others hereabouts ever since then, and there's never been so much as a hint of anyone bringing an *injuria* against her for any reason whatsoever."

He wiped away a trickle of sweat running down his fleshy neck. "But if it's some damning revelation you're seeking," he continued, "I will tell you this before any wag-tongues among the servants bring it to your attention. Our father left his estate equally to my brother and myself. Thus if the child and his mother were to join Damian, the entire estate would become mine. So there it is, Lord Chamberlain. I'm the only person I can think of who might be inclined to harm either or both of them."

John spent the rest of the afternoon interviewing the servants, who provided little of assistance to his investigation although he learned a great deal about their opinions of each other.

One of his last conversations proceeded along those very lines. The oldest estate worker, he was informed, was almost seventy and remained living there more from charity than from expectation of service, or at least according to Jason.

"They call Cepheus the head gardener, sir, but he spends most of his time pottering about and the rest of it reminiscing about the old days with anyone who'll listen. Of late, too, he's taken to loitering by the late master's mausoleum. Some of the others say he's preparing himself for when he must also leave the world, although personally I think he's just keeping out of sight of the mistress." As he spoke, the brawny man sporting a thick shock of glistening black hair continued to hoe savagely at the rock-hard flower bed where John had found him labouring, as if to prove to his highly placed interrogator that he, at any rate, was not just idly standing about.

"Perhaps that is the way Cepheus is being rewarded for his past service?" John suggested.

"You could say that, sir. Then again, some of us have to live by our labours while others gain softer lives by the goodness of Fortuna."

"Did you serve with Anthea when she first arrived here? You appear to be about her age."

The blunt question caused Jason to pause in his work and frown. "Sir, surely you don't think I resent Anthea's good fortune?" he blurted out, distress evident in his tone.

John pointed out that there was no doubt that many would feel that way. "But what I am more interested in is the tablet you found," he concluded.

Jason described again how it had appeared in a bucket of water he had drawn from the well. "I might not be an educated man," he went on, "but I don't take any heed of these country superstitions. I wouldn't pay a single *nummus* to have a few lines scraped on a bit of lead. But I was sorry that it upset the mistress. Will she be all right?"

John reassured the young servant and left him to continue his battle with the parched earth.

Just as Jason had predicted, Cepheus was discovered worrying at a spadeful of dry dirt beside a hedge not far from Damian's mausoleum, an unremarkable monument that, like many of its fellows, resembled a small Greek temple. Not surprisingly, the old gardener was quite ready to stop working and recall events long gone.

"Yes, your excellency, we have much to be grateful for these days," Cepheus piped, leaning on his spade. John gestured him to a stone bench set between a nearby pair of drooping laurel bushes. The old man limped painfully over to it and seated himself with a sigh of gratitude.

The gardener had once been big of frame, but now it was shrunken with age and his coarsely woven work tunic hung shapelessly from hunched shoulders. He did not need much encouragement to air his opinions.

"The old master, that is to say the father of Burrhus and Damian, he was a very difficult man indeed, excellency," he declared vehemently. "He was quick to anger and his wife was the same. A well matched pair, they were. Now, Helen was the old mistress's maid before she was appointed cook, or rather banished to work in the kitchen when the old mistress decided Helen had become aged and ugly. Not that she had, your excellency, she was just a little plumper than the comely lass she'd always been. But that was the way of the old mistress. Cruel in words as well as actions, she was."

He scowled. "She once accused Helen of stealing a bracelet," he went on. "A number of small valuables disappeared about the same time, mere vanities they were, just trifles. I seem to recall one of the house slaves was sold because of those thefts, or possibly that after the alabaster vase was broken . . . the details fade, I fear." Nor could he recall the slave's name when pressed. Requested to continue with his tale, however, Cepheus obliged with another spate of words.

"Well, the old master ordered Helen beaten until she admitted she had taken the bracelet. It was his right, excellency, I cannot deny that. But she hadn't stolen it, as she said all along. It was discovered a day or so later, fallen down behind something or other, I forget what it was, a chest in the mistress's bedroom, perhaps."

The incident had taken place years before but John noted that as the old man recounted it his veined and calloused hands had clenched into fists.

*   *   *

John was more concerned about the current threat to the family. At day's end, having spoken to every servant on the estate and listened patiently to their litany of petty grievances, he returned to the villa and again examined the tablet.

At first glance its pitted length of beaten lead appeared unremarkable, but its intent was as blunt as its inscription, or at least to anyone who could read the language in which was expressed. It began with a command.

> I call you and bind you, shade, by all the gods of this world and the next. Return and work this evil upon the master of the estate and all that he calls family. Take away their breath, torment them with pain, cause them to falter . . .

and so on down a list of similar dreadful afflictions and catastrophes.

John knew that none of the servants had the education necessary to write the curse in any language, let alone Latin. Nor could any of them have afforded to purchase a tablet. On the other hand, it was possible that whoever made it had merely copied the inscription from a book of magick, scratching its letters into the lead without understanding the words they formed. Yet the ill-wisher was obviously knowledgeable enough about the tablet's supposed workings – or had been instructed in them – to drop the small lead roll into the well, thereby placing it as close to the Underworld as possible.

John poured himself a cup of wine and retired to the villa's colonnade. He could just distinguish Damian's mausoleum at the far end of the garden, glimmering in the fast fading light. It would be pleasing to think that the man's shade was nearby, guarding his family, although as a Mithran John believed that a man achieved immortality only by ascending to the celestial home of the sun, not lingering in the world below.

His thoughts had just turned to examining one possible solution after another when an apparition came shambling out of the gathering shadows. John leapt to his feet, his hand automatically going to the blade at his belt. But it was only the gardener Cepheus, panting as he lurched along with painful slowness.

"Your pardon, excellency," the old man gasped in a panic stricken voice, "but the master has returned. I just saw him standing beside his mausoleum, staring at the villa. But I couldn't catch him, although I tried hard enough."

John grabbed a torch from the colonnade wall and ran to the spot Cepheus had indicated, cutting swiftly across flower beds and vegetable patches alike. Crashing through ornamental bushes whose thorns clawed at his tunic, he quickly arrived at the building. Nothing moved in the deepening twilight there or nearby and he could hear only his breathing and the increasingly loud night sounds of insects. The earth in front of the mausoleum was hard packed and showed no trace of footprints, either the apparition's or from the pursuit of it that Cepheus claimed to have made.

He informed the gardener as much when he returned to the colonnade.

"I didn't get too close to it, excellency. And a shade wouldn't leave footprints, would it?" Cepheus's voice quavered. He had collapsed on the bench lately vacated by John.

As John questioned him further, Hypatia emerged from the villa with wine for the shocked old man. Even as she placed the cup into his trembling hand, Anthea appeared, looking much like an apparition herself in a nimbus of white silk garments.

"I thought I heard Solon crying," she said, glancing around in a dazed fashion. "Hypatia . . ."

The woman sprang to her side. "He is well, Anthea. I sang him to sleep just a little while ago."

Anthea looked confused as John quickly explained recent events. "But the supposed apparition is nothing to worry about," he assured her, "It's more than likely it was just one of your servants off to a romantic tryst."

"But I saw it, excellency," Cepheus insisted from the bench as soon as the women had gone back inside, "and it was the master. I tried to catch him but I wasn't fast enough." He dropped the wine cup and it shattered on the colonnade's flagstones.

John put a reassuring hand on the old man's bony shoulder. "One of the servants will help you to your bed, Cepheus," he said gently. "But before you go, tell me, what makes you so convinced that it was Damian?"

Cepheus hesitated. "I . . . I don't know." He looked at the cup fragments at his feet. "I tried to catch him," he repeated. "But he got away and now he's wandering around the estate and it's my fault . . . old and crippled and useless as I am."

An enormous full moon, caught in the tops of the cedars along the estate's outer wall, was silvering the garden by the time Hypatia re-emerged. She told John that mother and child were sleeping and the servant who had been put in charge of Cepheus had reported the old man was now snoring safely on his pallet.

"If I may say so, master, I think that Cepheus is dwelling over much on the past," Hypatia continued. "When my grandmother grew old and her senses failed, she sometimes saw days long gone more vividly than the world around her."

"Anthea did not take Cepheus's imaginings seriously?"

Hypatia shook her dark head. "She was quite calm. Thankfully she's always been a sensible woman."

"Her marriage took place after you had left your employment here?"

"Some time afterwards, master." Hypatia paused. The shadow that passed over her face was not caused by the guttering of the torch set in a bracket on the colonnade wall. "I was here only a short time. But this afternoon Helen mentioned something to me that may be of interest perhaps."

John encouraged his servant to continue.

"She was talking about the family. It seems that Anthea and Damian were . . . familiar . . . before Anthea was manumitted. Damian's father freed her at Damian's request, for he genuinely wanted to marry her, according to Helen."

"He had the right to manumit her for any reason," John

replied. "He could have married her himself for that matter, if she had agreed to it."

"Yes, indeed. But it's . . . well, Helen says Solon was conceived before his mother was a freed woman."

"I can see that that would be extremely important to Anthea," John acknowledged, thinking of the comments Burrhus had made. In retrospect, it was not surprising that Damian had turned to John for occasional help rather than consult his own brother, himself a man of some influence. "But did Helen also happen to reveal anything of her own history, such as how she came to be cook or her contretemps with the old mistress?"

Hypatia expressed mystification at her employer's questions.

"It involved a severe beating and Cepheus at least is still angry about it," John explained. "It might have happened yesterday, the way he clenched his fists as he spoke of it."

Hypatia smiled. "I think I can explain that, master. Cepheus has always been quite taken with Helen. But she turned him away, it seems."

The rickety ladder creaked under John's weight as he descended into the well.

Looking up, he could see a small circle of light resembling one of the windows high in the dome of the Great Church in Constantinople. Below, where he tried not to look, the water was a black mirror reflecting the flame of the lamp he carried in one hand. The walls around him were constructed of the same rough stone as the subterranean mithraeum where he worshipped.

He took another reluctant step down. He had once seen a comrade in arms drown.

During the night Anthea had lost her calm demeanour. The tablet had been removed from its proximity to the Underworld and should have been rendered powerless, she had cried that morning. There must still be another in the well, for how else to explain the appearance of her husband's shade? Someone must investigate, and it must be done immediately.

John's grasp slipped on the rung. The pounding of his heart thundered in his head as he realized that despite the chill seeping into his flesh as he climbed downwards, his hands were slippery with sweat. He might indeed have been descending into the Underworld.

The water had fallen significantly during the drought and he was now below its usual level. He paused and moved his lamp about carefully, noting that the edges of the roughly hewn stones around him formed small ledges here and there. On one close to hand lay a *nummus* of a type no longer minted, on another a shard of broken pottery.

A little further down something reflected a gleam of lamplight. Trying to keep it in sight he descended another couple of steps, and then another, gasping as water swirled up over his boot. He swung the lamp towards the thing that had captured its light and peered intently.

A shape sprang towards him, dropping into the water with a splash. The largest toad he had ever seen.

Startled despite himself, he dropped the lamp on the creature's narrow stone perch. Oil spilled out and flamed, enabling him to see what some would say the creature had been guarding.

John felt a quick flash of relief that he would not have to descend further and fish around in the dark water.

For, just as Anthea had feared, it was another curse tablet.

The inscription scratched on the smooth lead was in Latin as before. However, this time it was specific, naming its victims as Anthea, wife of Damian, and their son Solon.

Rhea looked blankly at the small tablet, and then at John. The herbalist was a tiny woman, with a beak of a nose and the inquisitive, darting gaze of a magpie. "You tell me it is Latin. But what does it say, excellency?" She had a surprisingly strong voice for one so small of stature.

"Burrhus mentioned that you once worked for a colleague of his," John replied. "Was he also an advocate?"

"Indeed he was. But may I point out that while such men require Latin, their servants do not?"

"Where have you been these past few days?" put in

Hypatia from the kitchen window, fearing that the older woman's blunt manner of speaking might cause difficulties. "We may be needing more of your coltsfoot concoction soon."

"I thought your cough was nearly gone, my lady?" Rhea replied, addressing Anthea, whose arrival completed the crowd in the small kitchen.

"Almost," she replied. "If only you could help Solon as much! Although I will say he does look stronger this morning."

Rhea's bird-like gaze darted about the kitchen, lighting first on Hypatia, and then on John.

"I do know something about these curse tablets, Lord Chamberlain," she declared. "I know, for one thing, that none but an evil person would seek to use such a foul thing to force the shade of a father to injure his son." She paused to make the sign of her religion. "And though some may tell you otherwise, I have never indulged in such magick. I use only the fine plants blessing this world to work my healing."

Hypatia hastily requested Rhea to accompany her to the garden in hopes of finding a herbal gift that might be of some assistance to Solon. Anthea was at John's elbow immediately.

"Here's a strange thing," she whispered, glancing outside at the two herbalists, now deep in animated conversation. "When Rhea first came to treat me, Burrhus mentioned that she had transcribed all manner of legal notices for that colleague of his. Wouldn't such notices be written in Latin?"

John made no comment.

"It's plain the old woman's lying for some reason," Anthea went on. "I would never have suspected it of her, for she's done me nothing but good with her herbal remedies. Unfortunately we can't ask Burrhus about it right now. He went to the city this afternoon to plead a case. But he'll be back tomorrow morning."

John sat on the stone bench, deep in thought. The dry leaves of the laurel bushes shielding him from the moonlight rustled faintly in an evening breeze that had brought no respite from the day's heat.

Did Jason harbour ill will towards mother and child, he wondered. He had served with Anthea but was still a servant. Did he envy her good fortune? And he was her age. Perhaps he had professed affection and she had turned him away, as had happened with Helen and Cepheus.

He considered the elderly cook and gardener. Might deep resentment against their old master and his wife extend to the next generation, and the one after that?

Helen could easily have slipped something harmful into her mistress's meals. But equally Rhea would have had many similar opportunities. John had not discerned what her reason for such actions might be but the herbalist had admitted to some knowledge of curse tablets, and Anthea had already indicated her strong suspicion of the woman.

There again, Rhea would not have needed any reason at all if she had merely been consulted. By Burrhus, for example. He could certainly afford to purchase a curse table – and he definitely knew Latin.

John shifted on his hard seat, hunching over like an old man. Yes, everything seemed to point at Burrhus, a man who had seen half his father's estate pass to a woman he considered still a slave. A man who had much to gain by losing his sister-in-law and nephew.

There was movement in the moonlight beyond the mausoleum. It was a wisp of a figure, dressed in red. The apparition turned its shadowy face in John's direction before pivoting with otherwordly slowness to stare towards the villa.

John leapt up, the coarse, baggy tunic he wore – Cepheus's shabby garments – flapping on his lean frame with the sudden movement.

The figure darted away.

It was no apparition. John could hear it crashing through dried shrubbery as he gave chase. In his youth John had been a runner. He was still much swifter than the crippled old gardener whose clothing he had temporarily borrowed.

He lunged forward, grabbing a solid enough arm. The fugitive fell to the hard ground with a cry and in an instant John was tearing away a thin veil to reveal its face.

* * *

Cepheus let out a loud sigh. "Who would have thought that curse tablet would suddenly start to work years after I threw it down the well, and against the old master's grandson at that?" He shook his head sorrowfully and looked around the kitchen.

Most of the household had crowded into the small room. It had not been planned that way. Perhaps, John thought, they had gathered there because it was the one room where neither servants nor employers felt out of place.

Cepheus's bleary gaze came to rest on Helen. "I should never have stolen those trinkets to sell so I could buy that tablet," he went on sadly. "Others paid much too high a price for my thieving. But the woman, long gone now, who copied out the curse for me didn't tell me anything about the . . . er . . ."

His voice trailed away as he realized he had been about to refer to the unfortunate necessity that the tablet be concealed in the vicinity of a deceased person whose shade it could command. Damian's burial on the estate had obviously caused the tablet to begin to work its magick, he thought, but wisely did not say so.

"I never wished ill on the child or on you, mistress," he told Anthea, who sat on the stool Helen usually occupied. "I did it because of the way the old master and mistress treated Helen. I couldn't bear to see it. Yet I was only a slave myself, and just as powerless."

"What happened was not of your doing, Cepheus," John assured him.

Cepheus looked unconvinced.

"As I was about to say," John said, resuming the explanation the old man's outburst had interrupted, "upon comparing the tablets it was immediately apparent the first was much older, for it was pitted whereas the second was smooth. The first had been in the well for years, until the water level dropped enough to allow the bucket to scoop it up from where it had been waiting to do its mischief."

Cepheus sighed regretfully but remained silent.

"A man who carries anger for decades over injustice done

to a woman he cares about will seek revenge as best he can," John continued. "Given a slave's circumstances, the missing valuables, the more general wording regarding those wished ill by the first tablet as opposed to the specific names on the second, it was obvious who was responsible for the first tablet at least."

He glanced around the assembled company. "Yet I believed Cepheus when he said he saw Damian, or something like Damian, yesterday evening," he said. "The question was, could I catch whatever – or whoever – it was? So I borrowed Cepheus's tunic and used it to set a trap."

Anthea suddenly began to sob. "Burrhus hates me and he hates my son!" she cried. "He regards us as nothing more than slaves. He keeps saying my marriage to his brother was irregular."

"Anthea, your marriage was perfectly legal," John said gently, "and your son is free born".

She shook her head violently, tears running down her pale cheeks. "No, Lord Chamberlain. Burrhus is an advocate and those who practise law always find a way to get what they want by some lie or other, a tiny word or phrase that means something no ordinary person would dream it could."

"Burrhus isn't so unkind as you may think, mistress," Helen put in. "You surely remember his father's ways were often worse. But I must admit that considering all that has happened since the turn of the year, what with the young master's death and then your illness and young Solon born so frail, we were ready to believe the household was cursed as soon as Cepheus's tablet was found."

It was the tablet's discovery that had given Anthea the inspiration for her plan. Now she readily admitted her intention to point a finger at Burrhus, a man with so obvious a motive and the necessary linguistic knowledge. Aware of the belief that such curses enslaved the departed, forcing them to strike at the living, she had posed as her husband's shade, appearing only to crippled old Cepheus. His lameness would not, of course, have allowed him to catch her.

"I intended to lead Cepheus to Burrhus's office. I'd placed a third tablet there, knowing my brother-in-law would be staying in Constantinople tonight. I was only trying to protect my son's inheritance," she concluded tearfully.

The whole plan had been a hopeless scheme concocted by a simple woman and doomed to failure, but John did not say so. Having been caught in her own snare she had suffered humiliation enough, including the very public discussion now taking place in the villa's kitchen.

Hypatia, who had been standing silently in the doorway, now spoke. "You shouldn't worry about Solon, at least," she told Anthea, before addressing the others. "The child isn't so frail as he appears. Rhea was treating Anthea's cough with coltsfoot. Very effective it is, too, but I've heard that overuse during pregnancy can give a newborn infant a sickly, yellow colouring, although it passes quickly. Then too the heat is doubtless making him fretful, as well as affecting his appetite. But he is getting stronger every day and can look forward to a long life, a healthy life!"

At these kind words Anthea buried her face in her hands. "For all the good it will do him now," she wept.

"Don't worry," John comforted her. "I will speak with Burrhus when he returns. You've had a hard time these past few months, and the strange fancies that afflict pregnant women are well known. He will take no action against you."

As he finished speaking, Anthea wiped her eyes and looked gratefully at him.

Down the hallway, Solon emitted a loud, healthy wail.

Death of an Icon

Peter Tremayne

Peter Tremayne is the alias used by Celtic scholar Peter Berresford Ellis (b. 1943) for his mystery and weird fiction. The author of over sixty books, Tremayne is currently best known for his series of historical mystery novels featuring Sister Fidelma, which began with Absolution by Murder (1994). Fidelma is both an Irish princess and a qualified dálaigh, or advocate, of the law courts of Ireland under the ancient Brehon Law system. In addition to the series of novels, earlier Fidelma stories will be found in the collection Hemlock at Vespers (2000). The following brand-new story is set in the year 667.

"I cannot understand why the Abbot feels that he has to interfere in this matter," Father Maílín said defensively. "I have conducted a thorough investigation of the circumstances. The matter is, sadly, a simple one."

Sister Fidelma regarded the Father Superior of the small community of St Martin of Dubh Ross with a mild expression of reproach.

"When such a respected man as the Venerable Gelasius has met with an unnatural death, then it is surely not an interference for the religious superior of this territory to inquire into it?" she rebuked gently. "Portraits of the Venerable Gelasius hang in many of our great ecclesiastical centres. He has become an icon to the faithful."

Father Maílín coloured a little and shifted his weight in his chair.

"I did not mean to imply a censure of the Abbot nor his authority," he replied quickly. "It is just that I have carried out a very thorough investigation of the circumstances and have forwarded all the relevant details to the Abbot. There is nothing more to be said unless we can track down the culprits and that, as I pointed out, will be impossible unless, in some fit of repentance, they confess. But they have long departed from this territory, they and their ill-gotten spoils."

Fidelma gazed thoughtfully at the Father Superior for a moment or two.

"I have your report here," her hand lightly touched the marsupium at her waist, "and I must confess to there being some matters which puzzle me, as, I hasten to say, they have also puzzled the Abbot. That is why he has authorized me, as a *dálaigh*, an advocate of the courts, to visit your small community to see whether or not the questions might be clarified."

Father Maílín raised his jaw, slightly aggressively.

"I see nothing at all that is confusing nor which requires any further explanation," he replied stubbornly. Then, meeting her icy blue eyes, he added brusquely, "However, you may ask me your questions and then depart."

Fidelma's mouth twitched a fraction in irritation and she shook her head briefly.

"Perhaps it is because you are not a trained advocate of the law and thus do not know what is required that you take this attitude. I, however, will conduct my investigation in the way prescribed by the law. When I have finished my investigation, then I shall depart." She paused to allow her words to penetrate and then said, in a brighter tone: "First, let us begin with you recounting the general details of the Venerable Gelasius's death."

Father Maílín's lips compressed into a thin, bloodless line in order to disguise his anger. His eyes had a fixed look. It seemed, for a moment or two, that he would challenge her. Then he appeared to realize the futility of such an action and relaxed. He knew that he had to accept her authority however reluctantly. He pushed himself back in his chair, sitting stiffly. His voice was an emotionless monotone.

"It was on the morning of the sabbath. Brother Gormgilla went to rouse the Venerable Gelasius. As he grew elderly, Gelasius required some assistance to rise in the morning and Brother Gormgilla would help him rise and dress and then escort him to the chapel for morning prayer."

"I have heard that Brother Gelasius was of a great age," intervened Fidelma. Everyone knew he was of considerable age but Fidelma's intervention was more to break Father Mailín's monotonous recital so that she would be able to extract the information she wanted.

"Indeed, but Gelasius was also frail. It was his frailty that made him needful of the helping hand of Brother Gormgilla."

"So, this Brother Gormgilla went to the chamber of the Venerable Gelasius on the morning of the sabbath? What then?" encouraged Fidelma.

"The facts are straightforward enough. Gormgilla entered and found the Venerable Gelasius hanging from a beam just above his bed. There was a sign that a valuable personal item had been taken, that is a rosary. Some valuable objects were also missing from the chapel which adjoins the chamber of the Venerable Gelasius."

"These discoveries were made after Brother Gormgilla had roused the community having found the body of the Venerable Gelasius?"

"They were."

"And your deduction was . . .?"

"Theft and murder. I put it in my report to the Abbot."

"And to whom do you ascribe this theft and murder?"

"It is also in my report to the Abbot."

"Remind me," Fidelma insisted sharply.

"For the two days previous to the death of the Venerable Gelasius, some itinerants were observed to be camping in nearby woods. They were mercenaries, warriors who hired themselves out to anyone who would pay them. They had their womenfolk and children with them. Our community, as you know, has no walls around it. We are an open settlement for we have always argued that there is no need at all to protect ourselves from any aggressor, for who, we thought, would ever wish harm to our little community?"

Fidelma treated his question as rhetorical and did not reply.

"You have suggested that these itinerant mercenaries entered the community at night to rob your chapel," her tone was considered. "You have argued that the Venerable Gelasius must have been disturbed by them; that he went to investigate and that they turned on the old man and hanged him from his own roof beam and even robbed him."

"That is so. It is not so much an argument as a logical deduction from the facts," the Father Superior added stiffly.

"Truly so?" Fidelma gave him a quick scrutiny and Father Mailín read a quiet sarcasm there.

The Father Superior stared back defiantly but said nothing.

"Tell me," continued Fidelma. "Does it not strike you as strange that an elderly man, who needed help to rise in the morning as well as to be escorted to the chapel, would rise in the night on hearing intruders and go alone into the chapel to investigate?"

Father Mailín shrugged.

"People, in extremis, have been known to do many extraordinary things: things that are either out of character or beyond their capabilities."

"If I have the right information, the Venerable Gelasius was nearly ninety. In that case . . .?" Fidelma eloquently spread her hands.

"In his case, it does not surprise me," affirmed Father Mailín. "He was frail but he was a man of a very determined nature. Why, twenty and five years ago, when he was a man entering the latter years, Gelasius insisted on bearing the cross of Clonmacnoise in the battle of Ballyconnell when Diarmuid Mac Aodh was granted a victory over the Uí Fidgente. Gelasius was in the thick of the battle and armed with nothing but Christ's Cross for self-protection."

Fidelma suppressed a sigh for all Ireland knew of the story of the Venerable Gelasius which was why the old monk's

name was a byword for moral and physical courage throughout the five kingdoms of Ireland.

"Yet five and twenty years ago is still a quarter of a century
before this time and we are talking of an old man who needed
help to rise and go to chapel as a regular course."

"As I have said, he was a determined man."

"Therefore, if I understand your report correctly, you
believe that the Venerable Gelasius, hearing some robbers
moving in the chapel, left his bed and went to confront them
without rousing anyone else. That these robbers then overpowered him and hanged him in his own bedchamber?"

"I have said as much."

"Yet doesn't it also strike you as strange that these thieves
and robbers, thus disturbed, took the old man back to his
chamber and hanged him there? Surely a thief, so disturbed,
might strike out in fear and seek to escape. Was Gelasius a tall
man who, in spite of his frailty, might have appeared a threat?"

Father Máilín shook his head.

"Age had bent him."

"Then the Venerable Gelasius could not have prevented
the escape of the thieves nor even pursued them. Why would
they bother to take him and, presumably, get him to show
them the way back to his chamber to kill him?"

"Who knows the minds of thieves and murderers?"
snorted Father Máilín. "I deal with the facts. I don't attempt
to understand their minds."

"Nevertheless, that is the business in which I am engaged
because in so considering the 'why' and 'wherefore', often
one can solve the 'how' and 'who'." She paused for a moment
and when he did not respond, she added: "After this barbaric
act of sacrilege, you reported that they then removed some
valuable items and went calmly off into the night?"

"The itinerants were certainly gone by the next morning
when one of the outraged brethren went to their camp. The
emotional attitude of the itinerants, as to whether they be
calm or otherwise, is not for me to comment on. I will leave
that to you to judge."

"Very well. You say that Brother Gormgilla was the first
to discover the body of the Venerable Gelasius?"

"Brother Gormgilla always roused the Venerable Gelasius first."

"Ah, just so. I shall want to see this Brother Gormgilla."

"But I have told you all . . ."

Fidelma raised an eyebrow, staring at him with cold, blue eyes.

Father Maílín hesitated and shrugged. He reached for a hand bell and jangled it. A member of the community entered but when the Father Superior asked that Brother Gormgilla be summoned, Fidelma intervened. She did not want Father Maílín interfering in her questioning.

"I will go to the Brother myself. I have trespassed on your valuable time long enough, Father Maílín."

The Father Superior rose unhappily as Sister Fidelma turned and accompanied the religieuse from the room.

Brother Gormgilla was a stocky, round-faced man, with a permanent expression of woe sitting on his fleshy features. She introduced herself briefly to him.

"Had you known the Venerable Gelasius for a long time, Brother?" she asked.

"For fifteen years. I have been his helper all that time. He would soon be in his ninety-first year had he been spared."

"So you knew him very well?"

"I did so. He was a man of infinite wisdom and knowledge."

Fidelma smiled briefly.

"I know of his reputation. He was spoken of as one of our greatest philosophers not merely in this kingdom but among all five kingdoms of Ireland. He adopted the Latin name of Gelasius; why was that?"

Brother Gormgilla shrugged as if it was a matter of little importance.

"It was a Latinization of the name he was given when he was received into the Church – Gilla Isu, the servant of Jesus."

"So he was a convert to the Faith?"

"As were many in our poor benighted country when he was a young man. At that time, most of us cleaved to the old gods and goddesses of our fathers. The Faith was not so widespread through our kingdoms. Gelasius's own father was a Druid and a seer. When he was young, Gelasius told me, he was going to follow the arts of his father's religion. But he was converted and took his new name."

"And became a respected philosopher of the Faith," added Fidelma. "Well, tell me . . . in fact, show me, how and where you discovered his body?"

Brother Gormgilla led the way towards the main chapel around which the various circular buildings of the community were situated. Next to the chapel was one small circular building outside the door of which the monk paused.

"Each morning, just before the Angelus, I came here to rouse and dress the Venerable Gelasius," he explained.

"And on that morning . . .? Take me through what happened when you found Gelasius was dead."

"I came to the door. It was shut and locked. That was highly unusual. I knocked upon it and not being able to get or an answer, I went to a side window."

"One moment. Are you telling me that you did not possess a key to Gelasius's chamber?"

"No. There was only one key which the Venerable Gelasius kept himself."

"Was it usual for Gelasius to lock his door?"

"Unusual in the extreme. He always left it open."

"So the door was locked! You say that you went to the window? Was it open?"

"No. It was closed."

"And secured?"

"Well, I had to smash the glass to open it and squeeze through."

"Go on. What did you find inside?"

"I had seen through the window that which caused me to see the smashing of the window as my own alternative. I saw the body of the Venerable Gelasius hanging from a beam."

"Show me."

Brother Gormgilla opened the door and conducted her into a spacious round chamber which had been the Venerable Gelasius's living quarters and study. He pointed up to the roof rafters. Great beams of wood at the height of eight feet from the ground crossed the room.

"See that one, just near the bed? Old Gelasius was hanging from it. A rope was twisted round it and one end was tied in a noose around his neck. I think that he had been dead for some hours. I knew at once that I could do nothing for him and so I went to rouse Father Maílín."

Fidelma rubbed her jaw thoughtfully.

"Did you stop to search the room?"

"My only thought was to tell the Father Superior the catastrophic news."

"You have told me that the door was locked. Was the key on the inside?"

"There was no sign of the key. That was why I had to squeeze back out of the window. Our smithy then came and picked the lock when Father Maílín arrived. It was the missing key that confirmed Father Maílín in his theory that thieves had done the deed, locking Gelasius in his own chamber after they had hanged him."

Fidelma examined the lock and saw the scratch marks where it had been picked. There was little else to decipher from it, except that the lock had apparently not been forced at any other stage. Fidelma moved to the window, where she saw the clear signs of broken glass and some scratching on the frame which might have been made by a body pushing through the aperture. It was certainly consistent with Brother Gormgilla's story.

She went to the bed and gazed up. There was some scoring on the beam.

"Is the bed in the same position?"

"It is?"

Fidelma made some mental measurements and then nodded.

"Let me get this perfectly clear, Brother Gormgilla. You say that the door was locked and there was no key in the lock on either side of the door? You also say that the window was secured and to gain access you had to break in from the outside?"

"That is so."

"Let me put this question to you, as I have also put it to your Father Superior: his theory is that the Venerable Gelasius was disturbed by marauders in the night. He went into the chapel to investigate. They overpowered him and brought him back here, hanged him and then robbed him. Does it occur to you that something is wrong with this explanation?"

Brother Gormgilla looked uncomfortable.

"I do not understand."

Fidelma tapped her foot in annoyance.

"Come now, Brother. For fifteen years you have been his helper; you helped him rise in the morning and had to accompany him to the chapel. Would such a frail old man suddenly start from his bed in the middle of the night and set off to face intruders? And why would these intruders bring him back here to hang him? Surely one sharp blow on the head would have been enough to render Gelasius dead or beyond hindrance to them?"

"It is not for me to say, Sister. Father Maílín says . . ."

"I know what Father Maílín says. What do you say?"

"It is not for me to question Father Maílín. He came to his conclusion after making strenuous inquiries."

"Of whom, other than yourself, could he make such inquiries?"

"It was Brother Firgil who told the Father Superior about the itinerants."

"Then bring Brother Firgil to me."

Brother Gormgilla scurried off.

Sister Fidelma wandered around the chamber and examined the manuscripts and books that lined the walls. Gelasius had, as hearsay had it, been an extraordinary scholar. There were books on philosophy in Hebrew, Latin, Greek and even works in the old tongue of the Irish, written on wooden wands in Ogham, the earliest Irish alphabet.

Everything was neatly placed along the shelves.

Gelasius had clearly been a methodical and tidy man. She glanced at some of the works. They intrigued her for they concerned the ancient stories of her people: stories of the pagan gods, the children of the Mother Goddess Danu whose "divine waters" fertilized the Earth at the beginning of time itself. It was a strange library for a great philosopher and teacher of the Faith to have.

At a little desk were vellum and quills where the Venerable Gelasius obviously sat composing his own works which were widely distributed among the teaching abbeys of Ireland. Now his voice would be heard no more. His death at the hands of mere thieves had robbed the Faith of one of its greatest protagonists. No wonder the Abbot had not been satisfied with Father Maílín's simple report and had asked Fidelma, as a trained *dálaigh* of the courts, to make an inquiry which could be presented to the King himself.

Fidelma glanced down at the vellum. It was pristine. Whatever Gelasius had been working on, he must have finished before his death, for his writing materials were clean and set out neatly; everything placed carefully, ready and waiting . . .

She frowned suddenly. Her wandering eye had caught something tucked inside a small calf-bound book on a nearby shelf. Why should she be attracted by a slip of parchment sticking out of a book? She was not sure until she realized everything else was so neat and tidy that the very fact that the paper was left so untidily was the reason which drew her attention to it.

She reached forward and drew it out. The slip of parchment fluttered awkwardly in her hands and made a slow glide to the floor. She bent down to pick it up. As she did so she noticed something protruding behind one of the stout legs of Gelasius's desk. Retrieving the parchment she reached forward and eased out the object from its hiding place.

It was an iron key, cold and greasy to the touch. For a moment, she stood gazing at it. Then she went to the door and inserted it. The key fitted into the lock and she turned it slowly. Then she turned it back and took it out, slipping it into her marsupium.

Finally, she reverted her attention to the piece of parchment. It was a note in Ogham. A line, a half constructed sentence no more. It read: "By despising, denigrating and destroying all that has preceded us, we will simply teach this and future generations to despise our beliefs. *Veritas vos liberabit!*"

"Sister?"

Fidelma glanced round. At the door stood a thin, pale-faced religieux with a hook nose and thin lips.

"I am Brother Firgil. You were asking for me?"

Fidelma placed the piece of parchment in her marsupium along with the key and turned to him.

"Brother Fergal?" she asked using the Irish name.

The man shook his head.

"Firgil," he corrected. "My father named me from the Latin Vergilius."

"I understand. I am told that you informed Father Maílín about the itinerants who were camping in the woods on the night of the Venerable Gelasius's death?"

"I did so," Brother Firgil agreed readily. "I noticed them on the day before that tragic event. I took them to be a band of mercenaries, about a score in number with womenfolk and children. They were camped out in the woods about half a mile from here."

"What made you think that they were responsible for the theft and killing of the Venerable Gelasius?"

Brother Firgil shrugged.

"Who else would dare such sacrilege than godless mercenaries?"

"Are you sure that they were godless?" Fidelma asked waspishly.

The man looked bewildered for a moment and then shrugged.

"No one who is at one with God would dare rob His house or harm His servants, particularly one who was as elderly as the Venerable Gelasius. It is well known that most of those mercenaries are not converted to the Faith."

"Is there proof that they robbed the chapel?"

"The proof is that a crucifix from the chapel and two gold chalices from the altar are gone. The proof is that the Venerable Gelasius had a rosary made of marble beads from a green stone from the lands of Conamara, which was said to have been blessed by the saintly Ailbe himself. That, too, is gone. Finally, the Venerable Gelasius was found dead. Hanged."

"But nothing you have said is proof that these itinerants were the culprits," Fidelma pointed out. "Is there any proof absolute?"

"The itinerants were camping in the wood on the day before the Venerable Gelasius's death. On the morning that Gelasius was discovered and the items were found missing, I told Father Maílín of my suspicions and was sent to observe the itinerants so that we could appeal to the local chieftain for warriors to take them. But they were gone. That is proof that guilt bade them hurry away from the scene of their crime."

"It is circumstantial proof only and that is not absolutely proof in law. Was the local chieftain informed?"

"He sent warriors immediately to follow them but their tracks vanished in some rocky passes through the hills and could not be picked up again."

"Did anyone observe anything strange during the night when these events happened?"

Brother Firgil shook his head.

"The only person who must have been roused by the thieves was poor Gelasius."

"How many brethren live in this community?"

"Twenty-one."

"It seems strange that an elderly man would be the only one disturbed during the night."

"You see that this chamber lies next to the chapel. Gelasius often kept late hours while working on his texts. I see no strangeness in this."

"In relationship to the chapel, where are the quarters of the other brethren?"

"The Father Superior has the chamber next to this one. I, as steward of the community, have the next chamber. The rest of the brethren share the dormitorium."

"Is the Father Superior a sound sleeper?"

Brother Firgil frowned.

"I do not understand."

"No matter. When was it discovered that the artifacts had been stolen?"

"Brother Gormgilla discovered the body of Gelasius and raised the alarm. A search was made and the crucifix, cups and rosary were found missing."

"And no physical damage was done in the chapel nor to this room before Brother Gormgilla had to break in?"

"None, so far as I am aware. Had there been, it might have aroused the community and we might have saved Gelasius."

"Was Gelasius an exceptionally tidy person?"

Brother Firgil blinked at the abrupt change of question.

"He was not especially so."

Fidelma gestured to the chamber.

"Was this how the room was when he was found?"

"I think it has been tidied up after his body was removed. I think that his papers were tidied and his clothes put away until it was decided what should be done with them."

"Who did the tidying?"

"Father Maílín himself."

Fidelma sighed softly.

"That is all, Brother Firgil."

She hesitated a moment, after he had left, and looked at the area where Gelasius would have been working, examining the books and papers carefully.

She left Gelasius's chamber and went into the chapel. It was small and with few icons. Two candles burnt on the altar. A rough-hewn, wooden crucifix had been positioned in obvious replacement of the stolen one. She examined the interior of the chapel for a few minutes before deciding that it would tell her nothing more.

She left the chapel and paused for a moment in the central courtyard looking at the buildings and judging their position to the chapel. Again, it merely confirmed what Brother Firgil had said. Gelasius's chamber was the closest to the chamber.

She felt frustrated. There was something that was not right at all.

Members of the brethren of the community went about their daily tasks, either avoiding her eyes or nodding a greeting to her, each according to their characters. There was no wall around the community and, in that, there was nothing to contradict the idea that a band of thieves could easily have infiltrated the community and entered the chapel.

Half a mile away, crossing a small hill was a wood and it was this wood where Brother Firgil had indicated that the itinerants had encamped.

Fidelma began to walk in that direction. Her movement towards the woods was purely automatic. She felt the compulsion to walk and think matters over and the wood was as good a direction as any in which to do so. It was not as though she expected to find any evidence among the remains of the itinerant camp.

She had barely gone a few hundred yards when she noticed the figure a short distance behind her. It was moving surreptitiously: a figure of one of the brothers following her from the buildings of the community.

She imperceptibly increased her pace up the rising path towards the woods and entered it quickly. The path immediately led into a clearing where it was obvious that there had been an encampment not so long ago. There were signs of a fire, the grey ashes spread in a circle. Some of the ground had been turned by the hooves of horses and a wagon.

"You won't find anything here, Sister."

Fidelma turned and regarded the figure of the brother who had now entered the clearing behind her.

"Good day, Brother," she replied solemnly. He was a young man, with bright ginger red hair and dark blue eyes. He was young, no more than twenty, but wore the tonsure of St John. "Brother . . .?" she paused inviting him to supply his name.

"My name is Brother Ledbán."

"You have followed me, Brother Ledbán. Do you wish to talk with me?"

"I want you to know that the Venerable Gelasius was a brilliant man."

"I think most of Christendom knows that," she replied solemnly.

"Most of Christendom does not know that the Venerable Gelasius hungered for truth no matter if the truth was unpalatable to them."

"*Veritas vos liberabit*. The truth shall make you free," Fidelma quoted from the vellum in her marsupium.

"That was his very motto," Brother Ledbán agreed. "He should have remembered the corollary to that – *veritas odium parit*."

Fidelma's eyes narrowed slightly.

"I have heard that said. Truth breeds hatred. Was Gelasius getting near a truth that caused hatred?"

"I think so."

"Among the brethren?"

"Among certain of our community at St Martin's," agreed Brother Ledbán.

"Perhaps you should tell me what you know."

"I know little but what little I know, I shall impart to you."

Fidelma sat down on a fallen tree trunk and motioned Brother Ledbán to sit next to her.

"I understand that the Venerable Gelasius must have been working on a new text of philosophy?"

"He was. Why I know it is because I am a scribe and the *Delbatóir* of the community. I would often sharpen Gelasius's quills for him or seek out new ones. I would mix his inks. As *Delbatóir* it was my task to make the metal covers that would enshrine and protect the books."

Fidelma nodded. Many books considered worthy of note were either enshrined in metal boxes or had finely covered plates of gold or silver, some encrusted with jewels, sewn on to their leather covers. This was a special art, the casting of such plates called a *cumtach*, and the task fell to the one appointed a *Delbatóir* which meant a framer or fashioner.

"We sometimes worked closely and Gelasius would often say to me that truth was the philosopher's food but was often bitter to the taste. Most people preferred the savoury lie."

"Who was he annoying by his truth?"

"To be frank, Sister, he was annoying himself. I went into his chamber once, where he had been pouring over some texts in the old writing . . ."

"In Ogham?"

"In Ogham. Alas, I have not the knowledge of it to be able to decipher the ancient alphabet. But he suddenly threw the text from him and exclaimed: 'Alas! The value of the well is not known until it has dried up!' Then he saw me and smiled and apologized for his temper. But temper was not really part of that wise old man, Sister. It was more a sadness than a temper."

"A sadness at what he was reading?"

"A sadness at what he was realizing through his great knowledge."

"I take it that you do not believe in Father Maílín's story of the itinerant thieves?" she suddenly asked.

He glanced swiftly at her.

"I am not one to point a finger of accusation at any one individual. The bird has little affection that deserts its own brood."

"There is also an old saying, that one bird flies away from every brood. However, I am not asking you to desert your own brood but I am asking you to help in tracking down the person responsible for the Venerable Gelasius's death."

"I cannot betray that person."

"Then you do know who it was?"

"I suspect but suspecting would cast doubt on the good name of Gelasius."

Fidelma frowned slightly.

"I fail to understand that."

"The explanation of every riddle is contained in itself," Brother Ledbán replied, rising. "Gelasius was fond of reading *Naturalis Historia* . . ."

"Pliny?" queried Fidelma.

"Indeed – Gaius Plinius Secundus. Gelasius once remarked to me that he echoed Pliny in acknowledging God's best gift to mankind."

He had gone even before Fidelma felt that she should have pointed out that he could be ordered to explain by law under pain of fine. Yet, somehow, she did not think it was appropriate nor that she would be able to discover his suspicions in that way.

She sat for some time on the log, turning matters over in her own mind. Then she pulled out the piece of parchment and read it again, considering it carefully. She replaced it in her marsupium and stood up abruptly, her mouth set in a grim line.

She retraced her steps back down the hill to the community and went straight to the Father Superior's chamber.

Father Maílín was still seated at his desk and looked up in annoyance as she entered.

"Have you finished your investigation, Sister?"

"Not as yet," Fidelma replied and, without waiting to be asked, sat down. A frown crossed Father Maílín's brow but before he could admonish Fidelma, she cut in with a bored voice, "I would remind you that not only am I sister to the King of Cashel but, in holding the degree of *Anruth* as an advocate of the court, I have the privilege of even sitting in the presence of the High King. Do not, therefore, lecture me on protocol."

Father Maílín swallowed at the harshness of her tone.

He had, indeed, been about to point out that a member of the brethren was not allowed to sit in the presence of a Father Superior without being invited.

"You are a clever man, Father Maílín," Fidelma suddenly said, although the Father Superior missed the patronizing tone in her voice.

He stared at her not knowing how to interpret her words.

"I need your advice."

Father Maílín shifted his weight slightly in his chair. He was bewildered by her abrupt changes of attitude.

"I am at your service, Sister Fidelma."

"It is just that you have been able to reason out an explanation for a matter which is beyond my understanding and I would like you to explain it to me."

"I will do my best."

"Excellent. Tell me how these thieves were able to overpower and hang an old man in his chamber and leave the room, having secured the window on the inside and locking the door behind them, leaving the key in the room?"

Father Maílín stared at her for some moments, his eyes fixed on her in puzzlement. Then he began to chuckle.

"You are misinformed. The key was never found. The thieves took it with them."

"I am told that there was only one key to that room which the Venerable Gelasius kept in his possession. Is that true?"

Father Maílín nodded slowly.

"There was no other key. Our smithy had to pick the lock for us to gain entrance to the room."

Fidelma reached into her marsupium and laid the key before him.

"Don't worry, I tried it in Gelasius's lock. It works. I found the key on the floor behind his desk."

"I don't . . . I can't . . ."

His voice stumbled over the words.

Fidelma smiled sharply.

"Somehow I didn't think you would be able to offer an explanation."

Father Maílín ran a hand, distractedly, through his hair. He said nothing.

"Where are the writings that the Venerable Gelasius was working on?" went on Fidelma.

"Destroyed," Father Maílín replied limply.

"Was it you who destroyed them?"

"I take that responsibility."

"*Veritas odium parit,*" repeated Fidelma softly.

"You know your Terence, eh? But I did not hate old Gelasius. He was just misguided. The more misguided he became, the more stubborn he became. Ask anyone. Even Brother Ledbán, who worked closely with him, refused to cast a mould for a bookplate which carried some Ogham script because he thought Gelasius had misinterpreted it."

"You felt that Gelasius was so misguided that you had to destroy his work?"

"You do not understand, Sister."

"I think I do."

"I doubt it. You could not. Gelasius was like a father to me. I was protecting him. Protecting his reputation."

Fidelma raised an eyebrow in disbelief.

"It is the truth that I tell you," insisted the Father Superior. "Those papers on which he was working, I had hoped that he would never release to the world. He was the great philosopher of the Faith and yet he grew senile and began to doubt his faith."

"In what way did he grow senile?"

"What other condition could account for his doubt? When I reproved him for his doubt he told me that one must question even the existence of God for if God did exist then he would approve of the homage of reason rather than fear born out of ignorance."

Fidelma inclined her head.

"He was, indeed, a wise man," she sighed. "But for those doubts . . . you killed him!"

Father Maílín sprang to his feet, his face white.

"What? Do you accuse me of his murder? It was the itinerants, I tell you."

"I do not believe your itinerant theory, Father Maílín," she said firmly. "No one who considers the facts could believe it."

The Father Superior slumped back in his seat with hunched shoulders. There was guilt written on his features. He groaned softly.

"I only sought to protect Gelasius's reputation. I did not kill him," he protested.

"You, yourself, have given yourself a suitable motive for his murder."

"I didn't! I did not . . ."

"I will leave you for a moment to consider your story. When I return, I shall want the truth."

She turned out of his chamber and made her way slowly to the chapel. She was about to pass the Venerable Gelasius's door when some instinct drew her inside again. She did not know what made her enter until she saw the shelf of books.

She made her way across the room and began to peer along the line of books.

"Gaius Plinius Secundus," she muttered to herself, as her eyes rested on the book which she was unconsciously looking for – *Naturalis Historia*.

She began to flip through pages seeking the half forgotten reference.

Finally, she found the passage and read it through. The passage contained what she expected it would.

She glanced quickly round the room and then went to the bed. She climbed on it and stood at the edge, reaching her hands up towards the beam above. It was, for her, within easy arm's length. She stepped down again to the floor. Then she made her way to the chapel and stood inside the door as she had done a short time before.

Her gaze swept around the chapel and then, making up her mind on some intuition, she walked to the altar and went down on her hands and knees but it was not to pray. She bent forward and lifted an edge of the drape across the altar.

Beneath the altar stood a silver crucifix and two golden chalices. In one of them, was a rosary of green stone beads. Fidelma reached forward and took them out. She regarded them for a moment or two and then heaved a deep sigh.

Gathering them in her arms she retraced her steps to Father Maílín's chamber. He was still seated at his desk. He began to rise when she entered, and then his eyes fell to the trophies she carried. He turned pale and slumped back in his seat.

"Where did you . . ." he began, trying to summon up some residue of sharpness by which he hoped to control the situation.

"Listen to me," she interrupted harshly. "I have told you that it is impossible to accept your story that thieves broke in, killed Gelasius and left him in a room secured from the inside. I then find that you disapproved of the work which Gelasius was doing and after his death destroyed it. Tell me how these matters add up to a reasonable explanation?"

Father Maílín was shaking his head.

"It was wrong to blame the itinerants. I realize that. It seemed that it was the only excuse I could make. As soon as I realized the situation, I distracted the brethren and quickly went into the chapel and removed the first things that came to hand. The crucifix and the cups. These I placed under the altar where you doubtless discovered them. I returned to Gelasius's room and seized the opportunity to take his rosary from the drawer. Then it was easy. I could now claim that we had been robbed."

"And you destroyed Gelasius's work?"

"I only collected the text that Gelasius had been working on at the time and destroyed it lest it corrupt the minds of the faithful. Surely it was better to remember Gelasius in the vigour of his youth when he took up the banner of the Faith against all comers and destroyed the idols of the past? Why remember him as he was in his dotage, in his senility – an old embittered man filled with self-doubts?"

"Is that how you saw him?"

"That is how he became, and this I say even though he had been a father to me. He taught us to overthrow the idols of the pagans, to recant the sins of our fathers who lived in heathendom . . ."

"By despising, denigrating and destroying all that has preceded us, we will simply teach this and future generations to despise our beliefs. *Veritas vos liberabit!*"

Father Maílín stared at her quizzically.

"How do you know that?"

"You did not destroy all Gelasius's notes. Gelasius, towards the end of his life, suddenly began to realize the cultural wealth he had been instrumental in destroying. It began to prey on his mind that instead of bringing civilization and knowledge to this land, he was destroying thousands of years of learning. Benignus writes that the Blessed Patrick himself, in his missionary zeal, burnt 180 books of the Druids. Imagine the loss to learning!"

"It was right that such books of pagan impropriety be destroyed," protested the Father Superior.

"To a true scholar it was a sacrilege that should never have happened."

"He was wrong."

"The burning of books, the destruction of knowledge, is a great crime against humanity. No matter in whose name it is done," replied Fidelma. "Gelasius saw that. He knew he was partially responsible for a crime which he had committed against his own culture as well as the learning of the world."

Father Maílín was silent for a moment and then he said: "I did not kill him. He took his own life. That was why I tried to blame the itinerants."

"Gelasius was murdered," Fidelma said. "But not by the itinerants. He was murdered by a member of this community."

Father Maílín was pale and shocked.

"You cannot believe that I . . . I only meant to cover up his own suicide and hide the nature of his work. I did not kill him?"

"I realize that . . . now. The thing that had misled me was the fact that you and the real killer both shared a fear of the nature of Gelasius's work. But you both took different ways of dealing with it. When the killer struck, he wanted to make it appear that Gelasius committed suicide and so discredit him. However, you, believing that Gelasius's suicide was genuine, and would bring discredit on the Faith, then tried to disguise what you thought was a suicide and blame itinerants for murder."

"Who killed the Venerable Gelasius, then?" demanded Father Maílín. "And how? There was only one key and you say that you found it in the room."

"Let me first explain why I did not think Gelasius took his own life. The obvious point was that it was physically impossible for him to do so. He was old and frail. I stood on the bed and reached to the roof beam. I am tall and therefore could reach it. But for an elderly and frail man, and one of short stature, it was impossible for him to stand on the bed, tie the rope and hang himself.

"Yet one of your brethren went to considerable lengths to draw attention to the nature of the work that Gelasius was doing, pretending to express approval for it but, at the same time, hinting that Gelasius was so overawed by his revelations that he could not face the fact of his complicity in the destruction of our ancient beliefs and rituals. He even said that Gelasius had approved of a quotation by Pliny which, cunningly he left for me to find, having wetted my curiosity. It was the passage where Pliny wrote that, 'amid the suffering of life, suicide is the gods' best gift to men'. The murderer was Brother Ledbán."

"Ledbán?" Father Maílín looked at her in amazement. "The *Delbatóir*? But he worked closely with the Venerable Gelasius . . ."

"And so knew all about his work. And one of the mistakes Ledbán made was in pretending he had no knowledge of Ogham when, as you yourself testify, he knew enough to accuse Gelasius of wrong interpretation."

"But there is one thing you cannot explain," Father Maílín pointed out, "and in this your whole argument falls apart. There was only one key and that you confess you found inside Gelasius's room."

Fidelma smiled knowingly.

"I think you will find a second key. What is the task of Brother Ledbán?"

"He's the *Delbatóir* . . . why?"

"He makes the metal book plates and book shrines, casting them from moulds in gold or silver. It is not beyond his capability to cast a second key, having made a mould from the first. You simply take the key and press it into wax to form the mould from which you will make your cast. You will note, as I did, the key I found – Gelasius's own key – was covered in grease. A search of Ledbán's chamber or his forge should bring the second key to light if he does not confess when faced with the rest of the evidence."

"I see."

"However, it was wrong of you, Father Maílín, to try to disguise the manner of Gelasius's death."

"You must understand my position. I did believe Gelasius had committed suicide. If so, the nature of his work would be revealed. Would you rather Christendom knew that one of its great theologians committed suicide in protest at being responsible for the destruction of a few pagan books?"

"I would rather Christendom might learn from such an act. However, it was a greater guilt to fabricate the false evidence."

"My desire was to save Gelasius from condemnation," protested Father Maílín.

"Had Gelasius resorted to suicide, then he would have been condemned for his action," Fidelma said. "What was it that Martial wrote?

When all the flattery of life is gone
The fearful steal away to death, the brave live on.

"But, as you frequently remarked, the Venerable Gelasius
was a brave man and would have lived to argue his case had
he not been murdered. I will leave it to you to arrest Brother
Ledbán and await instructions from the Abbot."

She smiled sadly and turned towards the door.

"Must everything come out?" called Father Maílín.
"Must all be revealed?"

"That is up to the Abbot," replied Fidelma, glancing
back. "Thankfully, in this case, it is not in my purview to
make such moral judgments on what took place here. I only
have to report the facts to the Abbot."

King Hereafter

Philip Gooden

Philip Gooden lives and works in Bath and is the author of the Shakespearean murder mysteries Sleep of Death *(2000) and* Death of Kings *(2001), featuring his ac-tor-detective, Nick Revill. Not surprisingly, Gooden turns to the Shakespearean world for the following story, the world of Macbeth. The facts may be more Shakespearean than historical, but it's no less a puzzle for that.*

It was not until some weeks after I'd finally bedded the Lady Gruoch that we got round to talking about her husband. Naturally, we'd already chatted about him in a general way: that is, about his bed preferences and peculiarities. Not many of either, according to my lady. He was more the warrior than the lover. But now we started to talk about him as a man, with flaws and failings and weak points. His strengths we took for granted. I, the young cuckolder, found myself in the odd position of defending Gruoch's husband against his wife.

She leaned on an elbow and traced out my cheekbone with a long finger. The firelight gave a hectic gleam to her already flushed and naked chest.

"He is superstitious," she said.

"Most men are," I said, "more so than women in my experience."

"He won't go anywhere on Friday. He says it's an unlucky day to travel, for God's sake."

"There are other days to move in."

"He's afraid of the dark."

"Then he is sensible," I said, pinching one of her hard little nipples. "Why do you despise him so much?"

"He has no ambition. No hunger."

"*Now* we come to it."

"Not like you, Canmore," she said. Her tone was hopeful.

"A man situated as I am has no need of ambition. I only have to wait."

"You know what happened to the horse that waited for the grass to grow," she said.

"The proverb is something musty," I said.

"Huh," she snorted, horse-like herself.

The Lady Gruoch was fierce, impatient. That was the mood I liked her in best, the mood when we came together front to front, like two enemies in the field. As we did now.

She was right too. Of course I was ambitious. The notion that I was willing to wait until the prize fell into my lap was pretence, a necessary cloak in company. By instinct, I would rather have seized it.

She returned to the subject a few days later when we were out hunting. We were spending much time together at that period, uninterrupted time. Her husband was off in the west, fighting as usual, doing the King's business against a raggle-taggle bunch of mercenaries and rebels. It was a campaign that I'd participated in, my first in fact. I left the field when the only task remaining was cleaning up, an operation well suited to Gruoch's husband. He liked cleaning up almost as much as he liked fighting. The few trees along the western shores would be laden with the bodies of kerns and gallow-glasses, shrivelling in the sea winds like long, discoloured fruit.

I knew that he was more at home out there, campaigning and cleaning up, than he would have been in his castle with Gruoch. For my part I was happier here, on his side of the bed, than I ever was on the battlefield. Gruoch told me that she'd been waging her own campaign to bed down with me. Naturally I was flattered. Almost old enough to be my mother, she could have passed for my sister. Now I wanted her to enjoy the fruits of conquest for as long as possible. Let her husband hang and head the malcontents to his heart's content, I said to myself, as long as he stays away a little longer.

The hunting Gruoch and I had our own small deaths to attend to, out on the heaths and inside the wind-stunted copses. She dug her spurs in to be first on the scene as the spent hart faltered – regained his footing – stumbled once more – tried to rise – but too late, for the dogs were on him! She had her favourites in the pack (Blanche, Trey, Sweetheart, some of their names I can remember) and would egg them on at the kill, red and shrieking, her mouth flecked with unbecoming spittle. At such moments I wondered at her ability to lose herself in what she witnessed.

When we were riding back, with Blanche and the other braches bounding by our side, she returned to our bed-topic.

"Why should you wait?"

"He's old." I didn't pretend not to know what she was talking about. "He hasn't got much longer," I added.

"How do you know, Canmore? He leads a clear life. They're the ones that live longest."

"You mean God's in no hurry to get His hands on them?"

"I mean that they keep away from surfeit and sin. Pure livers live longest."

There was something in what she said. The old man did lead a clear life. He was oftener on his knees than on his feet. He spent more time with the priests in their chantries than the generals in their tents. He kept a battlefield at arm's length. That disturbance in the west I mentioned earlier – you may be sure he received report of it but stayed well out of ear- or arrow-shot. Unlike most of his predecessors, he was continent too, or continent now. *He* would not meet his end between a mistress's sheets.

"Yes," I said, raising my voice because we were trotting on either side of a peaty rivulet. "You're right. He'll die in his bed."

The Lady Gruoch looked round. At a respectful distance our retinues kept pace with us. Somewhere far in the rear, a little procession of carts and wagons transported our gral-loched quarry, our dead harts.

"Die in his own —"

"What's that?"

The breeze lifted her voice and carried it away.

"His own bed, I said," she said.

The wind gusted once more.

"Or ours," she said.

I thought I'd misheard again. It was growing late and the outline of Glammis was hardly distinguishable against the darkening sky.

"Ours. Die in our bed."

She'd overstepped the mark this time, I felt. All the same, a shiver ran through me, leaving me both hot and cold.

"I have something to show you when we get back, Can-more."

I took this as a promise of one kind of showing, especially as I knew that the animal spirits roused in her by hunting often carried over into our indoor life. So it proved on this occasion. In between bed-bouts, however, my Lady un-twined herself from my arms and legs, pushed aside the curtains, exited the bed and walked naked towards a heavily ornamented press in the corner of the chamber. There was a gap in the bed-hangings and I saw, by the lazy candlelight, how she bent down towards the bottom of the press and extracted from it a small gilded casket. This she bore back to the bed, holding it warily before her.

I thought at first that what she'd wanted to show me was the casket itself, a fine piece of work but hardly remarkable. Gruoch pushed back the sarcenet hangings to let in some candlelight and climbed into her husband's bed. Since she stayed sitting I raised myself up. Our shoulders touched. She stared down at the casket reposing on her naked lap.

"This is what you have to show me?" I said. "There is more treasure underneath it. A richer mine. See."

She brushed aside my rash, intruding hand and from somewhere, perhaps under the pillow, produced a small key. With a touch of ceremony, she opened the casket and took out a letter which it contained. She handed it to me. The letter was from the west, from the husband who was cleaning up after the campaign. He began with salutations: "Greetings, dear wife, I trust you are in health" and so on; quite formal. The rest of it was written in a stiff, warrior-like hand and style, and signed off in similar manner.

"So," I said. "Is this meant to make me feel guilty – a letter from your husband?"

"There's more."

She drew another sheet from the box and gave me this as well. By placing it over the first and seeing how the folds corresponded, I realized that they had been delivered together. The hand on this one was scrawled and wavering. There was no salutation. From her slow breathing, from the way I sensed her eyes on my face, I knew that this was the important communication, and that the other letter was just cover. Now we'd reached the quick of the matter.

"This is . . . interesting," I said after a time. I avoided looking at her.

"Is that all?"

"You believe him?"

She tapped the paper I was holding. "This is beyond him," she said. "He hasn't the imagination for even a small lie."

"And you?"

I looked at her now. Her sharp, pointy face was fixed on mine.

"Oh yes, I can lie, Canmore."

"No, I mean, do you believe what this says?"

I surprised myself with my level tone. After all, I was intimately concerned with the contents of her husband's letter, the second secret letter, wasn't I?

"I . . . am not sure," said Gruoch.

"Is this not the merest superstition? What you were so recently mocking your husband for."

But a little dread descended on me even as I attempted to make light of the business. Meantime Gruoch reached around so that I glimpsed her tawny flank while she stretched through the parted curtains and snuffed with her fingers the candle next the bedside. We were thrown into shadow.

"Yes," she said. "Now I believe it."

"And he will become king – like that – without his stir?"

"They have spoken," she said solemnly.

"What about –"

Something cut me off, like a cry choked in mid-course.

"My darling," she said, clutching at me in the dark, "it is you I'm thinking of, all the time. You that I'm planning for. Anyway it doesn't matter whether it's true or not, what matters is whether *he* believes that it is."

"I don't understand."

"Oh you do. But I will syllable it for you. If *he* believes, you see, then that will be enough, because we can . . . push him in a certain direction."

"The old man's direction?"

"A meeting can be arranged between the King and my husband – with my assistance."

"And afterwards?"

"Afterwards is ours."

"For your husband, I mean."

"Exposure, denunciation, execution – that will do for him."

"How long have you been brewing this?"

A note of admiration crept into my voice. I couldn't help it.

"Ever since I first set eyes on you," said Gruoch.

"I was a child," I said. "You were a woman."

"Even so," she said.

"Come here," I said.

"Wait."

She drew the bed-curtains so that the final fragments of light in the room were dimmed almost to extinction. Then she rubbed herself against me, her feral muzzle against me.

So, the story in the letter from her husband was this. That, returning from the western front with the Thane of Loch-quhaber, he had encountered three gyre-carlines (or hags, as I would have termed them) on a green. Now, Gruoch's husband must have been in an unusually mellow mood – or simply sated with battle-killing – because in other circumstances he might have strung the hags up merely for being in his path. Perhaps what made him pause was what they'd said to him, their predictions about his becoming king and all.

All this was in the second letter, the secret letter. Gruoch was right: he couldn't have made it up. He was too unimaginative. No more than a walking sword. Maybe that was what gave her the idea of what might happen next.

That, and what she told me after we'd made love again.

"He is coming here in two days' time."

"Coming. Who?" I said, drowsily.

"The King."

I slept and dreamed of the old man.

The next day Gruoch's husband returned and so I was compelled to leave her chamber and install myself in the guest-quarters of the castle. She promised me that it wouldn't be for long. That once her husband had done what was required of him and been disposed of, we'd be together for good.

I exchanged a few words with the cuckold when he entered Glammis Castle. He was glad enough to see me, the veteran war-oaf. Still sticky, still filthy from the campaign and the slog homeward across mountain and morass, he clasped his wife in the courtyard. I, who had so lately untwined myself from her limbs and torn myself from her bed, could see what he evidently did not. How she shrank in his mailed embrace. A charitable observer might have put it down to reluctance to have her delicately worked gown sullied.

Then Macbeth turned to me.

"Well, Canmore, I saw you last in the thick of battle."

"I am surprised you had the leisure to look about you, Macbeth, you were so busy parting souls and bodies."

"And now you have been enjoying my wife's hospitality."

For an instant I wondered, but only for an instant. He was too stupid to notice what was under his nose.

"She has been most gracious – and receptive," I said.

"Honour to her, and to you," he replied.

And with that he led her indoors while I made my way to my new quarters. She told me later how she had broached

the plan to him (after he had broached her – unenthusias-
tically, because he was tired and ever the fighter rather than
the lover) and of how he had responded, at first with
hesitation. But Macbeth really had no choice in the matter.
Not only was she on his back – and she would be more than
enough for any man – but the three gyre-carlines on the
green were behind him in spirit, harrying him with their
promises and predictions.

So, yes, he said yes. I'll do it.

We'll do it, she said. Kill the King.

The day after Macbeth's return the old man arrived at
Glammis Castle. He looked, in contrast to Macbeth, plush
and holy and old, like a prelate. In the King's train rode my
younger brother Donal, I'm sorry to say. Donal is as pious as
the King, but his boyish holiness is embalmed in a rake-like
body and a fierce gaze. You can be sure that my brother
pretended to be glad to see me and that I simulated a like
pleasure.

The King was gracious enough. He dismounted and
hugged his host and hostess in the courtyard while the
Glammis retainers stood around in liveried reverence. I
observed that Lady Macbeth was a better player than her
husband. She really did offer welcome in eye and tongue,
while he merely looked shifty.

We repaired to the audience chamber. Spices had been
cast on the great fire and a sweet, teasing scent filled the
air. Macbeth now remembered that he was playing the
part of loyal host and smiled and smiled like a stage
villain.

For his valour in battle, the King acclaimed him Thane of
Cawdor, a title that had belonged to one of those disloyal
thanes who'd supported the rebels from the western isles.
This struck me as a Greek gift. Who would choose a traitor's
name? But Macbeth seemed happy enough. As Gruoch said,
he hasn't much imagination.

Then the King turned to me.

"Now, my son Canmore, you too have fought most
bravely on the edge of our kingdom and, like our new Thane
of Cawdor, you deserve reward."

"Whatever I do, majesty," I said, bowing, "is done in your service, and that is reward enough."

I had to make an effort not to glance in my Lady Gruoch's direction as I straightened up after this effusion. I could imagine the red glint in her eye.

"Even so, Malcolm Canmore, you shall be honoured, and the more so for your loyalty and modesty."

He raised his right hand, palm outwards.

"Know therefore, thanes and kinsmen, that we hereby invest Canmore with the title of Prince of Cumberland, for him and his in perpetuity."

The court sent back the ritual cry: "Honour to him and to you."

I looked about, pleased or seeming so. It was a prize, Cumberland, but was there ever a man content with a single gold coin when a whole purseful of them lie nearby? A ring of Scotland's noblest lords and thanes stood round me, stamping approval with their feet, grinning wolfishly. Only the Thane of Lochquhaber fixed me with his steady gaze, as if he could see through to my inmost heart. Later, I wondered whether he had evinced a similar scepticism when he and Macbeth encountered the hags on the heath.

The old man stood up from the makeshift throne in the audience chamber. This was the signal for the court to disperse until supper. I went to my quarters and lay down, waiting for the knock on the door.

But she entered without knocking and within seconds we were tangled on the bed. Almost as quickly we separated ourselves, knowing that there was life-and-death business to discuss.

"It is arranged," she said. "He will do it tonight."

"You are certain?"

"Don't doubt, Canmore."

"I don't doubt you, my dove, but him."

"Listen. We have a small part to play in this. But otherwise our hands will be clean."

I waited. Looking back, it is extraordinary how ready I was to entrust everything to the Lady Gruoch. How I trusted her – as you would a mother, a sister.

"The King is two doors from here," she said, "in the royal apartment."

"You didn't house me there," I said, with mock grievance.

"You were housed in my bed," she said.

"A royal housing."

"Listen. To reach the King's chamber, Macbeth must cross the outer room where the two chamberlains are quartered."

"Kenneth and Rhun," I said. "I know them. And do *you* know that one of them is always supposed to remain awake while the other sleeps?"

"That is a custom going back to my grandfather's time," she said.

"So how do you propose to get round it?"

"After the King is safely in bed and asleep, we will make sure that the chamberlains enjoy a little rere-supper."

"A late collation which you will prepare of course?"

"And which we will both of us deliver."

"Both?"

"Because what they might look at askance from me they will readily take from you."

"There is a better reason than that, my Lady, and you know it."

She said nothing.

"You want both our hands to be a little sullied. So while your husband is covered in the old man's blood –"

"For which he must die."

"Agreed. He shall. But even as he is covered in blood, we too, or rather I too, must be a little implicated."

"You are the chiefest gainer, Canmore. Don't waver now."

"And do not doubt me, Gruoch. I am resolved."

So, it all went to plan – in the beginning. Once we knew that the King was safely installed in bed in his apartment, Gruoch and I conveyed a rere-supper of various dainties to the chamberlains who lay in the ante-room. They were pleased, if a little surprised, to see their hostess and the King's son personally bearing salvers of food and wine.

I knew Kenneth and Rhun. They were familiar with me from when I was a lad. They had served my father for many years and, though not as old as he, had grown grizzled in his service. They greeted me with affection, which in the circumstances I did not welcome. I am not a brute or a natural hypocrite. In the corner of the room Gruoch poured out goblets of red wine, two by two, courteously bringing the chamberlains theirs before serving me and herself. As she handed me a goblet, she gave me a furtive glance. I felt tight in my belly and the room suddenly grew airless.

Then it was simply a matter of waiting. We passed the time with the chamberlains, talking about the prospects for next day's hunting, but all the time quiet and low because we were mindful of the sleeping King Duncan next door. As the soporifics started to take effect, Gruoch slipped from the room to prepare her husband, whom she had left safely shut up on her side of the castle. I remained behind until Kenneth and Rhun, having drained their goblets to the dregs, slumped down, one awkwardly on a bench and the other flat on his back on the ground. Before I left, I eased the chamberlains' daggers from their sheaths and laid them out in plain sight on the rushy floor for Macbeth to pick up.

When I quit the King's apartment I should have turned left towards my own quarters, on the way passing my brother Donal's chamber. I'd barely spoken to him since his arrival with our father, noting only the disapproving glances he had given to all and sundry at the supper table. But I was possessed by a restless spirit – it is not every black night that one stands by while one's father is murdered – and instead of creeping back to my room and lying low until the deed was done I turned right to go down the stairs and into the open. The night was close, even though it was midway through autumn. I thought I wanted air. But in truth I was waiting for Macbeth to make his way across the yard and climb the stairs to my father's apartment. Although I didn't doubt Gruoch, and indeed had the highest respect for her persuasive powers, I still wasn't certain that Macbeth would actually be brought to do it.

I backed into a convenient doorway. From here I should

be able to see anyone approaching the guest area of the castle. As my eyes grew more used to the dark, I could discern the lineaments of several of the outbuildings littering the wide yard. There were no stars and the sky was low, pressing down like an eyelid on Glammis. Something flickered in the corner of my vision. A darker shadow moved among the shapes of the yard, accompanied by a faint glimmer. No, not one but two shadows, the second small and stunted as a dwarf. My heart leapt into my throat and I must have made some involuntary noise because the larger of the walking shadows stopped. The little glimmer of light was raised, and I realized its source was a shuttered lantern.

"What is it, father?"

"Wait here, I shall see," came a quiet but determined voice, and the shadow began to come towards the doorway where I was waiting.

To forestall discovery, I strode forward with confidence, as if I had every right to be there. And indeed I did have every right. I am a King's son, after all.

"Good evening, Banquo," I said.

I felt rather than heard the man in front of me breathe a sigh of relief. There was a scraping sound as he widened the aperture on the lantern and a measure of light spread over the place where I stood.

"It's Malcolm Canmore," said he, then remembering himself. "My lord."

The Thane of Lochquhaber is a brave man but like many men he is superstitious enough in the dark. I wondered to see him out so late.

"I couldn't sleep," he said. "Nor could the lad. Bad dreams."

So the short shadow now coming to join him was his young son Fleance.

"Nor I," I said. "I am out too – and having a piss here."

I shrugged over my shoulder at the empty doorway. Then resolved to say no more. Why should a King's son have to explain himself? There was a pause.

"Goodnight, and better dreams," I said, without stirring a foot.

"Goodnight, my lord."

He nudged Fleance and the boy aped his father: "Goodnight, my lord."

"Honour to you and to him," I said, thinking all this while *Begone, begone, Macbeth is due*.

Father and son moved off into the night, Banquo having reduced the lantern's gleam to a glimmer. But, as bad luck would have it, they had gone not more than a dozen yards before they collided with a third shadow. Literally collided. I heard the thump in the dark, the gasp and the oath. I sensed rather than saw hands reaching for swords. But identities were swiftly exchanged and a short conversation followed, of which I could gather only scraps, something to do with honour. I recognized Macbeth's broad tones.

I waited. Reduced to a bystander's role, I could do nothing else in this great drama. Whatever passed between them must have satisfied Banquo (who was of course an old friend of the new Thane of Cawdor) for after some moments two of the scraps of darkness split off from the third and Macbeth passed my doorway. As the warrior crossed in front of me, I heard him muttering to himself.

I did not stir or speak. This was his business. Gruoch's plan, which I had willingly endorsed, was that her husband, alone and unaided, should carry out the murder of my father in the belief (encouraged by the three hags and his wife) that he would become King hereafter. Then, the dirty work done, Macbeth would be "discovered", tried and executed as a regicide. In everybody's eyes he would be a devil, driven to that dreadful deed by overweening ambition. And this would leave the way clear to the throne for Malcolm Canmore, the elder son of King Duncan. This Malcolm would share his throne with Gruoch, Lady Macbeth, she who was the granddaughter of King Kenneth III and who was born to power if ever woman was.

I might have waited for my throne. I was young. I had time. But young men are impatient, and time is always passing.

So, my Lady Gruoch's plan offered the best road forward – for both of us. Despite the difference in our ages, she and I

were cousins. We were notional enemies too. My grandfather, also a Malcolm, had usurped hers. But it must have
been the cousinage – or is the word cozenage? – that accounted for something similar in our glances, our postures
(even though I am more than a head taller). Recently, before
her husband's return, rising in the early half-light in her
chamber, I caught sight of her in the polished metal which
stood on the far side of the room and in front of which she
was dressed each morning. Momentarily, I glanced round to
ascertain that she was still curled up in the marital bed. She
was. It wasn't her I was glimpsing, it was myself.

These things, or some of them, went through my mind as I
waited in the courtyard for Macbeth to do the deed. I could
not, for the life of me, have returned to my quarters to await
this night's event. An owl hooted and I jumped.

"Canmore."

An urgent hiss.

"Gruoch? Is it?"

"Has he finished?"

At that moment there came an unearthly low wail from the
floor above. My scalp prickled. Gruoch clutched hard at my
arm.

"Is that him?"

Her breath smelt winy, sour. So, probably, did mine.

"Who else can it be," I whispered.

"Is it finished?"

"Go and see."

I didn't mean her to do this – I was hardly aware of what I
was saying – but she at once moved across the yard and
toward the stairs. Before I could call out to bring her back
she had vanished.

Part of me thought: well, it was her plan before it was ours.

I might have counted to thirty but no more before she was
back by my side.

"It's all gone wrong," she said. "You must go and do
it."

"Not dead?"

"No."

"How do you know?"

"I looked into his chamber. The door's open. He's still sleeping. I saw him."

"Where's your husband?"

But she didn't have to answer. At that moment there rushed past us in the dark a frantic shape. It stumbled, picked itself up with much cursing, then flew on into the night.

"You must go and do it," she repeated, and when I didn't move away: "My darling, it makes no difference. Macbeth will still carry the blame."

"Where are the daggers?"

"In the outer room. He dropped them when I came in. He saw me in the doorway and the knives fell from his hand. He's in no state to kill anyone tonight. He was shaking and weeping."

She sounded oddly composed.

"I thought you'd prepared him."

"I had. But I've told you what he's like. Superstitious – and easily overawed. He can make a shambles on the battle-field and stare death in the face but evidently he cannot lift a finger against the King himself."

"Evidently," I said.

And so I moved off into the dark to do my duty.

I reached the entrance to my father's quarters. The fleeing Macbeth had left the door ajar and a few candles guttered in the interior. Kenneth and Rhun remained where they'd tumbled down.

At that point I might have continued walking along the passage and past my brother Donal's room until I reached my own. I might have retreated to the security of my couch and there passed an uneasy night, rising in the morning to greet Duncan and Gruoch and Macbeth with the pretence that all was normal. Not a word said. Then all I would have to do was wait . . . a month – or a year or three – or a little longer until my father paid his dues to Nature. With luck I might land the crown while I was still young enough to enjoy it.

But I did not choose this easy path. Instead, lured by the failing light in the antechamber and the slumped bodies of

the chamberlains, I entered the King's quarters, picked up
the wet, sweaty daggers from where Macbeth's nerveless
fingers had let them fall, strode into the inner chamber and
there killed my father.

My father as he slept.

I did not stand long by the bedside and watch the inert
figure before plunging the blades into his chest. I did not
suffer any scruple. Reminiscences of happy days spent
together – the way he had dandled me on his knee, or
steadied my childish hand as it held its first foil, or lovingly
watched as I formed my letters – not one of these reminiscences occurred to me, for the simple reason that we'd never
enjoyed them. I'd hardly ever seen my father. He was a King.
Kings have better things to do than to entertain, instruct or
love their sons.

All that the unstirring man on the royal couch represented
was a stumbling-block between me and the throne. Otherwise, he was nothing. To my mind he was already dead, the
sheets soaked in blood. So I stabbed home, with the right and
the left, again and again.

When I was sure that he was gone, I returned to the
antechamber. The chamberlains continued to mock their
charge with night-groans and snores. One of them turned
over and I feared he was about to wake. I hastily wiped the
daggers on the rushes to remove the grossest gouts and put
them back on the floor. Then I left the room, intending to
wash the murk and mire from my hands and to dispose of my
bloody clothes.

I had made only a few strides along the passage when a
white face loomed at me out of the dark.

"Brother!"

"Jesus save us!"

"I cannot sleep, brother Canmore. Come into my room
and pray with me, and then I may rest."

So, accoutred in blood as I was, I joined Donal Bane in
prayer. Luckily, only the feeblest candle flickered by his
bedside, no doubt for poring over some devotional text. It
was scarcely enough to light the tips of his fingers conjoined
in prayer. I knelt near him – but not too near for fear he

might smell our father's blood – while we prayed to our greater Father in Heaven. If I'd been a superstitious fellow like Macbeth, I might've been unable to mouth "amen" in answer to my brother's pious, fluty tones. But I found I was able to give a hearty "amen", and so returned in peace and quiet to my chamber. I'm pleased to report that I suffered no real ill effects from my murder, though I did shake a little as I climbed into my couch and lay watching for a while.

Unaccountable thoughts occurred: that my father might not be dead, and that I would have to get up and kill him all over again. And another: that he was already dead when I entered his chamber. But then these strange notions subsided, and I wiped a few tears from my face, and settled down for what remained of the night.

I was tugged out of sleep the next morning by the ferocious ringing of the alarum bell. There were the sounds of feet thudding backwards and forwards along the passage, followed by an uncivil thumping on my door. Strange as it may seem, it took me some time to realize what all this pother must be about and so I didn't have to pretend irritation and bafflement when I called, "What is it?"

By the time I'd dressed with a becoming haste and made my way down to the courtyard, the elements of the next act were in place.

There was my host, Macbeth, dumbfounded. His fair hair and beard were whitened in the early morning light while Gruoch's foxy features looked drawn. I had not seen her since quitting her in the courtyard last midnight to go and murder my father. Macbeth strode off somewhere and she glanced in my direction. The pity which she showed for a newly bereaved son was a lesson in playing. There were others milling about the scene. Banquo, the Thane of Lochquhaber, was talking earnestly to Macduff, the Thane of Fife. I soon gathered that it was he – arriving early at Glammis to escort my father abroad for the day's hunting and being dispatched by Macbeth to the King's quarters – who had found Duncan's body.

And then there was my brother Donal Bane, looking quite

shocked but wholly pious. He clasped me round the shoulders in fraternal style. Then he whispered in my ear, "What were you doing away from your room last night, Canmore?"

"Like you, I couldn't sleep," I replied.

"Did you see anything?"

For an instant I was tempted to answer "Macbeth" but caution chained my tongue.

"Only you, brother," I said instead.

"This is a sorry business."

I was prevented from replying by a great stir at the foot of the staircase which led to the guest quarters. It was Macbeth. He stood there, with a grim and angry visage, his naked sword in his hand. The reeking blade was clotted with red.

I could guess what had happened even before he announced that he had slain the two chamberlains as accessories to the King's murder. Apparently, they pretended that they had slept through the whole thing. But their bloody daggers gave them the lie. The other thanes clustered round Macbeth, whether in approval or disapproval of his action I couldn't tell.

Was this part of the plan or not? I couldn't tell that either.

I looked towards Gruoch. She looked away.

I felt the tightness in my belly. The sky suddenly grew darker, and a thin rain started to fall. Several of the thanes and their retainers now began to pace about the courtyard, half-drawing their swords as if they expected to be attacked any instant. I felt that, as the King's elder son, I should have stepped forward and spoken. If there was any moment to assert myself it was this one.

But I waited.

I should have been proclaimed.

You cannot proclaim yourself King.

By rights, I should have been proclaimed. I was the elder son. I had done the necessary work.

Macbeth walked towards his wife, waving the bloody blade more in display than threat, and she swooned into the arms of one of her gentlewomen. A curious kind of nothingness descended over the place.

I decided to quit the scene. Pulling a long face, and huddling into my clothes against the rain, I walked back to my room to contemplate the next move. The door was ajar. Hearing noises inside, I stopped on the threshhold. Then walked in, meaning to give the servant the thrashing of his life. It was no servant, however, but Lochquhaber. He was standing in the middle of the chamber. His face was flushed.

"Ah Canmore," he muttered. "Sir."

"Banquo."

"The door was open. I thought you were inside."

This was possible. Perhaps I had left the chamber door open in my haste to get downstairs and play the part of the grieving son. Then I remembered that the blood-boltered clothes I had worn last night were in a cedar coffer in the corner. There had been as yet no opportunity to dispose of them by burning or burial. Was the coffer locked? Again, I couldn't remember. I hadn't been in the mood for precaution six hours ago. I could dimly discern the coffer now in the chamber corner. Something seemed to be hanging from it.

I cast my eyes round the room, trying to see it as Banquo had seen it. He looked as shifty as I felt, and waited on his dismissal.

Eventually I said: "You wished to see me?"

"To commiserate with you, sir, on the loss of your father. And to know whether you saw anything last night. Did you?"

Had my brother put him up to that question?

"We met in the yard," prompted Banquo, as if it was likely I'd forgotten.

"I saw no one. Did you?"

"Only you – and Macbeth."

"Well then," I said, hoping he'd draw the obvious conclusion.

"There were four empty goblets in the anteroom."

"I expect my father was enjoying a drink with his chamberlains . . . if that's what you're referring to," I said a little too quickly. "Before he went to bed. They were old retainers, Kenneth and Rhun."

"Treacherous ones," said Banquo, but without animus.

"Well, they will never tell us anything now that Macbeth has given them their quietus. Where was he going last night when you met him?"

"To his wife."

"Good," I said.

"She is a delicate woman," he said. "Did you see how she swooned at his naked blade and the blood on it?"

"Yes," I said shortly.

"But *four* goblets, Canmore. Why four?"

"Lochquhaber, I must honour my father now in private."

"Of course," he said, relieved to be dismissed by a dead King's son. "Honour to him, and to you."

I bowed him out the door and locked it. Be sure I hastened to the coffer which sat in a dark corner of the chamber. The chest was not secured. Hanging down one side was a bloody sleeve. I gave a start, as if an entire corpse were immured in there. But it was only the shirt I'd worn the night before.

Had Banquo seen it? How could he not have done? He'd plainly come into my room to snoop around. Was he, even at this moment, alerting the other thanes in the courtyard? Were they about to move on me, swords drawn? Where was Gruoch in all this? Then I remembered that she'd swooned in the yard.

There was a creak behind me. The door opened. Impossible! I'd just locked it. I was still clutching the key in my hand. I felt the hair rise on my nape. Slowly, slowly, I swivelled round, still crouching. Gruoch, holding her own household key, stood in the doorway. Her whitened complexion was a fine foil for her dark red hair. She had recovered quickly from her courtyard faint but she looked older.

"My darling," she said, "you must depart –"

"Depart?"

"– for a time only."

"I did not leave this." I picked up the bloody sleeve where it hung limp from the coffer. "I am sure I did not leave it like this last night. I am afraid Banquo may have seen it."

"He must have done."

Again, she sounded quite composed.

"How did you know he was here?"

For answer, Gruoch merely looked at me.

"Someone has been here and opened this coffer and pulled out the sleeve. Look, it has snagged on a nail and torn," I said. Or had the sleeve been ripped as I stabbed my father? I couldn't be sure, couldn't be sure of anything.

Through my head there flashed the image that had shaken me last night on my couch: my father as he slept and I, his son, standing over him, two slippery daggers in hand. The body was still. The sheets were covered in blood. Was this about to happen – or had it already happened?

"Yes, Banquo must have seen the shirt," Gruoch said quickly.

I didn't immediately hear her. I was remembering the feel of the daggers when I first picked them up from the floor. Wet, sticky – but sticky with what?

"What?"

"They are saying that you were in the courtyard last night."

"Who is?"

"Banquo and his son Fleance. And Macbeth, my husband. They are all saying it."

"They were also down there. God knows who was about last night," I said, feeling matters slip out of my grasp.

"They had each other for witness, Banquo and Fleance," she said.

"And Macbeth? Macbeth has no one."

"Macbeth has me," she said deliberately. "He was by my side and slept sound after I wakened him from a nightmare."

I said nothing. There was more than one kind of treachery, I reflected.

Seeing I wasn't going to answer, she said, "It is safest if you depart – for a time. They are not going to proclaim you King today."

"Traitors!"

"Why don't you go to England?" she said reasonably. "Your cowardly brother Donal Bane has already left for Ireland. For a time."

"What did you tell him?" I said.

"I said he was in mortal danger – from you. He too saw you last night. He was easily persuaded."

"By you. Persuaded by you."

I almost spat these words. I opened the coffer, bundled up the bloody clothes and threw them at her feet.

"At least you can dispose of these," I said. "My hands are already as bloody as you can wish." On the way out of the room, I smelled her, rank as a fox.

I didn't go to England, not immediately. Instead I repaired to one of my boltholes and brooded, while Macbeth and Lady Macbeth were crowned King and Queen at Scone. I wondered whether she'd played me for a dupe all the time or whether she'd switched horses in mid-stream when she realised that her husband wasn't going to murder Duncan, and that I would have to do the deed instead.

If I had done it.

I couldn't rid my mind of that picture: myself standing above his bed, slippery daggers in hand and so far unused – *by me.* The sheets soaked through with blood . . . afterwards . . . or before as well?

Suppose Macbeth had carried through the deed. So that when I assailed my father I was stabbing a dead man.

I discerned a plot but could not be certain where its boundaries lay. My mind spun, trying to latch on to certainties.

Take Banquo, for example . . . Banquo, who'd received various king-begetting promises from the hags. Who'd been out and about that night. With his son Fleance. (But what good cover that would be, what colour, to have your son with you.) Banquo, who'd been in my room, finding my shirt, dragging it from the coffer so as to display it the world. If it was my shirt . . . foolish, trusting Malcolm Canmore not even to make sure of that.

And my brother Donal Bane . . . out of bed and watching. I'd thought I was concealing things from him. How convenient that dim candle was for both our sakes!

I recalled the chamberlains too, and the way one had stirred and seemed to wake. Had Gruoch actually given them a sleeping-draught? Or were they, like me, her conscious instruments. Perhaps *they* had done it after all, as Macbeth claimed, and been slaughtered for their pains.

If I was unable (at this moment) to lay my hands on the throne, could I at least claim my guilt? Guilt is something to be going on with.

In this mist only one aspect of the matter was clear, and that one hardly to my advantage.

Gruoch had won. She and her oaf of a husband.

But she was not infallible.

Her mistake was in allowing me leave Glammis Castle alive. She should have shrieked out, brandished my guilty garments (if they were mine); ordered me cut down at her gate; permitted the rain to handle my spilled blood. I don't suppose it would have stained her conscience for any longer than it took to wash away. It's what I would have done to her if circumstances had been reversed. It's what I will do to her – and to her oaf of a husband – in time.

But first there are other matters to settle. Banquo and his son Fleance, for instance, they shall not live.

Others will die too – the deserving and the undeserving. Women and children, I expect. Those who failed to proclaim me in the courtyard of Glammis Castle must pay for their hesitation. Of course, I will be careful to keep a distance between myself and the turmoil that I foster. I will use others as I have been used by the fox-faced woman.

Turmoil will lead to anger; anger to resentment; resentment to rebellion; and so to the unseating of Gruoch and Macbeth.

A King's son is not to be spurned.

The Death Toll

Susanna Gregory

Susanna Gregory (b. 1958) is the author of the mystery series featuring Matthew Bartholomew, a teacher of medicine at Michaelhouse, part of the fledgling University of Cambridge, in the mid-fourteenth century. That series began with A Plague on Both Your Houses *(1996). The following is not a Bartholomew story but is set over 300 years earlier at the start of the turbulent reign of Henry I and in the even more troublesome territory of the Welsh Marches.*

1

There was an uneasy truce between the English and the Welsh when Sir Geoffrey Mappestone returned to his home in Goodrich Castle after his second pilgrimage to the Holy Land. The year was 1106, and King Henry sat on the throne – a Norman despite his claims to have been born on English soil and to speak the English language. Under Henry's rule Norman noblemen held the best titles and the richest land: the English and Welsh alike had lost a great deal when the Normans had sailed across the Channel and seized the country four decades earlier. Geoffrey wondered why the Celts and Saxons had not combined forces to resist the invaders, rather than weakening each other with petty quarrels and the pursuit of ancient hatreds.

After years in the scorching dust of the Holy Land,

Geoffrey liked to climb to the castle battlements and look across the cool green hills that surrounded his home. Goodrich stood on a rocky promontory above the River Wye, on the English side of the border with Wales. Fertile fields rolled towards the muddy brown curl of the river, edged by the great Forest of Dean. In the distance, Geoffrey could make out the creamy stones of Flanesford Priory, and beyond that the leaning wooden spire of the village of Garron. Garron was Welsh and poor; Flanesford was English and rich. They were uneasy neighbours, and often even the powerful current of the River Wye had not been enough to keep monks and peasants from each other's throats.

Taking a last deep breath of crisp winter air, the knight left the battlements and descended the spiral stairs to the great hall. It was full of people, since it was the day of the month that Geoffrey's brother Henry collected tithes and heard petitions. Geoffrey saw that Prior Edmund of Flanesford, resplendent in white robes and thick riding cloak, had Henry's ear. His secretary was with him, listening to the conversation between baron and churchman with thinly disguised anger. Edmund's hands, encased in soft white gloves, gesticulated in agitation. Obviously, the discussion was not going well.

"The monks are here because of the tolls for crossing the river at our ford," came a voice at Geoffrey's elbow. "They want them for their priory. They've had greedy eyes on them for as long as I can remember."

Geoffrey recognized the dark, lean features of Rhodri, lord of the manor at Welsh Garron. Next to him was his burly cousin, Huw, the son of the local witch. There were rumours that Garron was not happy with Rhodri's rule, and that Huw was waiting to step in and claim the leadership. Both cousins wore short tunics and rough wool leggings. They carried sturdy broadswords in their belts, and Rhodri had a purse, although Geoffrey doubted it held many coins. Rhodri and Huw were not wealthy men.

"The ford tolls have always belonged to Garron," replied Geoffrey. "My brother won't give them to Edmund."

"What makes you so sure?" demanded Huw aggressively.

"Austin monks are powerful men – what they want they usually get, because people are afraid of offending them."

"But Henry doesn't want your Welsh raiding parties helping themselves to his English cattle, either," replied Geoffrey tartly. "Peace with Garron is important to him."

"Peace is an English preoccupation," said Rhodri distastefully. "We Welsh enjoy a good battle." Geoffrey saw him glance challengingly at Huw. So, he thought, the rumours were true: relations were not harmonious across the border.

Geoffrey pushed his way through the throng to the door. A dispute about tolls for using the crossing point over the Wye was none of his affair, and he had no wish to become involved. That was Henry's unenviable task, and went with owning the Goodrich estates. Geoffrey's only responsibility that day lay with his destrier, to ensure the animal was properly exercised. Warhorses were expensive, and many knights preferred to oversee their care themselves, rather than leaving it to a squire.

"The tolls should come to the *priory*," announced Edmund to Henry in a voice loud enough to arrest Geoffrey's progress and make him turn in surprise. "You're wrong to find in favour of Garron – yet again. But I'm a fair man. I'm prepared to accept your decision for now."

"No!" cried his pale-faced secretary in horror. "We cannot accept a decision that is so monstrously detrimental, Father! The ford adjoins *our* land. The tolls belong to *us*!"

Geoffrey saw Edmund rest his gloved hand on the man's shoulder to calm him. "It's winter, Aidan, when few people use the ford anyway. We'll take our petition to the bishop in the spring."

"I've already written to the King," said Aidan defiantly. "*He* will see justice done."

Geoffrey seriously doubted it, knowing very well that the King would not bother to embroil himself in a matter relating to a few penny tolls unless there was some advantage to himself. He would not even have wasted his time in reading such a plea.

"We'll petition the bishop," repeated Edmund, dismissing his secretary's futile attempt to secure royal favour. "But meanwhile, I long for the peace of my priory. We shall accept Henry's decision for the time being."

"Good," said Henry. He gestured for Rhodri and Huw to step forward. "I'll have the agreement drawn up and you can all make your marks."

Rhodri nodded curtly, and Geoffrey could not decide whether the Welshman was pleased or not. It meant he would have no excuse for stealing Henry's cattle, which was probably a more lucrative activity than collecting penny tolls. Huw's face was grim, and Geoffrey sensed he would rather Rhodri had failed, so that the loss of the tolls would further his own cause in securing the leadership of Garron. Geoffrey was about to escape from the hall into the invigorating chill of a clean winter morning, when Henry called him back.

"I need you to draw up this deed, Geoffrey. My clerk is ill and Rhodri refuses to sign anything the monks write. All those years of learning before you became a knight can come in useful at last. You can write this agreement for me."

Geoffrey complied reluctantly. He did not want to be indoors when the sun was shining, and he disliked the reek of burned food, animal manure and unwashed bodies that pervaded the hall. But his brother had been a generous host, and scribing a document was the least Geoffrey could do to repay him for his hospitality. He went to sit at the table, taking pen, ink and parchment from the pouch he carried at his waist. The two monks and the two Welshmen pressed forward to watch.

Rhodri was grinning, gloating at the clerics' disappointment. Huw watched intently, hoping for an argument that would see his cousin fall from Henry's favour. Edmund seemed resigned, but his secretary was seething. His thin lips were pressed into a tight white line, and his pale blue eyes were as cold as ice.

"The Royal Commissioners have recently imposed a new tax on the priory," he said furiously. "How can we pay it when we have no income from the ford tolls?"

"We have to pay this new tax, too," Rhodri replied immediately. "And *we* do not have chests full of gold crosses and silver chalices to fall back on."

"But neither of you has to pay as much as me," said Henry resentfully. "Because I own the land on which priory and village stand, I am expected to produce *twenty pounds*!"

There was a collective gasp of astonishment. Twenty pounds was an enormous sum of money.

"Why has the Treasury made this sudden demand on us?" asked Rhodri curiously. "Is the King thinking of financing another Crusade to the Holy Land?"

"It isn't sudden," replied Prior Edmund wearily. "The King is a man who likes his gold, and he has been imposing high taxes on his people ever since he was crowned. It has just taken him a while to reach this distant corner of his kingdom, that's all."

Geoffrey said nothing, and continued to pen the agreement. He knew from personal experience that the King was indeed a greedy man, and it did not surprise him that the shrewd monarch was happy to wring money even from the poorest inhabitants of his domain, as well as from the Church.

"I'm tired of being pestered with this toll business every month," announced Henry, abruptly changing the subject. He was a blunt man, not over-endowed with patience or intelligence. "I want you to add a bit on the end of that deed, Geoffrey: this agreement will hold for as long as everyone who signs it is alive. Their successors can petition me again, but I'll not hear another word about it until then."

Geoffrey regarded his brother uneasily, knowing that feelings ran high where money was concerned; even monks had been known to commit dreadful crimes in order to claim something they felt was rightfully their own. Henry's peculiar clause was just asking for someone to be murdered.

"Perhaps it would be better to say that the agreement will stand for five years, rather than the length of a man's life," he suggested tentatively. "It would be safer –"

"Do what Henry says," interrupted Rhodri, revealing white teeth in a wolfish grin. "I intend to live to a ripe old age, and it would be good to have this business resolved once and for all."

Huw's black expression suggested that his cousin might not live as long as he expected, while Aidan, was horrified at the prospect of signing away the priory's rights. Edmund was thoughtful.

"No Welshman can resist a fight," he said eventually. "Draw up the agreement, Geoffrey. The tolls will be ours before the year is out, because Rhodri will be where he belongs – in a pagan's grave."

2

Drafting legal documents was not something at which Geoffrey excelled, and it was some time before he had completed the task to everyone's satisfaction. Edmund and Aidan watched him like hawks, sitting side by side on the stone bench that ran along one wall. Rhodri and Huw stood opposite, as uneasy in each other's presence as they were in the monks'.

"Wine," ordered Henry, as he dipped his forefinger in the inkwell and drew a crude dagger on the completed document to signify his acceptance of its contents. "We shall drink to this agreement and hope it brings us peace."

"Our monks shall not be using the ford," said Aidan icily. "They will travel miles out of their way rather than give their money to Garron."

"That will not matter soon," muttered Edmund. "The Welshmen will fight each other, Rhodri will die, and the rights to the ford will revert to us."

"I have no intention of dying yet," said Rhodri cheerfully, unmoved by the prior's predictions.

"We shall see," muttered Huw darkly.

Geoffrey watched a servant carry goblets and a jug brimming with wine to the table. He set them down and retired, leaving the six men alone in the hall. The short winter day was coming to an end, and the sun flooded the room with rays of deep gold. Shadows darkened the corners, and Geoffrey looked forward to the time when the shutters would be fastened and a fire lit. It was cold in the hall.

Henry poured himself wine and gestured that the others were to do the same. He pushed a cup towards Geoffrey, who needed no second invitation. The knight filled his goblet to the brim before joining his brother at one of the windows, to stand in the light of the fading sun in the hope that there would be some warmth in it. Henry's favourite hound fussed around them, licking its owner's hands with a slobbering tongue, anxious for attention.

Geoffrey watched Rhodri step up to the table and dip his thumb in the ink. His confident, flamboyant mark covered a good quarter of the document. His treatment of the wine was equally colourful: he lifted the jug high, so that it fell in a noisy purple stream into the cup and splattered the table, and then snatched up the goblet with a victorious flourish.

Huw took Geoffrey's pen in both hands like a weapon, and sprayed ink all over himself and the document when his heavy grip snapped it in two. The clerics regarded each other expressionlessly, but made no comment. Huw then moved to the wine, pouring with his back to the others, as if he was afraid that he would spill it and embarrass himself further.

Aidan scratched his name with his own pen, then spent some time filling his goblet as high as it would go without spilling. Edmund was last. He signed his name without removing his gloves – not an easy task when the bone pen was shiny and slipped in his fingers. Geoffrey supposed the prior had grown chilled in the frigid hall, and did not want to expose his hands to the icy air. He sympathized: Geoffrey was cold himself. Edmund shook sand across the wet ink and went to the wine jug. When all six men had full cups in their hands, Henry lifted his high, so that it glinted in the last of the sun.

"To peace," he said. "And to an end of this squabbling over tolls."

"To justice," said Rhodri, eyeing the monks and Huw challengingly. "And to Wales."

"To a new beginning," added Huw ambiguously. From the unfriendly glance he shot in his cousin's direction, Geoffrey was certain he was not referring to the agreement he had just signed.

"To Rhodri's early demise," muttered Aidan, drinking heartily.

"To God," whispered Edmund piously. "May He have mercy on us all."

Geoffrey just drank his wine.

Once everyone had drained his cup and Henry was looking pleased with himself for finally resolving what had been a tiresome conflict, Geoffrey prepared to leave the acrimonious atmosphere in search of somewhere more pleasant to spend the evening. He was halfway across the hall when Edmund made a sudden retching sound and began to scrabble at his throat. The others regarded the prior uncertainly.

"I can't see," Edmund whispered. "I can't breathe." He dropped to his knees and vomited.

"What's wrong with him?" demanded Henry in alarm. "Is it a falling fit?"

"Poison," whispered Edmund. His eyes, wide in his face, fixed themselves on the Welshmen. "I have been poisoned."

"Do something," said Henry, appealing to Geoffrey. "Help him."

Geoffrey knelt next to the stricken man, but there was little he could do. He had seen enough of poisons on his travels to know that it was already too late to reverse the effects of whatever the prior had been given. Edmund's breathing was rapid and shallow, and a sheen of sweat glistened on his ashen face.

"Bells," he gasped. "I hear bells. And the room is turning green."

"Wolfbane," muttered Geoffrey, who had read about the effects of that particular plant.

He watched as Edmund struggled to breathe, each gasp an immense effort. Aidan muttered a final absolution; his voice shook with emotion and Geoffrey was sure his attention was not on the words he spoke. Edmund drew a final, agonized breath, although the terror in his eyes told Geoffrey that he was not yet dead. He knelt next to the prior until the final spark of life disappeared with the last of the sun.

3

"I need your help, Geoffrey," whispered Henry, pulling his brother away from the others. Aidan was praying, while Rhodri and Huw gazed at the dead prior as though they could not believe what was happening. Servants scurried here and there, closing shutters, lighting torches and stoking up the fire for the evening, all busying themselves in the hall so that they would be able to watch what was happening: it was not every day that a monk died in the castle.

"You have solved murders in the Holy Land and here, at Goodrich," Henry went on. "You must discover who killed Edmund, or the whole region might erupt into violence. The murder of a prior is a serious matter."

Geoffrey knew he was right. The monks of Flanesford would not calmly accept the loss of their leader *and* the river tolls, while the Welsh would bitterly resent the accusations that would inevitably come their way. Edmund's death would be the first of many, and the resulting feud might continue for years. People had long memories for crimes committed by their enemies along the borders.

"We know *what* killed Edmund," said Geoffrey. He stooped to retrieve the cup the prior had used and took it to a brazier, so that he could inspect it in the light. He pointed to a powdery residue at the bottom. "Someone put wolfbane in his wine."

"Who?"

"One of the five people who were in a position to do so," replied Geoffrey with a shrug. "Edmund was the last to fill his cup. You, me, Rhodri, Huw and Aidan poured our wine before him."

"Well, we know it wasn't you or me," said Henry. "So, that narrows the list to three."

Geoffrey inspected the jug. If that contained poison, then the culprit was Aidan, who had used it immediately before Edmund. But there seemed to be nothing amiss. Henry offered to test it on a servant; Geoffrey suggested using a mouse or a rat instead.

"But why didn't Edmund say something when he saw powder in his cup?" asked Henry, puzzled.

"The daylight was fading and he probably didn't notice. It doesn't take much wolfbane to kill a man, anyway. The cup wouldn't have been brimming with the stuff."

"The killer *must* be Aidan," said Henry. "When he took

his wine, there were only two cups left: his and Edmund's."

"He certainly has a motive," said Geoffrey thoughtfully. "With Edmund dead, the agreement you just signed is invalid. He was furious that Edmund had agreed to something detrimental to their priory. Perhaps he predicts that you'll feel guilty about Edmund dying under your roof, and that you'll give the tolls back to the priory to salve your conscience."

"I might have to," said Henry morosely. "But then Rhodri will rebel and I'll have years of border skirmishing to deal with. Can we charge Aidan with this murder, then?"

"Not yet. Remember that Edmund intended to see the bishop about the tolls in the spring. Would Aidan really murder his prior for a few pennies collected in winter?"

"But Rhodri and Huw had no reason to kill him," Henry pointed out. "They had just won their case."

"For now. But the bishop would almost certainly rule in favour of the priory come spring. Now Edmund is dead, he's in no position to petition the bishop or anyone else."

"But if Rhodri or Huw had put poison in one of the cups, they couldn't have been certain that *Edmund* would drink it. Aidan might have been the victim."

"True. But perhaps they didn't care which of the monks died. You want peace, but peace means that Rhodri and Huw are obliged to leave your cattle alone. Stealing cattle is more lucrative than collecting tolls, and perhaps one of them wanted the agreement to flounder. We know relations are strained in Garron. Perhaps this is Huw's way of damaging his cousin's reputation."

Henry sighed. "What a mess! You'd better solve this quickly, Geoffrey: all three suspects will leave Goodrich at first light tomorrow and we must have our killer before then."

Geoffrey beckoned Aidan to the hearth, where a servant was stoking the fire. The flames served to drive some of the dark shadows from the hall. But not all of them.

"Will you empty your scrip?" Geoffrey asked, gesturing to the leather pouch Aidan carried.

Aidan stared at him. "You think *I* killed Prior Edmund? I did not!"

But he flung the pouch on to the table, where Geoffrey emptied it. There was a pomander used when the clerk was obliged to enter particularly smelly places, a packet of salt to flavour his food, a horn spoon and a tiny knife. But there was no wolfbane.

Geoffrey called to the two Welshmen and asked them to do the same. Rhodri carried some coins and a lump of hard cheese in his pouch, while Huw sullenly claimed that he had no need to carry purses. Sensing that this made him appear suspicious, he removed his boots and shook out his tunic, to prove he had no incriminating packets hidden anywhere.

Puzzled, Geoffrey knelt next to Edmund's body. In the cuff of one of the prior's wide sleeves was the wolfbane. It comprised a small, neat packet, although the parchment was old and worn, as though the killer had possessed it for some time before finally deciding to use it. Geoffrey was disgusted with himself. Aidan had prayed next to the body, while the two Welshmen had been alone with it while he had searched Aidan. Since it was obvious that whoever possessed the poison was also the killer, it would make sense for the culprit to get rid of it as soon possible. And what better place than on the body itself?

4

All three suspects spent the night huddling near the fire in the hall, careful to keep a safe distance between them. Henry joined them there, afraid that the guilty party might make a bid for freedom and leave him with a reputation for allowing killers to evade the King's justice. Geoffrey sat at the dark end of the hall, thinking.

Aidan had the most to gain from killing Edmund, yet he also had the most to lose. A new prior would probably have his own secretary, and Aidan would lose his position of authority. And would Aidan really risk eternal damnation just to secure a few pennies in tolls?

Meanwhile, Rhodri had been the first of the three to take his wine. Had he simply put poison in one cup at random, reasoning that he would gain no matter who drank it? If Huw perished, he would rid himself of a dangerous rival; if one of the monks died, he would lose the tolls, but would gain the excuse to revert to the more lucrative occupation of cattle stealing.

Edmund's death also benefited Huw. It would be said in Garron that Rhodri had negotiated an excellent arrangement regarding the tolls, but then had lost it. It would weaken Rhodri's leadership and pave the way for Huw to step into his cousin's shoes. Huw's mother was said to be a witch, and so he would also have ready access to a substance like wolfsbane.

An uncomfortable thought insinuated itself into Geoffrey's mind. What about Henry? Had *he* poisoned one of the cups, hoping that it would spell the end of the dispute he had grown tired of arbitrating? Henry was not an intelligent man, and tended to regard matters simply. It was entirely possible that he believed the demise of one of the parties would make the dispute go away permanently. But would Henry have risked the life of his own brother in such a reckless gamble? With a start, Geoffrey suddenly recalled Henry's smile as he had pushed a goblet towards him, indicating which cup the knight was to take: Henry had not allowed Geoffrey to select his own.

Sleep was impossible with clues and questions tumbling around his mind, so Geoffrey left the hall and walked to the nearby church, where Edmund's body had been taken. The chancel was dark, except for the candles that stood at the prior's head and feet. Geoffrey approached the corpse and stared down at it. Edmund still wore his travelling cloak, white habit and gloves. Geoffrey examined him carefully, inspecting every fold in the robe and every inch of skin. Then he returned to the hall and studied the now empty packet of wolfsbane. By the time he had finished, he knew exactly who had killed Edmund and why.

5

The witching hour was no time to reveal his findings, so Geoffrey waited until morning, when the shadows of night were dispelled and sunlight streamed through the windows. Henry was the only one to have slept, despite the fact that he had promised Geoffrey that he would stand a discreet guard over the suspects. The others had been wakeful and restless, aware that even a short doze might mean a more permanent sleep.

"I shall take Prior Edmund home today," said Aidan, gazing around him accusingly. "There will be much grieving, and you will be hearing from the bishop. He will not stand by and allow clerics to be murdered by greedy Welsh peasants."

"I didn't kill him," objected Rhodri hotly. "I was happy with the way the tolls had been resolved and had no need to resort to murder."

"It wasn't me, either," growled Huw. "I have never heard of wolfbane, and would not know how to lay my hands on any."

"Liar!" sneered Rhodri. "Your mother is a witch; she always has an ample supply of poisons."

Huw bristled. "She should have used some on you. And then Edmund would still be alive."

Geoffrey stepped between them as daggers were tugged from sheaths. "Rhodri didn't kill Edmund."

Huw gazed at him in disbelief. "But he wants to resume his raids on English cattle, and the failure of these negotiations will give him just that excuse!"

Rhodri snarled something in Welsh and Huw stepped forward with a murderous expression on his face. Geoffrey dropped his hand to the hilt of his sword. It was enough to catch their attention: a Norman knight was a formidable fighter, and both Welshmen backed away quickly.

"I *am* innocent," said Rhodri, keeping a respectful distance from him. "But what convinced you?"

"I watched you as you took your wine. Unlike the others, you faced me, and made a showy display of pouring it from a height, splashing it across the table. You had no opportunity to slip poison into Edmund's cup: the killer was not you."

Rhodri's teeth flashed white in a triumphant smile. He pointed at his cousin. "It was him, then. Or the secretary. Both of them poured their wine with their backs to us. I remember it clearly."

"They did," agreed Henry. "Huw was almost furtive about it."

Huw's face paled. "But I didn't kill Edmund! You can't convict me on that kind of evidence."

"The killer hid the wolfbane in his pouch until he reached the wine," said Geoffrey. "Huw owns no pouch and his clothes are simple. There is nowhere he could have kept such a packet."

Henry looked doubtful. "He could have concealed it in his hand."

Geoffrey shook his head. "When Huw made his mark on the document, he took the pen in two hands, as though it were a dagger. He could not have held the poison at the same time. Also, he sprayed ink all over himself. Had he then touched the packet, there would have been ink on it." He tossed the wolfbane on to the table. "And, as you can see, it is clean."

Everyone looked at Aidan, whose eyes were wide with shock. "No," said the secretary, backing away. "Not me. I loved Edmund like a father!"

"You didn't kill him either," said Geoffrey. He was aware of the others gaping at him, and pointed to the poison on the table. "Look at that packet again. It is old and the corners are frayed; you can see where some of it has spilled on the table already. Therefore, we can conclude that some trace of it will be in the killer's pouch. Aidan's, like Rhodri's, contains no evidence that this leaky packet was ever in it."

"Who then?" demanded Henry. He became aware that people were regarding him uneasily. "Me?" he whispered, aghast. "Why would I want to kill anyone?"

"You were prepared to kill a servant to see whether there was wolfsbane in the wine jug," Aidan pointed out, quick to accuse now he was in the clear. "Life is cheap to men like you. You would not give murder a second thought."

"That may well be true, but he is innocent of this one," said Geoffrey, ignoring his brother's indignant spluttering. "Like Huw, Henry carries no scrip; he has no need to do so, because he is at home. But Henry is innocent, because immediately after he poured the wine, his favourite dog licked his hands. He would not have allowed the animal to do so had they been tainted with poison."

"Who did it, then?" asked Henry in confusion. He snapped his fingers as a thought occurred to him. "The servant who brought us the wine! I *should* have tried the poison on him!"

"Are *you* about to confess?" asked Aidan, regarding Geoffrey warily.

Geoffrey smiled. "During the night, I inspected Edmund's body. Remember that he wore gloves and that he never removed them? There are lesions on his fingers that suggest he was suffering from leprosy. He could not have kept the disease hidden for much longer, and we all know what would happen to him then."

"He would be banned from society and a mass said for his soul while he still lived," said Henry sanctimoniously. "It is a just treatment. We all know that leprosy is a scourge sent by God to punish the wicked."

"Better hope he didn't give it to you, then," muttered Geoffrey. Henry blanched and inspected his hands. But Geoffrey doubted his brother would become ill – he had seen many forms of leprosy on his travels and not all were contagious.

"*We* would have found him a place," objected Aidan tearfully. "Our Order is compassionate to the sick, and we have lazar houses to care for victims of that horrible disease."

"But he wouldn't have been prior," Geoffrey pointed out. "And Edmund was a man used to power. He decided to kill himself. The state of the packet suggests that he had carried it with him for some time, waiting for the right opportunity – or perhaps the courage – to use it. If you look in his scrip, you will see grains of the poison at the bottom, where it spilled. When he saw that his priory was about to lose the river tolls, he decided the time was right for him to end his life."

"He did it for us," said Aidan wonderingly. "He arranged his suicide to seem like murder, so that the agreement giving the tolls to Garron wouldn't be honoured. The bishop would assume the Welshmen had murdered Edmund, and they would have lost the tolls for ever."

"So, he poisoned his own wine," concluded Henry. "He was the last to drink, and he put the poison in his own cup."

Geoffrey nodded. "It was his parting gift to the priory he loved. It is just a pity that his act of sacrifice would have seen an innocent man hang for his murder."

Rhodri shuddered. "And it might have been me! Well, his plan didn't work. The tolls will stay with Garron."

"No!" cried Aidan. "That is an outrage! I will not allow my prior's death to have been in vain."

There was a sudden clatter of hooves in the courtyard outside, followed by footsteps on the stairs. Two men entered the hall, wearing insignia that marked them as the King's tax collectors. Henry groaned, seeing that he would be obliged to part with his twenty pounds sooner than he had anticipated, while Rhodri and Huw exchanged the kind of nervous glance that indicated they did not have what the King's men expected to be given.

"Why is the King taxing us so harshly?" demanded Aidan as the two men walked towards the little knot of people near the hearth. "We are poor folk, and cannot afford to pay for Crusades to distant lands or for wars in France."

The agent regarded Aidan in surprise. "The King does not want your money for fighting. And *you* should know why he has taken an interest in the Goodrich estates, Brother Aidan. It was you who wrote to tell him about this dispute over the tolls."

"I wanted to see justice done," said Aidan, aware that he was on the receiving end of looks that were far from friendly from his neighbours. "I wrote to ask the King to ensure that the tolls went to the priory, where they belong." He swallowed nervously. "I wrote in the heat of the moment, actually. I didn't seriously expect an answer from a busy man like the King. But what has my letter to do with the taxes?"

The agent smiled. "Can you not guess? He's going to use the money to build a bridge across the River Wye – just to the south of Garron. It won't matter who owns the ford tolls in a few months, because people will use the bridge instead."

"And who will have the tolls from the bridge?" asked Geoffrey curiously. "Henry, because he will finance the bulk of its construction? Rhodri and Huw, because the ford tolls currently belong to Garron? The priory, because Aidan wrote to appeal its case?"

"Of course not," said the agent scornfully. "The King will have the tolls. He is a clever man: he has resolved an age-old dispute and will provide you with a new bridge in one decisive action. How could you begrudge him a few pennies in tolls?"

"How indeed?" asked Geoffrey, laughing at the King's transparent opportunism and the abject dismay on the faces of his brother, the Welshmen and the secretary. "How indeed?"

The Isle of Saints

Kate Ellis

Kate Ellis (b. 1953) is the author of the fascinating series of West Country crime novels featuring amateur arche-ologist and Detective Superintendent Wesley Peterson. Although set in the present day the series creates intriguing links between modern crimes and past events. The series has reached five novels: The Merchant's House *(1998),* The Armada Boy *(1999),* An Unhallowed Grave *(1999),* The Funeral Boat *(2000) and* The Bone Gar-den *(2001). The following story does not feature Wesley Peterson but takes us back over 800 years to the time of the great traveller and theologian Giraldus Cambrensis or Gerald of Wales (1146–1220).*

Many years ago I heard strange and wonderful tales of an island where nobody dies, except in extreme old age: an isle of saints where violent death never walks abroad and all live in peace and brotherhood. In the innocence of my youth I believed in this blessed place. But on that journey we made through Wales in that distant spring of 1188, I learned that there is no place on this earth untouched by death and evil.

In Lent of that year Baldwin, Archbishop of Canterbury and Gerald the Welshman, Archdeacon of St David's, jour-neyed all through Wales calling men to fight for the Holy Land. And although Archbishop Baldwin spoke no Welsh, he drew the crowds to him wherever he went.

In those days I, Maelgwn, was a young novice of Strata
Florida Abbey, shortly to make my vows, and on the second
day of April I joined up with the travellers in the company of
my abbot and two other brothers of our house.

There is little comfort in lengthy travels – as I know now
that I am advanced in years myself – and as we journeyed I
relied on my new companions to distract me from the
discomfort of a hard saddle. It was Gerald the Welshman
who drew my particular attention. Even on short acquaintance I liked the man and shared the high opinion he seemed
to have of himself. He was handsome and tall with delicate
features, and a tongue as sharp as his quill pen. And in the
arrogance of my youth I flattered myself that he had deigned
to notice the lowly young brother who rode an aged pony
near the rear of the party. But looking back now, I doubt if he
was aware of my existence until the night when blood was
shed.

It was on the ninth of the month, on the eve of Palm
Sunday, that we crossed the Traeth Mawr and the Traeth
Bychan at low tide and came to the Lleyn peninsula with
great relief that we had encountered no quicksand that would
drag our laden animals downwards to the bowels of the earth.

As we rode toward the town of Nefyn I fell into conversation with two monks of Whitland, fellow Cistercians, who
had their Abbot's permission to ride with the party and be of
use to Archdeacon Gerald and Archbishop Baldwin on the
journey. One was called Deiniol, a small, wiry man who was
quiet and modest in his manner. I liked him for he said little
and listened much and the words that he did say were full of
gentleness and good sense.

But I can think of little good to say of his companion
whose name was Hywel. He was a Welshman of Lleyn, or
so he said, but there was something about him that I did
not like. Perhaps he smiled too much with no mirth in his
eyes – or perhaps his thin face reminded me of a death's
head.

As Deiniol rode on ahead with Archdeacon Gerald, Hywel
hung back and stayed beside me. It was plain that he had
taken a liking to me. I was a good-looking lad in those days,

eighteen years of age and on the lookout for any distraction from my abbey's dull routine of prayer and labour.

This Hywel told me many tales of what had happened on the journey before I had joined them. He told of widows who had given their blessing to their only sons' desire to fight in the Holy Land and he spoke of other, more stubborn, women who had prevented their menfolk from going and who had thus incurred the wrath of the Almighty. I told him that I intended to volunteer myself, if God so willed it. He smiled and said that with the Archbishop's powers of persuasion, I might have little choice in the matter.

Young and naïve as I was, I babbled on to Hywel about my admiration for Archdeacon Gerald. He smiled again, that mirthless smile, and said that he had noticed how I listened intently to Gerald's stories and how I was so eager to sharpen the quills he used for his writings. It was true – I had never met a man so full of stories as Gerald the Welshman and I drank in his every word.

Then, as our ponies rode side by side across the rough terrain, slightly behind the rest of the party, Hywel put his hand on my bridle.

"A word," he said, leaning over so that his face was close to mine. His breath was fresh – like most Welshmen he cleaned his teeth diligently.

I backed away slightly, uneasy, and I saw that Deiniol had turned and was watching us with a look of gentle concern on his face. I suspected that he too felt no liking for his fellow monk of Whitland and I wondered to myself how they got on together in their day to day life in the abbey.

"So, young Maelgwn, you admire the Archdeacon?" Hywel whispered in my ear.

I nodded, uneasy.

"You wish to impress him? Gain his favour?"

He saw my discomfort as I prepared to deny it.

"Come on, boy. Only a blind fool would not notice that you hang on his words like a lovesick maiden. Would you not like to earn his gratitude?" He smiled, the death's head baring its teeth.

"I find him . . ." I searched for the word. "Interesting. His skill in writing . . . the tales he tells . . ."

"And his sharp tongue wielded like a sword against those he dislikes?" Hywel hissed. I suspected then that he had been at the sharp end of Gerald's wit more than once during the journey.

I felt myself blushing and I looked round. We had fallen further behind the others and Deiniol was now riding ahead. I noticed that Gerald was engaged in deep conversation with the Archbishop.

Hywel spoke again, leaning towards me still, his voice lowered so that it would not carry to the others. "If you wish to please him, I can tell you how to do it."

My curiosity was aroused. I looked at him and waited.

"There is a book," he said after a long pause. "A book he has said many times that he longs to see. You know his nature: he has a scholar's inquisitiveness about all matters but this one in particular. He has been searching for this volume for many years, or so he tells anyone who cares to listen."

"What is it?" I heard myself asking. I wished Hywel would get to the point so that I could be out of his company.

He looked around, as if to check that he could not be overheard. "The writings of Merlin. Have you heard of them?"

I nodded. I had heard tell of Merlin, the magician of legend and Archdeacon Gerald had mentioned his writings. But Hywel's talk was strange and I felt uneasy.

"Merlin lived at the time of King Arthur and made many prophecies," Hywel began patiently. "It is said that he was buried on Ynys Enlli, a holy isle near here."

"So?" I tried to feign indifference. I did not like this talk of magic from a man of God.

He was smiling, the grinning death's head. "I know where to lay my hands on Merlin's book."

I looked at him, wary. Archdeacon Gerald had spoken of the book more than once in my hearing and he had said that he had searched for it and longed to see it. "Where is it?" I asked.

"I cannot get it myself, you understand," Hywel said smoothly. "But nothing prevents you from fetching it." He paused, watching my face. "And if you do, I can guarantee you'll be high in Gerald's favour. Maybe he'll speak well of you to your Abbot. Or, as you haven't yet made your vows, he might even take you into his household."

I felt a warm glow of temptation as I contemplated such preferment. "Why can't you get the book for him yourself?"

Hywel hesitated, showing discomfort for the first time. "Because it is in a place where I am known. It is not far away, just outside the town of Nefyn where we are bound. You would be there and back before your Abbot missed you. When we reach the town, take the road south-west that leads to Ynys Enlli and you will see a house, the last before the open country. Go into that house and in a niche in the wall near the doorway you will find a box of strong oak. The box contains an ancient volume: the writings of Merlin."

"How do you know?" I asked. Now that I think back on it, I curse my naïveté.

"I know because I have seen it."

"Who lives in the house?" I had no wish to be chased off by an angry householder and I had an uncomfortable feeling that I was not being told the whole story.

"Just an old man. Nobody who matters. You ask too many questions," he hissed at me, the spray of his saliva hitting my cheek. "The book is mine, you need not fear that I am making you a thief," he added as if he had read my thoughts.

When we reached the town of Nefyn, Hywel grabbed my pony's bridle. "Go now, boy. There is the road. It is not far."

I looked up. I could see my Abbot ahead with the two other brothers of our Abbey who were with us. I was far behind the party and my departure would not be noticed. I gave my pony a firm kick and rode on, down the road which led towards Ynys Enlli, the isle of saints.

It was so easy, my first and last attempt at theft. The house was not large, nor was it small. It was built of stone, standing alone at the very edge of the town, and I guessed that its owner, if not a wealthy man, was at least comfortably off, and yet there was an air of neglect about the place. I pushed at the heavy oak door. It opened smoothly and when I stepped inside it was some time before my eyes adjusted to the gloom. There was no fire lit in the central hearth. And no sign of the old man Hywel had spoken of.

I wondered who the old man was, who owned such a place. And how Hywel had come to leave a precious possession here, if indeed he did own the book of Merlin he had spoken of. But I thought then that it was best not to ask too many questions.

I found the niche and the wooden box easily enough; it was there just as Hywel had said. I opened the box and lifted the shabby, leather-bound book from its resting place. It wasn't until I was outside again, riding off towards Nefyn with the book hidden beneath my cloak, that it occurred to me that my ambition, my desire to please Gerald the Welshman, had turned me into a thief: a thief who would sneak into a house and steal a precious thing from it unsuspecting inhabitants. Then I began to justify my actions by telling myself that Hywel was indeed its rightful owner. But somehow I knew deep in my heart that I was deceiving myself.

I endeavoured not to dwell on my sin as I rode into the town of Nefyn to rejoin my fellow travellers. And I did not suspect then that I had been followed from the house by someone who was tracking my progress as a huntsman tracks a deer.

There was no sign of Hywel among the travellers thronging in the main street so I made straight for the house where I was to lodge for the night. Several good people of the town had offered us their hospitality, for in Wales nobody begs and everyone's house is open to all: for the Welsh generosity is the greatest of all virtues, as Gerald the Welshman boasted on many occasions.

I and the other brothers of my abbey were to lodge in the house of a widow called Nest. But Hywel, I knew, was to stay with Gerald in the priest's house on the other side of the main street. How I longed to be part of that learned man's household, to sit at table with him listening to his talk and his ready wit, or rest around the dying fire in the evening listening to his tales.

I hid the book of Merlin's writings beneath my discarded cloak which I folded carefully around it. I had resolved to keep it from Hywel as I intended to take the credit for its discovery myself and present it to Gerald before Hywel had the chance to take it from me. I am ashamed to think of my vanity now, in the days of my wisdom and maturity, but I longed for Gerald's good opinion and for the praise and notice that I would receive for finding the volume he had been eager to see for so long. How foolish we can be in this mortal life.

But my plans did not go smoothly. Hywel arrived at my lodgings when the meal was beginning, just as the sun was descending into night. I hurried to the doorway to meet him, not wishing him to enter and search for the book I had so carefully concealed.

"Did you get it?" he asked, putting his face close to mine.

"Of course." I drew myself up to my full height, an inch or so shorter than my adversary's. "But as I took the risk of retrieving it, I intend to give it to Archdeacon Gerald myself," I said with a courage I did not feel.

He smiled, a death's head grin. "But how will you explain your actions to your Abbot . . . or to Archbishop Baldwin himself? What will they say when they know that a novice monk is a common thief who broke into a house and stole a precious treasure? Give the book to me and you can rely on my silence. If not . . ." A smile played on his lips. He was enjoying himself, relishing the discomfort of a lad so naïve that he'd committed foolish sin to impress a superior.

I hated Hywel then: hated him for encouraging me, for tricking me into doing his dirty work for him. My thoughts as I looked into his smug, mocking eyes, were hardly worthy of one who planned to take holy vows. I turned away before I yielded to the temptation to strike him and wipe the smile from his gloating face.

"Your part in this is best forgotten. If you give me the book, I guarantee that your Abbot will hear no word of this," he said smoothly. "But now I have more pressing matters to claim my attention. The Archbishop is anxious to recruit as many as he can to fight in the Holy Land. How I will rise in the favour of my superiors if it is known that I persuaded some willing fools to die in the heat." He gave a bitter laugh and I shuddered.

He edged further into the house, peering through to where the household were eating, sitting around in groups of three as is the custom. My hostess, the widow Nest, spotted him and bustled over. She was a small woman with a round, apple face.

As she approached he leaned towards me. I felt his warm breath on my ear and shifted away.

"I have heard that this widow has a son," he whispered. "He looks a likely lad to make the journey to the Holy Land. I will talk with him, work on him before the Archbishop preaches in the morning." He stared beyond the approaching woman, his eyes focused on a boy who was sitting with an older man and a girl. I knew the boy to be our hostess's son but I had paid him scant attention. It was the girl by his side, his elder sister, who interested me more. She had hair like spun copper and a delicate face dotted with pale brown freckles. I had learned from one of the men that her name was Awena and for a moment, as I watched her, I forgot that I was supposed to be in that place on the Lord's business.

The widow Nest brought water for Hywel's feet. This he declined, saying that he had only dropped in for a word with his fellows and did not intend to stay there for the night. Nest looked relieved that the customs of hospitality didn't oblige her to feed another hungry mouth. I watched her as she walked away and paused to speak to her son, her face all love and concern. He was her only son, I had heard, and she clearly held him most dear in her heart.

But Hywel made straight for the lad and his companions. Squatting down to talk with Nest's son, Hywel looked like some great bird of prey in the habit that hung loosely off his thin fame. What honeyed words of persuasion he used I do not know to this day, but I saw the fire of zeal appear in the boy's eyes. Another recruit for the Holy Land, I thought fleetingly. Then my thoughts turned elsewhere.

I retrieved the book of Merlin from its hiding place. Now was the time. While Hywel's attention was focused elsewhere I would save the situation by presenting Gerald the Welshman with the book he had sought for so long. I would be in his favour and I would tell the truth about Hywel if necessary. Hywel, the death's head, would laugh on the other side of his ugly face.

I slipped from Nest's house and crossed the street to the house of the priest where Archdeacon Gerald and the Archbishop were lodging for the night. I opened the door and crept in like a scurrying mouse, not wishing to draw attention to myself.

But I need not have feared. Gerald the Welshman was sitting nearest the blazing hearth, all eyes upon him as he recounted some tale. I waited in the shadows at the edge of the hall until he had finished, the book clasped beneath my cloak which I had folded lightly around my body as the night was chilly.

When some of the party began to drift into chattering groups and the Archbishop announced that he intended to retire to the church for an hour of prayer, I seized my chance. Gerald was sitting alone, gazing into the fire's leaping flames, so I approached him quietly. But he must have heard my footsteps because he looked up, his eyes sharp and darting, noting everything he saw and storing it in his formidable memory. I hesitated, conscious of my gaucheness, knowing that the faults and weaknesses of others were only too apparent to this great man.

"Come, boy. If you have something to say to me, then get on and say it," he said with a hint of impatience that robbed me of my confidence.

I stepped forward and drew the ancient volume from the folds of my cloak. I held it out to him, too nervous to speak. He took it and turned the pages as I waited. After a while he spoke. "Where did you come by this, boy? Speak up now – I don't eat novices during Lent." A smile played on his lips and I sensed that he was trying hard to suppress his excitement.

"I cannot say, sir. But I knew you were searching for it so I . . ."

But he wasn't listening. He had opened the book and was now devouring its contents with greedy eyes. I knew there would be no more questions. I stepped back into the shadows and watched him, hoping that he'd remember my face and that he'd one day decide to favour the one who'd found the treasure he'd been seeking.

But for the moment I had no word of thanks. I looked round and saw that Deiniol was standing in the shadows near by, watching me. He looked worried – but Deiniol, I thought, often looked that way. I returned to my lodgings across the street, resolving to ask Gerald in the morning how he'd enjoyed the book so that I wouldn't be forgotten.

But such is ambition that it is so often thwarted. When I awoke the next morning, stiff and cold in the huge communal bed I shared with the rest of the household, news had already come that Hywel was dead.

He had been found outside in the street, face down on the cold damp stones. A dagger or a sword had been thrust between his ribs and into his beating heart but there was no sign now of the instrument of death: the murderer had drawn the blade out of Hywel's body leaving no clue behind.

As I took in the news my thoughts returned to the last time I had seen him alive. When I had returned to my lodgings the previous night, he had been leaving. He had asked me where the book was and I took great delight in telling him that Gerald was reading it as we spoke. He had reddened first, clenching his first in fury, then he had leaned toward me and hissed like a snake spitting venom, "You will pay for this treachery, boy."

I confess now that I had been afraid. I had thought to outwit him, to earn Archdeacon Gerald's good opinion. But I feared that Hywel would never forget how I bested him.

Those bitter words of his still echoed in my head as I watched his lifeless body being carried to the church where it would lie until it received Christian burial. But I was distracted by Awena who stood beside me and touched my arm, gentle as a butterfly. I looked at her and felt a stirring in my loins.

She spoke to me, standing on tiptoe so that her soft mouth met my ear. "He will not be missed," she whispered. "He was a wicked man."

Shocked by her bluntness, I asked her what she meant.

"My brother is not yet fifteen," she replied. "A man who would persuade a child to leave his home to face death in a foreign land and break his mother's heart is wicked in my eyes."

I muttered the familiar words. It was in the service of Our Lord. It was to avenge the insult done to His name by unbelievers. But I knew that there was hesitation in my voice. Did Our Lord not pity a widow and her children? I would not have uttered these doubts to anyone in our party, yet I wondered whether I was alone in my thoughts. Did men put words into holy mouths for their own ends and glory?

But I had no more time to talk with Awena, even though the prospect was enticing. It was the hour when the Archbishop was to preach in the church and there were whispers in our party that Hywel's murderer had been discovered and was about to be brought to justice.

Reluctantly, I left Awena's sweet presence and hurried to the stone church. The Archbishop was standing before the altar, next to Hywel's lifeless body. Archbishop Baldwin was a swarthy man, of moderate height. He was thin and had about him an air of abstinence and self-control. But his face was gentle and good-humoured as he gazed out upon his congregation. Archdeacon Gerald stood towering beside him, his eyes fixed on the doorway where the townsfolk were pushing their way into the building.

The heat from the packed bodies and the smell of sweat created a warm fug in the small, packed church but when the

Archbishop began to speak, there was complete silence.
When Baldwin preached, all the town wished to hear.

"Our brother has been most wickedly done to death," he
began. "And we have the guilty one."

He paused as a murmur of voices rose from the crowd. A
man standing next to me muttered that the widow Nest had
been taken to the priest's house. She had been seen following
Brother Hywel last night after angry words had been exchanged: her guilt was certain. My mouth gaped open. I had
been talking to her daughter only fifteen minutes before and
there had been no hint then.

I pushed my way out of the church and found the street
outside deserted. I had to find Awena again; I had to discover
what was happening. I ran to her house and looked inside but
the place was deserted. Then, when I was heading back to
the church, I spotted a figure lurking in the shadows – a
cloaked man, bent and old. He stood still for a while and he
seemed to be staring in my direction. I began to walk away
slowly and, glancing round, I saw that the old man had
begun to follow. I swung round to face him but he moved
away quickly, flitting like a moth down the side of the
church.

Something made me follow. Curiosity perhaps – or perhaps a desire to solve the mystery, for mystery there was
about Hywel. I had had the uneasy feeling ever since I had
met him that Brother Hywel wasn't quite what he seemed.

The old man slipped down an alleyway, still moving fast
for one of his apparent age. I followed and fortune favoured
me that day as the alley came to a dead end. He stood with his
back to me, like a cornered beast trying to find an escape
route.

When I neared him I found I was lost for words. I was a
mere novice monk and no pursuer of suspects. Then I had a
sudden fear that if this was Hywel's murderer then it would
be only too easy for him to swing round and plunge a knife
into my own heart. But he made no move towards me.
Instead he turned slowly and I saw his face. There was
something familiar about his features, an echo of someone I
knew. But I had no time to think as I recognized the fire of

madness in the old man's bloodshot eyes. I began to back away as he spoke.

"My son was the devil." The old man spoke in Welsh, a strong musical voice with none of the hesitancy of old age.

"What do you mean?" I stammered, suddenly afraid.

"He slithered into that holy house as the serpent slithered into Eden. Wicked, he was – even as a boy." He raised his eyes to heaven. "And I must bear the shame of fathering such a one."

The old man would have made a fine preacher for there was a fire in his words that made me tremble. "Who are you?" I asked.

The old man stared at me. "I am Meredudd ap Dafydd ap Merfyn ap Idwal and, to my shame, I fathered a thief and a liar. But now he is dead, down in hell with the others of his kind. The Lord knows the heart of every man. It is futile to hide behind a monk's cowl."

I shuddered at his words, knowing the shortcomings of my own heart. My thoughts about Awena in the night had been far from pure. Then the truth dawned and I realized why the old man's features had seemed so familiar. "You are Hywel's father?"

The old man looked at me slyly. "You are the one he sent to my house. I watched you take the book. I thought he would come for it himself but I should have known he'd send another. He lacked even the courage to face his own father."

I swallowed hard. This explained how Hywel had known the whereabouts of the book but I had not suspected that I had been observed. "Tell me about the book," I asked. I had to know the truth.

Meredudd stared at me, as though deciding if I could be trusted. He seemed calmer now and my fear began to ebb away. He began to speak. "My wife, God rest her soul, bore me two sons, Hywel and Cynan. Hywel was a spiteful, sly boy and Cynan was good and honest. Fruit of the same tree, one wholesome and one appearing wholesome but eaten from within by the worms of corruption."

Meredudd looked around as though he feared that he

would be overheard. "Eight years ago Cynan went on pilgrimage to Ynys Enlli, which the Saxons call Bardsey Island. It is the most holy of places and it is said that the monks there are as pure in heart as mortal men can be. Pilgrims flock there and they say that nobody dies there except of extreme old age. It is a place of peace – a place of saints."

"I have heard of it." I willed him to get on with his story.

"Hywel suddenly decided to go with his brother. I was glad and I hoped he would make penance for his many sins on Ynys Enlli; I even allowed myself to think that he intended to make a new start and turn from his wickedness. But Hywel had other plans in mind. He was a sly boy, giving a virtuous face to the world to hide the foulness within."

I knew what he meant about Hywel. I had seen the truth beneath the mask.

"Cynan did not return," he said in a low whisper. "And later I went to the island myself to seek the truth." Tears appeared in his eyes.

"Go on," I urged, impatient to hear the end of the story.

"I was told by the monks there that Cynan and Hywel had visited them but that Cynan's drowned body had been found on the mainland, on the beach at Aberdaron near where the pilgrims embark for the island. They said that kind pilgrims had carried him back to Ynys Enlli for burial so that he could join the rest of the island's saints in eternal rest. I spoke to a young monk there who was all kindness and gentle speech." He hesitated. "But I knew that he was hiding something: he was not a good liar and I suspected that he knew more about Cynan's death than he claimed."

I said nothing, hardly believing that monks with such a reputation for holiness would be involved in a violent death.

He continued. "I went back to the mainland and asked more questions at the pilgrim's guest house at Aberdaron, near where the monks claimed that Cynan had been found. I was assured that no drowned body had been discovered near by – but the people there had heard rumours that a precious book had been stolen from the monks on the island at around the time of Cynan's visit. Hywel hadn't yet come home to tell his version of the story and I feared that he was somehow involved."

"So what had happened to Hywel?"

"He returned home weeks later and he swore to me that he had found Cynan's body on the shore of Ynys Enlli itself and that he had drowned accidentally. My first instinct was not to believe him: Hywel wasn't the most truthful of men and I feared greatly that he was responsible for his own brother's death. But one part of Hywel's story fitted with what I had learned at Aberdaron on the mainland and I began to wonder why the young monk would lie about the place where Cynan's body was found. What did he have to hide?"

I was starting to feel more confused. What motive would the reputedly saintly monks of Ynys Enlli have for covering up the drowning of a young pilgrim on their island? "What about the missing book?" I asked.

"Hywel left an old book with me when he returned – the one you took from my house," he added with a hint of reproach. "I told him about the rumours of theft I had heard at Aberdaron and I asked him if he'd stolen the book from Ynys Enlli. But he denied it and said that he'd bought it from some monks at Bangor. Then he told me that he intended to join the brothers of Whitland Abbey as penance for his former crimes and that he intended to present the book to his abbey one day in the future. I was glad at this news. But when he said that a man could prosper in the church and the presentation of the book would earn his Abbot's favour, my blood ran cold. The church has such men in it, I know – they work like worms in an apple against the will of God and use His church for their own advancement." Meredudd shuddered and I stayed silent. Then he stared at me, his eyes piercing through mine. "He used you to do his will. Were you his friend?"

I shook my head. "He asked me to fetch the book because the Archdeacon wished to see it. That is all." To my shame I tried my best to sound innocent, to hide my own ambitious thoughts. The protection of my reputation was important to me then, setting off as I was on life's path.

"I mourned Cynan but I will not mourn Hywel," the old

man spat out suddenly. "Death was the only way to stop his wickedness."

Meredudd turned and walked swiftly away and I made no attempt to stop him. But I realized then that the widow Nest was not the only person in Nefyn who had good reason to rid the world of Brother Hywel.

I heard later that the preaching of Archbishop Baldwin was an inspiration to all who heard it. Although I could not vouch for this myself as the sermon was over by the time I returned to the church. But I saw that many men came forward to take the cross, vowing to fight in the Holy Land. Nest's son was amongst them. If Nest had indeed killed Hywel for his powers of persuasion, then her offence had been in vain. I looked for Awena but I could not see her and I didn't blame her for her absence. As I pictured her I felt a sudden and urgent longing but I knew I had to banish all thoughts of her from my mind.

When I left the church Deiniol caught up with me and said that Gerald the Welshman wished to speak to me about an urgent matter. I asked him if there was any more news of Hywel's killer. Deiniol shook his head sadly and said that the widow Nest had admitted to following Hywel from her house to beg him not to press her son to fight in the Holy Land. I saw a sadness in Deiniol's eyes and I suspected that, like me, his regrets were for the widow and not for Hywel. As he hurried away, I spotted Awena across the street and she glanced at me then looked away. I walked towards the priest's house with a heart full of sadness. Does violent death always spread its dark misery to everyone around?

But Gerald had asked to speak to me. I confess now that this honour – and the fact that the great Archdeacon had remembered my existence at all – raised my spirits a little. I strutted to his lodgings with as much dignity as I could muster, my head held high with sinful pride.

Gerald awaited me, his face solemn and I was surprised to see that Archbishop Baldwin was with him, sitting by his side and watching me with good-humoured eyes. I stood before those two distinguished men and any youthful confidence I had felt, ebbed away rapidly.

Gerald spoke first. "You were seen talking to Brother Hywel. What do you know about him?"

At his coaxing I stumbled out the whole story. I told him everything I had learned from Hywel's father, about the pilgrimage to Ynys Enlli, Cynan's death and the story of the stolen book. I noticed that he kept the book of Merlin by his side and that he was fingering it lovingly.

"So this precious book may have been taken from Ynys Enlli?" He glanced at the Archbishop. "I would not have it known that I was in the habit of receiving stolen treasures."

"Indeed not," the Archbishop said sternly. "If it belongs to the monks there, it must be returned at once."

Gerald frowned. "What you have told us casts some doubt on the guilt of the widow Nest. Several witnesses saw her with him outside her house but she swears on everything holy that he was alive when she left him. She insists that she is innocent and I tend to believe her. Do you not agree?"

I swallowed nervously and nodded. I wanted to believe that it was not my attraction to Nest's daughter that made me sure of the widow's innocence. I thought of the woman, her apple cheeks, her affection for her children. But love can drive people to kill as much as hate – nobody protects like a mother.

Gerald stared into the fire for a while without speaking. Then he broke the silence, looking me in the eye. "You show initiative, my young brother. If I were to ask you to remain in Nefyn to make some inquiries on my behalf . . ."

"Anything you ask, Archdeacon," I said. "But my Abbot . . ."

"Has agreed," said Gerald, a smile flickering around his lips. "We travel now to Bangor, proceeding part of the way on foot to rehearse the hardships we will encounter on our pilgrimage to Jerusalem. Our journey will be slow which will allow you to catch us up. I will leave Deiniol here to help you. He is a man I can trust. Will you do it?"

I nodded, lost for words, and prayed that Gerald's faith in me would not be in vain.

I watched the travellers depart and at that moment I wished I was with them. I felt that my burden was too heavy for one so young and I feared that I was bound to fail – or worse still, to make a fool of myself. But with prayer all things are possible, I told myself and I went with Deiniol to the church to make our petitions to God.

We knelt there before Hywel's body in the flickering candlelight. I had expected Meredudd to come forward and claim his son's mortal remains for burial but, according to the priest, there had been no word from him. Perhaps Hywel's father had rejected him in death as well as in life. Or perhaps Meredudd feared discovery for it is said that a corpse bleeds afresh if touched by its murderer – the more I thought of it, the more convinced I was of his guilt.

Before the Archbishop's party had left Nefyn, the Widow Nest had willingly come to the church and touched the body of the murdered man to prove her innocence before the whole town. The corpse had not bled, nor had there been any other signs of her guilt. Most in the town seemed satisfied by her actions. But, as a pursuer of truth, I kept an open mind.

How seriously I took my task, watching, questioning and listening. And yet I felt alone. Deiniol was a quiet man whose mind was far more active than his mouth and, although I liked him, I missed the chatter and gossip of my fellow travellers, especially the tales and sharp wit of Gerald the Welshman. As the life of the town returned to normal after the Archbishop's departure, I felt that I was somehow left behind and that the excitement of the journey was continuing elsewhere without me. But if Gerald expected me to clear the matter up quickly and catch them up at Bangor, I wondered what he knew that I didn't.

Deiniol and I were to stay at the house of the priest and when I carried my meagre possessions from Nest's house, I was surprised to find Deiniol sitting by the fire in my new lodgings with the book of Merlin in his hand. I said I was surprised that Gerald hadn't taken it with him.

"The Archdeacon knows that it was not yours to give," Deiniol said gently, making me feel a little guilty. "The priest here has offered to return it to Ynys Enlli where it belongs."

"Is it certain that it was taken from there?"

"It is certain," said Deiniol quietly.

"Then the priest must return it." It was a satisfactory solution to the dilemma.

"But what about our other problem?" Deiniol sighed, staring into the flames. "How are we to find the one responsible for Brother Hywel's death?"

I shrugged my shoulders. I feared that Gerald's faith in me was sadly misplaced as I had no idea where to start. I would, most likely, have to rely on Deiniol for ideas. He was older and more experienced – and probably knew more of human nature.

"I think we should visit Meredudd, Hywel's father." I felt myself blushing as I recalled my last clandestine visit to his home. "I fear he had good reason to hate his son. He told me with his own lips how he suspected that Hywel had killed his brother and stolen the book, how he had always brought shame to the family. It may be that . . ."

Deiniol nodded. "You should question him but I will stay here. Meredudd will talk more freely with one he already knows."

I opened my mouth to object but Deiniol had turned his attention once more to the flames. I had no desire to face Meredudd alone again – he who was unbalanced at best . . . and at worst, the murderer of his own son. Deiniol was a coward – a fine partner for a man who had been charged with uncovering the truth about a murder. However, I controlled my tongue and walked from the room with my head held high. I would face Meredudd alone and trust in the Lord to protect me.

But when I stepped out into the street I saw Awena leaving her mother's house and I fell into step with her. With such sinful thoughts in my heart, I feared that the Lord would hardly look upon me with favour at that moment. Yet I could not help myself. I walked close to her and felt the forbidden thrill in my loins. I told her how relieved I was to hear that her mother's innocence had been proven and I asked if her brother intended to keep his vow to fight in the Holy Land. But her answers were evasive and there was no hint now of the pleasure she had appeared to take in my company the night before. I felt she was trying to hide something – or was I fooling myself and failing to realize that she had merely lost interest in me?

She walked across the rough ground and I quickened my steps to keep up with her. Then she stumbled and I grabbed her. I told myself that it was to keep her from falling but in reality I was seizing the chance to touch her warm body. I held her, longer and closer than was necessary for I had never held a woman before. Then, to steady her, my hands strayed inside her cloak. She pushed them away with swift efficiency but not before they had touched the belt slung around her slender waist. She stepped back and I saw the fear in her eyes for, concealed beneath Awena's cloak, was a long, sharp dagger. I said nothing. I needed time to think. I watched her hurry off down the road and wondered what I should do.

Meredudd was waiting for me, almost as if he were expecting my visit. This time the fire was lit in the hearth and the smoke swirling around the room stung my eyes. He said nothing as I entered, uttered no greeting or question. I stood before him, not knowing where to begin.

But he spoke first. "You are here because you think I killed my son." There was no hint of madness in his words. His eyes met mine and I looked away. "I have never broken God's law in that way – although I have been tempted many times. I did not kill him."

To this day I don't know why I believed him. But some instinct within me told me that he was telling the truth. I stood there, wondering what to say next. I was a boy then and no expert in extracting the truth from the guilty or the innocent.

But I feigned a confidence I did not feel. "It is said that a murdered corpse bleeds if touched by its killer. Will you touch your son's body?"

I stared down at the man boldly, but with uncertainty and fear in my heart. I wondered why Gerald had charged me with this task.

"I will undertake any test you care to name," Meredudd said quietly. "But the Lord may still judge me a murderer because I have wished Hywel dead a thousand times."

I was suddenly afraid that if Meredudd's innocence was proved, then Awena would come under suspicion of killing the man who had quarrelled with her mother and tried to lure her beloved brother away to a hot death beneath foreign skies. And I knew that I would probably do everything in my limited power to allow that lovely girl to evade justice. I shuffled my feet, unsure of what to do next. Meredudd stared into the smoking fire for a while before looking up at me.

"Has the brother told you anything?"

"The brother?" I hoped the old man wasn't slipping into madness again.

"The brother from Ynys Enlli: the brother I met there who did not tell me the whole truth about Cynan's death. I saw him in Nefyn. If you speak to him he may tell you more than he told me. He may tell you what he was hiding from me eight years ago."

My heart began to beat faster. "Where did you see this brother?"

Meredudd told me and I hurried back along the track to the town. There was one person I had not yet questioned.

I found him in the church, kneeling by Hywel's body. He looked up when he heard the church door open and my eyes met his.

I walked softly across the church and his expression was wary as he watched me approach.

"Touch him," I said when I was standing by his side.

I saw that there was fear in his eyes.

"Touch him," I repeated.

"I cannot."

I took hold of Brother Deiniol's large hand and thrust it towards the white-covered shape that had once been Hywel.

"No," he cried before pushing me aside and rushing from the church.

But I knew where he would go. He would not leave Nefyn without the precious book. I ran to the priest's house and I found him there, gathering up his possessions with frantic haste. He swung round and stared at me like a cornered animal. But there was no violence in him and I had no fear for my safety. I walked towards him, holding out my hand reassuringly. I told him I just wanted to speak to him and that I was in no position to do him harm.

He looked at me and nodded. Then he sat down by the fire and clutched the precious book of Merlin close to his chest. "It is not as you think," he said softly.

"Tell me," I said.

Deiniol hesitated for a few moments. But when he spoke his voice was clear and unemotional. "Eight years ago a young pilgrim called Cynan was murdered on the shore of Ynys Enlli on the same day that a precious book was taken from the brothers' library there. The brothers of the island agreed between themselves to give Cynan a quiet burial amongst the saints and not to speak about his death to anyone."

He must have seen the look of surprise on my face as he began quickly to explain. "The island's reputation as a peaceful, holy place where nobody dies except of old age would hardly have lasted if word of a murder had got out, and the pilgrims who were our livelihood would have stopped coming. The brothers there all agreed it would be best. The culprit had escaped by then and our abbot said we should leave his punishment to God." He hesitated again. "We did not lie – we just did not tell the whole truth. Without the pilgrims and their offerings, how could our community afford to carry on?"

"You lied to Cynan's father. You said that his body had been found on the mainland."

Deiniol nodded sadly. "A small untruth."

"Go on," I prompted with the impatience of youth.

"I had witnessed Cynan's death from a distance. I had seen a man holding the young pilgrim's head beneath the waters, bringing violence and murder to our sacred place, but I was too far away to help the unfortunate victim or to see the murderer clearly. As the months passed, I found that I was reminded of the evil I had witnessed, and my lack of power to prevent it, each time I passed the scene of Cynan's death or his humble grave. So after a while, I decided to leave the island. I said farewell to my brothers there and, knowing no other way of life, I joined the brothers of Whitland which I thought would be far enough away to allow me to forget."

He stopped and stared at the fire, his lips pressed together in anger. "Then a brother called Hywel joined our house. From the start I never liked him but I begged the Lord's forgiveness because I thought the fault was mine. There was something familiar about Hywel, something which I could not place. Then I realized that his colouring and build, the way he moved, reminded me of the man I had seen from afar killing the young pilgrim on Ynys Enlli. I told myself that this unfortunate resemblance was causing my irrational dislike, but of course it never occurred to me that Hywel and the murderer could be the same man. Later, however, I came to discover that Hywel's virtue was false and that he did indeed come from Lleyn, so I began to watch him but I never voiced my suspicions as I had no proof."

Deiniol looked at me with clear blue eyes which were started to brim with tears. "Then we came here and when the book of Merlin – the treasure stolen from Ynys Enlli – was presented to the Archdeacon yesterday, I knew that Hywel was indeed the man who had taken it from the brothers there . . . and the killer of the pilgrim, Cynan. My instincts had been correct all along. I followed him last night and challenged him, as I could no longer remain silent. I had to expose his wickedness which had no place in a house of God."

"What happened then?"

"When I told him I knew what he'd done on Ynys Enlli, he drew his knife. He said that he'd killed once: he'd drowned his own brother who had caught him stealing

our precious book. I admit that I was afraid. I grabbed at the
knife and in the struggle which followed he was stabbed. It
was all so quick that I don't remember exactly how it
happened." He turned his eyes towards the flames of the
fire and sat for a few moments in brooding silence. "He
realized I knew the truth about him and he was going to kill
me. I merely defended myself."

I stared at Deiniol and wondered what to do. I could
hardly bring this gentle monk to justice because he defended
himself from a murderer. And I believed he told the truth.

"What will you do now?" I asked him.

"That is up to you, my young brother. Archdeacon Gerald
instructed you to discover the truth. Now you have done it."

I stared at the book of Merlin resting on the stool beside
Deiniol. "I think the Archdeacon intended that the book
should be returned to its rightful place. That's why he left it
here instead of taking it with him. And I suspect that he knew
the truth already and selected a mere novice to seek it out so
that you might go free." I smiled at him. "You are no
murderer, Brother Deiniol. And I think you should return
this volume to your brothers on Ynys Enlli."

I left him there. I walked out of the house into the street,
mounted my aged pony and coaxed the hardworking beast to
a trot. Then I rode out of Nefyn, taking the road to Bangor
and I was not to hear of Deiniol again for many years.

Some time later, when I read Gerald the Welshman's
account of his journey through Wales with Archbishop
Baldwin, I noted with some amusement that he boasted of
having discovered the works of Merlin – which he had long
been looking for – himself. But he had added the words "or
so I would like you to think," as a tantalising hint at the
truth. He made no mention of Hywel's death or the task he
had set me and I blessed him for this. Deiniol would, after
all, be able to live out his days in peace in the service of his
Maker. Gerald was ever a man with a ready wit and I think of
him now and smile.

A year ago I went on pilgrimage and crossed the racing
tides to Ynys Enlli. There I met a frail and aged monk, about
ten years older than myself. I recognized Brother Deiniol,

even after the fifty years that had passed since our last meeting, and he greeted me like a long lost friend. He had returned to his blustery island and had at last found peace. And the memories of Hywel's crime had faded with the passing of time.

As I was leaving Ynys Enlli, Deiniol put his hand, now thin as a skeleton, on my weary shoulder and told me how he was longing for the day when he would sleep with the saints on the island where nobody dies.

A Perfect Crime

Derek Wilson

Derek Wilson is the author of over forty books, and is a leading writer of popular history, biography and fiction. Amongst his books of naval history are The World Encompassed *(1977) and* The Circumnavigators *(1989). He is also the author of a series of mystery novels featuring art specialist Tim Lacy, which began with* The Triarchs *(1994), and he has recently embarked on a series of novels about the Intelligence war. The following story, though, takes us right back to the time of the Crusades and the Knights Templar and a particularly devious crime.*

I n the high summer of the year of our Lord 1265 I, Brother Thomas of the Order of Saint Francis, was chosen to accompany the ill-fated mission which set out from the Temple in London for the Holy Land. Now that more than a quarter of a century has passed I can, indeed I must, write down a true account of all that happened on that journey.

It was a time of chaos. A time of vengeance. God's judgment was being visited on the whole of Christendom for its violent rejection of Christ's teaching of peace and poverty. Kingdom fought against kingdom. In England Henry III was the captive of Simon, Earl of Leicester, and paraded around the country like a tame bear. In Outremer disaster had fallen on the Christian knights. All the triumphs of the one whom men called Louis the Pious had been reversed by the Infidel. The self-styled Poor Knights of Christ and of the Temple of Solomon were losing castle after castle. Hundreds of defenders were being put to the sword in their vain efforts to defend the Holy Places. I recall clearly a letter received by the Master of the Temple in England that I was called on to read to the brethren gathered in the great church towering proudly over the river and the streets huddled against the city wall. He understood well the fate falling upon the gold-glutted Order. "Rage and sorrow possess my heart so firmly that I scarce dare stay alive," he wrote:

> It seems that God himself is on the side of the Mameluke Turks. Outremer has lost so much territory that it can never regain its position. They will turn holy Mary's convent into a mosque while her Son looks on approving. To fight against the Turks is madness when Christ himself does not. They have conquered and they will continue to conquer, for God sleeps and Mohammed waxes powerful.

It fell to me, a priest brother of the poor Franciscans, to announce these dire tidings because none of the Templars knew their letters and, as confessor to the Master, Hugh de Tremblay, I enjoyed his complete confidence. De Tremblay had received from Thomas Berard, Master in Jerusalem, an urgent appeal for funds. This presented no problem to his brother Templars in London. They might live frugally (though of true poverty they were ignorant), but their coffers so bulged with the income from lands and trade that they were the envy of every prince in Christendom. The decision was immediately made to send succour to the beleaguered knights of the Holy Land, and Simon de Benville, the Master's close friend and comrade in arms, was appointed to lead the mission. I begged leave from my superior and from de Tremblay to accompany the party in order to make a long-hoped-for pilgrimage to the land of our Saviour and this was granted.

Reluctantly – I can say that in all humility, for it is true. I

had made myself very valuable as priest and spiritual counsellor ever since my transfer to the new Franciscan house in
London. As one who had drunk at the pure well of Assisi I
had attained a certain reputation and my austerities were
applauded by those who had no desire to emulate them.
There is no need to burden whoever may read this in years to
come with details of my own early history. It is enough to say
that, at a very early age I understood with a passionate
certainty the path to holiness and purity my life must follow
and this drove me from my native Carcassonne, where such a
life was no longer possible, to walk barefoot to the mother
house of the Franciscan order and beg admission.

Preparations were made quickly and we set out on a day of
heat and dust to travel to Dover where we would requisition
a ship to carry us across the narrows. "We" were a party of
fifty-six souls. Simon de Benville was a pious and dedicated
Templar. As a younger man he had seen crusading service
against the Cathars and been well rewarded with lands in
Languedoc and Provence. Soon after that he had joined the
Order and assigned all his estates to the Templars. By 1265
he had long reached the age when active men turn philoso-
phical, seeking reasons behind orders and purpose beyond
deeds. He and I had spent long hours debating the state of
the Church, the spread of heresy and the seeming success of
the Infidel.

Not so de Benville's younger brother. Were it not for the
respect in which Simon was held Philip would have long
since been expelled from the Order. He possessed the
braggadocio which is possibly an asset in a newly fledged
knight but which is tiresome when flaunted by a warrior
past middle years. In truth "warrior" is scarcely an appropriate word for Philip de Benville. If he had been involved
in half the chivalric exploits of which he boasted he would
certainly have been a hero. In fact most of the heads he had
broken had been in tavern and whorehouse brawls. The
severest penances had not deterred him from his tumultu-
ous way of life or separated him from companions drawn
from the lees of London life. Everyone on this expedition
knew why Philip de Benville had been included: to remove

him from the fellowship in which he was a disruptive influence.

Simon de Benville's designated lieutenant was Geoffrey de Vaux, another veteran of Templar campaigns. He had been to the Holy Land before, having accompanied Louis IX in 1248 on the crusade which had resulted in the King's capture and the appalling suffering of many of his companions. It was said by those who had known de Vaux since before that expedition that his head had been turned by the tortures inflicted on himself and by the death of many comrades in the desert sands. Certainly by the time I came to know him he was a morose man with few, if any, friends whose thoughts and feelings were not for sharing.

The captain of our fifty strong body of men at arms was William Leyburn, the younger son of an honourable Kentish family. He was not a member of the Order. The English Templars could not put a large body of military knights in the field as they had once done. The majority of the brethren, even at that time, were farmers, administrators and bankers whose energies were fully employed (when they were not at their devotions) in scrupulously husbanding the vast resources of the Order. When soldiers were needed in a holy cause the Templars never failed to provide them – by purchase. Mercenaries are always to be had – at a price – and the golden well of the Poor Knights was deep.

This, then, was the party which hastened towards the coast in those July days. The de Benvilles rode in front attended by de Vaux, myself and Simon's squire-cum-body servant, John Barnet, a young man whose only virtue was his dedication to his master. Leyburn followed, keeping an eye on his men who guarded the single closed wagon which contained the treasure-chest and all our equipment. We wasted no time on the road, anxious to get to sea while the weather was still favourable.

Dusk on the second day brought us within sight of the walls of Dover and we presented ourselves at the Franciscan house which at that time was just outside the town. We were, of course, hospitably received, though the Prior was full of apologies that he was unable to accommodate all our num-

ber. Some of the soldiers had to be sent to find their own
lodgings in Dover while ten of them were appointed to do
sentry shifts over the wagon in the convent's inner courtyard. The rest of us were made comfortable in the guest
quarters and invited to share fully in the life of the community.

Food was prepared for the company and most of them
were only too glad to fall to their victuals after a long day in
the saddle. I, of course, joined the brothers at Compline.
Nourishment of the soul is more important than providing
for the body. I had grace from the Prior to miss the last daily
office but explained that I have trained my body in the
rigours that lead to perfection. As we filed into the chancel
from the cloister I happened to glance sideways into the body
of the church and noticed that other members of the party
had come to share the worship. Simon de Benville was there,
kneeling close to the chancel step, and de Vaux was beside
him, determined, I thought, not to be outdone in deeds of
piety by his comrade. Farther back, in the uncandled dusk,
John Barnet leaned against a pillar. His presence there
surprised me. He was a surly, foul-mouthed fellow who
certainly loved his belly. As I peered along the length of
the church I gained the impression that he did not want to be
seen for, observing me turn in his direction, he pressed
himself back against the stonework. The next time I looked
round he was gone.

The short office concluded, I left with the other members
of the community. As they dispersed, yawning, to their cells
I lingered for a while in the cloister and enjoyed the cool of
approaching night. I sat on the low wall in one corner of the
court and silently recited the 139th psalm, *Domine probasti*. I
had just reached the end when a figure strode briskly along
the ambulatory opposite me, his form clearly visible in the
moonlight – de Vaux, returning from the church. A few
minutes later I followed. The route to the guest quarters took
me across the inner courtyard. Leyburn was there, checking
the guard – and none too pleased with what he discovered.

"Lout!" he bellowed, striking the man full across the face
with his gauntleted fist. "Do you think you can doze on duty

just because you're in a house of holy men? Never heard of light-fingered friars? For that you'll get no relief. You stay here – *awake* – till dawn. And I shall be around from time to time to make sure your eyes and ears are wide open."

The captain fell into step beside me and we walked together the last few yards. "See what dregs they've given me, Brother. Soldiers? More like children in play armour. That one's no more than fourteen. If he survives as far as Acre I'll pay for a dozen masses. Still, better he should be here than serving our lord the King. Henry is in enough trouble without relying on babes in arms to get him out of the barons' clutches."

"What news of the King?" I asked.

"Still with de Montfort in Wales but Prince Edward besieges Gloucester and if he can only raise enough men he'll control all the Severn crossings. The traitor will be trapped and forced to sue for peace. Would to God I were there to crush a few disloyal skulls. Well, goodnight to you, Brother."

We parted and I went to my bed thankful that another day, another milestone had been passed on the journey to heaven. The dim lamplight played on a crucifix at the bed's foot so that the last thoughts in my mind could be of death and the release of soul from body into the pure realm of spirit. I was ready for that transition, readier than I had ever been.

I emerged, as was my custom, into full consciousness. Still in the flesh. Automatically my mind turned to preparation for the first daylight office. But there was to be no Lauds that day. Scarce was I out of bed when the door of my cell was flung open by a young friar in great distress.

"Come quickly, Brother! Father Prior wants you in the chapel. Something terrible . . ." He turned and was away across the courtyard before completing the sentence.

I scurried after him. Others were crossing the open space between the living quarters and the towering bulk of the church. As I turned through the archway leading to the cloister I was aware that I had seen something amiss but, whatever it was, the gathering commotion and confusion ahead drove it from mind. Brothers, servants and visitors were converging on the narrow door into the chapel and struggling in their eagerness to reach whatever was within.

I pushed my way into the dim interior. The atmosphere was immediately different, as though we had all passed through a curtain shielding some holy secret from profane eyes. And, indeed, we had. Stumble-footed we blundered into the presence of death. I moved to the front of a circle gathered round the chancel step. The Prior, cowl thrown back from his corona of white hair, knelt beside a sprawled face-down figure, the upper part of which was heavily stained with blood. I took a step forward and looked down at the body of Simon de Benville.

The Prior looked up at me, dazed, shocked, affronted. "Stabbed! Here of all places!" He pointed to the narrow dagger embedded in the Templar's neck as though begging me to provide him with some explanation.

I moved forward to crouch beside him and reached out to touch one of the dead man's hands stretched forward on the grey stone towards the distant high altar. It was tomb cold.

While I was struggling to find some words, heavy boots crunched on the floor beside me. "By Mary and all the saints what mischief is this?" Geoffrey de Vaux had appeared and immediately took charge. "When was he found?" he demanded.

"The sacristan discovered him when he came to prepare for the service not twenty minutes since," the Prior explained, rising stiffly to his feet.

"God rest him," de Vaux exclaimed. "A soldier of Christ to die thus! He shook his head and fell silent. But only for a moment. "Clean him and lay him out properly. He will be buried here in the chapel," he ordered. Turning to me, he said, "The Master must be informed without delay. Find Leyburn. Tell him to send men to London with the news."

I hurried off to do his bidding but the captain was nowhere to be found. I stood in the middle of the courtyard, gazing helplessly round for some sign of Leyburn or his men. Several huddled groups of brown-robed figures, their routine disrupted, stood discussing the tragedy in hushed tones. Then I realized what was wrong, what I had sensed but not identified a few minutes before. There was the wagon, where we had left it the previous evening, but there was no guard keeping watch over the Templar treasure. Quickly I strode across the dusty yard. My fingers trembled as I unfastened the strings holding the canvas coverings. I pulled the flaps back as far as they would go and peered inside. There were piles of luggage and harness neatly stacked on the boards. Of the sealed chest containing the gold there was no sign.

I rushed back to the chapel and whispered the news to de Vaux. The old knight swore loud and long. Colour poured into his already ruddy cheeks and his bulging eyes glared round at the little crowd of friars. "Father Prior," he thundered, "I want every door out of this place locked and every window watched. No one is to leave until I've searched the last inch! Brother Thomas, come with me!"

As I hurried after him, he muttered, "I never did trust Leyburn. His father's been ruined in the King's service. Did you know that?"

"He's never concealed the loyalty of his father and brothers, nor what it cost them. But you surely cannot believe that he would murder de Benville and steal . . ."

We crossed the cloister, almost running as de Vaux answered. "De Benville is brutally cut down. Our gold disappears. Leyburn disappears. How would you explain those 'coincidences'?" He went ahead of me through the doorway into the great courtyard. "We'll make a thorough search of the priory, though I doubt we shall find anything: the rogue's had several hours to escape with the treasure. At the same time we must send down to the harbour. That's Leyburn's most likely escape route. If we have no success there . . ."

He stopped. A small mounted cavalcade was entering the courtyard through the main gateway opposite. It was the military escort and William Leyburn was riding at its head.

Seeing us, the captain jumped from the saddle and ran across the yard. "Where is de Benville? I have grave news for him."

De Vaux's hand went to his sword hilt. He unsheathed the weapon and pointed it at Leyburn. "You know well enough where he is! Thief! Murderer!"

The captain fell back, drawing his own sword. "What are you saying, man?" He lifted the blade to parry the Templar's blow.

"I'm saying that you killed our leader and made off with our treasure!" Metal clanged as the heavy swords met.

Leyburn circled, watching for his assailant's next thrust. "Made off? Made off? Do you not see me, man?"

"Where have you been at this hour?" De Vaux faltered and I took the opportunity to step between the antagonists.

"Brothers," I protested, "this solves nothing. Monstrous sins have been committed in this holy place and we must pool our energies if we are discover the truth and uphold justice." I explained in a few words that de Benville had been murdered, several hours before, judging by the temperature of the body. Leyburn seemed to be honestly shaken by the news. "And you, Captain, where have you been this morning?"

The soldier resheathed his weapon. "I came out to check the guard about half way through the hours of darkness. I found the man on duty trussed up in the wagon – and the treasure gone. Immediately I roused the rest of my men here in the priory. Three of them were missing. It was obvious why. I rode out with the rest and we spent a couple of hours scouring the countryside. A mile away we came across the Templars' chest by the roadside – forced open and empty. The rogues must have divided up the booty and gone their separate ways."

De Vaux looked dubious. "Why did you not check the harbour? The thieves are sure to try getting away by ship."

"Two of my men are making inquiries there now. I left them in Dover when I collected the rest of my company at first light."

De Vaux continued to gesture with his sword. "Well, I am in charge here now and I hold you personally responsible for the recovery of the gold. I shall want two of your men to ride as fast as they can for London to report to the Master and bring back his instructions. The rest of our forces we'll divide into small parties to make a thorough search for the criminals."

At that moment there was movement in the gateway. Another rider entered the courtyard, swaying heavily in the saddle as his horse ambled forward. Philip de Benville reined in his mount and gazed, bleary-eyed at the assembly. "What's all this," he sneered, "shouldn't you all be in chapel?"

De Vaux scowled at the newcomer. "And where have you been – as if I needed to ask? You'd better sober up quickly. You've family responsibilities to attend to. Your brother's dead."

The mounted man stared back with a puzzled frown. De Vaux turned from him in disgust and walked away with Leyburn to talk over details of the search. It was left to me to explain to the younger de Benville what had happened and to take him to see the body. It was only the sight of Simon's blood-stained corpse, lying now in a side chapel with the Prior saying over it the prayers for the dead that finally banished from his brain the fog of a night's carousing.

He fell to his knees weeping, then tugged at my robe for me to pray beside him. "You've always liked me, haven't you, Brother Thomas? You understand that I'm not made for all this praying business. You can say what you like about me but I'm not a hypocrite. It was Simon who wanted me to join the Templars. He was the holy one and what good did it do him? Look at him. He always said that I would end up killed in a tavern brawl. But he's the one . . ." Sobs overwhelmed him as he slumped forward.

"He died at his prayers," I explained gently. "His soul must have been borne away by angelic spirits."

"You think so?" He turned to me, pathetically appealing for comfort. "Well, Brother, here and now I make this solemn vow. I dedicate myself to the Order, just as he was dedicated – after I have done one other thing."

"What's that?"

"I will make sure Simon's killer suffers for his crime."

The next day we buried Simon de Benville before the high altar of the Franciscan Priory of Dover. It was not the interment he would have wished – after an heroic battle fought beneath the Cross or laid to rest in the company of other poor knights in the vault of the London Temple – but it was done decently. For us it made an interval in the search for the killers and thieves.

Late on the following afternoon our messengers returned on lathered horses from London. De Vaux ordered the company to assemble in the frater to hear the Master's instructions. He handed me the sealed letter which had evidently been dictated in great haste to a scribe and I, with some difficulty, translated the scrawled Latin. After conventional tribute paid to the dead man the leader of the English Templars ordered that no effort was to be spared in tracking down those responsible for de Benville's death and the theft of money designated for the relief of his hard-pressed brethren in the Holy Land. Geoffrey de Vaux was to bring the party back to London as soon as he was satisfied that no purpose could be served by remaining in Dover. But the investigation was to be entrusted to another member of the expedition, and everyone was enjoined on pain of eternal damnation to answer truthfully whatever questions he might wish to put to them. Here, to my surprise and consternation, I read my own name.

There was a deal of murmuring among the party but de Vaux strongly supported the Master's decision and ordered all present to be available to me as and when I might wish to speak with them. They all looked at me expectantly and in my confusion I had no idea what to say. After a long pause I expressed my unworthiness of the solemn trust reposed in me by the de Tremblay but pledged myself to do my utmost, with the help of God, to find the truth and clear away the foul miasma of suspicion hanging over the brotherhood. Perhaps, I suggested, it would encourage the other brothers to be frank with me if de Vaux were the first to be interviewed. The surprise that flitted over the old knight's face told me that he had regarded himself as exempt from the Master's fiat but he obviously could not refuse and, as the company dispersed, he and I walked across to a window embrasure to converse quietly.

"There's nothing I can tell you," de Vaux said as soon as we were alone. "However, the Master has great confidence in your intellect, so if you think I can shed any light . . ."

"Thank you, Brother. As you say, there's little that I need to ask you. However, it does occur to me that you might have been the last to see Simon de Benville alive. At the end of Compline you and he were together in the chapel, were you not?"

"We were both praying, yes."

"Who finished first?"

"I did."

"And you left the chapel immediately?"

"Yes, shortly after the end of Compline . . . ten minutes perhaps."

"And de Benville was still at his devotions?"

The other man nodded. "He seemed much burdened. The heavy responsibility of the mission . . ."

"Of course. He was well past the prime of his life. His energies not what they had once been. As an old comrade-in-arms you must have been aware of that."

"He was certainly approaching that time of life when a man should be preoccupied with preparing his own soul for death. Tragically, that consolation was denied him."

I stared down into the courtyard, musing. "I suppose you are now the obvious choice for next Master."

He spluttered with indignation but I hurried on, as though not realizing the implication of what I had said. "Was there anyone else in the chapel when you left?"

He reflected briefly. "I don't think so."

"I fancied I saw someone in the nave during the office. It might have been John Barnet."

The possibility appealed to him. "It was dark, of course, but I suppose . . . Barnet's a scurvy fellow who's come within the shadow of the gallows more than once. Simon took him into his service out of pity. I think he would have been quite capable of forming a compact with some of the soldiers. The whole scheme might have been his idea."

"But why kill his master? And are we really sure that the two crimes are necessarily connected?"

"Well, surely . . ."

"I'm puzzled. If you were going to steal the gold why would you need to kill de Benville?"

"That's obvious. Simon must have surprised the thieves while they were emptying the wagon, so they struck him down."

"And carried his body to the church?"

"Knowing that it would not be discovered until everyone assembled for Lauds."

I gave the impression of considering this possibility carefully. "In that case there will be blood in the courtyard." We both peered down from the window. Around the wagon the dust had been stirred up by scores of feet over the last couple of days. "I'll look carefully later," I said. "Thank you for the suggestion, Brother. It may be very helpful."

I left the frater and sought out the Prior in his lodging. I could not help noticing how comfortable his quarters were. He had several chambers at his disposal, furnished with tables and chairs and even a woven wall hanging. So much for the poverty St Francis had enjoined on *all* members of the Order. I did not trouble him long. All I needed from him was the weapon that had been used to kill de Benville. With that concealed in my sleeve I went in search of John Barnet. I had a shrewd suspicion where I would find him and I was not mistaken. He was in the kitchen, chatting with the brothers who were preparing the evening meal and scrounging scraps.

He looked sideways at me as I stood in the doorway, silently beckoning. "No good talking to me, Brother. I know nothing."

"If you know nothing you have nothing to fear by answering a few questions. Come with me. We'll take a turn around the cloister."

Since all the brothers were at their work the enclosed area with its rectangle of sun-scorched grass was deserted. We walked slowly around the arcade and I decided on a very direct approach. "What were you doing in the chapel during Compline on the night your master was murdered?"

He shook his head vigorously. "Me? At Compline? No, Brother, I leave the praying to them as understands such things. Not that I've anything against you lot . . . or the Templars," he added hurriedly. "My master was very good to me. I wish I knew who did for him."

"And if you did know, my Son, what would you do about it?"

Again the sideways glance. "Why I'd tell what I know and make sure he swung for it."

"You'd not be tempted to take the law into your own hands? It wouldn't be the first time, would it? Wasn't there a nasty affray in Cheapside a couple of years ago? Two foreign merchants killed as I remember, and you'd have gone to the gallows with three other villains if your master hadn't put in a word for you."

The swarthy little man was sweating. "That was all a mistake. I was nowhere near Cheapside that night."

"Or so you convinced your master, which is why he vouched for you. However, that's nothing to the matter. You were in the chapel during Compline. How long did you stay?"

Barnet swore roundly. "I keep telling you I wasn't there."

"Just as you weren't in Cheapside when another murder took place?"

"That's right. Why won't you believe me?"

"Perhaps because I'm not as trusting as your late master. You don't have him to protect you now, to help you conceal the truth. Well, I mean to have the truth. Since you won't tell me let me suggest something to you. You were spying, keeping a watch on the Sieur de Benville and the Sieur de Vaux. You wanted to know exactly where they were at all times so that you could let your friends know when the coast was clear to break into the treasure wagon."

"NO! No, Brother! That's not right! I'll swear it on all the holy relics in Christendom. I wasn't watching out for no thieves. I was . . ."

"Yes?"

"Nothing!" He gave me a glance of surly defiance.

I had to break him. I grabbed him by the shoulder and forced him to face me "I command you, as you value your immortal soul, tell me why you were in the chapel and what you saw."

"I saw nothing!" I could feel the fear trembling through

his body. "Yes, I was there – just for a few minutes . . . Because my master told me to keep watch."

"To keep watch? What for?"

"He'd been troubled with dreams of late. He thought some-one was out to kill him. Revenge, or some such nonsense."

"Perhaps it wasn't such nonsense."

"Oh, yes it was. Just a crazy notion. Anyway, just to humour him I followed him from time to time. That's why I was in the chapel. But I reckoned no one was going to do anything to him in there, so I left. I was exhausted after all that travelling. I went straight to bed."

"You slept in your master's chamber?"

"Yes on a mattress by the door."

"So that you would wake and attend to him when he came in?"

"That's right. Only he didn't come in that night."

"When did you realize he hadn't returned?"

"Not till morning. I told you, I was worn out. I slept like a drunk dog."

I had one more test for the servant. I whisked the dagger out of my sleeve. "Have you seen this before?"

He jumped back, caught his heel on the low cloister wall and sprawled on the grass. I stood over him, holding the stiletto's point close to his chin. "Well?"

Now he was really frightened. "Is that . . .?"

"Yes. Do you recognise it? Did it belong to your master?"

"No, I don't think so."

"Take a good look." I held out the narrow blade, now cleaned of blood, for his inspection. "Castillian workman-ship. The sort of thing that's very common north of the Pytenees where the de Benville estates were. You're sure you've never seen anything like it among the possessions of your master – or perhaps his brother?"

"Yes, that's possible." He accepted the lifeline readily. "Philip de Benville likes that sort of thing. He's got quite a collection. Why don't you ask him about it?"

At that I let the fellow go. He was obviously lying but I would get no more out of him at that point and what he had revealed called for careful thought.

The next day de Vaux ordered the return to London. Intensive enquiries in the area had yielded no information about the missing gold or the thieves, a fact which, in itself, I found interesting. Leyburn left a few of his men behind to continue their search but he returned with the main party to accept responsibility for the loss and to face the wrath of the Master. The hot weather continued and we made a long rest in the deep shade of some woodland on Barham Down. I took the opportunity for a quiet talk with the captain. Or, rather, it would be truer to say that he took the opportunity. I was sitting by myself meditating with the aid of *The Interrogation of John* – perfectly safe amidst that illiterate company – when he sauntered up and crouched beside me.

"Well, Brother," he began, "these Templars have placed a heavy burden on you. Are you making any progress?"

I closed my book and looked him in the face. What I saw was an honest, straightforward soldier, a youngish man loyal to simple, easily formulated ideals. "One or two interesting facts have come to light. I think de Benville's man holds the key to the business. He witnessed the crime; I'm sure of it but he is very scared and at the moment I can't get him to tell all he knows."

"No problem there, Brother. I'll get the truth out of him for you."

I shook my head. "Thank you, my son, but my experience of torture – and I have had some in my time – has taught me that the victims say what their persecutors want to hear rather than what is true. Tell me, where did you raise your troop of soldiers?"

"Most of them are my father's tenants from our estates near Maidstone."

"Which we shall pass close by on our journey."

"Yes, tomorrow."

"So you know well the perpetrators of this foul murder?"

The question shocked him. "Murder? You're not suggesting that my men had anything to do with that? All I can tell you is that the three who have disappeared were unknown to me until a few days ago. They were from London. They were men who had served the King here and in Gascony and had suffered for it. They were near-destitute and I took pity on them – the more fool I. They are blackguards. They deserve to hang and hang they will when I track them down. But for robbery, not murder."

"The two crimes must be connected, do you not think? It seems to me that de Benville must have come across the thieves in the act of removing the treasure. They overpowered him, killed him and carried his body to the chapel in the hope that we would not connect them with so unspeakably foul and cowardly a deed."

"But there would have been evidence of the crime in the courtyard – blood, signs of a struggle."

"Carefully covered up by the murderers. They had time to brush dust over any telltale marks."

Leyburn stood up and leaned against an ash bole. "A neat theory, Brother, but I'm afraid it's wrong. I've questioned my men very thoroughly, especially the wooden-headed idiot I left on duty. You remember the lad, Brother? I was reprimanding him for dozing at his post the other evening. His story is that three of his colleagues went to sit with him in the middle of the night. They brought wine but he refused it, knowing the trouble he would be in if I caught him with the stink of it on his breath. When they found that they could not befuddle him they knocked him senseless, tied him up and threw him in the wagon. I found him there in the morning. He would have heard if anyone had come up to challenge the thieves."

"How so? By his own admission he was unconscious." The captain fell unhappily silent and I pressed home my advantage. "No, it must be the thieves who committed this more infamous crime. How did you make their acquaintance? The Master will want all the details we can provide. Rest assured that the long arm of the Templars will reach out to these miscreants and their accomplices wherever they are. The vengeance of the poor knights is legendary."

"I still think you're wrong, Brother, but the one you should talk to is Philip de Benville. It was he who recommended those men to me – doubtless some of his drinking cronies."

It was to be the following day before I could put the captain's suggestion into effect. The bereaved brother was hard to approach. He rode alone in morose silence and swore gruffly at anyone who attempted to bear him company. In Canterbury, where we passed the night, he disappeared among the city's stews and our departure in the morning was delayed while men were sent in search of him. We had been an hour on the road when I drew my horse alongside his. His sins had left their mark on the wretched knight. He looked dreadful – bleary-eyed and dishevelled – and smelled worse. I apologized for intruding on his grief but pointed out that my only interest was to discover his brother's killer. I took his grunt as permission to ask my questions.

First of all I showed him the knife. Did he recognize it, I inquired.

He shrugged. "I've seen several like it."

"But not in England, I think."

"No, more like the ones they use in Languedoc and Provence."

"Where you fought the Cathar heretics?"

He nodded. "Where our lands were."

"A beautiful country. I know it well. The swelling hills; the abundant vineyards; the sun; the wind from the mountains."

"Beautiful, indeed, Brother." I noticed that tears had come to his eyes.

"What a sacrifice you made for the Order, giving up such fair estates, estates won at great cost fighting the enemies of the Church."

"Simon's sacrifice, not mine."

"You did not approve of him granting away the patrimony?"

De Benville shrugged. "He was the elder brother. He had no sons."

"Still, he might have left some land for you. As you said to me the other day, you were not designed to be a poor knight. It's a vocation. Simon's but not yours."

For the first time he turned to me, maudlin gratitude in his eyes. "You're a good man, Brother. You try to understand.

But you can't know what it's like to be a prisoner, shackled to someone else's piety.''

"I understand that a man may come to hate the one who fastens fetters upon him. I have seen it often: the boy put to a life of religion by devout parents who have no concept of the burden they are piling on him. With every penance, every paternoster, every recitation of the holy office resentment grows and slowly love turns to hatred." The tears were now streaming down de Benville's grimy cheeks. I changed the subject abruptly. "These villains who have made off with the gold – were they the murderers, do you think?"

"It's what everyone supposes."

"You knew them, I believe – in London, before we set out on this terrible venture?"

He scowled suddenly. "Who told you that?"

"Captain Leyburn mentioned that you had recommended them to him."

"The man's a liar!" de Benville shouted. "Leyburn came to me. I remember it well – it was in the White Lion at Queenhythe, next to the Salt Wharf. He was having difficulty hiring men. Any who had experience of arms were away fighting for de Montfort or the Prince of Wales. I told him that the only 'soldiers' he was likely to find along the waterfront were ruffians and fugitives. That was the beginning and end of my advice to him. Leyburn's the one who employed thieves and murderers and he can't shrug the blame off on to me. If we don't track down the men who stabbed my brother to death I'll require vengeance at their paymaster's hands, as he well knows."

"Oh, we shall find the murderer," I said, confidently.

De Benville looked at me sharply. "You sound very sure of yourself, Brother."

I allowed myself a smile. "Not of myself; of the one who witnessed the crime."

"Someone saw? Who?" he demanded eagerly.

"Your brother's servant. He's too frightened to tell at the moment but I shall have the truth out of him before we reach London."

It was soon after our midday rest that John Barnet went missing. He was observed eating with some of the soldiers at the roadside and someone swore that they had seen him mount and set forth at the rear of the train. As we approached the village of Sittingbourne I turned and went in search of him. The column had become well spaced out as it wound through thick woodland and the servant was not to be found. In response to my earnest inquiries men told me that they had not seen him for an hour or more. I went urgently to de Vaux, told him that I feared that Barnet had fled and that it was vital that I talk to him. In response to my pleading our leader ordered a group of Leyburn's men to ride back along our way in search of the missing man.

When they rejoined the column towards evening they came bearing Barnet's body tied across the saddle of his own horse. We were traversing a stretch of open heathland and the entire party gathered in a circle as the soldiers told their mournful tale. They had first come across Barnet's mare tethered close to the spot where we had rested. Probing further among the trees they discovered the corpse in a clump of bracken. There was no mystery about how the poor man had met his violent end: a deep gash across his throat had all but severed head from neck.

It would be foolish to claim that this second death deeply shocked the company. Barnet was a mere servant and no one had had much to do with him. It was only when I pointed out my conviction that Barnet had been murdered by one of our own number because he had vital evidence about de Benville's assassination that de Vaux ordered anyone who knew anything to speak. The appeal was fruitless and, as we rode on the leader mournfully suggested, "I suppose we shall now never know what happened to poor Simon."

"On the contrary," I assured him. "I can now make my report to the Master. But I beg you to say nothing of this to a living soul. It is vital that the murderer should believe that my investigation has been frustrated."

The outcome of all this can be briefly narrated. When I had reconstructed the crimes for the Master he placed Philip de

Benville in custody and within days personally conducted
the knight's trial on a charge of fratricide. The prisoner, of
course, denied the crime with fervent oaths but his own
character was the most effective prosecutor. His brethren
knew well his mode of life, his dislike of the cloister, his
resentment against his brother. Leyburn repeated the story
of de Benville recommending London ruffians for service
on the expedition. I explained how I had, regrettably, told
the younger brother that John Barnet was a witness to the
crime, not, at that moment, knowing myself the identity of
the murderer. Thus, unwittingly, I had doomed the hapless
servant, for de Benville had wasted no time in silencing him.
The Templar jury did not hesitate in reaching their verdict.
They concluded that Philip de Benville had plotted with
some of his city cronies to kill his brother and make off with
sufficient money to enable him to live in that style which he
believed was his due. His own absence in the fleshpots of
Dover was meant to distance him from the crimes. To the
very last, on the scaffold, the convicted man protested his
innocence but no one was moved by his tearful entreaties.
The Master was relieved to be able to bring the painful
sequence of event to a swift conclusion and also to rid the
Temple of a very unsatisfactory member. And he had other
reasons for rapidly veiling the affair at Dover, as only I, his
confessor, later discovered.

Thus was I the instrument of God's vengeance on the de
Benvilles. Not a day has passed during the last twenty-six
years when I have not recalled to mind the invigorating
events of the summer of 1265. But still more vivid is the
memory of 1249. Of a terrified fifteen-year-old boy watching
through a tear in the hayloft thatch as the de Benvilles and
their armed men rode through the village brandishing their
holy banners, crying "Death to the Cathars!," "Death to the
heretics!," and hacking down indiscriminately men, women,
children and even animals before setting their torches to our
homes and barns and crops.

I was the only survivor, somehow crawling out of the
blazing building to safety. I think I knew then, that very day,

that I had been spared for a work of importance to the Father of Spirits. My total devotion to him had already been recognized. Months before I had received the *Consolamentum*, admitting me to the number of the Perfect, the small band of Cathar holy ones enabled by divine grace to live here on earth a life of purity. The only approximation to that life that I could find after our brotherhood had been all but destroyed was among the Franciscans, the best of whom embrace a pale sort of piety.

I did not deliberately seek out the agents of Satan who had butchered my family and our peace-loving friends in Carcassonne but when we were brought together in London I knew why and I only had to await my opportunity. When I learned that both the brothers were making a journey to the Holy Land I had to make sure that I accompanied them. Still I had conceived no plan; I attended only on divine prompting.

In the Franciscan priory at Dover the moment came, the moment for which I had waited most of my life. There was nothing of high art about my scheme. I simply lingered in the cloister till the chapel was empty, fortifying myself with the words of Psalm 139:

> Wilt thou not slay the wicked, O God
> for they speak unrighteously against thee?
> Do I not hate them, O Lord, that hate thee?
> Yea, I hate them right sore
> even as though they were mine enemies.

Then I slipped inside and struck down Simon de Benville who was still kneeling at prayer. Having, as I thought, fulfilled my destiny I was fully prepared for death. I believed that I would that very night be freed from my mortal body. When I woke still in the flesh it was in my mind to confess to Geoffrey de Vaux but the theft of the treasure threw everything into confusion. I was still praying for guidance when the Master's instructions came ordering me to investigate my own actions!

What followed was play acting – solemnly asking all those

questions! But through this foolish mummery I learned what I still had to do. John Barnet had obviously, as I half suspected, remained lurking in the chapel to guard his master. I was glad to hear that Simon de Benville had been given a premonition of his end. Barnet must have seen everything and was terrified that I might realize this. I let all my "suspects" know that the serving man had vital information. I suppose it occurred to me that one of them might silence Barnet because of something he might have discovered about the theft. In the end it was I who had to conceal myself in the woodland and waylay him on the pretext of further discussion. It was all made absurdly easy. Barnet was deliberately hanging back, with the obvious intention of running away. When I confronted him he became almost incoherent with terror. He still insisted that he had left the chapel before his master's death. By that time it mattered nothing whether or not he was telling the truth. His murder was a part of my plan, a perfect plan, the plan of a Perfect. Thus God avenged himself for the massacre of his people. He continues to punish the perfidious Templars. This very day news has arrived of the fall of Acre and their expulsion from the Holy Land. But the time of their final visitation is yet to come. May I be spared to see it.

I had almost forgotten – the Templar's gold: who stole it?

Why, the Templars themselves. This was what I learned from the Master months afterwards in the confessional. These deceitful and cowardly "poor brothers" who are wealthier than all the kings of Christendom had made a pact with Henry III. They were to help his chief henchman, Roger Leyburn, seize control of London. However, they were far too fearful of Simon de Montfort to come out in open support of the King so it was arranged that William Leyburn, Roger's son, would counterfeit the theft of the treasure and smuggle it back to London via the family estates in Kent. There it would be used to buy troops and bribe officials to declare for the royal cause. Simon de Benville was, of course, one of the few men privy to the plot. I believe it weighed on his conscience that money pledged to the Templar cause in Outremer was being thus diverted. That is probably why he spent so long in prayer during that last hour of his life. How unfathomable are the ways of God!

On Wings of Love

Carol Anne Davis

Carol Anne Davis (b. 1961) was born in Dundee, Scotland but moved to the south of England in the hope of being "globally warmed", which may explain all this freakish weather we've had in recent years. Her crime novels include the mortuary-based Shrouded, *the sociopath-exploring* Safe As Houses *and the killing-the-neighbours-from-hell* Noise Abatement. *She has also published a book about female serial killers,* Women Who Kill *(2001). Compared to all that, the following story, about a lost falcon, seems remarkably calming.*

The guilty were expected to hang when the King's best gyrfalcon went missing. His lordship had been hawking with the bird and had freed her to fetch a large duck on the wing. The prized falcon rose *highe* in the skies and set off as *swyfte* as she was wont to do, and seemingly as *mery*. King Edward waited patiently on his mount but the raptor never returned.

As the days became a week there was much excess in the humour of blood in our warrior king for he missed his gyrfalcon sorely. The huge, rare bird had been as white as the finest rose and, in keeping with its purity, had been fed on the sweetest white doves. I myself – the King's chief falconer – had raised these doves in a cote in the enclosed garden that my master had built especially for his birds.

I wasn't the only man who lived in the chamber there – the

other falconers also made much of King Edward's patronage. And each handsome bird had the most ornate of cages in the garden and an aqueduct that brought them fresh water every day.

At first we wondered if the Welsh could have magicked away the snow-white prize but in time it was decided that this was beyond their dwindling powers. We knew, though, that the gyrfalcon couldn't have gone innocently missing for it was written in law that if anyone found a bird of prey they were to hand it over to the sheriff who would seek out the owner with due haste.

And no one but a king could own a gyrfalcon anyway – so it was clear that this was Edward's very own creature. Lesser nobles had to restrict themselves to a *fawcon gentills* (peregrine falcon) whilst a cleric might risk owning a *musker* (a male sparrowhawk) though canon law forbid the clerics to hunt and hawk. A coward might invest himself of a kite that, rather than soar to pluck fresh flesh from the skies, contents itself with the dead prey of other beasts. And a lady might at best have a merlin on her arm.

The King tried to interest himself in his many other hawks but I could see that he pined in his noble way for the powerful white bird that had so often accompanied him through the fields of our beloved England. And I begged leave to hunt down the person that was responsible for this untimely loss.

But where does a man like myself start in so wretched a search? Who brings him succour? Uncertainty gave way to jubilance when my wife heard tell of a woman who had no need of purses but who could turn the wheel of fortune a certain way.

I went to her at dead of night. We spoke through stones for not everyone approves of such luminaries.

"Did someone with empty saddlebags thieve away the bird?" I whispered.

"Someone without a horse," she agreed, I thought with some reluctance.

"Can you describe his countenance?"

"No, the stars can only softly light your way." She would

not be drawn further so I had to hold on to her words about the horse, words that told me the thief was impoverished. And so my first forays were into some of the most wretched hovels in the land. My task was slow for even poor wretches tend to have a jay or a dawe in their quarters. Every tale of feathers shed and squawks emitted had to be investigated and in truth it was a loathsome task.

"Have you heard tell of the King's white gyrfalcon?" I asked again and again but the peasants just shrank back in fear, shaking their heads so forcefully that I feared they might lose them. As well they might have done had the enormous golden-beaked beast been found in their fetid abodes.

Not that a pauper would have wanted the bird simply for its own sake. No, the creature had had the bluest sapphires and the most blood red rubies in the land attached to its jessel, jewels that would keep a common man in land and food and ale for several times his own life.

I returned from the homes of the poor to find the lord king gazing sadly at the swivelling perch where his falcon had once rested. He had fixed the jewelled ring known as a terret back on the perch as if awaiting the bird's return. Her hood, resplendent in its heraldic colours, also awaited her presence, being used to calm her into sleep.

In truth there was no calming her master now. He had grown used to the loss of the creature – but not to the loss of face that its theft had caused him. Someone had kept or killed the purest bird in Christendom, knowing that it was a royal bird. Someone had to pay for so blatant a deed.

There were other men keen to track down the culprit, but none knew the bird's ways as well as I. I knew that she had been enamoured of a particular tercel so now brought him from his vast cage and took him out into the kingdom. We rode for many a day, his bells jingling as he clung to my leather clad arm and my trusty mount galloped over hill and dale.

This time I stopped every destitute poacher I espied, assuring the bedraggled men that I didn't want to take away the deer that they'd just slain or sue them in a common law court on an action of trespass. "The very elements stay agitated whilst the King's bird is hidden away," I lamented. But they were men more used to trapping fowl than to hawking with raptors so I accepted their trembling denials about knowing the bird and let them be on their way.

Again I returned to the women who knew many things. Again we spoke hushedly and rapidly.

"You said the culprit was poor."

"I said they had no horse."

"But surely . . . ?"

At that very instance her infant cried as if the Devil himself had entered its body and she had to scurry away. I pressed my lips to the stone and spoke some more but she dared not answer. Dread of ecclesiastical censure fastens many a tongue.

A culprit without a horse . . . You are doubtless thinking that I visited the clerics next, but you would be wrong. Edward himself had the ear of his best friend, the episcopal officer Robert Burnell, and very little of the religious life escaped that fine chancellor's notice. And Edward himself had at this time given generously to his monastery at Vale Royal.

No, it would not be a monk who had taken the gyrfalcon for they had all the ale and eggs and bread – with many days of pork and mutton – that a man of prayer could ask for. And though it's true that some monks were fishers not of men but of money, word soon reached our ears, like iron attracted by a magnet, as to what these particular monastic men were about.

Someone who wasn't poor, who didn't poach, who wasn't a monk. Someone who didn't have a horse . . . Noble men usually owned fine mounts of course, but some of these nobles had been ruinously injured whilst hunting or were so melancholic that they could not ride a strong steed. They, then, were next for my inspectorate for truth to tell they cheated and lied and stole and lacked the capabilities and piety that my king, the beloved Edward Longshanks, had.

And so many weeks of entering sculpted doors and majestic arches became my way of life, for the nobility loves its vast ornate houses. And often I entered a palatial residence, only for a knowing squawk to give my tumult pause. But it was always a popinjay brought from foreign shores at great cost to please a lady, yet so beautiful that its ownership was beyond price.

Some of these men even offered me their popinjays to gift the King, usually at their wives' protestations. But I explained that Edward only wanted his own white raptor back – or the punishment of he who had stolen it away.

My task unfulfilled, again I returned to the mystic, my heart wounded to bitterness. "Is anyone in the wrong?"

"Sire, only in a way."

"Someone who doesn't have a horse yet is not a poor man or a poacher or an injured nobleman?"

"Someone who is poor yet rich in many ways."

"You seem to hint at the spiritual life but no one has heard tell of a monk or cleric behaving this unseemly."

"It is not a monk you seek, sire," the woman said through stones.

My search, so nobly and royally begun, seemed at an end as I made my way back to the raptors' garden.

"If *you* cannot tempt the bird back," I said to the gyrfalcon's favourite tercel, "then perhaps no one can." He came gladly to my gloved hand and his bells tinkled beautifully with his every movement. The sound made me think of the sacred music of the nuns. Most of these nuns came from families of wealth and breeding, homes of the finest silks and rarest diamonds. Would that ongoing longing for luxury make one grab the jessel of a gyrfalcon as she feasted on her ground-brought prey?

This time I had to make my inquiries especially discreet for no one wants to anger an abbess or her sisters. I spoke to those who understood the religious life of the women, who knew their ways.

It transpired that the Archbishop of Canterbury himself had at one stage ordered a Benedictine abbess to stop keeping dogs in her monastic chamber. Truth, it turned out that the nuns went to church with squirrels on their shoulders and little hounds and monkeys playing in the folds of their skirts.

As they had vowed to live in houses of strict order, these pet creatures were frivolous and not in keeping with the religious life.

More tellingly, it wasn't in keeping with the need to keep the food bills frugal as so much went on the diets of these monkeys and hounds that the women themselves ran out of food.

And so there was a ban and though some rebellious girl might keep a rabbit in her cell, no one had heard tell of a white gyrfalcon. And how would a nun tempt such a bird to stay in her modest chamber when the raptor was used to the finest royal cage and whitest dovemeat in the land?

"Is the gyrfalcon in a nun's monastery?" I asked my source.

"No, sire."

"Where, then?" It may be wrong to tax the Muse but I was worn out with talking after dark in whispered riddles.

"Within our good country yet further away than many men have ever been."

Further than many men have ever been. I understood she must be talking of the nation's hermits for truth to tell they were foot-wearyingly hard to find. But no man can hide completely from another so I stopped weary travellers on my journey and they pointed out various hermit's abodes. Some lived in caves, closer than I'd ever dare live to the restless dark waters. Others had taken to tall trees so I called through the branches, knowing that if the gyrfalcon was there she would answer me or credit the tercel attached to my arm. And many lesser birds did reply to me but none had her special distinctive call.

These reclusive men had their spiritual strengths, but had no sweet white doves or gilded cage to offer. Who could take so magnificent a raptor and make her disappear from God's sweet earth?

It was as I rode across the furthest reaches of England's earth that I found my answer. For the tercel started to strain sideways in a particularly urgent manner so I bade my horse to plunge through the foliage to create a path. And in time we went through forests that hadn't seen a hoofprint for many a season and we crossed rivers that were undrunk by human lips.

Finally we came to a lawn sweet with ox-eye daisies, primroses, iris and marigold. And the scent embraced me and my mount so sweetly that I wanted to stay there in that clearing for the rest of time. But there was a small stone accommodation before me demanding my attention so I dismounted and walked towards the entrance that had no door.

And then I heard a sound that was a thousand times sweeter than the flowers that assailed my senses, a sound that made my spirits lift towards the very skies. It was a sound of such purity, of such joy, that I could scarcely believe it was a human voice.

I stayed transfixed as a hare before the stoat for an eternity before peering into the shadows to see the source of this perfection. The song came from a slender young woman sitting on the earthen floor. Her eyes were closed and it seemed that her mind was far away as she sang her sweet psalms – but the white gyrfalcon's eyes were open and it was staring straight at me.

Its jessel had been removed and it wasn't tethered in any other way to the rock that it sat on. I already had the tercel on one arm so offered the other to the huge white bird that had so often been my companion. But after glancing at me it returned its strong gaze to the songstress, ignoring I who had raised it, who had tended its early sicknesses and later wounds.

All too soon the young woman's song came to an end and she opened her eyes – eyes that were as large and brown and trusting as a newborn fawn's. She bid me welcome and I accepted a pitcher of water from her as any passing traveller would. We spoke of the tallness of the trees and the richness of the monasteries but the time came when I had to broach the reason why I was there.

"That's a beautiful gyrfalcon," I said.

As if knowing that it was under scrutiny, the raptor rose from its stone and flew carefully over and perched on her slender arm. I could see that she had wrapped miniver skins around the limb to protect herself from its talons.

"Yes, I love her dearly," the girl said.

"And she appears to love you too."

In some ways I had just been forming pleasant words but even as I said them I knew they were true. There was something about the way that the huge creature looked at her that made me profoundly envious. None of us falconers, for all our offerings of doves and fresh water, had ever inspired such devotion in our hawks.

"Have you had her long?"

"Long enough to grow to love her."

"Who did you buy her from?"

"I have no money – I have chosen to live simply in retreat."

By dint of slow questioning I found out all I needed to know about her life. She had been born noble but had chosen the religious path, at first entering a nunnery. Then, in time, she had realized the goodness to be had in the simplest and most solitary of livings, in a diet of seeds and fruits rather than manmade bread. She saw how the bodily humours could regulate a person's temperature without need of fire. She heard for herself how the singing of a single voice in the darkness spoke more loudly than fifty nuns following a psalm.

"I gave up all I knew," she explained, "And walked here relying on the kindness of strangers. I brought with me a handful of seeds to start the garden of contemplation you see before you. Still I lacked . . . *something* and often asked the heavens to grant me this missing element if it was right for me. And one day this wondrous creature came down from the heavens as I was singing and she has stayed close by my side ever since."

The tercel moved restlessly on my arm as the woman told her tale and its bells tinkled compellingly and the gyrfalcon put its head to one side and closed its eyes in a fair imitation of human rapture. And I realized then that the white bird hadn't been enamoured of the tercel but of the bells that played on his feet whenever he moved. The falcon clearly loved music in a way that few higher beings love music – and she had flown for as long as a bird can fly to seek out the most breathtaking voice in Christendom.

I asked the nun if there was anything that she needed but she had sweet nuts to eat, spring water to drink and primrose leaves to ease her hurt from long hours working in her garden. And she had the gyrfalcon for company and it had the freedom of the skies to find its food.

I left then, holding her song close to my heart. I spoke not another word about the King's lost avian creature. Truly, you cannot own a bird like a raptor – it had chosen her and it was not my place to interfere with that.

I went home to tell untruths to my beloved Edward but he had by now forgotten about his favourite bird and had tournaments to regulate and taxes to raise and monasteries to run out of funds for. And he had many fortified castles to build in Wales.

I've never forgotten the young nun, the magnificent songstress. I think of her every time I hear a nightingale or a swallow plight its troth. She sang as sweetly as a skylark and her heart was as pure as the heart of a newborn child. Who stole the bird? It stole away itself to live a life of goodness and simplicity – and had I not the many burdens of a married man I would follow its example and do the exact same thing.

A Lion Rampant

Jean Davidson

In my anthology Royal Whodunnits, *Jean Davidson introduced the character of Father Gregory, a spy during the reign of Edward I. The following is a sequel to that story, set a few years later when his past catches up with him.*

You may try to escape the past, but its long chilly fingers can stretch out to touch you whenever and wherever you least expect. I'd thought myself free and clear, reborn and reinvented as Scotland was reborn with Robert the Bruce as king. I thought I was so safe in my new life and new identity I'd even started courting a Highland girl.

But who should have known better than me? You can never be safe.

And now here I was, clattering up Tower Street past All Hallows Church under armed escort. The walls of the Tower of London loomed on my left, ahead the River Thames sparkled in the early morning summer sunshine. I shuddered as we turned and crossed the first drawbridge and entered through Lion Gate. Long ago in my old life I'd been instrumental on several occasions for sending other men on this route. They'd not come out again and I could only pray that I would escape a similar fate. But first, I had to find out what I stood accused of before I could talk my way out of it.

As we walked our horses past the Barbican and towards

Middle Tower I heard a terrible growling behind us. Even my guards, tough men that they were, looked alarmed and our horses jittered uneasily. Then came the shout of one man, followed by howling, then more shouting and finally a horrible cacophony of wild animal cries.

"The King's Beasts are restless. Has old Osric forgotten to feed them or is he no longer Keeper?" I remarked to the least taciturn of my own keepers. I'd hardly been able to get a word out of either of them about the weather, let alone anything more interesting, on the week's journey south from Scotland, which meant they'd been the right men for the job, unlikely through compassion or bribery to allow me to escape and make their own lives forfeit.

He muttered something indecipherable in his native Welsh and I shrugged. At least I wouldn't have to face him and his companion over breakfast any more.

"Ho – what have we here!" a voice challenged as we entered Middle Tower. I was in luck. Alfred, Sergeant at Arms, was hurrying towards us followed by several of his men. A short wiry man, his face knocked about and scarred, his men feared and respected him. "As I live and breathe – Gregory Deschamps. That is, if you're Gregory today and not wearing some other guise." He gave a sly grin as he referred to my former life as spy for John Droxford, head of the King's Wardrobe and ultimately, the old King, Edward I. But these were new times, with a new King, and I thought I called no man master any longer.

"No counterfeit but the real Gregory," I told him. "You recognize me after all these years."

"Not that many and anyway, once seen never forgotten. Are you here on business or pleasure?"

"Possibly the King's pleasure. The new Lieutenant of the Tower wants to see me, and then I'll know."

"Ah – in that case come with me. I'm on my way to him now – you two take the horses and report in."

I had no time to stretch my stiffened limbs. Alfred hurried me down a stone staircase and I realized we were heading for the menagerie, back the way we'd come, to the Lion Gate, but through an underground passageway. "What's happening, Alfred? Has one of the animals escaped?"

"I'm no wiser than you are." He clapped me on the shoulder. "Come and drink some ale with me later. We'll talk then."

The stench of the caged animals hit me as we approached the circle of cages set in a stone wall under individual arches around an exercise area open to the sky. Gutters on either side carried away their excrement into the Thames. There were lions, leopards, bears and other strange wild creatures not seen in England, all sent as gestures of admiration and pride from foreign rulers to the English kings and queens. The roar and snarl of a lion greeted us as we rounded a corner and saw two men examining something lying on the ground.

They moved aside to reveal their secret. It was the body of another man, but who he was I could not tell. His face had been bitten away and his body badly mauled – at a guess by the very lion who was venting his anger at being thwarted of his meal. I recognized one of the men as Osric, the gnarled, bandy-legged Keeper of the King's Animals. The other, a slender man of medium height with straight black hair, wore expensive clothes and had to be the Lieutenant of the Tower, de Lisle, the man who had ordered me to be brought here.

"Who is this?" he asked, regarding me from hooded eyes and fastidiously holding up his long sleeves edged with fur to keep them from dangling in either the drainage gulley or blood from the dead body.

"Gregory Deschamps," I informed him. "You sent for me."

He snorted. "Hardly. I had you arrested, and at just the right time. This man – do you recognize him?" he nodded at the body on the ground.

"No. Do you?"

"You should do. This is – or was, until a few scant minutes ago – William de Kellseye. It was you who gathered enough evidence against him five years ago to have him condemned to the Tower for life. When I became Lieutenant six months ago he approached me and told me that you had falsified evidence against him and that he was now in a position to prove it. It was not easy, but I had you tracked down and 'sent for' as you so delicately put it."

I made a noncommital noise. I had been under armed escort and outside the Tower when de Kellseye had met his death and had indeed forgotten his existence. But I had learned long ago that innocence and ignorance were no protection in this brutal world of ours. I would have to wait and watch and listen, and pray I would survive.

"And now, at the very moment of your arrival, here he is, dead. Convenient wouldn't you say?"

"I can hardly be accountable for a man foolish enough to wander too close to an uncaged lion," I pointed out reasonably. "And what was the animal doing out of its cage – or did he open the cage himself and climb in there with it? Even old Osric here thinks twice before doing that."

"The animals don't get fed until mid morning – now, in fact. Everyone knows that. This lion is a gentle beast."

De Lisle ignored him. "Either someone forgot to close the lion in, and Osric assures me he checked all the cages personally last night *and* first thing this morning, or the cage door was deliberately opened. You could easily have bribed someone to do that."

I sought another line of attack. "Is there a guard on these cages night and day? No. And lords and ladies are not always above," I pointed up to a rampart, where curious onlookers had indeed gathered now, looking down on us, "to see what is going on. Anyone could have been down here, and sheltered from view under these arches before making good his escape. And what was de Kellseye doing down here anyway? I think –"

"Don't think to sharpen your wits against me, Master Spy, because you've met your match." His smile was tight-lipped. "See here," he pointed to what was left of the chest on the mangled body. "Look closely – a knife or sword thrust killed him and the lion released to cover the misdeed. Only Osric came by and the animal didn't have time to finish his meal."

"I heard him growling. 'Twasn't the right sort of growl. I knew as something was up," Osric contributed.

I crouched down to examine de Kellseye's torn clothing then, with permission, lifted it and examined the narrow chest sprinkled with grey hairs underneath. One thrust right to the heart. Probably a short sword, as used for close combat, judging by the size and type of wound, and from the front too. His attacker was a friend then, or so he thought, to allow him so close. De Lisle was right, he'd been slaughtered in cold blood and then the big male lion, who was kept in a separate cage from his lionesses, released to hide the deed.

"Give me one good reason," de Lisle said, enjoying this moment to the full, "why I should not have you arrested, tried and executed – preferably hung, drawn and quartered – before the week is out."

"I've never come across de Lisle before, except by hearsay, and that wasn't much, but he's definitely got a grudge against me. I wonder why." I stretched my feet a little closer to Alfred's warm fire. These quarters in the Tower were often chilly in the evening when the mist rose up from the river, as it did even in the height of summer, and summers now were not hot like they used to be.

"You won't like to hear this, but he's the first honest Lieutenant I've served under. Couldn't handle himself in a fight, but he can run this place and keep the men happy and prisoners in order. Not to mention the King himself. He wants to make his mark, prove himself." He poured us some more ale. We were alone in his private quarters for, after I had stolen a kiss and a squeeze of her ample body, his wife Matilda had tactfully withdrawn to her sewing to give us time alone together.

"Shame young King Edward doesn't visit the Tower much. I'd like to have seen the man he's grown into. He was never anything like his father, but a few years in power may have changed him?"

"He's up in the fens. Likes to go there for rowing and those rural pursuits he's so fond of. Thatching, I ask you! But he's a brave man, good swordsman. You'd always find him in the thick of the battle. Bad choice in friends, though."

"Mmm. Talking of his friends, what of his other pursuits?"

"Ah. So news did reach you amongst those heathen savages north of the border. What on earth possessed you to stay up there, squatting in the heather and thistles when you could've been in London –"

"King Edward's other pleasures?" I reminded him.

He gave a short dry laugh, almost like a cough, which was the most that ever escaped him. "He has a pretty French queen for a wife, though I hear she's strong-willed. Piers Gaveston," he made a face, "is safely out of the way in Ireland ordering the savages there about, instead of lording it over everyone here. He's the King's 'good friend'," he glanced over his shoulder as if checking we weren't being overheard, "and I don't know how much further it goes than that, but he's anyone else's friend."

"I don't suppose the Irish want him lording over them much either, but he's doing a good job I hear."

"Where's all this leading, Greg? What's it to do with your dead man?" He shook his head. "I don't like it when one of our prisoners dies on us like this. Looks bad – like I've fallen down on the job."

"Hardly my dead man – I take no responsibility for him. As for the King – let's say I have my reasons. He may be brave but he doesn't know how to unite the country behind him. There's plenty want him off the throne already and not just because of his taste in bed partners, rumoured or not."

"I think you're wasting your time there, and wasting your time drinking ale here. You've got one night to come up with a story to prove your innocence, and it had better be a good one. De Lisle is no fool."

"I can see that." I drained my beaker and set it down on the hearth. "What I want to know is, why was de Kellseye down by the animal pens? You know everything that goes on in here. Was he an animal lover?"

"Hah," he gave his short coughing laugh again. "He was a forgotten man, wasn't he? Model prisoner, wife visits him every Saturday, prayers every day in the chapel. Didn't mix with the wrong sort, no conspiracies. Wasn't even mixed up in the crown jewels' robbery. So now he wanders about just as he wants and no one pays him any attention."

"A forgotten man – yes, I'd certainly forgotten him. Yet he remembered me." I frowned. "Why was he so keen to blacken *my* name? I was completely unimportant in this game. An expendable underling."

"Revenge?" Alfred suggested. "Not that he looked to me like he was brooding. Seemed to have accepted his fate."

"Nothing fits together – yet. But it will. If only I had more time – just a few hours to clear my name and ensure I make it back to Scotland and the bonnie lass waiting for me there."

"Bonnie lass!" Alfred spat into the fire. "Some thick-headed peasant girl when you could be warming the silken sheets of a fine lady or writing poems of courtly love to your true heart. That King Robert as he calls himself has turned your brains to porridge."

I grinned. "I doubt any fine lady would let me air her sheets, let alone lie in them with her. I have no riches and no standing these days, and that's just how I like it," I said lightly, to cover the clutch at my heart that always came at the thought of a certain lady fate had decreed could never be mine, despite the love we had for each other. "Now, will you trust me out of your sight? I know the curfew bell has rung and the gates are locked but there is someone in the City I want to talk to."

He snorted. "Trust? I gave that up long ago. And you're more slippery than any eel I can snatch out of the Thames. But you know if you don't return to my custody you'll have an unhappy and very *short* life. And it won't be the botched job that someone made of de Kellseye's end."

As I walked down the Inner Ward past the White Tower towards the royal apartments the first pale stars were beginning to appear though the sky still held the blush of the setting sun. The prisoners had been locked in for the night when the curfew bell had been rung, and those men who were not on duty had either returned to their families, or were gathered together to drink and play dice into the night.

Alfred was right. William de Kellseye's death bore all the hallmarks of a botched job. My suspicion was that he'd been silenced, but had the murder been deliberately botched in order the easier to implicate me, the person who appeared to have the biggest reason to kill him. As I'd said to de Lisle, "Yes, I could have somehow heard of his accusations, I could have planned his death. But if I had, I would have made a far better job of it. I'd've made it look like an accident, or that someone else was to blame. I wouldn't point the finger at myself."

De Lisle regarded me carefully. "I believe you," he said at last, "I heard you were a clever man. Now prove it to me. You have one day before I turn you over to the Sheriff of London for examination. He's on his way here now with the Coroner who is going to examine the body."

I'd been given into Alfred's safekeeping, but it was only now, after all the due administrative processes were over, that I was free.

My first target was de Kellseye's prison, and I'd persuaded Alfred to part with the key. He'd told me that Mistress de Kellseye, the widow, had been too distraught to attend today. I hoped the room would be untouched and just as he had left it – as long as none of Alfred's men had sneaked in and plundered it first.

The room was small, but comfortable, and on the first floor with a slit window with open views to the south across orchards and vineyards. It was well furnished with two colourful tapestries on the walls, a bed made up with linen, blankets and furs, a table and several chairs. Using the light of a candle I walked around slowly, looking not only for anything out of the ordinary but also to develop a portrait of the man and his life in the Tower. He may have been a model prisoner, but something had happened. Something had changed and given him the hope that he could overturn his conviction. Had he kept the evidence here?

Nothing seemed to have been disturbed. I went to the cold fireplace and sifted through the ashes, but they gave nothing away but dark embers of wood. Systematically I searched his bed, behind the tapestries, and in every crevice, saving his coffer until last. I recognized the type – once it had been my job to know as many types of lock and key and ways of preserving secrets as any good locksmith could devise. After going through his few – but good quality – clothes I reached down inside and found the lever I was looking for. A slender drawer slid out from underneath the chest. Here were his quill, ink and parchment, as well as his personal seal, wax and candles. There were a few coins too.

I sat down and turned the seal in my hands, recalling how and why I'd hunted this man down. Surely there must be some event, some clue, in what took place then to have led to this moment when, from beyond life, de Kellseye had reversed our roles and put me in greater jeopardy than he had ever been.

It was about money. What else? The old King, the cold-hearted monster Edward I who'd nevertheless ruled with an iron grip, could not give up his dream of conquering Scotland. He could not bear to have his will thwarted. But the war was a costly one. The Crown borrowed a huge amount of money, and the Jews of the City of London had proved exemplary financiers. But then came a new source of revenue, the Frescobaldis, bankers from Florence in Italy. Not only did this give Edward the chance to reform the currency to make things easier for himself, but the Frescobaldi family was distantly related to Piers Gaveston's family through Gascon connections. There was a link. So Edward accused the Jews of clipping coins in order to reduce their power over him.

However, not everyone liked the Florentines' influence.

William had been a middle man. He carried messages and brokered loans and deals. But Edward discovered he was being short-changed somewhere along the way. Was it the Jewry, to tarnish their new rivals' name? Or were the Frescobaldis not to be trusted after all? I was told to infiltrate this financial world and find out, without disrupting the flow of cash into the Crown's Treasury, who was defrauding whom.

It was delicate work but eventually I narrowed in on de Kellseye as the point at which the money went missing. I held the evidence in my hands right now. His private seal on his signet ring. I'd intercepted, by devious means, one letter which was carefully worded but, when taken in context with other transactions, confirmed his secret negotiations. And he'd sealed it with this seal. Easy to prove as it had a small crack on one side which showed up in the wax.

At the time he had not protested. I'd sat at his trial and been surprised at his demeanour. He neither accepted nor denied the charges, but took his sentence without a murmur. He'd been rewarded with this fine room and freedom to have his family in and to roam the Tower as he wished.

But what was the ring doing here? I jumped up and, candle in hand, began to search the room even more minutely. He would surely not leave without it. Take it off at night, perhaps, while he slept, but I remember he always wore the ring – hence he could not claim that someone else had used it on the incriminating letter.

And then I found something. Brushing aside the rushes on the floor near the bed I saw dark stains. They looked like splashes of blood. I looked more closely at the rushes, straining my eyes, and was certain I could see stains on them too. Recent drops of blood then.

He could have been killed right here and his body carried to the menageries. It would have to be done quickly, for the blood still to be flowing. How? Rolled inside some linens or sacking perhaps. Easy enough for two strong people to do. This knocked aside my first theory, that he'd received an invitation to meet someone – someone known to him – and was killed there. I hadn't noticed that stiff morbidity in him you get in bodies some time after they have died – most noticeable when visiting a battlefield the day after to gather up the dead – but perhaps the lion's mauling had done away with that. The blood pointed to two very brazen men who had walked quite openly through the Tower grounds. I would have to ask Alfred to question everyone whether they had noticed any such thing. But act with confidence and often you are not noticed.

Who would have gone to such elaborate lengths? Why not simply kill him and leave the body to be found in his room?

And why had de Kellseye only now decided to protest his innocence? Although he'd allowed us to believe he'd acted alone perhaps he'd had a partner in crime who now, afraid of exposure, had killed him? That could have been his new evidence – to blame an accomplice. Or maybe the accomplice was double-crossing him after all this time. Someone associated with the Frescobaldi bank? I could guess that his timing had been due to the appointment of the new Lieutenant of the Tower. A new broom who wanted to sweep clean and make his mark. That dangerous thing – a zealously righteous man.

I liked the direction of these thoughts because they led directly away from me. I too had been a forgotten man and had made it clear I wanted to stay that way.

The only puzzle I could not even begin to figure out was why de Kellseye had refused to produce his new "proof" until I was present?

The animals of the King's Menagerie were quiet now, but their scent was just as noisome. Old Osric was not in the tiny cubby hole he called home, so I went down to the cages. He was talking to a big brown bear that sat contentedly licking at honey on a twig he'd given it. He'd always given his bears a treat because he said they were the ones that hated cages the most.

He did not look pleased to see me. After I'd tried to ask after his health and close the gap of the past five years and he'd answered in monosyllables, preferring to look at his bear rather than me, I asked, "What news of the lion? Will he be punished for attacking de Kellseye?"

Suddenly animated, Osric now looked me in the eye. "Oh no. He were only doing what comes natural to such a kingly beast. I told the Lieutenant straight, this was dead meat to him. He thought it was his feeding time. Right?"

"Was this lion especially greedy? Would the murderer have chosen this lion, for example, instead of one of the others, or a leopard – a bear even?"

Osric looked at me oddly and sucked on his yellow-grey moustache. "I always feeds them a few hours after sun up, you know that. 'Course he was hungry, but no more than any of the other beasts here."

"So whoever it was did know your routine and that the animals would be restless and hungry at that time, expecting their food. But they didn't necessarily know the individual animals. Is that what you're saying?"

He looked away again. "If you say so."

"And you and your helpers didn't see anyone at all – not even de Kellseye himself. You see, I'm wondering how he – or they – could have approached the pens unseen. Even perhaps, two men carrying a dead body –"

I had his attention again. His eyes gleamed with interest. "Brought him in you say? You say you think he weren't stabbed here in front of Hannibal's – the lion's cage?"

"That's right. The next problem is – how did they manage to stop the lion chasing them once they'd opened his door and also escape without passing you on the way?"

"First question's easy. Smell of fresh blood. Lions can smell scents from miles away. Much better noses than us. 'Sides, they're lazy. Why chase after something when a meal is all ready in front of you? Specially males, they eats what the female hunts for, or so I've been told."

"That makes sense. Are you sure you and your lads saw and heard nothing?"

"We was getting the food ready so they could 'ave gone past us easy. And it weren't none of us that killed him, neither."

Obstinately he clung to this version of events, but when I left I had at least extracted a promise that he would talk to his assistants again.

I made my way to the postern gate now. Alfred had promised that he would give orders to allow me out – and back again. I knew he did not trust me fully. But then it's only those who have never been betrayed who can trust completely. Both Alfred and I had seen so much in our lives that it was a wonder either of us had an ounce of trust left.

London's streets were still busy and noisy even at twilight. The inns were as full as ever and in dark corners bawdy women offered their services. I breathed in the strong odours of humanity mingled with overflowing sewers and the River Fleet and held more than a hint of the many industries that brought the City much of its wealth, like tanning and brick-making. This was my home town, and the excitement was still there, of human lives pitched one against another jostling for money, fame, attention. But it was no longer the home of my soul, I realised.

I moved to a quieter area of darkened homes and knocked on a door. After a moment, a peep-hole was swung aside and fearful eyes looked at at me. Then the door was hastily unbarred and swung open and I was clasped in a hug.

"Elias," I said, "You recognized me."

"One doesn't forget a friend. Come in, come in. Rachel will get us something to drink – see what a beauty she has grown into."

"Your father is telling the truth," I greeted his youngest daughter, who kept house for her father since her mother had died, her brothers and sisters all being married. Rachel smiled shyly, poured us some rich ruby wine and placed nuts and fruit at our elbow then sat quietly to one side working on copying a manuscript while we talked. Elias believed that woman had a brain as quick as a man's, and she joined in as we caught up with each others' lives. Finally it was Elias who said, "Is it true? I heard that William de Kellseye is dead – and on the same day, here you are."

"I know, but the link doesn't extend as far as his death." I told him everything that had happened, including my own half constructed theories.

He scratched his beard, thinking. "So de Kellseye had an accomplice after all. One of the Frescobaldi family, or one of their men, perhaps."

"Who else could it be? I know that when the King accused you and your community of defacing his coinage and clipping it to make money for yourselves that must have been the only thing on your mind but think back. Does any name spring up that was associated with de Kellseye? He always seemed to me at the time to be nothing more than a clerk, and perhaps I was right. Or was he being doubly clever in hiding his true nature?"

"Beware of looking only at the outside of the container. It's what the vessel contains, what is hidden within, that carries the true spirit." He touched his head and his heart, while Rachel nodded in agreement. "I remember that time only too well – I could have been in the Tower, if it hadn't been for you – the irony is, the way things are now we might have been safer in there. Now we're afraid to go out in the streets, and must continually hide our true selves and our true worship. Many of us have been attacked."

"Life has been hard for you. But you have had champions – Judge de Bray for one, and there will be others."

"True. You must never doubt, Gregory, that de Kellseye *was* guilty. You found the proof. The seal was his and he never denied it. It is possible that he's been shielding someone else all this time. But more likely he's been shielding the money. I never believed his story that he'd spent it all on good living, fine wines and garments, dowries for his children. There was far more missing than that."

"He didn't spend it on his apartment in the Tower. It was comfortable but plain. He didn't have expensive habits but lived a simple life, with his wife visiting him every week."

"Perhaps he was murdered by his accomplice because he would not reveal to them where he'd hidden the money. Or perhaps you're right, he was killed to silence his tongue. Even a cracked bell can be heard. Rest assured, my friend, I will talk to everyone and send a message immediately if one name is spoken too often."

Our farewells were emotional ones and not to be our last, I hoped, as I returned through the dark streets. I kept my head down and moved fast wishing Alfred had allowed me to keep my dagger. I could hold my own face to face in fair combat, but against two or more from behind I would be vulnerable. Several times I looked over my shoulder, sure I could sense a shadow slipping silently behind me, but I reached Tower Street without incident and without being accosted. At that moment I relaxed and looked up at the bulk of the walls, and consequently never heard the soft footfall behind me. I only felt the violent pain at the back of my head followed by a sickly falling into black unconsciousness.

When I came to my head was throbbing and my body felt bruised all over, as if I'd been thrown down a flight of steps. I was lying on a thin mattress of straw on a hard stone bench. I was in one of the darkest, dampest cells in the Tower. The sort people are put in when they've seriously displeased someone. I tried to sit up and promptly felt so sick I lay down again. My groan was loud enough to bring someone to the door. It was John, my taciturn companion on the journey from Scotland.

"You're awake then," he said, passing me a jug of water through the bars.

"What happened? Why am I in here?"

"I'll fetch Alfred."

Alfred brought stew and bread and thin red wine. He settled himself on the stone bench opposite and regarded me with relish. "Nasty crack that was," he said. "Surgeon looked at it. Said you'd live."

"Maybe there's someone'll be pleased to hear that," I said through a mouthful of meat and vegetables. "So what happened?"

He shrugged. "John was on duty and expecting you back. Kept looking out for you, saw you lying there with someone stopping over you so he raised the hue but they made it away over the river. He carried you in. Who, what or why I'm none the wiser. You?"

I thought of the shadow I'd sense behind me, but if there had been someone there they would have been plainly visible or audible out on Tower Street. It had to be someone either lying in wait for my return, or a robber after my purse. If the latter, he'd've been sorely disappointed. "No, nor me. Are you sure you didn't ask John to give me a going over?"

"You're slipping," he grinned, shaking his head. "In the old days you'd've been waiting for their move and slipped a knife in their ribs first. Told you all that fresh air was bad for you."

"I didn't do much knife slipping, as well you know. Alfred – I can't do much from in here, and I haven't learned anything yet that's going to save me from the gibbet. I thought I had a whole day's grace."

"Said it was for your own safety. De Lisle, I mean."

I groaned. "Try and get me out again."

He gathered up the empty bowls but left me the jug of wine. "I'll try," he said, but he didn't look as if he'd succeed.

There was nothing for it but to try and work out what I was going to say to the jury of my peers the Sheriff and Coroner were no doubt assembling right now for a hearing later today. They'd be so resentful of this interruption to their lives they'd no doubt recommend me as guilty within minutes just so's they could get home in time for their supper.

There was only one answer to the whirling in my mind, the pain in my head, the misery of my surroundings: I slept. My last sight as I closed my eyes was of dull grey stones and a thread of light at the window. My first sight on being roughly reawoken by John was of an extremely beautiful woman, her expression ravaged with grief but wearing the most sumptuous of clothes, her mantel worked in gold thread and lined with the softest fur, the fillet on her head of purest damascene and held in place with twists of gold.

I staggered to my feet feeling distinctly dirty, tousled and disadvantaged.

"Mistress," I said, attempting my best courtly bow despite the nausea I suffered, "I'm sorry, I have no seat to offer you."

"I prefer to stand for what I have to say to you," she said, her voice harsh with distress. John was lingering in the background gaping at her till I scowled. He went, leaving the door open.

"My husband told me everything," she said. "You are the evil man who caused his downfall and made us live this unhappy life and now, not content with that, you – you have killed him careless of what will happen to his family."

"Mistress de Kellseye, please don't distress yourself so, sit down and drink this." I gently pushed her in the direction of my mattress and poured some of the wine Alfred had left. She buried her face in her hands and I could hear her ragged breathing as she struggled to contain her emotions. She was much younger than I had expected and breathtakingly beautiful. Had it been her idea or her husband's to keep out of sight until now? She certainly hadn't attended his trial. I'd've remembered.

"I had no hand whatsoever in your husband's death," I

began, but this only inflamed her. She glared at me with tear-filled eyes.

"You hounded us unmercifully. He never had a chance and now, now when he was old and – and a broken man, you destroyed our final days of happiness."

"He was a broken man?"

"What do you expect after years of living in this terrible place?" she accused me. "And now I will be destitute and without my dear husband." Her breath caught and she stopped and took a sip of wine.

"He always told you he was innocent," I said slowly, my eyes never leaving that lovely face. "If you believed him why did you never speak up for him? And what was this new proof he had, did he tell you that?"

"I obeyed my husband in all things and in turn he shielded me," she countered, her voice rising in distress. "And I have no intention of helping you. I hope they stick your head on a spike where I can spit at it until it rots –"

"It's not me you'll be helping but yourself. If your husband's honour is restored then so will his worldly goods and estate be restored to his family, something that would surely ease your widowhood." I wanted to keep her talking, anything rather than contemplate the thought of my head on a spike for crows to peck at and humans to scorn.

She took a deep breath and composed herself, though she still regarded me suspiciously. She drank some more wine and I waited, holding myself still to stop the pain in my head flaring up again.

"This is what he told me," she said eventually, "That is he now believed he had nothing to fear except for God his Maker," she made the sign of the cross, "That it was time to put our affairs in order and he *would* speak out. 'I held my peace before,' he told me – those were his exact words – 'but I will take care of you now'."

"That was it? Nothing else? And he didn't give you anything – no object however small – for safekeeping against my arrival?" I demanded in frustration.

She shook her head. "He told me that was all I needed to know."

After she had gone I went over to the tiny slit of a window and gazed up at the thin sliver of bright blue summer sky, letting my mind roam over everything I'd heard. He had nothing to fear. Did that mean that his accomplice had had some sort of hold over him but was dead now and he could speak out? No, not if it was the accomplice who'd murdered him. Then was there a rival, who sought revenge for being double-crossed or who feared betrayal at this late hour?

But I was sure he was guilty. He had betrayed the King's trust and defrauded him time after time. I had to continue to believe in myself and my own judgment.

It was when I'd stopped thinking about de Kellseye's death and started dreaming of Scotland and whether I would ever see it again, that it came to me. A faint echo of Elias's words set off an answering resonance in my mind: what lies within, what is contained within . . .

Immediately I rushed to the door and yelled for Alfred. After much arguing and then waiting on permission from de Lisle, I was allowed to examine de Kellseye's body.

The surgeon had already looked at it but as the cause of death was quite apparent he had not cut or manipulated the body in any way. Touching dead flesh was not my favourite pastime, but it had to be done or I would be next on this table. It had a strange waxy feel to it, and I could not get used to the whitish-blue pallor. Nor am I a surgeon and I had no clear idea of what I was looking for but I felt his whole body very carefully, inch by uncomfortable inch. I even lifted the cloth that covered his mangled head and looked at what remained of his skull. But my patient search yielded results even more obvious than I'd been hoping for. I covered him up, offered up a brief prayer for his soul and then left the mortuary. I had two people to talk to, then was ready to face de Lisle.

I asked for a private interview. He agreed to meet me in the guard-room with Alfred and his own private clerk in attendance to take a faithful record. De Lisle sat behind a carved oak table. His clothes were of the finest materials but austere in cut and decoration. I stood facing him and he regarded me coolly and steadily.

"What have you learned?" he asked.

"I have learned that William de Kellseye was not murdered."

He immediately started to rise. "What utter nonsense is this –"

"Hear me out. After all, my life depends on this. Now, no one saw anyone enter the menagerie and particularly, no one was seen to leave. Osric could hear the lion growling and snarling and went to him immediately. I was entering the Tower at the time. I saw no one running away. This is what I believe happened."

De Lisle slowly sat down again, the clerk's pen was poised over his parchment, Alfred looked hopeful.

"De Kellseye knew he was very ill and was dying. His window gave me the clue. He told her he longer had anything to fear but God. He wanted to protect his beautiful wife and have his estate restored to her in her widowhood. His plan was to pretend he was going to establish his innocence and make it look as if he were murdered to keep him silent. He started laying the foundations of his plan some months ago, and I believe he bought himself time by saying I had to be found. He still had to choose his method. At first, when I found drops of recent blood in his room I thought he'd been murdered there and taken to the menagerie to cover up the deed as an accident. But there was a complete lack of evidence. What did I know about the man himself, both from the past and the present? He was a thinker, a planner. He made himself as inconspicuous as possible – a model prisoner. At night, of course, he was locked in his room. Nor could he plan an escape from the Tower because that might endanger his wife and family. Otherwise he moved about freely. He would know the routine at the menagerie, and when Osric and his assistants would be busy and he could slip in unnoticed.

"When I examined the body I found he had a huge and prominent tumour in his abdomen." I had been lucky there. His illness could have been far more hidden. "I suggest the surgeon opens up his body, and that you question those who served him – he was probably eating very little. I also found marks on his arms from copious bleedings. The doctor confirms he attended him yesterday morning, that de Kellseye had complained of a weakness of the humours, but did not mention his stomach. Also, de Kellseye said he would dispose of the blood in the bowl. This was where the blood on the floor came from. He smeared that blood on his tunic before going to the menagerie."

I stopped. They were all gaping at me.

"Well," de Lisle prompted me. "What happened then?"

"It was a brave and wild act, but maybe the knowledge he only had a few days left in this earthly sphere gave him the necessary courage. He unbolted the lion's cage, exposed his tunic, and must have taunted the lion."

There was a choking sound. Alfred looked white. "I hope it were quick," he said. "But, the sword wound?"

"Ah," I hesitated. I'd hoped he'd forget that. "He must have stabbed himself just as he entered – perhaps threw his sword into the sewers or the river."

"Hummm." De Lisle stared down at the oak table, frowning. "I don't like it at all. The man killed himself – that is against the laws of God."

"That's why I asked for this private interview. He did it for the sake of his wife and family. He sacrificed his own honour for them. Proclaim it an accident – he was faint from bleeding and his illness and didn't know what he was doing. The lion was provoked and only followed his natural instinct for blood. Meet Mistress de Kellseye. Talk to her and then make your decision."

I now had to wait. Would de Lisle investigate further or would he, in a manner of speaking, throw me to the lions?

Was it my imagination or did the air smell sweeter once I had crossed the moat and passed through Lion Gate and was on the outside again, alone this time and a free man? Even the lump on my head did not feel so tender. I knew exactly where I was headed. There were old friends to visit, old ties to inspect, before I headed north again . . . yes, of course I was going north again. Wasn't I?

I wanted to run, just in case de Lisle changed his mind, but

I forced myself to walk. The tumour had indeed been a big one and further questioning confirmed my suspicions. The surgeon said de Kellseye would indeed probably have lived only a few more days. De Lisle and the surgeon and those others of us who were asked to speak told the Coroner and jury that it was an accident. The widow and family were safe, though I sensed de Lisle would be keeping an eye on her just in case the missing money mysteriously resurfaced.

As I walked I recalled the last conversation I'd had before leaving the Tower.

"That was quite a blow you gave me the other night," I told Osric. "You must have been worried I'd find out what really happened and give you away."

"Don't know what you're talking about," he said, but his eyes betrayed the truth.

"I know it was you who put the sword in. You arrived first and alone and saw in an instant what de Kellseye had done and that he was dead. You feared that Hannibal would be destroyed for attacking a live man and so you drew your sword and stabbed him – to save your lion's life by making it look like murder. You chased Hannibal into his cage some- how – that lion must really love you – and tossed the sword into the bear's cage, under the straw, retrieving it later when I saw you."

Osric sucked on his moustache and all he would say was, "I've heard that once they gets a taste for human flesh they wants it again. But he's a gentle beast that one. I thinks his taste'll be enough to put him off for life."

Osric always had preferred animals to humankind, and who's to say he's wrong?

The Amorous Armourer

Michael Jecks

For over six years, Michael Jecks (b. 1960) has been producing the popular series of West Country novels featuring former Templar and Keeper of the King's Peace, Sir Baldwin Furnshill, and his colleague, Simon Puttock, bailiff of Lydford castle. The series began with The Last Templar *(1995) and continued with* The Merchant's Partner *(1995),* A Moorland Hanging *(1996),* The Crediton Killings *(1997),* The Abbot's Gibbet *(1998),* The Leper's Return *(1998),* Squire Throwleigh's Heir *(1999),* Belladonna at Belstone *(1999),* The Traitor of St Giles *(2000) and* The Boy Bishop's Glovemaker *(2000). The following is a brand-new Sir Baldwin story.*

When he crouched at the body's side and studied the small, insignificant-looking wound, Sir Baldwin Furnshill, Keeper of the King's Peace for Crediton in the county of Devonshire, was struck by the melancholy atmosphere of the place.

Often a murder scene felt cold and sad, as if the departing soul had removed all warmth as it fled, but here, in the small hall down an alley off Crediton's high street, there was a sense of poignant gloom that Baldwin had not experienced before and he looked about him for a moment, wondering where the feeling came from. Certainly it was cold. The fire had been out overnight and there was a damp chill in the air, as though the house had been deserted for months. Apart from that there was little to differentiate the room from many another prosperous artisan's property, except for its comparative emptiness.

Usually there would be tapestries, cushions and flowers and occasional scatterings of fresh herbs among the rushes to disguise the more distasteful odours where a dog or hog had soiled the floor. Walls would have paintings on them or tapestries to keep the cold at bay, tables and cupboards would have good linen spread over them, chairs would have cushions – but not here.

Baldwin was honest enough to admit to himself that the decoration was remarkably similar to his own before his marriage. It was unremittingly masculine: there was no indication that it had ever enjoyed the influence of a woman's hand, as if the dead man wanted nothing that might remind him of feminine comforts.

The table tops were plain, scraped wood; stools and benches bare, the fireplace was a rough circle of fire baked clay on the earthen floor delineated by moorstone rocks. The sole evidence of luxury lay in the man's upper chamber. He had so valued his sleep that he had constructed a bedchamber reached by ladder.

"You recognize him, Sir Baldwin?"

Baldwin nodded as he reached inside the shirt to study the stab wound more closely. There was a rough oval mark about in, and Baldwin considered it thoughtfully before answering. "Yes, Tanner. Humphrey the armourer."

"He came here little more than a year ago," Tanner said, his gaze moving about the room. "Poor bastard."

Baldwin grunted agreement. "No wife?"

"He came here when she died. Some disease or other she got in Exeter." His tone showed that he was unsurprised by people dying in such a terrible place. Tanner was a heavy man with a square, calm face weather-beaten to a leathery toughness. He always asserted that there were many more vicious and evil creatures in cities like Exeter than in the wilds of Dartmoor.

"And he left behind all his memories," Baldwin murmured, looking about him once more. It was as if Humphrey had intentionally eradicated all trace of her. Baldwin thought it sad. If his own wife were to die, he would want to remember her.

"Some men try to forget dead women," Tanner suggested. "Makes it easier to snare another wife."

"You think he was a womanizer?"

"Not really. There were rumours he liked the whores, though."

Baldwin noted the gossip. Any clues could help find the killer. "Was he robbed?"

"There's a chest up in his bedchamber. His purse is empty."

Baldwin grunted to himself, then made his way laboriously up the ladder. He had never liked heights, but today the corpse distracted him enough for him to be able to get into the small bedroom before realising how far from the ground he was.

The chamber was large enough for a thick palliasse and chest, which he opened. Inside were clothes and some plate. A thief would have stolen them. There was one other thing Baldwin noticed. By the side of the palliasse was a cloth, a square of fabric with careful embroidery all about the edge. "A pretty kerchief, Tanner," he said, letting it fall to the constable.

Back on solid ground, Baldwin took the kerchief back and smelled it. There was a faint odour of perfume about it. "Whose was this?"

"I've never seen it before," Tanner said.

"No? It is a decorative little scrap, though. And out of place in a bachelor's hall. Keep it by, Tanner. We may need it."

"*He* won't, will he?" The Constable observed, stuffing it into his belt.

"No, Humphrey is beyond caring. Shame he wasn't wearing some of his armour when this happened," Baldwin said. Blood had flowed thinly from the dead man's wound, but there were one or two smudges, as if someone had stood in the gore. Perhaps it was the killer? he mused. No matter. The prints were too indistinct to be able to tell anything from them. "The door was open?"

"No, Sir Baldwin. Locked. We had to come in through the window."

Baldwin looked up at the unglazed window. It was high in the western wall to catch the dying sun without allowing a thief to clamber in with ease, and now he looked he could see that the timber mullions had been broken. "You got in there?"

"Yes. But when I got here, there was no key in the door."

"Where was it?"

"On a ring of keys on his belt. Here."

Tanner passed him the heavy keyring and Baldwin stood weighing it in his hands. "You suggest somebody was in here, stabbed the armourer, left, and the armourer then obligingly rose and locked the door after him? Not with that wound."

"No," Tanner agreed. "He couldn't have got to the door and locked it. He must have died almost immediately."

"So someone else locked the door. From outside, or from in here?"

"There's no other way in or out that I've found."

"Good! So they left by the door," Baldwin said. "And that means that they must have had a key of their own. Who would have been friendly with this man?"

"That I don't know, Sir Baldwin."

"Neither do I, so let us speak to the neighbours."

They were all waiting outside under the suspicious gaze of a watchman who held his wooden staff like a man keen to show his expertise. No one would dare to run away.

Not that there was much point, Baldwin reminded himself. There was nowhere to run to for people whose business and livelihood was tied up with Crediton. However all the neighbours must be kept until they had been *attached*, made to pay a surety that guaranteed that they would attend the Justice's court when he next appeared. All of them would be fined anyway, because any man who lived near a murder was taxed for the infringement of the King's Peace, which was why the men shuffled resentfully.

"You have sent for the Coroner?" Baldwin asked Tanner quietly.

"Yes. The messenger left at the same time as the man sent to fetch you."

"Good. So we need not keep these folk too long, hopefully." Baldwin said. "Although the dull-witted fool may take his time."

"He usually does," Tanner growled.

Both knew the Coroner. Sir Roger de Gidleigh had been a useful ally in Baldwin's previous investigations, but he had been thrown from his horse earlier in the summer and was confined to his bed, a shrunken, twisted reminder of his previous hale and powerful self. In his place Sir Gilbert of Axminster had been installed.

Compared with Sir Roger, Sir Gilbert was a weakly and insipid youth. Sir Gilbert had never taken part in a battle, nor had he earned his rank from proving his honour. No, he had become a knight under the ridiculous rules by which any man who owned an estate worth more than £40 each year could be compelled to take up knighthood; it led to cretins like Sir Gilbert wearing the golden spurs, Baldwin thought contemptuously. Feeble-minded doddypolls who were scarcely capable of lacing their enamelled sword-belts. And once knighted, Sir Gilbert's puerile sense of humour and effeminate manner had led to his advancement to Coroner. With a King like Edward II, who preferred favourites like Piers Gaveston and Hugh Despenser to his own wife, it was no surprise that men like Sir Gilbert found senior posts.

It hurt Baldwin particularly because he had been a "Poor Fellow Soldier of Christ and the Temple of Solomon", a Knight Templar, who had risked his life in the hell-hole of Acre in 1291 as that great city fell to the Saracen hordes. The Templars had been honourable, devoted monks who had taken the threefold oaths of poverty, chastity and obedience, and yet they had been slaughtered for personal gain. The French King had covetted their wealth, so he unleashed a storm of impossible accusations against them, having them arrested and then burned at the stake like heretics, all because he wanted their money.

That was the prick that drove Baldwin to investigate crimes: he had been the victim of persecution; he had suffered from the lies of politicians; he knew how difficult it was to deny the claims of bigots. All made him determined to protect others who suffered from injustice.

The memory of his dead friends brought a scowl of disgust to his face; the memory of his comrades' foul deaths made him wear an expression of glowering bitterness, which lent his dark features a ferocious air, a fact which was brought home to him when he caught the eye of a young girl, who recoiled as though from a blow.

Abruptly he turned and glanced again at the dead man's hall, trying to drive away the memory of burning Templars.

"Looks new still, doesn't it?" Tanner said, following the direction of his look. He was still unused to his Keeper's sudden mood swings, even after six years.

Baldwin grunted assent. The hall shone, showing the gleaming white of fresh limewash. The oak timbers were light-coloured, fresh and had hardly twisted or cracked yet. It would need a couple of good winters to weather them.

Alongside was the man's place of work. Before talking to the waiting neighbours, Baldwin entered it.

It was a long, low building, as new as the hall. At the far end were the huge hammers which were tripped by cams beneath, driven by the massive wheel outside in the leat. A large anvil sat in the middle of the floor, standing upon a tree's trunk, and all about were sheets of metal, tools and the detritus of the forge: broken blades, offcuts from helmets or plate armour. At one corner stood straw dummies with armour bound to them. A trestle contained two helms and various farming implements: scythes, hammers, axes, and blades for wooden shovels.

Everywhere there was the stench of the armourer: the sharp tang of metal and rust, the insidious odour of oil, the brackish, unpleasant scent of the filthy water used to quench the red-hot metal and temper it, but above all there were two smells: the sweetness of the beeswax which was rubbed over the metal while still hot to prevent rusting, and the noisome stink of animal excrement, almost human in its foul pungency.

"He has a pig?" Baldwin asked. There was no sign of it.

"Everyone has a pig," came Tanner's laconic reply.

Baldwin nodded, but walked to the corner where the smell came from. "Nothing here."

"Maybe it's out in an orchard or woods?"

"Odd time of year for that," Baldwin said. Hogs were usually left to rootle about in yards on their own, which was why they so often escaped and caused such mayhem in the roads. They were such a nuisance that if someone caught another man's pig, he could demand its execution and claim its trotters as reward.

He could learn nothing from a pig's excrement. Baldwin peered about him again. It was a remarkably clean, well ordered smithy. Blacksmiths he had known tended to work bare-chested, apart from their leather aprons, in black, sooty rooms. They were invariably wiry, lean men with hands scarred from gripping hot metal, their faces weathered and crazed with wrinkles from staring into white-hot charcoal as they tempered blades and armour. Humphrey's forge was almost clean and tidy. Only by the anvil itself were there the fine silvery flakes which showed that red-hot metal had been worked.

"Massive hammers, those," Tanner mused.

"You need them to make blades," Baldwin said, then he paused. "I wonder if it was one of his own which killed him?"

Back outside, he studied the shuffling, anxious men.

"Who lived nearest the armourer?" Baldwin called out. Although there was a general movement among the men standing before him, no one cared to volunteer information to the Keeper of the King's Peace. He was the most powerful and important of all the King's local officials, and as such inspired fear. It was a constant cause of irritation and near-despair for Baldwin. He could never understand why he should be viewed with such alarm. However today he was aware of a certain lethargic dullness growing within him. It was not his place to investigate and report on murders – that was the Coroner's duty – and Baldwin wished to be gone from here. In truth it was tempting to go and leave Sir Gilbert to his task – but if he did, he knew he could fear that the wrong man could be arrested for the murder. He had no faith in Sir Gilbert.

With a sigh, Baldwin accepted that he must inquire himself, just to make sure that the innocent could walk free.

The crowd was a curious blend of people. Two poor-looking churls, Ham from Efford and Adam Weaver, and one more affluent serf, Jaket the Baker. Ham and Jaket's women clung to their husbands with terrified eyes, while Adam's wife Edith stood proudly apart. Children mingled with the adults, plainly fretful, and a pair of dogs fought, egged on by two lads with sticks.

Baldwin could smell the fear rising from them. It was like a sour miasma that crept to his nostrils and made him feel tainted. Poor people always stood to lose when they were investigated, he reflected: the rich could afford a lawyer to lie for them.

Picking a man at random, he pointed to Ham. "You! Come here!"

Ham started, nervously smiling, a weaselly fellow with sallow complexion framing sunken dark eyes and pinched cheeks. "My Lord?"

Baldwin beckoned. Ham had been standing with his wife and two young girls. He left them reluctantly, approaching Baldwin with his eyes downcast.

"You are Ham from Efford, aren't you?" Baldwin demanded. He vaguely remembered that the man had been working with a cloth-maker some while ago.

"Yes, sir."

"You work with John in . . ."

"No. He let me go when he took on an apprentice. An apprentice is cheaper than a trained man."

Baldwin nodded, and his voice became more gentle. "Where do you live?"

"In that house," he pointed. "My family has a room at the back."

It was two doors along the alley from the armourer's place. "How well did you know Humphrey?"

"Hardly at all. He was a cocky bastard, making his bloody metal all day. You could hear the din ten miles off, I reckon."

This was declared in a wheedling tone, like a beggar whining for alms. Baldwin raised his voice. "Who else disliked him?" There was no answer and he spoke coldly to Ham. "Perhaps the dead man was not so troubling to others, Ham?"

"They thought the same," he said sulkily. "Jaket? You had enough trouble with him."

Baldwin beckoned the man. "Jaket, what can you tell me about Humphrey's death?"

"Sir Baldwin, I know nothing about his death," Jaket said. He was a large, pudding-faced man with sparse hair and a large gut. Baldwin recalled seeing him often enough in taverns and inns, always with genial beaming features. Jaket always seemed to be the first man to lead singing or to call for fresh ales, a good companion for an alehouse.

"Did either of you see Humphrey yesterday?" Baldwin asked.

Ham shook his head. "I was working all day, logging in the Dean's garden."

Baldwin nodded. He could check with the Dean of Crediton's Collegiate Church later. "What of you, Jaket?"

"I think I did see him, yes."

"Where?"

"In the alley, near his door. He was with a tall, foppish young fellow, fair haired, wearing a rich scarlet tunic. He must have been a knight, from his belt and spurs."

Baldwin was struck by the similarity between this description and Sir Gilbert. "Did you hear them talking?"

"I didn't go close to them."

Ham spoke up. "He never got on with the armourer. They've been fighting in courts for ages. Ever since Humphrey first came here."

Baldwin could recall hearing of their battles in the court. "What was the dispute?"

Jaket had reddened. "It was nothing much. He built his forge on my land, but when I told him he refused to stop building, said he had bought the land fairly and it was nothing to do with me. I couldn't fight with him, so I paid a lawyer to argue my case in the Church court. Dean Clifford chose to find in favour of Humphrey."

"And that rankled," Baldwin observed.

"No. Not much," Jaket protested.

Baldwin did not believe him. Jaket had realized that admitting to an unneighbourly dispute could make him the most obvious suspect. " 'Not much'? Does that mean that you were happy to lose your land? How much did he take?"

"Half the forge is on my land," Jaket said, throwing a fierce glare at Ham. "And he never even offered to buy it. How would you feel? Anyway, I didn't talk to them because they were arguing. Something about money."

"Who else could wish to harm Humphrey?" Baldwin asked.

It was Jaket's turn to implicate someone else to deflect attention from himself, and he jerked his chin at Edith Weaver. "Ask her."

"Edith?" Baldwin asked with surprise. "What have you to say for yourself?"

"Nothing, Sir Baldwin," she said, casting a cold glance at the watchman, who had prodded her forward with his staff.

She was a comely woman, a brunette of maybe twenty years, of middle height, with an oval face that, although it was not beautiful, had the attractions of youth and energy. Slanting eyes met Baldwin's with resolution, but also a slight anxiety. However Baldwin would not convict anyone for appearing nervous in front of a King's official.

By comparison, her husband was a pop-eyed fool of some thirty years, with the flabby flesh of the heavy drinker who scarcely bothers with solid food. He had the small eyes of a rat, but set in a pale, round face. Baldwin had never liked him, and liked him even less when he thought of Edith.

"Ask anyone here," Jaket said. "She's got a common fame for whoring. She's notorious."

"Edith?" he asked. "Have you anything to say?"

"What can a wife do when her husband has no work and spends his days in taverns?"

"Shut up, you stupid bitch," Adam snarled.

"When did you last bring money for me and your children?"

"I'm going to get work soon."

"Oh, yes? For six months you've given me nothing for food or drink, but have taken everything you could to fill your guts with ale, you drunken sot! What did you expect me to do? Watch my children starve?" she sneered.

Baldwin stared at him coldly. "Adam, I shall question you in a moment. For now, be silent!" He faced Edith. "So you do not deny your trade?"

"Why should I? Don't most wives have to turn to selling their bodies at some time or other?"

Baldwin reflected that his own wife was born to a more fortunate environment. "Did you see Humphrey yesterday?"

She was quiet a moment, as if choosing whether to lie, and Baldwin snapped his fingers to Tanner. The Constable pulled the kerchief from his belt and passed it to the knight.

Adam cried out, "Edith, your kerchief!"

Baldwin said, "This was beside his bed. It is yours?"

"Yes. It's mine," Edith said.

"Where you there last night?"

She paused again, but this time Baldwin had noticed something else. "What is that?" he asked, pointing at her foot.

On one sole of her thin sandals he had seen a mark, and there was a corresponding smudge on the inner side of her foot below her ankle. Edith gazed down at it with a kind of weary resignation.

"It is blood, is it not?" Baldwin said sternly.

She sighed and nodded. "Yes. I had to flee after I saw him die. Humphrey was here in the yard yesterday morning, and he asked me to visit him last night. I knew Adam would be in the tavern till late, so he wouldn't care, and Humphrey always paid me well, so I agreed."

"When were you to go to him?"

"At dusk. But when I arrived, he was in the forge talking to the man Jaket described. I walked into the hall and drank some of his wine. When I heard him leaving the forge and talking outside, I went up the ladder to his chamber and began to doff my clothes. He was talking angrily, I think. I wasn't sure if he would still want me, but I was desperate for the money, so I prepared. My kerchief and skirts were already off when I heard him come in, and a gust blew out the candles. I could see nothing in the dark. I took off my other garments thinking he would join me. Then I heard it."

She lifted her eyes to meet Baldwin's serious gaze. "It was like the thud of a clod of soil thrown at a man's back. I heard Humphrey curse, then cough, and I heard him say, 'You have killed me!' and there was a tumbling noise, then a rough, rattling sound as of a man with too much phlegm in his throat. I remained silent up in my chamber, not daring to move, until I heard the door slam. I donned my clothing as quickly as I could, and rushed down the ladder to him, but I was too late."

"He was dead?"

"Yes. There was nothing I could do. And I feared that if I called the Constable, I would be suspected. What else could I do? I ran."

"The door was locked," Baldwin said.

"I locked it."

"Where did you get the key?"

"He had a spare key in the forge, hanging with his tools. Everyone knew about it. I went there to fetch it, locked the house, and put the key back in the forge. I was scared – but I'm no murderer."

Which explained why the forge was open, Baldwin thought. "Did you see whom it was that entered the hall with Humphrey and stabbed him?"

"No. I swear it."

Jaket interrupted eagerly, "Surely it was the tall knight I saw with Humphrey earlier."

"Perhaps," Baldwin said. "But there is no proof of that."

"Proof of what, Sir Baldwin? My Heavens, have you decided to hold the inquest without me? Eh? Won't do, Sir Baldwin. No, it won't."

Sir Gilbert, Baldwin sourly told himself, could scarcely have picked a better time to arrive.

Baldwin sent Tanner to fetch bread, wine and some roasted meats, then joined Sir Gilbert in the hall. They sat at Humphrey's table and while they waited for their meal to arrive Baldwin summarised the evidence he had heard so far.

Sir Gilbert appeared unconcerned by Humphrey's death. "He wasn't a terribly good metalsmith."

"But you chose to buy from him."

"I didn't know how poor his work was. Not that it matters. I have an almost complete suit of armour and have paid nothing."

"Why not?" Baldwin asked in surprise.

"I was here to collect it yesterday, but the helm didn't fit snugly. It was shoddy, quite shoddy, so I told him to fix it before I would pay him. He wasn't happy, of course, but then who ever is? Serfs nowadays are so surly. They hardly ever show the manners they were born with." He yawned, adding petulantly, "Where's that damned fool with the food?"

"He will not be long," Baldwin said. "What time did you leave Humphrey yesterday?"

Sir Gilbert had curious eyes that remained half-lidded, as though he was in a perpetual state of confused lethargy. It was one of the reasons why Sir Baldwin disliked him, but now he also found himself distrusting the knight as well.

"Are you suggesting that I could have had any part in his death, Sir Baldwin?"

"I said no such thing. I merely inquired when you left Crediton yesterday."

"I should take it very ill should you accuse me of murder, Sir Baldwin."

Baldwin leaned back and stared unblinkingly at Sir Gilbert, his left hand on the table top, his right near his belt where he could reach his small riding sword. "If I were to accuse you, I would be happy to allow you trial by combat, Sir Gilbert."

Sir Gilbert chuckled. "I think you would find the combat

rather short, and I would find it not to my liking," he said frankly.

Tanner entered with a pair of cooks and soon Baldwin and the Coroner were tucking into their food. As they ate, Baldwin admired the small dagger which Sir Gilbert used to cut his food.

"This knife? I bought it from the armourer," Sir Gilbert said when Baldwin asked.

When they were finished Baldwin asked, "What time did you leave? After all, your servants can confirm when you left."

That was no threat. Any knight could guarantee his own servants would perjure themselves to support their master.

Sir Gilbert sipped wine from his mazer and then steepled his fingers under his nose. "I see no reason not to answer you. I left almost immediately after seeing my armour. It was quite late."

"You had angry words with him outside the forge?"

Sir Gilbert's eyes widened marginally. "Who told you of that?"

"A witness."

"Let us say, he was not happy that he would have to wait for payment."

"Not happy enough to come to blows?"

"You overstep your mark, Sir Baldwin," Sir Gilbert grated.

"I would hear an answer."

"And I would not answer impertinence," he snapped. "Now, if you have no objection, Sir Baldwin, I wish to conduct my official inquiry."

Baldwin stood behind the Coroner as the town's jury shuffled in. Every man from the age of twelve was brought in and stood nervously at the wall, their eyes reflecting their consciousness of the seriousness of the matter. A cleric from the Church had already taken up his post at Sir Gilbert's side, reed in hand, to record the inquest. That was the Coroner's first duty, after all, to record all the facts about a murder so that the justices could try the murderer later.

Adam, Ham and Jaket were led in, Edith at their rear. The four were taken to a point between the jury and Sir Gilbert, who sat on a low seat and studied them.

"Sir Baldwin de Furnshill has informed me of your evidence," he began. "First, jury, you must agree how this man died."

He walked to the body and stripped it with Tanner's help. "See? One stab in the chest, by a blade probably an inch broad at the hilt. It reaches in," he added, shoving a finger into the hole, "oh, not more than four inches. I think it's fair to say he died almost instantly: it went straight to his heart."

Rolling the body over and over, he showed that the corpse had no other wounds.

Tanner glanced at Baldwin. "Sir, there are no cuts on his hands."

"No," Sir Gilbert said sharply, drawing Tanner's attention back to him. "So we can assume this murderous attack happened swiftly, before he could think of protecting himself. He didn't have time to grab the blade and push it away."

He turned from the body and returned to his seat. "The question is, who among you could have so hated this man that you killed him? My first thought is you, Adam."

"Me?" The squeal was like that of a pig, Baldwin thought, and with that thought, he wondered again about the excrement in the forge.

"Yes, *you*! You knew that your wife was whoring about the place, didn't you? You knew that Humphrey was enjoying her, didn't you?"

"No, I didn't!"

"You didn't know your wife was selling her body?"

"Well . . . I knew that, yes . . ."

"So you took revenge on him."

Adam shivered slightly. "I'd have beaten *her* if I'd guessed she was lying with a neighbour, yes, but not him."

"You expect me to believe that?"

"We needed the money," Adam said simply.

"You mean," Sir Gilbert's voice reflected his disbelief, "you mean you'd happily allow her to whore her way around the town so long as she didn't sleep with a near neighbour?"

"It'd be hard to look a neighbour in the face, if she had," Adam said apologetically. "I'll thrash her for that later."

Baldwin had to control a chuckle. Sir Gilbert was being confronted with a different set of rules and principles of honour. To have one's wife lie with other men was all right, but not if her clients were close neighbours! But then the thought of the pig returned to him and he watched the men with interest.

"Jaket, you must have detested this man because of your litigation against him."

"Oh, you expect that kind of problem," Jaket said off-handedly. "It's not as if it was a huge dispute."

"It went to court? You had to pay lawyers?"

Jaket licked his dry lips and tried to wear a smile. "The money a lawyer charges cannot be laid at Humphrey's door. I knew how much they could cost before I started the case."

"And he won the matter, keeping the forge on your land."

Jaket shrugged. "It happens."

Sir Gilbert pressed him. "Weren't you angry? Didn't you complain about the noise?"

"I don't deny that. Almost everyone in the alley complained about it. They shook the foundations of all our places, those hammers, and the smoke! You should have seen this alley on a windless day. Smoke and fumes all over. You couldn't hardly breathe."

"Sir Gilbert, may I ask a question?" Baldwin inquired.

He was rewarded with an expression of annoyance, but then the knight gave him a dismissive wave of the hand, as if Sir Gilbert was indulging him. "Please do," he said.

"Thank you. Jaket, do you have a pig?"

"Yes. It's out in the orchard."

"Did Humphrey keep a pig?"

"No, he didn't have space for one."

"And yet his forge has sheltered one. Whose would that have been?"

"Ham's. His hog went wandering a couple of days ago and Humphrey managed to catch it."

"Ham? Is this true? Baldwin asked.

"Um. Yes." Ham had his fingers intertwined, and he twisted them as he tried to meet Baldwin's eyes.

"Did he demand the trotters?"

Ham suddenly flinched as though someone had struck him. "It wasn't fair! The pig is all we have left! Since I lost my work, I've had nothing, but what I could afford, I've shoved into the pig to fatten him, so that come winter there'd be enough for us to eat, and then Humphrey, God rot his balls, comes and tells me he's taken my hog and stuck it in his forge, and unless I agree to have it killed and give him the trotters, he'll keep it. I couldn't let him do that."

"So instead, you went to him, stabbed him, and rescued your pig," Sir Gilbert said sneeringly. "How much fairer and more just."

"No, I didn't! I went to his house to try to argue with him as darkness was falling, but the door was locked and he wouldn't answer it no matter how hard I banged on it. And then I heard my pig, and I thought, well, if he's not here, I could get my pig back. But I didn't even have to break down the door because it was open already. I fetched my pig and took him home."

"You expect us to believe this?" Sir Gilbert demanded. "Pathetic! It's the most unbelievable tale I have heard in many years!"

"I swear it is true, Sir."

"You had the motive and you had the means," Sir Gilbert said gleefully, pointing at Ham's belt. "Your knife!"

Baldwin walked to him and held out his hand. "Give me your knife."

Ham reluctantly pulled it from its sheath and passed it to him, and Baldwin studied it. "No blood," he said, and then held it up for all to see. "And the blade is a good nine inches long."

"So?" Sir Gilbert asked.

"So it was not used to kill Humphrey. There is one additional thing about the deadly stab wound," Baldwin said, walking to the corpse and pointing. "About it there is a ring like a bruise. I think that it means the killer stabbed with main force, driving the blade in sharply as far as he could. The hilt struck Humphrey's flesh and marked it in this manner."

"And what does that tell us?" Sir Gilbert asked suavely.

"That the handle struck him, which means that a long blade like this would probably have gone right through him," Baldwin explained.

"It might not," Sir Gilbert said. "It could have struck his shoulder bone and thus not penetrated his back."

"If that were the case, the hilt would not have struck his chest," Baldwin pointed out. "No, Humphrey was killed with a shorter blade."

"Who had a shorter blade?"

"Sir Gilbert, you have a shorter blade, don't you?" Baldwin said mildly, pointing to the blade on his belt.

Sir Gilbert was suddenly very still. "You accuse me?"

"I do not accuse any man," Baldwin said pointedly. "I only wish to get to the truth. I would like to call another witness. Do you object?"

"I . . ." Sir Gilbert was white-faced with rage, but seeing the interested attention of the whole jury and the reed poised over the paper in the clerk's hand, he swallowed his ire with difficulty. "Call whomever you wish," he rasped finally.

"Let us hear your servant," Baldwin continued, and when the man had been brought in, Baldwin made him stand before the jury, his back to his master.

"I want to ask you about last night," he said.

"Sir."

"Were you with your master?"

"Yes, sir."

"From dusk?"

"Well, all afternoon, sir."

"So you were with him here when he came to see Humphrey?"

"I was holding his horse for him at the entrance to the alley."

"I see. When your master appeared, how was he?"

"He was angry, sir."

"Because the armour was no good?"

"Not only that . . ."

"Why, then?"

The servant tried to turn to look at his master, but Baldwin brought his fist down on the man's shoulder. "*Answer!*"

"Because he'd made an offer for the man's woman, so Humphrey grew wrathful with my master."

Baldwin looked at Sir Gilbert. He appeared almost to have fallen asleep. "Your master offered Humphrey money for his woman?"

"Yes, but Humphrey said he wouldn't accept all the gold in the Pope's palace at Avignon for her."

"Did your master have blood on his tunic?"

"He was wearing his scarlet tunic, Sir Baldwin."

"The perfect clothing for murder," Baldwin observed.

"I killed no one," Sir Gilbert snapped.

"Then who killed Humphrey?" Baldwin asked.

"The girl said that the candles were out. I left before full dark. If I'd been there, she would have seen me," Sir Gilbert protested.

"Did Ham collect his pig after Humphrey's death? The house was locked." Baldwin mused. "Was it full dark then, Ham?"

"No, it was as the light was fading. It was dull, but not dark yet."

Baldwin glanced up at the west-facing window, puzzled. "How long was your master gone?"

Sir Gilbert's man considered. "Not long. I could hear them. Then Sir Gilbert came hurrying. He jumped on his horse and spurred away and I had to hurry to mount my pony and ride off to catch up. As I left Crediton, all I could see was the fading sun catching his harness in the distance."

"So it was not full dark, even then?" Baldwin asked.

"No, sir."

Baldwin faced Sir Gilbert. "And you had not paid the armourer, you told me?"

"I refused to pay him until my helm was ready. What would you have done?"

Baldwin ignored his question, instead turning to face the four suspects again. "This murder was committed by someone who was well known by Humphrey. That was how the killer got so close to him."

"A thief might have waylaid him," Sir Gilbert said.

"Behind what would the thief have hidden? Humphrey was killed in the open, in the middle of his floor. No, he was with someone he knew. He didn't expect to be murdered. He thought he was safe."

Baldwin stood still, contemplatively staring up at the window.

"The trouble is, so many of his neighbours disliked him. But they could have killed him at any time. They had no reason to kill him last night. Only one person could have wished to kill him last night, and only one could have got close enough."

"Do you accuse me?" Sir Gilbert said, his voice low and dangerous.

"Sir Gilbert, please calm yourself. I know you are only recently dubbed knight, but it is not chivalrous to lose your temper," Sir Baldwin said scathingly, and as Sir Gilbert swelled as though about to explode he continued, "No, it was the Coroner's argument with the armourer which points us to the murderer. The Coroner wanted to offer money for the woman he had seen going to warm Humphrey's bed, and that enraged Humphrey."

"He didn't attack me, if that's what you're leading to," Sir Gilbert snapped.

"No. He went inside and spoke to his whore, an attractive young woman for whom he felt a very warm affection. Him, a man whose wife had died some while before, a lonely man, living almost in a barn. Look at this place, you can see, you can *feel* his loneliness! What more natural than that he should want a woman to share this with him? And what could be more natural than that he should want the woman who so regularly comforted him to share his life?"

"I couldn't do that, sir," Edith said modestly. "I am already married."

"We all know of women who can and do leave their husbands," Baldwin said gently. "And a man in love may even think of disposing of a rival. Did he suggest that to you?"

"Me, sir? Why should he do that?"

"Because he loved you, Edith. And he probably thought you loved him too, which was why he didn't think you would mind when he told you he could not pay you."

"Of course he could pay me," she said, but her face had paled.

"No. He had nothing in his purse. There was plate in his chest, which a robber would have taken, but he had no money. Perhaps he was relying upon Sir Gilbert's cash to pay you."

"No! I couldn't have hurt him!"

"You say it was dark, but all others were here at dusk. Ham was here after the murder, if your story is true and you locked the door before going. Before that Jaket saw Sir Gilbert here. Sir Gilbert left without entering the hall. But you were here."

"He threatened me, sir, what could I do?" she said, throwing caution to the winds and falling to her knees at his feet. "He wanted me to leave Adam and live with him, wanted me without paying. I couldn't do that! I was bound to Adam by my vows. I had to draw my knife in defence!"

"He thought you loved him. He thought you would willingly agree to sleep with him for free. And you stabbed him to death."

"He was killed because I didn't pay for his armour?" Sir Gilbert said, shocked.

"Edith needed the cash. He made his use of her, but then failed to reimburse her. In a rage, she lashed out with her little dagger."

Sir Gilbert glanced down at her belt and saw her delicate knife. "Which is too short to penetrate both sides of his body."

"But was long enough to puncture his heart," Baldwin agreed.

Sir Gilbert motioned to the clerk at his side. "Record that the woman Edith has confessed her guilt."

Edith stood up and allowed herself to be gripped by Tanner. Baldwin took her dagger and studied it. "Blood," he said, tossing it to Sir Gilbert.

*   *   *

"I do not understand how you decided that it was her and not one of the other people," Sir Gilbert said, pouring wine.

Having completed the public aspects of the inquiry, now the two sat at the table, having supervised the removal of the body, while the clerk took an inventory of the dead man's belongings.

"It did not make sense to me," Baldwin explained. "Why should any of his neighbours suddenly kill him? Surely there must be a striking event which gave someone cause to murder him yesterday."

"The pig?"

"I thought of that, but Humphrey had taken his pig. You can be sure that Humphrey would not let Ham get close. If Ham had been there, Humphrey would have had defensive wounds on his hands and arms, as he would if it was Jaket or Adam. He would be on guard. As he would have been with you. Especially since you refused to pay him. No, that did not seem credible. But the thought led me to think that of all people, a man is at his most defenceless with women. The argument with you about his woman left him furious, and perhaps he was more determined than ever to rescue her from the degrading life of a whore."

"And she turned upon him."

"How else would a whore react? He tried to persuade her of his love as soon as you left – when Ham came it was still dusk, and Humphrey was already dead, so he had had no time to bed her. But she assumed he was trying to avoid paying her. In a rage, she stabbed. Maybe she only meant to hurt him, to show that she was not so foolish as to be taken in."

"Why did she leave her kerchief there?"

"Now you test me," Baldwin said. "It was by the bed, so I think she agreed to let him keep it as a momento some time ago. Perhaps she thought it would be a good way to keep her client bound to her. He would have something to remember her by even when she was not with him."

"Why did she lock the door and go through that charade of leaving the forge open?"

"Panic. Her first instinct was to bolt, but then she thought that anyone could come in, and too many knew she had been there. Better if she leave the body hidden for a while."

"But left the key in the forge where anyone could get it."

"That was clever. If anyone could get it, anyone could have killed him."

"She is plainly a dangerous woman."

"Yes." Baldwin said, his gaze travelling about the room once more. His voice dropped and he spoke as if to himself. "But only to sad, lonely men who thought her body could be taken as a gift when it was merely a commodity she traded for money. That is the sadness. That Humphrey truly loved her. Did you see how similar her knife was to yours?"

"They could have been twins."

"They are. She told me that he gave it to her. It was a gift."

He glanced at the window once more, and shivered.

"Can you imagine how he felt? A lonely man, missing his first wife, who at last declared his love for another woman only to be stabbed with the very token he had given her. It's no wonder he didn't protect himself. He probably didn't want to."

Benefit of Clergy

Keith Taylor

*One of my favourite characters in history is Sir John
Mandeville, who lived in the mid fourteenth century and
who may or may not have experienced all or some of the
adventures he relates in his book of* Travels. *The Mandeville family were well known during the Middle Ages, and
no doubt Sir John Mandeville (if this was his real name)
was descended from Geoffrey de Mandeville, constable of
the Tower of London during the reign of King Stephen and
first Earl of Essex. The Baron Munchhausen of his day,
Mandeville was a great yarn-spinner and an ideal character to become a crime-solver, in his own inimitable way.*

*Keith Taylor (b. 1946) is an Australian writer with an
interest in history and myth. He is perhaps best known for
his series of historical fantasy novels set at the time of the
downfall of the Roman Empire in Britain which began
with* Bard *(1981).*

Anne had seen bizarre things since she took to the roads
of England in a boy's disguise. Parades of bleeding
flagellants, knightly bandits riding to plunder, a golden hart
in a forest, that changed (she was game to swear) to a man at
the moment of dawn – Anne had beheld it all on the high-
ways and byways. Still, the two pilgrims she met on the
Bristol road made her blink.

"If this doesn't look very dire I'm a lurden, Squire
Mandeville," she said. "See you these fellows behind us?"

Her mentor turned his large russet head. "Mai foi! This does look evil, Martin."

Even in private, he always maintained her role as Martin Chinnock, herald. Always, he behaved to her as to a boy, and called her "lad" or "Martin". She was well accustomed to playing the part by now. Half of her revelled in the freedom and safety it gave, while half hated the constant pretence of being something she was not.

"Here, fellow," Mandeville called out sternly, "we're an honest company on lawful business. Shoulder that great axe and walk easily if you'd pass among us."

The man so addressed gave back an unfriendly stare. Rangy, with great lean muscles and fleas hopping on his wolfskin jacket, he carried a long-hafted woodcutter's axe, and trod (at times literally) on the heels of a man nearly as large as himself. This person, though, was better fed, with the general look of one who had known comfort and ease.

He clearly had none in his soul now. He clutched a wooden cross in both hands and often glanced back, pop-eyed with terror. Whenever he did, the second man would glare and snarl, his hands closing more fiercely on the axe. A pure craving to kill blazed in his bloodshot eyes.

"My business is honest and lawful too," he answered roughly. "Don't meddle in it, my smooth clerk, or you may wish you hadn't."

"Lawful!" croaked the man with the cross. "Lawful! Over in Bedfordshire this man is known as a highway-thief! Cut him down, I beg, or call those who can!"

"Stay fast!" the axe-man roared. "I'm Bartholomew Ainslie, an honest woodcutter! This gallows-meat here is the thief and slayer, for which he's been tried and found guilty — over in Bedfordshire, as he says. In his whole tale those are the only true words."

Ainslie had marred the truth himself in calling Mandeville smooth, unless he meant smooth by comparison, for Ainslie rather resembled a walking bramble. The herald's russet beard might be short, neatly barbered, and grow on a fresh-skinned rubicund face, but it was respectably thick and virile. His dubious frown as he looked from one stranger to the other showed that he had yet to be filled with confidence in either.

Pitching her voice to its now-accustomed male depth, Anne asked the obvious. "Convicted of such crimes, why isn't he dangling high?"

"Benefit of clergy!" the man with the cross nearly screamed. "I'm chaplain to the noble Sir Oliver Ketters! The bishop's court alone had power to hear my case, and he has commanded that I walk to Bristol –"

"Aye!" Ainslie interrupted. "Walk to Bristol holding that cross, and there take ship on a far pilgrimage. Then he's absolved of his crimes. My nephew's murder among 'em!" With a dreadful grin, he whirled the axe in his labour-toughened hands. "Carelessly drop that rood, though, you dog, or leave the road by one yard, and you're outlawed. Then are you mine! By Saint Swithin, I will split you like a log on the chopping block."

The entire party of travellers had gathered to listen by now. Chapmen, a cloth-merchant, a half-dozen shipwrights on their way to Bristol, a fur-trimmed prioress, and the rest, all heard with interest. Their sympathies seemed to lie with Ainslie. The chaplain, the dullest among them had noted, made no denial of being a highway-thief, or of having murdered Ainslie's nephew.

Ainslie, glaring around at them, asked if they had had their complete fill of staring.

"Peace, fellow," Mandeville said. "A chaplain? Can you show written proof of your office?"

"I have it here! The Bishop himself appointed me and sealed my warrant!"

"May I see it?"

Ainslie snorted. "What are you, then? Some sleek lawyer who robs with a quill instead of cudgel or knife?"

"I'm a herald," Mandeville said equably. "A good one. I was at Crécy, and then a year at Calais. Except for the Black Death, I would not be adrift on the roads bearing with your foul lack of courtesy."

Maybe impressed, and maybe somewhat influenced by Mandeville's cutting words to Ainslie, the chaplain passed over a rolled parchment. Mandeville scanned it, and his eyebrows rose.

"It's the Bishop's name and seal right enough. It confirms all you say, master chaplain. If indeed you are Leonard of Dunstable."

"That's my name," the chaplain said. "Restore me the Bishop's writing, for nothing else restrains this man's hand, and let me travel with you for protection of numbers, I beg."

"What, afraid of bandits, you bloody dog?" snarled his nemesis. "Be afraid of *me*."

"It appears," lisped the Prioress, "that if we accept you, master chaplain, we take this rough fellow besides, and that is asking much."

"I'm Leonard the Chaplain's shadow to the ends of the earth," Ainslie said implacably, "or until he forfeits Church and law's protection, and I may do justice."

"We have all heard you," Mandeville said dryly. "In the meantime, how if you surrender the axe? In exchange we will halter the chaplain so that he cannot take to his heels."

"Why should I do so?" the chaplain countered with a derisive grin. Anne did not care for it. "The Bishop's court spared me hanging at the price of a pilgrimage. As a true son of the Church, I bow to its rule."

Ainslie laughed harshly. "He doesn't wish to leave England. He'd defy his sentence and become outlaw, without me behind him! And well he might! If God gives justice, he'd fall overboard and drown before clearing the Severn, or be eaten by dog-headed men in Spain. Yet I'd liefer save God the trouble."

"No, not in Spain," Mandeville amended. "The Cynocephales, I can tell you, do not dwell in Spain, but much further, in the island called Nacumera, among the Isles of Ind. They fight well, and if they take any man in battle, in due course they do eat him. But your way will not take you there. Unless the Bishop has commanded that you travel beyond Cathay."

"He has not," answered Leonard the Chaplain. Hardened rascal though he appeared to be, he had listened to Mandeville with a child's fascination. "How do you know all this?"

"I voyaged there with my uncle as a boy," the herald answered casually. "Now then, Master Ainslie, you have not answered me."

"I keep the axe."

"Not while you travel with us, and there are six lusty shipwrights and a clothier's bodyguard to support me," Mandeville told him. "The axe?"

Ainslie glowered. Then, with a shrug and short laugh, he spun his weapon into the roadside grass. Its edge bit into the soil and the long haft stood up.

"Take care of it, herald, if you like a whole skin. By Saint Paul! I apprise you all that this dog has a purse crammed with gold florins, spoil of his robberies. I make it known to all we meet in the hope that some rogue will slay him for it."

He received a malign look from the chaplain. "And in return I apprise all that whosoever will kill this man may have my gold with no need for robbing."

Ainslie laughed scornfully. Anne reckoned his contempt might be well founded. He didn't look like a man who would be killed easily.

"That's a merry pair to have joined us," she murmured to Johan later. "I cannot like either. Which one do you believe, squire?"

"I cannot say I wholly believe either. But the tale of the big rough one rings more true. The chaplain looks to be as shifty a liar as I've encountered."

"I haven't been in Bedfordshire," Anne said, "and don't know Sir Oliver Ketters, but is it right that robber lords often have their worst henchmen appointed castle chaplains? Finding it useful to have them, through benefit of clergy, exempt from hanging?"

"Right as rain. It's full often done. Indeed, you may say that being a chaplain reflects very badly on a man's character."

Anne cocked her head and stuck her thumbs in her belt like a jaunty youth. She was practised in such attitudes by now. "Aye, Johan. It's a great shame what naughty rogues there are."

Johan de Mandeville, who finding himself masterless after

the plague had survived among jugglers, minstrels and fair-ground riff-raff, and penned for coin many a false reference, writ of exemption from armed service, or certificate of freedom, had lost the knack of blushing.

"Lamentable," he agreed, "but not our concern. What we must do, Martin, my lad, is gain steady employment as heralds again. With Lord Winchlade, maybe, once we reach Marlborough. I reckon that purple and silver livery would become us."

"And steady eating more so." Anne's stomach rumbled. A wild cry interrupted them. Turning, Anne saw a wrinkled old woman hobbling across the resilient turf of the downs, lugging a covered basket and calling out with more spirit than coherence. Splashing through the roadside ditch, she favoured them with an all-embracing glare.

"Rascals! I ask for justice! Ill-doing – slaughter! *My pig!*"

"I cannot tell what your pig is to do with us, old woman," the cloth-merchant said testily.

"Some rascal in this train has killed him!"

"We'd smell roasting pork a mile if that were so. None here is breaking his fast with fresh pig. I wish we were!"

"I'faith, I agree with that," Anne said fervently.

"Did I say stole? Did I say ate? Nay, the devils stuck him and let him lie! Why, I know not. He was my only meat for the winter. See here!" The crone uncovered her basket and showed a bloody pig's head. "I cry for justice!"

"Salt him or smoke him, then. That's justice, for the meat will still be yours. D'you think we'd slay a pig and be such fools as to leave the carcass?"

"It's a cogent argument, old dame," Mandeville assured her. "Have you enemies who might do such a thing to spite you? Withal, I will give you a silver crown for that pig's head here and now, to spare you the exertion of lugging the burden back."

The woman accepted his offer gladly. A shilling would have been enough, not that Anne begrudged it. That Mandeville was generous to poor folk helped her stomach his triple-dyed rogueries. His traveller's tales of Cathay and the Isles of Ind were harmless by comparison, though to the best of Anne's knowledge he had not been further than France, and maybe a principality or two in the Low Countries.

"Dinner!" he said delightedly of the pig's head.

"Yes, and I'm glad to have it. Still I'm puzzled, for squire, why would anyone kill the old woman's pig only to leave it on the earth?"

Mandeville shrugged. "Spite, as I said. Or someone disturbed them before they were done, and they scuttled away craven. Lad, if you wonder why folk do a tithe of the idiot things they do, you will lose your wits fretting over it."

The party travelled on towards Marlborough, beside the Kennet's clear waters, with Savernake Forest to the north of them. Ainslie, black-bearded and dire, strode never more than arm's reach from Leonard the Chaplain.

At mid morning they passed a patch of green oakwood. Ainslie said abruptly, "I'm going yonder. Watch *him* well."

Anne felt astonished that he would leave the man he hated even for a call of nature. Still, he made for the oakwood with a long urgent stride that left small doubt of his need. The chaplain stared after him with sulphurous hatred.

Then he cried out. Before Ainslie quite reached the wood, two tall figures burst from cover and attacked him with cattle-killing spears. Roaring furiously, he fought back with a heavy sax-knife he pulled from his belt, but the long spears drove into his body so that blood spurted in freshets. The chaplain howled with delight.

Johan, disgusted, struck him so that he fell in the roadway. Despite his stocky form and short limbs, the herald carried useful muscle under his plumpness. Leonard lay groaning.

By the oakwood, Ainslie had gone down and nothing could be seen but his legs kicking, as his two assailants drove their spears down time and again. Mandeville seized the woodcutter's axe, then made for the oakwood with his short legs pumping. Three shipwrights and the clothier's bodyguard soon overtook, then distanced him. Anne ran with them, whirling the sling with which she had become skilful since she left home. Although she had nothing to add to the puissance of five strong men, she passed for a man herself.

To show a white feather was to risk being bullied and perhaps exposed as a girl.

The murderers fled into the oakwood. They dragged Ainslie's reddened body with them, for some reason Anne could not conceive. What use had they for his corpse?

Mandeville, a scowl of loathing on his rubicund face, knelt by the patch of gory grass and inspected it closely, even touching a splash of blood and rubbing it between his fingers. Then he lifted it to his nostrils and sniffed several times. A frown of astonishment took the place of his scowl. After thinking deeply for a moment, he tasted the blood, which rather repelled Anne. Nor did he explain why.

She knew him well enough to be sure there was a reason. She copied his actions, all but the last. Perhaps having just witnessed a brutal slaying disordered her mind, but she learned nothing. Mandeville still made no comment.

Anne sought a clue in his face. Oddly, he looked as puzzled as she felt, and a good deal less grim, almost as though his heart had grown lighter since he saw Ainslie die. Why should that be? Ainslie had not been likeable – a harsh, violent man bent on revenge – but he'd had strong cause to hate the chaplain – his nephew's murder. Leonard did not even protest his innocence. Ainslie at least observed the law and would take no more than it allowed. Dogging the chaplain's footsteps all the way from Bedfordshire, he must have had many an opportunity to brain him in secret – as he yearned to do – and yet had refrained.

"Let's see whether we can track these murderers," Mandeville said. "I've hunted often enough in noble company, and so have you, Martin."

In Yorkshire, Anne had been a baron's daughter. Like other highborn girls, her part in noble hunts had been more decorative than anything else, but her role as a young man had to be maintained. She stayed close to Mandeville and avoided treading on any tracks he might discover.

They proved to be few, and Mandeville lost them a furlong into the oakwood. The ones he saw he studied with care. Again, Anne was hoping for a comment, but Mandeville made none. She stared at three footprints he had found in a patch of leaf-mould, for they seemed to interest him more than anything else, but they told her little. Just footprints, and so vague she could not even discern what sort of shoes had made them, though the man who left them must have been legging it energetically. The stride was long and his feet had come down hard. Certes, that was only to be expected from a man fleeing the scene of a murder.

"This wood is not large," Anne said. "The men in our band of travellers would suffice to search it, and the slayers are two; not enough to give us trouble if we caught them. Meseems that would be better than going ten miles to raise the posse in Marlborough!"

"True." Mandeville rubbed his chin. "Go fetch the rest of the shipwrights, lad. That brawny mason, too. Just for mischief, ask the banker's messenger with his silk, plume and dagged mantle to lend a hand. He'll refuse, no doubt, but it'll put him to the blush, saying no."

The most thorough search they could make did not flush the murderers out of the little oakwood. Stranger yet, they found no trace of Ainslie's corpse. Anne reckoned that baffling to the highest degree.

"I can believe the murderers might escape clear," she said in dudgeon. "We have neither dogs nor archers, and the stream is not far distant. With a boat waiting, they could don't, but a man's dead carcass can't vanish. And why should they take it with them?"

"That's indeed the question," Mandeville agreed. "Why take a dead carcass with them? Plainly enough they slew him to earn Master Leonard's purse, but if I know rogues they must have come to some sort of firm arrangement with him first, for what would they do if he reneged? Bring his Nemesis back to life to plague him again?" He shook his head. "I must have a word with our holy chaplain."

His "word" was not mild.

"You precious villain, this is *your* doing!" he raged. "The devil's in it, but these two murderers were among those who heard of your promise to reward any who'd slay Ainslie!"

"What if they were?" the chaplain retorted. "I stood lawful trial and am carrying out my sentence; it was not for him to hinder. He's crow's meat now. Should I pretend to grieve? What affair is it of yours, master herald?"

"I'm a squire, from a family of coat-armour," Mandeville barked, "and not the king himself would 'master' me. Withal, to answer your question, it's my affair and that of all these good folk, because the murderers are like to track you for the dirty payment you offered. And, *Master* Leonard – *I* shall not prevent their cutting your throat if they don't receive it."

"You need not fret." Master Leonard grinned unpleasantly. "Meseems they were hard men, to dispose of Ainslie. I'll yield them my purse if they come for it. Why, they'd slay *me* else."

"Yea," Mandeville said ironically, "that would be woeful sad."

He turned away in dudgeon. Despite his own rogueries, the chaplain's depraved and utter lack of principle repelled him. He was scarcely the only one. The pretty Prioress would not look at Leonard, and even the clothier's body-guard, a rough, ill-looking fellow, kept his distance.

"It's as though those two wolf's-heads had vanished from the earth," he growled to Anne. "What do you make of it? They must desire to be paid for their murder from the chaplain's fat purse, and they must remain close to him to receive their due. In their place, what would you do, my chick?"

"In their place? I'd follow and seek a chance to talk with him privately. I'd also be wary lest he hand me over to the law. After all, I should be guilty of Ainslie's murder, and the chaplain is not – or not that any man can testify. It's a foul business, Johan."

"Oh, granted. It distresses you, Martin, doesn't it?"

"Sieur Jesu!" Anne erupted. "Bloody murder done before my eyes, and I helpless to stop it? Yes! It distresses me, rather."

"Yea, you're a sweeting," Mandeville said indulgently, making Anne fume thereby. "Yet think, as you haven't done yet, and there are aspects of that bloody murder which must strike you as curious. Ainslie was going into that wood – to relieve himself, I suppose – at the time those wolf's-heads attacked him. Why did they rush out? Wouldn't most murderers wait until he entered the trees and slay him there, rather than do the deed before witnesses, in high daylight? Apply the wits God gave you, and you will find several other things about it equal odd."

Anne knotted her brows. What Mandeville said was very true, and he had made it clear by now that the murder of Ainslie was more than it appeared. Also that he felt disappointed in her acumen.

Beaming across his ruddy, chestnut-bearded face, Mandeville added, "Let me tell you something about Master Leonard, too. It's nothing direct to do with the murder, but I ought to apprise you. His sentence was light because he has benefit of clergy, he told us, and so can be tried in ecclesiastical courts only, which cannot condemn malfeasors to death. He even displayed the bishop's warrant that appointed him a castle chaplain."

"Well?" Anne prompted.

"It's not worth a sheep's dag. No Bishop's clerk made it out. I ought to know. I penned it myself, oh, three years ago, during the plague. Told you I've been in Bedfordshire. By the Host, so I was! I was Sir Oliver Ketters's captive and clerk all that winter. Moving, eloquent ransom notes I wrote at his orders, Martin. Besides forging that chaplain's appointment for Leonard. By the way, this is not the same man, which is why I didn't know him, nor he me. We must take it the original Leonard of Dunstable is dead."

"This rascal succeeded to his place with Sir Oliver and assumed his name also?"

"It's probable."

"The Bishop's court never knew this when he came before it on charges? Hades, what a muddle! I suppose half its former members were dead in the pestilence, though. You are saying this impostor has no entitlement of any sort to benefit of clergy?"

"No. He has it. Another man's entitlement that was counterfeit anyhow. Ainslie neither knew it nor could ever have proved it, I daresay. I copied the Bishop's seal well."

"Saints, what a tangle!" Anne rounded on Mandeville

with her eyes blazing. "And where are you going to put justice?"

"What justice?" the herald asked patiently. "Benefit of clergy is a bad custom whether a man enjoys it under false pretence or not. We have agreed on that."

"The fellow murdered Ainslie's nephew and then Ainslie! Or might as well ha' done! He should have danced on air!"

"That's passion, not thinking," Mandeville complained. "How often must I say to you that you are not using your wits?"

"Johan! Your forging pen saved this rogue from the gallows! We saw a man done to death by his contriving! Will you do nothing about it?"

"Yes," Mandeville said with sudden energy. "I shall. That long woodcutter's axe of Ainslie's is ill to have around me. It shivers with bloody, vengeful intent. Bad luck only can attend the thing, and I mean to bury it in the earth at the first convenient moment. Martin, my comrade, you may help me instead of carping. Now stint your noise."

Anne gritted her teeth. However, if Johan had not explained all, he had still been explicit that there was more to this matter than met the eye. What had she not seen? The murderers had been madly rash in letting witnesses see them kill Ainslie, and witnesses, at that, who might pursue. (As they had.) But she had thought no more of it than that. Some men *were* both bloody and rash.

Why, though, had they carried away his body, and what was there about his gore on the ground that had interested Johan so? Anne cast her mind back to that hour. She tried to see the dark blood on the grass, to feel and smell it once more. Johan had found some great meaning in it, she knew, and she had studied the blood herself in an effort to discern what.

Oh.

Anne, remembering the precise look of those dark and sticky stains, splashed about, drawing flies, felt a blaze of enlightenment.

Oh!

No wonder Johan had said, more than once, that she was not using her wits.

Nothing was as it had seemed, nothing at all. Johan's avowed intention to bury Ainslie's axe included. Anne, staggered, sought to regain her presence of mind and paint her entire picture of the situation again, in other colours. A dozen questions came to mind while she did so, some concerning the two men she had seen spear Ainslie in such a savage onslaught. Would the chaplain (she might as well continue to think of him as one) see them again, after all, and would they dare come to him demanding their blood money for the slaying? Unless Master Leonard (his real name might be anything, and Anne did not care) turned from the highway, the pair would have to venture upon it to confront him. Anne did not envision their doing that until they could catch him alone. They would require to watch him very closely, though, lest he give them the slip meanwhile. They must be skulking after the band of travellers, waiting for the time they and Master Leonard would part.

"Johan, I see now what you have been hinting at," she murmured as they walked, the clothier's pack-horses clopping behind them, the clothier himself and the Lombard dandy riding ahead. "Do not tell me it is late! Just tell me what you wish to do. Anything? We reach Marlborough today, and you and I go no further. Can we leave this business as it stands?"

"Oh, saints and devils!" Mandeville said, exasperated. "I can't suppose your maiden-tender conscience still troubles you – Martin."

"No. Na'theless, if we do nothing we leave the affair unsettled."

"It's not for us to settle, lad. Even the law can do nothing to settle it. Remember, Lord Winchlade is the law in Marlborough, and I wish to find a place with him, not be a witness before his bailiff. And neither do you!" Mandeville lowered his voice. "Are you still mindful of all *you* have to hide?"

"I cannot spend the rest of my life hiding it!"

"This is scarcely the time or the place to disclose."

"No, to be sure not. Then what are we to do?"

"Bury that accursed axe and be rid of the thing. It's a nasty reminder."

Anne knew he meant to be rid of it. But not to bury it. Mandeville recovered the axe from one of the pack-horses and walked briskly to the nearby riverbank. Anne accompanied him, one hand close to the hilt of her knife. Although she had a sling, too, and could use it with practised skill, it would be of no use among the willows and alders fringing the Kennet's banks. She kept sharp watch while Mandeville began cutting a long narrow hole in the riverside earth with the axe itself. She had no wish to be surprised by the sort of men they were dealing with.

She was, however. A weed-covered head rose out of the water by a mass of twisted willow roots, and a large hand gripped her ankle. Anne's heart nearly sprang out of her mouth.

"That's no way to treat a good axe," the man growled. "Cease."

Anne cursed heatedly and pulled out her knife. "Hands off, you! I've had a bellyful of your tricks."

The man heaved her into the stream and ducked her. With water in her nose, Anne sought to slash him, not sure how harmful the man's intentions might be, and less than eager to learn. He caught her wrist and twisted her arm behind her back. Finding his footing again, he hauled her above the surface.

Mandeville met them at the bank, the axe lifted in his short but hard-muscled arms.

"Let Martin go, or I split your skull, you lurden," he barked. "I've no great quarrel with you. *Yet.* Do not make one."

The man hauled himself out of the river, streaming and dripping. Even naked, he looked formidable, with his great raw-boned limbs and scowling brows. He fumbled among the willow roots and produced a heavy quarter-staff. It would crack a head as well as the axe.

"You know then. How? And who else knows? I went to much trouble wi' this plan."

"Where are your friends?" Mandeville countered. "The pair who pretended to murder you?"

Ainslie snorted. "Yokels I met at Newbury. Paid 'em my

last coin. Likely they have blabbed the tale all over the town by now, but I'm not returning there and nor is the chaplain, so I care not. But you? You're a different matter." He glowered, looking ugly and dangerous. "I *thought* you knew. I ask again. How?"

"Sit yourself down, and I'll tell you."

Ainslie, still glaring, did so. To avoid being recognized, no doubt, he had shaved himself clean and chopped his hair to the nape, which somewhat lessened his wild appearance, though not wholly. Anne could believe he had gone to much trouble to produce his plan. He didn't seem very clever. She wondered if he was even right in the head. Still, he had fooled her. She granted that.

"The first thing was the blood," Mandeville said, like a scholar enunciating points in an argument. "When I looked closely, I saw it was dark and stale. Hours old, my friend. Ergo, it was not yours, even though I had seen it spurt out of your body! You had it in a bladder under your jerkin, eh?"

Ainslie gave a sullen nod. "Mixed it with wine so that it wouldn't clot too soon. It came from an old woman's pig."

"I remembered. She had come traipsing down the road that same morn to complain of't. She was much displeased – and yea, I smelled the wine. Then, within the wood, I saw three footprints in a patch of loam, two of them marking a full stride. The long stride of a tall man. Taller, it seemed to me, than either of your assailants – tall enough for *you*. Few men stride when they are dead."

"Huh." Ainslie ruminated, worried. "So you knew from that first day?"

"I was certain when two other things struck me. If they were brigands and that was a real murder, they were foolish to assail you in the open where we could all witness. And having been seen, why did they go to the labour and risk of dragging your body away?"

"Because you wanted us to believe you had been murdered," Anne interjected, "and because you could not have us learning that you were alive."

"I haven't spoken to you, boy," Ainslie snarled. "You've had little to say for yourself until now. Keep it so."

"Manners," Mandeville said sharply. "And tell me this. Why wish to be thought a dead man? To deceive the chaplain, yes, but what good is't to deceive him?"

"I know the dog. He doesn't wish to face the dangers of pilgrimage! He'd leave the road, flee, stay in England even if it means outlawry, and find service with some other robber-lord – if he sees his chance. I wish him to think he has that chance. Then he'll break the terms of his sentence, *and I shall have him*."

The bitter words hummed with menace.

"All within the law," Mandeville said on a note of marvel. "I will not say that he isn't deserving. We have not warned him, and all I came to do was give back your axe."

He tossed it down by the willow tree with a thump. Ainslie, staring, did not seize it at once. He said on an almost placating note, "He slew my sister's son. But I'll not touch him unless he forfeits the protection of law and Church. I'm an honest man."

Mandeville supposed he was. He still scrambled up the river bank in some haste to put distance between them, gripping Anne's arm to assist her. She shivered a little.

"If the chaplain breaks the terms of his sentence –"

"If, instead, he takes ship from Bristol," Mandeville reminded her, "he will live."

The Pilgrim's Tale

Cherith Baldry

Cherith Baldry (b. 1947) is a former teacher and librarian who has written a number of children's books as well as several Arthurian fantasies, of which the most recent is Exiled from Camelot *(2001). In "The Friar's Tale" in* Royal Whodunnits, *Cherith introduced Geoffrey Chaucer (1340–1400) as spy and crime-solver. Chaucer returns here in a new mystery.*

A north wind was whipping off the sea with a sharp sting of sleet. It might have come, thought Sir John Burley, straight from Ultima Thule, across the marshes and sand dunes, until it battered the harbour walls at Calais and any poor fools doomed to be standing there. He turned his back on it, and on his two men-at-arms, who were grumbling quietly together, pulled his cloak of good English wool more tightly around him, and peered out over the tossing waves.

A ship – the *Maudeleyne* by the cut of its sails and its unhandy wallowing – was working its way through the harbour mouth. Sir John waited, stamping his feet and blowing on freezing fingers, until it dropped anchor and a small boat put out from the side.

He had been requested to give all assistance to the King's emissary – or, given the King's dotage, to the Duke of Lancaster's emissary. The two were not the same.

Besides, by all reports, the man they were sending had little knowledge of war, or the weighty matters that divided

France and England. A wool clerk, a jumped-up scrivener, and – God save the mark! – a poet. Sir John had been a King's man since Edward took Calais for the English, and he was too old to change now. He would do his duty as best he could; no one said he had to like it.

He watched the progress of the small boat bucketing over the waves, and strode to the edge of the quay as it tied up and its passenger stepped out. He held out a hand. "Sir John Burley, Captain of Calais. You're Master Chaucer?"

The newcomer nodded. He was a small man, with sandy hair and beard, dressed in a russet cloak and hood over a tight-fitting cote-hardie and woollen hose. Not the court popinjay Sir John had feared; nevertheless, the Captain eyed him warily, half expecting him to break into verse.

"I'll take you up to the castle," he said brusquely, gesturing to his men-at-arms to fall in behind him.

Master Chaucer inclined his head. "My thanks, Sir John," he said, and added, "It's wild weather for a crossing."

Sir John grunted agreement. He had seen hardened soldiers green and vomiting when the sea ran high; to do this fellow justice he was bright of eye and brisk of step as he hurried along the quay at Burley's side.

"And . . . the man I am to meet?" Chaucer inquired delicately.

"I sent a courier to the French king. His envoy should be with us shortly." Pausing in his swift progress along the quayside, he added, "This city is my responsibility. Am I allowed to know what your business is?"

He was prepared for a rebuff, but Chaucer met his eyes steadily. "The Black Prince is dead, God rest him," he said. "His father cannot live much longer, and his heir is no more than a child. There must be . . . accommodations with the French."

"You seek for peace, then?" Sir John said.

Chaucer nodded. "And that may not be popular. Too many men cry 'War!' when they know nothing of what war means."

"True." Perhaps, Sir John thought, there was more to this poet than met the eye. "You'll not find a soldier to disagree with that."

He was turning off the quayside, leading the way to the castle, when he heard a commotion coming from a little way up the street. Something crashed over, there was the sound of trampling feet, and voices raised in anger.

Burley paused, and jerked his head towards his men-at-arms. "Go and see what that is."

The two men quickened their pace, and disappeared through the archway that led into the yard of the Three Feathers. Seconds later, the noise died.

When Sir John approached the archway, with Chaucer hard at his heels, he saw his two men holding a prisoner, who stood quietly between them, breathing hard. He was a squat, toadlike fellow with a flat nose and dark hair grizzled like a badger's. He wore a leather jerkin with a crossbow slung over one shoulder and a short sword in a scabbard at his belt.

"Your pardon, Master Chaucer," Sir John said as he strode into the yard. "I'm responsible for good order here. I'll not keep you waiting more than need. Well?" he barked at his men. "What's all this?"

"Murder, Captain," one of the soldiers said. "And this here's the murderer."

The prisoner said nothing, but his eyes flashed anger.

"And who's dead?" Burley asked.

At the other side of the yard, huddled beside the main door of the inn, was a small group of men and women. One of them broke away from the others and hurried across the yard in time to hear Sir John's question: Thomas Marley, host of the Three Feathers.

"One of my guests, sir," he said. His broad face was red with agitation. "A decent young fellow, on his way home from pilgrimage. Strangled, with a crossbow string."

"And this fellow did it?" Sir John looked the prisoner up and down. In the cross-bow case, he knew, would be several spare strings. A crossbowman risked garrotting himself if his bowstring snapped under strain.

"Who are you, fellow?" Sir John demanded. "What's your business?"

"My name is Bertrand," the prisoner replied, speaking

English in a gravelled voice with an execrable French accent. "And my business is not to be spoken of here."

"He's one of these damned rutters." Sir John flung the words over his shoulder at Master Chaucer, who was staring at the prisoner in shock. "Soldiers they call themselves; bandits is closer to the mark. Any of them would kill his own grandmother for a groat." He nodded to his men-at-arms. "Take him away." He added, muttering to himself, "He'll hang for this."

As the men started to drag their prisoner away, Chaucer laid a hand on Sir John's arm and said, "No, wait."

There was such quiet authority in his voice that Sir John's men hesitated, glancing uneasily at their Captain as if they were not sure whom they should obey.

Sir John was taking breath for a blistering curse when Chaucer added, "We have no evidence that he is guilty."

"Evidence? He's a damned Frenchman, what more evidence do you want?"

"To be accurate, *mon ami*," said Bertrand, "I am a Breton."

There was a gleam in his dark eyes; if Burley had not known it was impossible, he would have said the fellow was amused.

"Frenchman, Breton, what's that to me?" Sir John turned on Chaucer. "It's clear what happened. He strangled this fellow for his purse. Why isn't that enough for you?"

Chaucer's shock at the sight of the Breton mercenary was ebbing away, leaving behind an air of calm good sense. "Is he carrying a stolen purse?" he asked.

At Sir John's order, the men at arms began to search, pulling roughly at the prisoner's jerkin. Bertrand stood still, with an exaggerated air of patience.

"You observe, Sir John," Chaucer murmured, "that he carries crossbow, sword and belt knife. Why would he choose such a comparatively complicated way to kill someone as strangling him with a bowstring?"

"How do I know why a damned Frenchman does anything?" Sir John growled.

The men finished the search. One of them held out a shabby leather purse, too flat to contain much coin.

"That is my own," Bertrand said.

"It's true, sir," said Master Marley. "He paid for wine from it, before ever Master Buckton was found dead."

"Then whether he killed or no," Chaucer said, "he did not steal."

Sir John let out a curse. Irritably he reflected that if he had not been saddled with this poet, he could have finished this matter without trouble, and no one would have been a penny the worse. Except for Bertrand the Breton mercenary, he reminded himself.

"Master Marley," he said. "Show my men a store room with a good stout lock. We'll keep this fellow safe while I try the matter further." To the soldiers, he added, "Keep him well guarded, or I'll slit your noses with my own dagger."

He pulled Bertrand's sword and belt knife from their sheaths, and his crossbow from the case on his shoulder. Bertrand did not try to resist, only saying, "Take good care of my weapons, English Captain. I shall require them of you later."

His eyes met Sir John's with that same impudent, amused look.

"You may yet require a gallows, Breton," Sir John snarled, and strode off across the yard.

The group of people beside the inn door stood back to let Sir John and Chaucer enter, and then crowded in behind them.

The door led into the common room of the inn. Opposite, near the fire, a woman was sitting, her body shaken with sobs. On one side a young man was trying to persuade her to drink from a cup he held, while on the other side an elderly nun clasped her hand and murmured words of comfort.

The woman was young and pretty, with dishevelled chestnut hair. The lacing of her kirtle was open, and the reek of burnt feathers suggested that someone had recovered her from a faint.

More people were seated in little huddles all round the common room. The usual group of pilgrims, Sir John observed: a couple of priests, a friar in a grey habit, several men in the solid finery of merchants, and one young sprig of the nobility, lounging in the window seat and fitting a new string to his lute.

They all broke off low-voiced conversations as Sir John entered and turned their faces towards him.

"I am Sir John Burley, Captain of Calais," Sir John announced, planting himself in the middle of the room. "Who can tell me what happened?"

A chorus of voices answered; Burley cut them off with a movement of the hand, and pointed at the nearest man. "You."

The man he spoke to was tall, dark-haired and dressed in good but unfashionable clothing. He had an air of competence about him that Sir John liked.

"We're all pilgrims, sir," he began. "We met on the road to the shrine of St James, and we travelled home together." He half smiled. "It's good to hear your own tongue in a foreign land. We've been here two days," he went on, "waiting for a ship to take us home to England."

"And then, Master . . . ?"

"Henshawe, sir, Nicholas Henshawe. I'm steward of a manor near Ashurst in Kent. We were waiting for Master Marley to call us to dinner. Mistress Buckton –" he indicated the weeping woman by the fire – "went to bring her husband down from the bedroom. We heard her screaming, sir, and when we went up there we found Master Buckton dead."

"And when did you last see him alive?" Chaucer asked.

Master Henshawe looked slightly startled at the change of questioner, but he answered readily enough. "At morning Mass, sir. Afterwards, when we broke our fast, he complained of heaviness, and went upstairs to rest."

Chaucer nodded, and said to Sir John, "Perhaps we had better see Master Buckton for ourselves."

"I'll take you." Master Marley led the way through another door on the far side of the common room, and up a flight of stairs. On the landing the first door stood open, and Marley gestured for them to go in.

Inside the room were several beds. On the nearest, a man was lying; bending over him was a hugely fat woman, who turned as they came in and gave them a wide, gaptoothed

smile. "I'm laying him out, sir, and doing all that's proper."
She dipped in a ponderous curtsey in front of Sir John, and
added, "Margery Bolton, sir. I'm a midwife by trade. I bring
'em into the world, and I see 'em out."

She would have continued with her work, but Sir John
said to her, "Thank you, mistress. We won't trouble you
further."

Margery went off with an offended sniff, and the host
followed her downstairs. Sir John gave his attention to the
dead man.

He was young, a little too plump, with a florid complexion.
His hands were folded on his breast and his limbs were
decently composed. The only sign of his violent death was a
thin red line running around his neck, where the bowstring
had dug into his flesh.

"Damn Mistress Margery!" Sir John said. "No one
should have touched the body."

Chaucer murmured agreement. He was bending over
Master Buckton, examining him carefully, and prodded with
one finger a fat purse that hung from his belt.

"His body was not robbed," he said.

Sir John grunted. For some reason, the little poet did not
believe the Breton mercenary was guilty, and the more Sir
John saw, the more he began to think that perhaps he was
right. If theft was not the motive, then more likely Master
Buckton had been murdered by someone who knew him than
by a chance some Breton who had never set eyes on him
before.

All the same, Sir John resolved, he would keep tight hold
of the mercenary until he was sure of the fellow's innocence.

While he pondered, Chaucer had been examining the
room, but he found nothing.

"The murderer took his weapon away with him, no
doubt," he said.

Sir John let out another noncommittal grunt. He could, he
supposed, have everyone searched, but what point, when a
bowstring was so easily tossed into a fire and destroyed.

"There's no sign of struggle here," Chaucer said, surveying the room again.

"Maybe Mistress Margery righted it," said Burley.

"If he had struggled and cried out," said Chaucer, "some-one would have heard him. Maybe he trusted his murderer, let him come behind him . . ."

"He would not have trusted the Breton," Sir John admitted.

Carefully and quietly, for he did not want any interruptions from the pilgrims down below, he searched the room, and the two others on the same floor, looking for weapons. He found two swords, one of superbly forged steel that he guessed was the property of the young aristocrat, one rusty with a jagged edge, that might have belonged to anyone. But Buckton had not been killed with a sword. He had been strangled by a bowstring, and there were no bows.

Returning to the first bedroom, where Chaucer waited for him, Sir John stared down at the body for a moment longer, frowning as if the name of the murderer might appear written on the dead forehead. Then he led the way downstairs again.

In the common room, Master Marley and a couple of potboys were handing round mugs of steaming Hippocras. The pilgrims seemed to have relaxed, as if their stunned calm at word of the murder was wearing off.

"Sir Simon!" someone called. "Give us a tune on your lute!"

The young nobleman tossed back golden curls and looked the speaker up and down, an expression of disdain on his handsome features. "Not in a house of mourning," he said.

He got up, took his lute, and fitted it into its case, while Master Marley himself came over to offer the hot, spiced wine to Sir John and Chaucer.

"Master Marley," said Sir John, "have you weapons in this house?"

"I've longbows, sir. Me and the lads practise at the butts, as is our duty."

"And where are the bows kept?"

Master Marley grinned. "In a room over the stables, sir. Locked up safely, and the key kept here." He patted the bunch that dangled from his belt. "I'll not risk some fool of a stable boy getting drunk and shooting someone. Whoever used that bowstring brought it with him."

"It might be well to search the inn," Chaucer suggested.

For a second Sir John felt irritated that a poet should presume to tell him how to do his job, but Chaucer had spoken courteously, and there was sense in the idea after all.

He gave a grunt of agreement, and went out to look for his men. When he had found them, and made sure that they had the Breton safe behind a good, stout door, he set them to the search and returned to the common room.

By this time, Geoffrey Chaucer had joined the little group beside the fire, and was speaking to Mistress Buckton. Sir John came up to hear the last of what he was saying.

". . . anyone who was your husband's enemy?"

Mistress Buckton had stopped crying, and took a sip from her cup of Hippocras before she replied.

"James had no enemies. Everyone liked him." She appealed to the young man beside her. "Isn't that true, Francis?"

The young man hesitated, flushing awkwardly as if he was reluctant to agree, and then said, "No one had cause to kill him, truly."

Looking more closely at Francis, Sir John could see a distinct resemblance to Master Buckton, though he was younger, and thinner, with a scholar's face and hands.

"Are you related to Master Buckton?" he asked.

"His brother, sir."

"And his heir?"

Francis half rose, opened his mouth to utter a protest, and sat down again with the protest unspoken. He muttered, "Yes."

"Your brother was a wealthy man?" Sir John persisted.

"He owns . . . owned a manor in Hampshire," Francis said. "Good land – prosperous. But I didn't envy him!" His voice rose shrilly. "I'm to be a priest!" He shook his head, baffled, and went on, "The manor's mine now, and it's the last thing I want. And I had no bowstring . . . I carry no weapons, but a knife for meat. I –"

"Keep calm, lad," Sir John said. "No one has accused

you." *Yet*, he added silently. Turning back to Mistress Buckton, he asked, "You know of no one else who might have wanted your husband dead?"

"No!" Tears welled up in Mistress Buckton's eyes. "He was a good man, a kind husband . . . Oh, Dame Cecily, what shall I do without him?" She dissolved into sobs again and rested her head against the elderly nun's shoulder. Dame Cecily, her sweet, wrinkled face framed by her white wimple, put an arm around her and gently smoothed the tumbled chestnut curls,

Half embarrassed, half annoyed that he could not go on questioning her, Sir John drew back, to find Nicholas Henshawe at his shoulder again.

Softly he said, "Sir John, don't take too much heed of the sorrowing widow."

"Oh?" Chaucer was there, too, surveying Henshawe with bright-eyed interest. "Was James Buckton not a good man and a kind husband?"

Henshawe bared his teeth. "We're told not to malign the dead, but when he was alive he was an arrogant young snot. And he quarrelled often enough with Mistress Isabel. Now he's dead, she canonizes him." He coughed. "For all that, he didn't deserve to die."

"And Master Francis?" Chaucer inquired.

"Wears out his knees with praying," Henshawe said. "From all I've seen, what he says is true. He talks of nothing but his priesting."

"And you know of no one else who —"

A tap on his arm distracted Sir John. Beside him was standing another of the pilgrims, a wizened elderly man with grey hair and a neatly clipped beard.

"A word with you, sir." His voice was unexpectedly deep.

Sir John inclined his head. "Speak."

"My name is William Warton. I am a doctor of physic. I carry a chest of my remedies, and on the road I treated anyone who fell ill."

"That was charity, sir," Burley said.

Master Warton waved the praise away irritably. "Sir, a vial of poppy syrup is missing from my chest."

Sir John's eyebrows shot up. "And Buckton complained of sleepiness after Mass," he said. "Did someone drug him?"

"It makes you think, does it not?" Warton said sardonically. "But he didn't die of it," he added. "He died of strangulation."

Sir John exchanged a glance with Chaucer.

"Sleepy . . . unaware . . . unable to struggle," the poet murmured. "Thank you, Master Warton. This is weighty news indeed."

The doctor nodded and withdrew, looking pleased with himself.

"Master Henshawe," Sir John asked, "after Buckton went upstairs, did you see anyone follow him? Or did you notice if anyone was absent for any length of time?"

Henshawe shrugged, smiling. "Who can say? We were all moving around. And before you ask, Sir John, I didn't see anyone put poppy syrup in Buckton's wine, either."

Sir John grunted. He had to admit, it would be impossible to work out where everyone had been, between the time Buckton withdrew and the time his wife went to look for him.

The door to the kitchens opened and Thomas Marley reappeared with a huge platter of roast fowl. His potboys followed with bread, pasties, fruit and more wine.

"Sit, sirs, be my guests." Master Marley gestured Burley and Chaucer to a small table a little apart from the others. "I'll be grateful all my life if you can come to the truth of this, and prove it was none of my doing."

"No one blames you, Master Marley," Sir John said, taking the offered seat.

Marley shook his head. "A death on the premises is bad, sir." He set food on the table, and departed.

Disgustedly, Sir John stabbed his belt knife into a slice of roast capon. "Come to the truth!" he said, repeating the host's words. "I feel the truth is hidden so deep we'll never come to it." Wryly he added, "If only you had let me hang that damned Breton!"

"The truth may yet come to light," Chaucer said tranquilly.

"Then tell me how! If we believe Master Henshawe – and

I see no reason not to – Francis would not have murdered his brother. And who else had reason to want James Buckton dead? He might have been stabbed in a quarrel, but this – drugging and strangling – means forethought. What did Buckton have, apart from the estate that his priestly brother inherits?"

Chaucer eyed him across the table with a trace of amusement in his face. He said, "A beautiful wife."

Burley brought down his fist on the table, and then glanced round in embarrassment as he realised that several of the pilgrims had turned to look at him.

"You're out of your mind!" he said. "True, she's beautiful, but is she stupid enough? If any man here asked to wed her, she must guess that he killed her husband."

Chaucer nodded, and applied himself to stripping neatly a wing of capon.

"Then why would he take the risk?" Burley went on, struggling to keep his voice down when what he really wanted was to shout. "Unless . . ."

"Unless she had already consented," Chaucer said. "Unless she knew."

Burley could not help swivelling round for a look at the widow. Mistress Isabel was still seated between Francis and Dame Cecily, prettily dabbing her lips with a napkin before she sipped from her wine cup. Sir John had to admit to himself that she did not look grief-stricken.

His gaze roved over the rest of the pilgrims. "Supposing you're right," he said grudgingly. "We're looking for a man who might have been tempted by Mistress Isabel – but damn you, that's every man here, excepting the priests, and maybe some of them as well!"

"You mistake, Sir John," Chaucer said softly. "We are not looking for a man who would be tempted by Mistress Isabel. We are looking for a man who would have tempted *her*."

Sir John took in a mouthful of air and did not know what to do with it. Chaucer's eyes were levelled at the handsome young aristocrat.

"I have seen him at court," the poet said. "His name is Sir Simon Havering. An old family, and an honourable one . . .

his grandfather died at Crécy. But Sir Simon is a younger son, and his patrimony is small. As Master Buckton's widow, Mistress Isabel has the right to a third of his estates."

Sir John gaped, a venison pasty half way to his mouth. "And she . . ."

Chaucer gave a slight shrug. "She would be 'my lady'."

Burley could hardly keep his eyes off the young knight as he drained his wine-cup and pushed his chair back from the table.

"God's nails!" Sir John said. "I can almost believe you. *But he has no bow*. Where did he find the weapon?"

"I think I can tell you that," Chaucer murmured. "With your leave, Sir John . . ."

Burley hesitated, and then gave a curt nod. At once Chaucer rose to his feet and attracted attention by banging his wine cup on the table.

Everyone in the room turned to look at him. Their voices died.

The little poet permitted himself a faint smile. "I will tell you a tale," he said, "for tales are good to while away the hours of a pilgrimage. Forgive me that this tale is a tragedy, for it tells of the death of Master Buckton."

A stifled sob from Isabel punctuated his words.

"Not long ago," Chaucer went on, "someone in this room now went upstairs and strangled James Buckton while he was drugged with poppy syrup and unable to resist."

"But how could they?" Nicholas Henshawe called out. "None of us has a bow."

"But Master Buckton was not strangled with a bow-string," Chaucer said. "Not a bowstring," he repeated. "A lutestring."

A chair crashed over as Sir Simon sprang up. "You point at me? How dare you!" His voice was outraged.

"Strings break," said Chaucer. "A lute-player always carries spares. And with one of them you followed Master Buckton upstairs and strangled him."

Sir Simon looked scornful. Snapping his fingers, he said, "I know you. Master Geoffrey Chaucer, so-called poet. God, I'll destroy you for this!"

"I think not," Chaucer said calmly. "Not when Sir John examines the string you fitted to your lute just now."

For the first time, fear leapt into Sir Simon's eyes. He turned to the door, but Nicholas Henshawe was in the way. Sir Simon drew his belt knife. "Stand aside."

Henshawe glanced at Sir John, who had risen and was trying to shift unobtrusively behind Sir Simon to grab his weapon from behind. Sir Simon whipped round to face him. His face was feral, snarling.

At that moment, Sir John's two men-at-arms tramped in from the yard. One of them started to say, "Sir, we've searched from cellars to attic, and –"

The other, a bit quicker on the uptake, launched himself at Sir Simon, and chopped the knife out of his hand. Chaucer darted forward and retrieved it while both the soldiers grabbed Sir Simon. He fought, cursing, but he could not break free.

"This was for you!" he spat at Isabel. "You led me into it. God, I was a fool to listen to you!"

Mistress Isabel was staring at him, her face white, her eyes huge with fear. "No – no!" she screamed. "I knew nothing about it, nothing!"

"You bitch!" Sir Simon said. "Who put poppy syrup in his wine so that he would feel sleep coming on him? Who made sure he would be upstairs alone, and too drugged to fight for his life?"

Isabel did not reply. Her screams spiralled up into a bout of hysterical shrieking. She clawed at her hair and face, and left red streaks down Francis's face when he tried to restrain her.

"Damn you to hell!" said Sir Simon.

"Take him," Sir John said to his men. "And release the Breton. Tell him to come here and collect his weapons."

The men-at-arms went out, Sir Simon gripped firmly between them. After his first bout of struggling, he went with dignity, his head high. Dame Cecily managed to calm Isabel enough to coax her out of the room and upstairs to lie down.

"What will you do with her?" Chaucer asked.

"Nothing." Burley let out a curse. "What can I do? She's guilty as he is, but how to prove it?"

"There may be punishment," Chaucer said quietly. "She will never be 'my lady'. And if this story follows her to Hampshire – as assuredly it will – she might find men are less than eager to wed her."

As he spoke, the Breton mercenary walked into the common room and stood surveying his surroundings with a faint smile on his swarthy features.

"And as for you . . ." Sir John turned on him. "Thank God and His saints that Master Chaucer was here, or you'd be gallows meat by now. Take yourself off, or you'll find my boot behind you."

Bertrand moved to recover his weapons from the table by the door, but he showed no desire to leave.

"Sir John . . ." Chaucer sounded embarrassed. "Allow me to introduce Messire Bertrand du Guesclin, Count of Longueville and Constable of France. The King of France's envoy."

"What!" Sir John realised he was gaping, and shut his mouth with a snap.

Bertrand's thick lips were twisted in amusement, and his eyes shone.

"You could have told me," Sir John said accusingly to Chaucer.

Chaucer shrugged apologetically. "If I had, you would have freed my lord Bertrand from the charge of murder, but so many people would have known of it that his name and his purposes would have been quite uncloaked. Lord Bertrand himself gave me a clear hint right at the start that I should remain silent. To discover who killed the pilgrim was the only way to preserve the secret of his name and his mission here."

"And to preserve the good will of the King of France," Bertrand added. "I assure you, *Messire Jean*, my lord would have been seriously annoyed if an English Captain hanged me for murder."

Sir John shuddered. "Heaven preserve me from the French!"

"No, *mon ami*." Bertrand stepped forward and held out his hand. "For you are an honest man, and honest men of all nations should honour one another. Is it not so?"

Sir John stared at the offered hand, and did not move. He felt a powerful sense of injury, without knowing exactly why. If Chaucer had spoken out, the news would have spread through the Three Feathers like fire through corn, and then through Calais and beyond. The hoped-for peace would have been broken. God's blood, the wretched fellow was right!

Chaucer clapped him on the shoulder. "Come, Sir John. Let us share a cup of Master Marley's good Hippocras. And let us drink to an end to war and murder, and to peace on God's earth."

Slowly, Sir John nodded. Slowly, still with a shade of reluctance, he reached out and grasped his enemy's hand.

And What Can They Show, or What Reasons Give?

Mat Coward

Mat Coward (b. 1960) has been writing for over fifteen years and his books include such diverse titles as Success . . . And How to Avoid it (2001) and The Best of Round the Horne (2000). With Up & Down (2000) he began a series of crime novels featuring DI Don Packham and PC Frank Mitchell. His work has appeared in all the major mystery magazines and anthologies. The following story is set at the time of the Peasants' Revolt in 1381 and sets a special dilemma for its protagonist.

"With whom hold you?"

"Stand aside, child," said William. "We're in the middle of Jack Straw's Castle, we don't need watchwords."

The sentry – a boy of about thirteen – trembled a little, and bit his lip, but still he stood his ground, his spear pointing towards us. "With whom hold you?" he said again.

I admired anyone, man or boy, who might stand up to my cousin William (a large and noisy man, where I am small and quiet), so I spoke before William had a chance to bark again.

"With King Richard and the True Commons."

"Pass, Captain." The lad gave me a smile of gratitude, lowered his weapon, and stood smartly to one side as William and I entered the tent.

The smell of blood, of life's blood spilt, was one I knew well enough; there were few men in those days who didn't. For all that, the scene within the tent shook my soul. This was not death on the battlefield, nor yet death from the plague. This was something more terrible by far. A man of thirty years or so lay lifeless upon the ground, face-down, his blood all about him. "Murder," I said. "This is murder."

William nodded. "Without doubt, John. A cry was heard from this tent, and a man seen leaving it, as bold as dawn, with blood upon him. I was sent for, saw what you now see, and set that silly boy to guard the tent while I went to fetch you."

Me . . . yes. They called me Captain, and had elected me so, though I was by trade a pigman. I knew all about pigs that any man might know, but I knew nothing of murder. I said as much to my cousin, as we returned to the sweeter air of the Heath. Spring was surrendering to summer, and the early evening was mild and pleasant.

"Who else can we turn to, John?" he answered. "Our situation is such that we cannot call on the usual authorities. You are our leader, here in this camp."

"Leader?" I laughed. "John Ball preaches that there are no lords; that we are all the descendants of Adam and Eve, each equal to the other."

William was always a man of short temper, and his tone was one of irritation. "You know what I mean."

"I know what you mean," I admitted. Back home in the county of Sussetter I had been, for the last twelvemonth, an organizer in the Great Society. I collected pennies from the commons in my village, and those neighbouring it, and encouraged them to refuse to work for any lord for less than sixpence per day. The moneys amassed were used to pay the fines of any member who stood true for his rights, and was persecuted for doing so.

Had I known that this would result in men calling me *Captain* – expecting me to lead them in this uprising against the traitors and bloodsuckers who held our King in thrall – I should never have accepted the commission.

"I am no Wat Tyler, cousin."

He grinned, and threw a huge arm around my shoulders. "You are *our* Wat Tyler. There are 300 men upon this Heath today, many of them strangers to you and to me, but all of them know you by reputation, John. A steadfast man, and a just man. If we are to hold the men together in this great undertaking, then this horrible matter must be settled quickly, and justly."

"By me?"

"By you. So, Captain – let us make a start."

I accepted my destiny, and collected my thoughts. "The bloodied man seen leaving the scene of the crime – he was taken?"

"He is held."

"Then," I said, "let us begin with him."

All around London, that night, there were camps like ours – some bigger, some smaller. The next day, all would assemble together, under the counsel of Wat Tyler, to meet with the young King; and, God willing, all would be put right. The poll tax would be lifted; the bloodsucking, high-living traitors, who so cruelly suppressed the porail, and waged foreign wars for their own enrichment, would be removed from office and arrested; the Church would be dispossessed of its great wealth, and its numerous bishops defrocked; most important of all, the state of villeinage itself would be abolished. There would be but one lord in the kingdom, under God: the King himself.

Our band, drawn from a number of villages in the far west of Sussetter, had made camp there on the northern heights overlooking London for no better reason than that one of our number had family in the nearby village of Hampstead. Near a mill pond we set up, alongside some ancient earthworks upon a hill. According to the locals – as best we could understand through their thick accents, that is – this used to be a castle, hundreds and hundreds of years ago. So, naturally, the lads began calling it "Sir John Ball's Castle" or "Sir Jack Straw's Castle".

The merchants of the neighbourhood made us welcome enough, and sold us good provender at fair prices. The old system of lords and serfs was not to their liking at all. They would have us all freemen, earning good wages – that we might spend those wages on their goods, and also that they and the manufacturers upon whom they depended, might find the labour they needed, when they needed it, at a price set in the market place, not in the manor house.

All in all, considering the serious business upon which we were embarked, it was a jolly scene there up on the Heath, with camp fires sparkling in the dusk, men drinking and singing, and the good, godly aroma of fellowship and brotherhood enveloping all.

Who sort of man would befoul such a scene with bloody murder? And for what reason?

As to the first question, I soon had an answer. The man who sat on the ground inside William's tent, his wrists roped behind him, was tall, of middle years, his head entirely bald, and wore an expression that was at once severe and calm.

"I don't know you, do I?" I said. "I am John Cable, of Middlefield."

"I know who you are."

I waited for the prisoner to say more but he did not. "And *you*, brother?"

He looked at me for a moment, as if deciding whether or not my question was worth answering. "I am Edmund Bull," he said at last, "not of Middlefield."

"Well then, Edmund Bull," I said, sitting opposite him, and wondering how on earth one went about interrogating a suspected killer. It was not a skill much honed by pigmen. "You have blood on your clothes. Have you killed a man today?"

I suddenly realized that I did not know the name of the departed soul. William, standing immediately behind the prisoner, must have had the same thought at the same moment, for he spoke now. "The man who was killed, Captain, was one Richard Hunt, of the village of Three Oaks."

"I know the place. I have been there once or twice, upon the business of the Great Society. And you, Edmund – you are also from Three Oaks?"

Bull merely shrugged; that was two questions he hadn't answered, I noted. Two crucial questions. If he maintained this policy of silence, I should soon be forced to make a decision concerning his fate. This far from home, and in such conditions, there could be only one outcome. The thought filled me with revulsion.

"Edmund, I shall say this bluntly. If you refuse to speak to me, then tomorrow's dawn will find you hanging from a tree on the Heath. Without your testimony my hands are as tied as yours."

He looked away into nothingness for a while. When his gaze returned to meet mine, I thought I saw a sparkle of amusement in his eyes. "I shall hang anyway, Captain. Such speech as I might offer would serve only to pass the time until your hanging-tree receives its burden."

The prospect did not seem to dismay him. I could see about him nothing of rage, or triumph – nor yet of remorse, nor fear. Yet by his words, surely, he had confessed to the crime with which he was charged? One thing seemed clear, if nothing else did: that there was a story here, and that I would sleep uncomfortably for a long time to come, should I send a man to the rope without knowing *why*.

"Let us start with simple fact, Edmund. You killed this man, Richard Hunt?"

The accused nodded. "Yes," he said, "I am from Three Oaks."

"What?"

"You asked me, Captain, if I was of the same village as the dead man. The answer is yes." He smiled.

"You little turd!" yelled William, clouting Bull around the head with a hand the size of a horse's buttock. "The Captain asked –"

"All right, William." I held out one of my own, much smaller hands, to prevent another blow falling. "Edmund Bull may tell us his story in whatever manner pleases him, so long as he tells it true." I turned to Bull, whose expression had not changed, despite the rivulet of blood trickling from his upper lip. "Will you do that, Edmund? Tell it true?"

He merely smiled again, and shrugged his shoulders. I was making no progress against his obstinacy, his apparent lack of concern for his fate. Watching him while he watched me, I saw how I must appear to him: a man of nearly forty years, of unimpressive physical stature, tired and confused. Well: Edmund Bull was not to know it, but I had fathered three sons and two daughters in my time, and I flattered myself that I knew something of the methods by which a smile may be wiped from a naughty face.

"Has the prisoner been searched?" I asked. "Has he been stripped of his clothing, to discover what it might conceal?"

"He has not," William replied.

"Then see to it now, please." I left the tent without another word, and without even a glance at the accused man. I walked back to the place of murder, and looked again at the horrors to be found there; more calmly this time. Exposure to vileness deadens the involuntary reactions, as any man whose workaday world involves the slaughter of animals will readily attest.

By the time I returned to my cousin's tent, Edmund Bull was naked, other than the rope re-tied around his wrists. His look was less confident, now.

"Did you find it, William?"

Whether or not William had guessed what *it* was, he betrayed no hesitation in his answer. "We found nothing, Captain."

I remained standing this time, for the purpose of looking down on the supposed murderer. "You cannot kill a pig with bare hands, Edmund," I said. When he did not reply, I added: "Nor yet a man – at least, not one who died so bloodily as Richard Hunt."

After a moment, Bull said: "He did bleed mightily, didn't he? So much blood."

"A cry was heard," I said. "A terrible cry, the sound of a man dying. Several people rushed immediately towards the tent from which the noise came. As they did so, they saw you emerge from that same tent, with blood upon your hands, arms and clothing. You were taken and held by those men, and from there you were brought to this tent – a distance of

200 paces. Will you grant me, at least, the accuracy of the story so far?"

Bull nodded. "That much is true."

I leaned down until my face was only inches from his. "And yet you sit here, naked, your clothing having been investigated by my cousin . . . and no sign is there of the weapon with which you killed Richard Hunt."

I looked up and met William's eyes; he nodded. So, he had understood what I was about, and his search would have been thorough and purposeful.

The accused stretched his spine, and flexed his arms as if to bring back the feeling to his bound wrists. "This would seem, Captain, to speak prettily of my innocence."

I did not respond directly to that comment; I would play him at his own game for a while, and see where it took me. "I would say that poor Richard was slain with a short dagger. I have seen such wounds before, while on the King's service abroad. But there is no dagger inside the dead man's tent – I have just been to look, myself – nor on the ground outside his tent. And there is no dagger in *this* tent."

"Perhaps," said Bull, "it was taken from me by the men who first arrested me. Or perhaps I cleverly dropped it whilst being led from that place of arrest to this place of confinement."

"If you had been holding a weapon in your bloody hand when you were taken, Edmund, I have no doubt that it would have been seized from you. But if it had been, it would surely have been turned over to my cousin, here, and he would have spoken of it to me. As for your second suggestion – William?"

"I'll set men to search the route taken from there to here." He left the tent, and I heard him giving orders. I could not hide my smile; Cousin William was a blacksmith, and used to having his instructions obeyed.

"I don't think they'll find the dagger, will they, Edmund?"

Bull shrugged his shoulders. "If it's there to be found, perhaps they will."

"Without that dagger, I should be most reluctant to hang you."

"Then I shall pray that their search is in vain."

"I do not ask again whether or not you killed Richard Hunt, for it is clear to me that that is a question you do not intend to answer. But will you tell me this? Did you see him die?"

"You have heard the account of events, Captain. A scream; my exit; a dead man behind me. This would seem to answer your question."

"And yet *you* do not answer it. I can think of other explanations which would as well fit the facts, and which would point to your innocence. It may be, for instance, that you went to visit your neighbour, Richard Hunt, found him murdered, and ran in terror."

"I see. So the scream which was heard would have been mine, not his?"

"Why not? One man's scream sounds much like another. An old soldier like yourself would know that, I fancy."

Bull laughed, softly. "I have not told you that I was once a soldier. Perhaps I was –"

"And perhaps you weren't. Quite. But I tell you that you *were*, Edmund. It takes one to know one."

"Then, if no dagger is found, I have merely to repeat the tale you have just suggested to me, and my neck will likely retain its current length."

"Or," I said, turning away from him, to give my words a falsely casual air, "I might decide that, at a moment of great destiny for England, I have no patience for trifling matters such as the lost lives of two strangers. And having so decided, I might then hang you without delay, that more important thoughts might occupy my mind."

There was a long silence within that tent. I did not look at him, though I was sure he was looking at me. When he spoke, it was with a calmness that seemed to me unnatural for the first time. "I do not believe you would do that, John Cable. Your love of justice is visible in every line on your face."

Now I faced him. "Yet, it would not suit you, would it? To be hanged this evening, rather than in the morning."

"It would not suit me to be hanged at any time, Captain. I am sure most men would take the same view."

Nonetheless, I thought, *I have pierced your shell at last*.

"I shall go now to fetch food and drink for us both, Edmund," I said, "and then we shall talk again."

Food and drink could wait a little longer. Leaving a man to guard the prisoner, I went first to confer with my cousin. No dagger had been found, cunningly dropped between the victim's tent and the makeshift jailhouse.

"As I thought," I said. "It is increasingly my belief – or suspicion, at any rate – that Edmund Bull is innocent of this crime."

William shook his head, in part from amusement, I thought, and in equal part exasperation. "You always want *everyone* to be innocent, John."

"However," I continued, "I do believe that the identity of the real killer is known to him, and that all his current actions and inactions have one design – to allow that killer time to escape. That's why he is not frightened of being hanged, William: he knows no evidence can be found against him, because no evidence exists."

"Evidence can always be found," William said, his voice dark as midnight. Many of us had personal reasons for taking part in this crusade.

"That is the point: Bull trusts in our justness, since justness is the only cause of our being here on this Heath at all! We are gathered for the King, and for true English law, and for Christ's mercy. He knows we will not hang him without proof."

William snorted. He was not impressed. "If Bull's aim is to enable the killer to escape justice, then Bull is as guilty as the other, and should answer for it."

"I know. Which is why I still hope to persuade him to talk to us soon, before his hesitation damns him utterly."

"If he is not the killer," said William, after a moment's thought, "then what was he doing in the victim's tent?"

"Well, they came from the same village."

"So he says."

"Yes, so he says – I can't see why he would lie about that, can you? Assuming it's true, then it is no mystery that he went to visit Richard Hunt, who was his friend, or neighbour, or relative."

William scratched at his beard. "No, John, there's no sense in that. If Richard were his friend, why will Bull not name his murderer?"

I thought I had an answer to that. "Because the murderer is also a friend?"

"Could be, I suppose. Yes, that fits. Ah, but it reminds me of something else! I've asked around amongst those camped nearest to Richard Hunt, and no one seems to have known him, or our prisoner. The dead man's name and home village were known, only because he had offered it when he arrived here – after the rest of us, by the way – casually, as anyone might, when meeting a stranger over a campfire."

"You have asked people from the same village, Three Oaks?"

"From there, or nearby."

I wasn't sure what that signified. "That is a puzzle. I shall ask Edmund about it."

Again, William snorted. "You might as well ask Hob the Robber what has become of the King's treasure while he has had stewardship of it!"

"For now, Cousin, I would have another look at the scene of the killing."

As we walked towards Richard Hunt's tent, William asked: "What are you looking for? There's nothing there, I can tell you that: tent big enough for one man, one small parcel of clothes, and a corpse. Nothing else."

"That is just it, William. What I am looking for is something which, I suspect, is not there."

"Riddles! Perhaps John Ball might hire you to write his sermons."

I smiled. "I think not. I have no gift for rhyming." At that moment, on the mild evening breeze, I heard the men at archery practice chanting "*When Adam delved and Eve span, who was then the gentleman?*" He had a talent for saying much with few words, did the people's preacher. They looked cheerful, those archers, in their smocks and stout boots. The whole camp somewhat resembled a holiday fair – only the banners of St George, flying here and there, suggested a more solemn purpose.

Having spent a few moments in poor Richard Hunt's tent – during which unpleasant time I noted amongst other things the wounds inflicted on his belly and hands – I returned to my prisoner, along the way collecting a roast fowl and a jug of beer. I untied Edmund's hands so that he might dress himself and eat, tied them again when he had finished, and then said to him: "Tell me, Edmund Bull, why are we here, on this Heath far from home?"

"To protest against the poll taxes," he said. "To put our grievances to the young King, so that he might set right that which is ill in the land."

"I meant – how has this come about? That a people must rise up like this, in great numbers, and do violence against men and property, only so that our voice shall be heard, which should have been heard without the need for such measures?"

"The Death," he said, his tone suggesting that anyone who did not understand that must be an idiot. "That terrible plague killed a third of the men in the entire kingdom. Thus, we have enjoyed twenty years in which the value of a man's labour has risen and risen. Jakke Trueman and John the Miller have tasted power – power which the lords believe is rightfully theirs alone. Now, with their poll tax, and their Statutes of Labourers, and their enclosures, the lords fight back. So, this rising shall be kill or cure – at its end, we shall either be returned to the bondage known to our grandfathers, or else we shall have broken serfdom for ever."

His words were unremarkable; similar speech might be heard in every cowshed, field or tavern in the country. Yet his manner of speaking struck me as oddly lacking in passion; as a child might recite a lesson from Scripture, which he has learned but does not yet understand.

"Our demands are just, Edmund, would you not say? No more serfdom, homage or suit to any lord. Each man to pay fourpence an acre rent for his land. No man to be compelled to serve another, except freely by his own will and on terms of regular covenant. The law to be enforced against the traitors who have stolen the young King from his people."

Bull smiled. "Everyone to be free and equal."

"A pretty dream, you think? Never to be reality?"

He met my eyes. "It is why we are here, Captain."

"William found no dagger," I said.

He was not thrown by my sudden change of direction. Without pause, he replied: "As you expected."

"As we both expected. The sun is sinking, Edmund. Will you tell me the truth now? Has enough time passed for your friend to make his escape?"

Bull's face became guarded, but his lips opened to reply – and at that moment, to my irritation, William entered the tent, and gestured urgently for me to step outside.

"What is it, William? I am sure Edmund was about to –"

"Time is running out, Captain. Word has spread around the camp that Bull will not talk – that he is playing for time. Most of the men believe that can only be because he expects rescue; that the Mayor's soldiers are coming for us tonight."

"I see . . . I see."

"Therefore they demand summary justice for Richard Hunt's killer – they want his head on a pole this hour. And then that we should be up, and march to Blackheath to join the Chieftain's host."

"Will the camp act against me?"

"They will not act against *us*," said William, and I loved him well for that. "Not yet. But this matter must be brought to resolution soon."

"I understand. Do what you can to calm the commons. I will put this to Bull."

Back in the tent I saw by Edmund Bull's face that he had overheard our conversation; my cousin's whisper was louder than many men's shout.

"So, Edmund?"

He nodded. "Very well. The truth. I killed Richard Hunt, but I had reason. He was a quest-monger."

"Ah." I had begun to suspect something of the sort. The evils of our bondage followed us wherever we went. The law was clear, though not always enforced: it was unlawful to leave a lord's service without his permission, just as it was forbidden to receive a wage higher than that which might have been paid before the Death – this despite the great increase in the price of goods. "He was hired by a vengeful lord to find a serf who had affirmed himself free of serfage?"

"Just so. And the runaway was, of course, me. Indictment had been laid against me by jurors, and I was in my absence put in default. Richard Hunt – I don't know truly who he was or where he was from – tracked me to this gathering, and confronted me. But he offered me terms. If I could pay him, he would leave me be. I told him that I had money, and would go to fetch it."

"Instead you killed him."

Bull said simply: "I had no money, Captain."

"Any man in this camp would have only sympathy for such a tale, Edmund. Why did you not tell it at once?"

"I did not kill him in a fight. I killed him by subterfuge. This, I feared, might lessen men's sympathy."

"Yes," I said. "And then, of course, there is this point: the man you killed was unarmed."

At last, I had spoken words that surprised my prisoner! His mouth fell open in what could only be genuine astonishment. Then came understanding; until that in its turn was replaced by something more familiar – calculation. "What? Unarmed? No man in this camp is unarmed!"

"Nonetheless, no weapon was found in the victim's tent. Not that which slew him – yours, presumably – nor his own."

"As to mine, I threw it in the millpond."

"Impossible. There was no time. The death scream was heard, and an instant later you were seen to leave the tent."

His mask of confidence had returned fully now. "Not so, Captain. The scream was mine; a pretence. I first left the tent, supposedly to fetch Hunt's payment, then re-entered stealthily and cut his throat from behind. He died at once, and without voice. Then I left his tent again, rid myself of the murder weapon, came back yet again to that horrible place, screamed and made my final exit."

"Why come back when you had already got away?"

"I had been seen coming and going, more than once. Someone would have identified me later. But this way, without the knife, I knew you had no proof against me. This is no King's Bench that will hang a man without proof. Besides, we march to London tomorrow to parley with the King. Thus, having failed to convict me overnight, in the morning you would either exile me from this band, or else let me march with you and take my chances in whatever may follow."

No, I thought: this is not yet the entire truth. A man unused to murder would not behave with such cool subtlety in its aftermath. "What about Hunt's missing weapon? You said yourself, such a man would never go unarmed."

"He had a knife when last I saw him, a fancy one. Perhaps it was stolen by the men who seized me. In any case, I do not see its great significance?"

"Is this, too, insignificant: that we have spoken to men from Three Oaks, and they do not know you?"

"That means nothing. As men go searching for higher wages, the old, immutable communities are changeless no more. There are strangers everywhere these days."

That, in 1381, was undeniable. In my own countryside, one man in ten was unknown to me. The England I had been born into was dying, one way or another. We lived now in a frightening land where one might not know the names of a neighbour's children, though they lived but a mile away.

Which thought gave birth within my mind to another.

I rose. "Your story stands well to any questions my poor mind can conceive, Edmund. But you understand the mood of the camp – if I am to protect you, then I must ensure that all believe in your innocence. I will ask my cousin William if he has any more questions to put to you."

I made one last visit to the victim, after which I would order him buried. Again, I inspected the wounds to his belly and hands. There was blood everywhere, but by washing gently with a cloth, I saw that his throat was intact. I fetched William and told him what I had heard, and showed him what I had found.

"William, is the victim's name and home village known throughout the camp, as well as the manner of his death?"

"Probably not."

"Then please see that it becomes so, without delay."

"I will, but why?"

"Something that Edmund and I were speaking of."

I walked a while in the gloaming, my eyes on the ground, not the heavens. After some time, William caught up with me. He had with him an old man who, when shown the body, was able to identify it as Richard Hunt of, indeed, Three Oaks.

"Haven't seen him for a few years, Captain, but I've known his family all my life, and the resemblance is unmistakable."

"Thank you, brother. Why have you not seen him in so long, if he is of your village?"

The sadness in his voice gave way to pride as he replied. "Richard was a man as did free himself. His lord didn't like that, it lodged in his arse like a wasp, but there was little enough he could do about it, for Richard was gone and none knew where."

The old man left, and I wept. William put a huge arm round my shoulder. "Do you weep for the dead, John, or . . ."

"For the dying," I said. "William, go and find a stout rope."

I untied Edmund's hands.

"Am I then free, Captain?"

"No. This is so that you might pray. A man cannot make his last prayer bound like that, it is not seemly."

After a long silence, he said only: "I see."

Most lords in those days did not bother to chase after runaways. They might make solemn vows between themselves, to hold firm against the demands of the working man, but when a lord's own fields stood ready for harvest, he would pay what wages he needed to pay, and to Hell with his fellow landowners.

Some, however, let their pride dictate their actions; or perhaps they were the far-sighted ones, who saw that if they did not stand together, they would lose their realm to merchants and freed workers. Sir Simon Burley, for an example, had been so determined to retake a fled serf, that his stubbornness had led to the rising in Gravesend, the sacking of Maidstone, the siege of Rochester Castle – and, in large part, to our own presence on the heights of London.

"Richard was no quest-monger," I said. "It is you who are the informer, the man-hunter. Richard was your prey."

He said nothing, as I had expected.

"His throat was not cut. You meant to cut it, I daresay, but he defended himself. It was indeed his scream that was heard. Much else, I think, is as you have said. You hoped that, with no weapon, no witnesses and no confession, I should have to acquit you come morning. If I dismissed you, you would make your own way back to the lord who hired you. He didn't care whether or not you brought his man back alive, only that the rebellious serf was punished for his disloyalty. If I made you come on the march, then you would have slipped away at the first opportunity, to join the Mayor's men."

"Not necessarily," said Bull, his calm manner having reasserted itself now that all hope had fled. "I have no love for mayors and archbishops, any more than for your own mad preachers and wild malcontents. It may be that I would have joined with Tyler and Ball – should they win, which perhaps they will. Though I must admit, I doubt it."

I peered at him in the fading light. "Do you know something?"

He laughed. "Whatever it is, Captain, I shall take it to my grave. Now, is my tree ready?"

I could not but be saddened by such bravery, for it was not merely courage in a wrong cause – it was courage *without* cause. Bull laughed and jested, knowing himself minutes from death, and yet he had fought, and would die, for nothing more than a bag of coin.

William brought the rope, and we walked a way across the Heath to the tree that he had chosen as suitable for our work. As my cousin and some others made their preparations, I stood aside with the condemned man. Softly, I said to him: "Was it your son?" He said nothing, so I continued. "You must have had a confederate, to take the dagger away with him – and, unthinkingly I suppose, to take also Richard Hunt's knife, which he had lost during the struggle. This confederate then made his escape from the back or side of the tent, while you, making sure to attract attention to yourself, appeared from the front. And for you to act so, this confederate must have been someone close to you. A son, I thought, or perhaps a brother?"

Edmund nodded, and smiled once more. "My nephew, Captain. My only living family, and a reluctant if loving lieutenant in this business. He is long gone, and need trouble your thoughts no more."

"Then you would have me hang the murderer's accomplice, yet leave the murderer to go free?"

Fear. In an instant, his eyes filled with fear. And fear for another – which is the worst kind. "What do you mean?"

"The fatal knife-work was your nephew's, not yours."

"Why do you say so?"

"You told me you had cut Richard's throat – yet, as I have said, his throat was intact. Perhaps this is how it was: you sent your nephew into the tent first, to hold Richard's attention. You would then enter quietly, and slice your victim from behind, silencing him and killing him with one action. But at the crucial moment, you were distracted, perhaps by a noise from without. You turned, peeked from the tent-flap to see that no one was approaching – and when you turned back, at the sound of Richard's scream, it was to discover that your nephew had done the job for you."

Bull said nothing, but stared at me, as if trying to make me out from afar. I continued.

"He was eager to please his uncle, no doubt. To prove himself to a man he loved and admired. In any case, you did not witness the killing itself – only its aftermath, which was bloody and indistinct. The corpse lay on its stomach. You did not know that your nephew's blade had entered poor Richard by the belly, not the throat."

He placed a hand on my arm, gripping it with the passion almost of a lover, or an assassin. "Captain, I beg of you – don't search for the boy too hard. And in return I shall do you a kindness, with these words: do not go to the parley tomorrow."

"What *do* you know?"

"Only this, that people who have power never in history have ever parleyed honestly with those who have none."

Was he murderer or murderer's accomplice? It was likely I would never know, nor ever know if it mattered.

"That is hardly a kindness, Edmund – to set me tossing and turning, torn between my duty and my skin, all through what may well be my last night on earth."

I hanged him instantly thereafter, not wishing unpleasantly to prolong the business.

The next morning we marched to Blackheath, to join the great mass of our fellows, and the rest is known to all, I suppose. That Wat Tyler, our lovely chieftain, was murdered; that not only the King's men, but our young King himself, betrayed us; that hundreds of honest men died in the months that followed, their crime being only a dream of freedom.

And this too is known, I hope and trust: that the great lords thought they had defeated freedom for all time, and that slowly they were taught that they had not.

Heretical Murder

Margaret Frazer

Margaret Frazer started out as the pen name of two co-authors, Mary Margaret Pulver and Gail Frazer, but since 1996 the name has been used solely by Gail. Starting with The Novice's Tale *(1992), they created the character of Dame Frevisse who has appeared so far in eleven novels and several short stories. Both authors have contributed several stories to my anthologies and I was delighted when Gail received the Herodotus Award for the Best Historical Mystery Short Story of the Year from the Historical Mystery Appreciation Society for "Neither Pity, Love Nor Fear" from* Royal Whodunnits *(1999). The following is not a Dame Frevisse story, though it is set in the same period, in 1431, and introduces us to Sire Pecock, who went on to later fame and notoriety as Bishop Pecock. Reginald Pecock was born in Wales and became both a priest and a fellow of Oriel College, Oxford. In 1431, he was in his early forties, and made the rather bold move of leaving the scholar's life of Oxford to become Master of Whittington College in the heart of London. He was there for the next ten years, turning his learning towards convincing heretics of the error of their ways through the use of Reason. This made him unpopular with a great many people but he was nonetheless made Bishop of St Asaph's in 1441 and, in 1450, Bishop of Chichester. He continued his writings, became more unpopular, and in 1457 was falsely and illegally charged with being a heretic himself. In keeping with his teachings, he bowed to the verdict made against him by the Church, most of his*

*writings were burned, and he died imprisoned and in
obscurity a few years later.*

The bright rain spattered down, silver in the sunlight, its
thin cloud barely casting a shadow as it swept over
London on a warm breeze, taking the rain shower with it that
mid April morning in 1431. Barely dampened, young Dick
Colop dodged out of College Hill Street into narrow Paternoster Passage and along it toward the hardly wider yard
at its end closed in by St Michael Paternoster's Church and
churchyard on one side and Master Whittington's Almshouse on the other. Richard Whittington, three times Lord
Mayor of London and dead these ten years, had left money
for charities and among them was the building and endowing
of this row of almshouses and the keeping in comfort there of
thirteen poor men and women for all time to come. To
oversee them and tend to their souls and pray for the souls
of Master Whittington, his late wife Alice and others, a
college of five priests had been founded with the Almshouse
and built across the churchyard from St Michael Paternoster
that had been given over to the good of the College and the
Almshouse together.

Dick Colop, all of twelve years old and neither poor nor a
priest, had place here, first, by his father's thought that he
might make a scholar or even a priest and anyway would not
be harmed by more schooling, and then by the help of his
uncle John Colop who had persuaded the priests to take on
an able boy to run their errands and help the servants in
return for his keep and lessons in Latin and penmanship –
"Useful if he goes on to university or to be a lawyer or even,
God willing, a priest," his uncle had said.

"And useful anyway," his father had said, "if all he does is
follow me into the trade." Which was the making of books –
Books Fine and Plain said the sign over his father's shop in
Fryda Street.

Therefore Dick was here and mostly glad to be, since he
enjoyed learning and books, and the College's priests, re-

quired by its charter to be learned men, provided both. The only steady blight on his life was the Almshouse's poor folk. They seemed to think he was their servant, which he was not, and never saw him without demanding he do one thing or another for them. So as he dodged into Paternoster Passage he was reckoning his chance of skimming past the Almshouse without being caught and didn't think there was much chance. Nor was there, he saw as he came into the paved yard. The morning being more fair than not, the pensioners were lined like jays on the benches in front of the Almshouse, facing south into the sun, old Henry thumping his cane on the stones and saying something at deaf Stephen but breaking off to call, "Hai! Boy!" at Dick but too late. Dick had veered aside to the nearby side door into the church, was through it and closing it even as old Henry shouted and able to pretend he hadn't heard.

Mostly he didn't do that but just now he needed time to gather himself and the church was his surest place to do it. This was the quiet while of the day – after morning Mass and between early and midday prayers – and he moved into the choir end of the church, hoping one else would be there but unhappily discomfited to find Sire Pecock, one of the College's priests, was.

Not that Sire Pecock in himself was a trouble. He was newest-come to the College and so far was the least demanding of the priests, never thinking of something for Dick to do simply to have him doing something. Sometimes he even made a jest over Latin lessons, and if he had been in prayer here, he would have been no problem now either, because when Sire Pecock prayed he prayed deeply and would have ignored Dick. But he wasn't praying; he was sitting in his particular choir stall gazing somewhat towards the raftered roof with the furrow between his eyes that always brought Sire Thomas to say, "He's gone off again." Not in a fit but with thinking. Even for someone who had his degree from Oxford, Sire Pecock seemed given over much to thinking, Dick thought; he could do it for longer at a stretch than anyone Dick had ever seen. But he stopped now, turned his gaze from the rafters to Dick, and asked, "What's the matter, young Richard?"

Since his thick, wooden-rimmed spectacles were lying in his lap and he was exceedingly short-sighted without them, his question made Dick, a full ten feet beyond where Sire Pecock could see him clearly, ask back, startled, "What makes you think aught is the matter?"

"Because, faithful though you are to your prayers, I've never noted you come to them panting with eagerness. Yet you're here and panting . . ." Dick tried uselessly to steady his quick breathing. ". . . And that suggests the possibility of that something is the matter." Sire Pecock picked up his spectacles and put them on, looping around his ears the ribbons that kept the frame astraddle his nose while going on, "So what is the matter? Come and sit down and tell me."

Dick went, pulled down the hinged seat in the choir stall next to Sire Pecock's, and sat with a deep heave of breath but no words.

"Go on," Sire Pecock encouraged. "Say it and maybe it won't weigh so much. Ah." The priest leaned a little forward, peering at Dick's face. "You've been out and about, being part of this stir, and you're feeling the pain of stay-at-home? Is that it?"

"No," Dick said, sharp with self-defence.

Sire Pecock's eyebrows – they were very impressive eyebrows – lifted questioningly, the way they did in lessons when he was doubting Dick fully understood what he was saying.

"It isn't!" Dick insisted. "I didn't go on purpose to see any of it anyway. Sire John sent me to St Lawrence Jewry with that book he'd borrowed and I couldn't help but see, going across Cheapside." Where the London men going to join the Duke of Gloucester's army against the rebelling Lollard heretics in Oxfordshire had been gathering before going to their muster in Moorgate Field outside the walls. The men's talk had been loud and overbold, the crowd around them loud and ready to cheer them on their way, and at first Dick had felt the way Sire Pecock had said. To go back to lessons and the church's quiet and the old men's talk had seemed a miserable thing compared to hanging a sword on his hip, shouldering a pack, and setting off on a bright spring day to see the world with a great many others in high, good spirits. But then he had seen a woman crying, a baby on her hip, and a man trying to tell her goodbye while she clung to his sleeve; and an old woman staring into the crowd after someone, her whole face bleak with the fear she'd never see him again; and after that Dick had seen more and more of the sorrowing amid all the noise and eagerness and his own eagerness had gone out of him. But he couldn't say all that to Sire Pecock, could only manage, "It was just that I had this thought that if there's fighting, some of the men there might never come back."

"They'd be killed, you mean."

Dick nodded.

Sire Pecock tapped him firmly on the knee. "If that's what you mean, then say it. Always say straight out what you mean, because words are the only way we have to reach each other in this life and if we're false to them we're all too likely to be false to one another. Still, you've moved past seeing only the surface seeming to what lies behind – in this case past the pleasure people take in the glories of war to the plain truth that those glories require killing and that those killed may include men on one's own side as well as on the other. Now . . ."

Knowing that Sire Pecock tended to turn any talk into a long-sentenced lecture unless stopped, Dick interrupted him – almost everyone did and Sire Pecock never took offence – with, miserably, "The trouble is, I don't think I much want anyone to be killed on the other side either."

"Young Richard," Sire Pecock said sternly, "the other side are heretics. Are you saying you don't want heretics killed?"

Dick sat up straight with indignation, "I've heard you say in talk with my uncle and with Master Carpenter that you think it's better to reason with heretics instead of killing them. That someone who's not saved before he dies is damned afterwards and that it's better to save a man's soul than send it to Hell. I've heard you!"

Sire Pecock's laugh was rich and full with pleasure and

approval. "Well said. I wondered if you ever heeded when we talked."

"Of course I heeded." Dick was still indignant.

"And, better than heeding, you understand and, moreover . . ."

He would be away at lecturing again in another moment, and before he could be, Dick said, "There was something else, too. I saw a dead man in Watling Street when I was coming back."

Behind his spectacles' thick glass Sire Pecock's eyes widened. "Just lying there in the street with no one heeding him?"

"Oh! No. There were people all around and Father Alard from St Mary Aldermary and a sheriff's man came as I was leaving." In truth, after sidling and weaving his way through the crowd to come close enough to see the man crumpled down in a spread of his own blood on the paving under an inn gateway, he had had time for only one long look before the sheriff's man was ordering the crowd back but by then Dick had gone gratefully because he had never seen someone dead like that before, all sprawled in his own blood. Where so many people lived so close together as in the middle of London, with everyone knowing everyone else's business for three streets and more in every direction, someone dead was not an uncommon matter; but the dead that Dick had seen in his few years had always been laid neatly out on their beds with family and friends gathered mourning around them. Not like the dead man in the gateway with his arms and legs flung careless around him and his head a-loll, with people crowded around staring and jabbering as if at a Corpus Christi show. "But I knew him. He was Master Furseney."

"The scrivener with a house in St Mildred Close?" Sire Pecock asked, and at Dick's nod, he started to rise.

Dick caught hold of the side of his dark gown. In the short while Sire Pecock had been at the College, he had taken it on himself to learn St Michael Paternoster parish fairly well and a goodly portion of London beyond it but he didn't know everything and Dick said quickly, by way of warning, "His wife and he, they're not much for coming to church. There's talk . . ." Dick dropped his voice to almost a whisper: ". . . that they're Lollards."

The same as were in revolt in Oxfordshire, heretics who claimed they knew God's meaning in the Bible better than any priest could and that the time was come to put down the rich clergy in favour of poor men, if rumors and their pamphlets to be found in London these past few weeks were anything to go by. They were both stubborn in their beliefs – one of them had been burned at Smithfield last year for his – and dangerous, as their present rebellion showed.

But Sire Pecock twitched loose of Dick's hold and kept going, saying, "Talk is talk but deeds are deeds and duty is duty and whether he was heretic or not makes no difference in my duty. Come you, too. I'll maybe need you."

Dick made after him, both willing and unwilling and trying, "Father Alard will have done all there can be done for him."

"Very like, but he was still of our parish and one of us should be there, too."

At least, going with Sire Pecock, there was no trouble in passing the Almshouse. The men called out greetings to Sire Pecock and he gave them a smile and signed the cross in the air for blessing towards them without losing stride, and a quick stride it was, considering the first grey was showing in his dark hair around the tonsure. Dick had to trot to keep at his heels as they went up the street, where everything was the familiar busyness of a London morning. There were house-wives and servant-women, alone and hurrying or in pairs and talking, some with children holding to their skirts and almost all with their market baskets on their arms, with the day's purchases of new bread from the baker and maybe a cut of meat from the butcher and whatever the greengrocer might have in this early in the growing year, along with anything else needed for the day's running of their households. An apprentice from the draper's shop in Thames Street was cheerily whistling along, trading nods with another appren-tice going somewhere else with a bundle in his arms. At the foot of the street the water carrier was rounding the corner with his daily cry of "Water, water, clean and cool" and his cart and its clanking load of water cans, while the ale-seller at the other end of the street was letting down his shutter to turn his shop's front window into the counter of his stall for the day, singing loudly and off his tune that summer was a-coming in.

It was all as if everything was as it always was and that unsettled Dick the more, because things weren't as they always were and it wasn't right for them to seem so. There were heretics in rebellion and men going off to fight them and a man dead who hadn't been an hour ago . . .

"Good," Sire Pecock said when they reached Watling Street and sight of the small gathering of men outside the gateway to the Rising Sun tavern's yard. "They've not gone." Undoubtedly meaning those to whom Master Furseney's death was their business – the undercrowner and his clerk, the sheriff's man with a clerk of his own, and Father Alard – not the few men and women left from the crowd there had been, a dozen or so folk who really did have nothing better to do than stand around watching other people at a sorrow. They were keeping well back now, on orders from the sheriff's man, surely, and not in Sire Pecock's way as he joined the small group around the body.

Dick went with him not very eagerly. Master Furseney's body had been moved aside, out of the welter of his own blood, on to a length of rough cloth for carrying away. It had been straightened, too, been laid out on his back and though his mouth still gaped, his eyes closed by someone, making it easier for Dick to look at him, if only in a brief glance and away. No one else was looking, their business with him apparently done, the undercrowner telling his clerk, "Go let Master Drury know we're having the man taken away now. He can have his gateway back. Good morning, Sire Pecock. A sad business."

Good mornings and agreement to that were exchanged all around before Father Alard said, "Sire Pecock, by your leave I'll go with the body. I know the family and his wife wants him at home before he's buried."

"That's most reasonable," Sire Pecock assured him. "I'm

very new here. I leave it all to you." Making it clear he wasn't
going to quarrel over the body and the pence for the prayers
over it. But as Father Alard moved away, to find men among
the onlookers to carry the body, he went to stand over it and
look down into the dead man's slack face. Dick, somewhat
ashamed of his unease, kept with him and made himself look,
too, and was as surprised as he always was by how little was
left when someone was dead. Only a body and it no longer
seemed to matter much. But then Master Furseney had
never seemed to matter much when he was alive. From
the little Dick had ever seen of him, he had been a vague
man – vaguely there, vaguely busy, vaguely competent – and
he wasn't even that. He was just dead, his body there and
everything else about him gone. In a day or so his body
would be buried into London ground, displacing the bones
of someone buried there before him, and later, when his little
stretch of ground was needed for someone else, his bones
would be moved in their turn into the churchyard charnel
house, to keep company with all the others waiting there for
resurrection on Judgment Day.

"What happened?" Sire Pecock asked at the undercrowner
who was just starting to turn away.

The man – Dick could not remember his name but he was
presently the deputy of the king's crowner for London,
required to be called in to any unexpected death – stopped
with a shrug. "There was some sort of brawl in the tavern
yard. One of those sudden things. Mostly fists but someone
used a knife and . . ." He tipped his head toward the body:
". . . there he is. Stabbed in the back."

"Is it known who did it?"

"From all anyone has said, they were all strangers here but
him. Likely they were Kentish men, mustering to the duke of
Gloucester's army. These days it seems there's five times as
many strangers around as men I know and most of them
quarrelsome, I swear. This lot took off, are surely somewhere back with the army by now and lying low. We'll not
find them." He shrugged again. "He picked the wrong men
to brawl with is all."

The man moved away, his clerk with him, and before Sire

Pecock could do the same an elderly man from among the
onlookers sidled over and said low-voiced to Sire Pecock's
back, "That's all wrong, you know."

Sire Pecock turned to him. "What is?"

"About Furseney being done that way. Couldn't have
happened."

"No?"

"I've known William Furseney as boy and man and he was
never in a brawl in his life."

"You were here?"

"Wasn't," the man said. "But I know him. He was never a
tavern brawler. Was never a brawler at all, was William
Furseney."

"You've said so to the undercrowner or the sheriff's
man?" Sire Pecock asked.

"Tried. They don't want to hear it. It's enough he's dead
and they can say why and be done with it."

While he was saying so, a woman with a full market-basket
on her arm but no haste to be home joined them. "He has the
right of it there," she said. "There's too much else a-foot
these days to worry over somebody like William Furseney
being dead. He wasn't anybody."

"Not in the world's eyes maybe," Sire Pecock said firmly,
"but in God's eyes he was as much as you and I, good wife.
Were you here when they were brawling?"

"I came at the end of it. Not in time to see much." Her
regret for that was open.

"Did you see Master Furseney fighting?"

"That I didn't. I'd just come up, was on the edge of
everyone crowded into the gateway to watch and just
asking Mistress Emmys what was toward, when the
men that were fighting – you know how they are, not
paying any heed, just all clotted together and hitting at
each other and yelling – lurched right into crowd and set
us a-scrambling to be out of the way. Then somebody
started yelling about somebody being stabbed. 'He's
stabbed,' I heard someone yell that."

"Aye, so did I," said another woman who had come close,
a servingman behind her, and been all ears with listening.

"Somebody said that and all of a sudden most everybody was scattering . . ."

"The men who had been fighting," Sire Pecock said.

"Them and some who'd only been watching and should have been somewhere else anyway," the first woman said with a sniff.

"Those as had been fighting, they took to their heels," her servingman said.

He was a gangling youth, tall enough to have seen over heads better than most, and Sire Pecock asked him, "Did you know any of them?"

The youth shook his head that he didn't.

"How many were there?"

"Five or six, like."

"They were away before anyone could think to stop them," his mistress said.

"And some other folk disappeared up and down the street," said the first woman. "Such as didn't want the bother once the fun was over. But I stayed, on the chance there'd be questions asked." Making a virtue of it.

"Not that they were interested," the second woman humphed, and they both gave dire looks toward the sheriff's man and the undercrowner in talk beside the gateway.

"Couldn't be bothered," the old man put in. "Too much else in hand these days."

"Did any of you see Master Furseney among the men fighting?" Sire Pecock asked again, this time of the women and servingman. None of them had. "Or any daggers out?"

"No, sir," the servingman said, "but it was all happening fast, like. They were all clotted together. You couldn't see anything clear except they were fighting."

"Richard." Sire Pecock turned to Dick, who had kept close and been listening hard. "Go to everyone still standing around and ask if they saw Master Furseney before the fight or in the fight and who among the men had a dagger out."

"Sir," Dick said with a bow and went willingly to the task.

He returned from it puzzled, rejoining Sire Pecock just as he finished talk in the tavern doorway with Master Drury and turned away, beckoning with his head for Dick to follow him away along the street. Master Furseney's body had been carried away, the officers were gone and most of the onlookers wandered on their way. Except for a servant sluicing a bucket of water over the blood on the pavement to wash it away, nothing out of the usual might have happened here.

"So, Richard?" Sire Pecock asked. "What did you learn?"

"That almost nobody, at least those still here, saw Master Furseney at all." That was no puzzle; Master Furseney had been a man easily overlooked. "Only one woman says she saw him coming along the street with a man not much before the fight. She didn't know the other man."

"Did she see them go into the tavern yard?"

"She says she didn't. There were a lot of folk coming and going along the street, the way they do this time of day and more than usual because of the muster. Master Furseney and the man with him passed her, that's all she knew, and then she heard the fighting and turned back to see what was happening. Otherwise all anybody else I talked with knew is that there was a fight and Master Furseney was killed. What did Master Drury say?"

"That the men were strangers to him – some of the Duke of Gloucester's men out of Kent, he thinks, from the way they talked. They were at the inn only a little while, had been quarrelsome with each other when they came and all he meant was to let them have a few drinks and send them on their way." Sire Pecock began to walk back the way they had come along the street, Dick at his side. "He was indoors when the fight started and didn't see Master Furseney with them, but he says none of his servants saw him either. Or doesn't admit to it anyway. One must always leave room in one's considerations for lying." At the jog in the street where Watling turned into Budge Row, Sire Pecock stopped and faced Dick. "What do you make of what we've heard so far, young Richard?"

Used to the priest's way of suddenly demanding that he think, Dick answered, with barely hesitation, "Nobody saw Master Furseney with the men or in the fight. Or they're not saying they did, anyway. But we don't know of any reason why any of them would lie about it so probably we can take it as truth." Sire Pecock nodded approval of that, and Dick went on, encouraged, "So, if the woman was right about seeing him in the street, he doesn't seem to have had chance to meet them before the fight started. He was just there and was watching in the crowd and somehow was stabbed."

"Somehow?"

"Well, the men staggered into the crowd while they were fighting. One of them had his dagger out and, instead of stabbing one of the others, he stabbed Master Furseney. By accident, it would have been."

"Hm," Sire Pecock said, committing to nothing. "Clumsy of whoever did it, wasn't it?"

Dick had been thinking the same and readily nodded agreement.

Sire Pecock began to walk again. "Tell me about Master Furseney. You said he was a scrivener. What else do you know of him?"

Because Dick's father's trade was the making of books and Dick was good at listening to what was said around him, he knew something of Master Furseney and told it to Sire Pecock, little though it was. Master Furseney had his own shop but not much work of his own. What he mostly did was take the overflow of copying work from more important scriveners. "They'd hire him, see, to . . ." said Dick.

"It is not a matter of sight, young Richard. You're telling me this. I'm hearing, not seeing it. Please be precise."

Keeping his sigh to himself, Dick said, "They'd hire him to do work when they'd taken on more than their own people could manage fast enough. He was good at it, must have been, because my father used him sometimes. He just didn't have ambition to be more. Some men don't, my father says. He got by and that was enough for him, like."

"Like enough or exactly enough?" Sire Pecock asked crisply.

"Exactly enough," Dick muttered, but he knew he wasn't being bullied, he was being educated, and repeated clearly, "Exactly enough," before he could be told to do so.

"Very good," Sire Pecock approved, giving Dick nerve to ask, "Where are we going?"

"To Master Furseney's window, to see how likely she thinks it is for her husband to be dead this way. But first we stop here." And on the word Sire Pecock did, outside Master Hansard's scrivening shop with its sign hung out above the street of a silver quill pen crossed slantwise with a bright red parchment roll. "Do you know if Master Hansard," who came to St Michael's and was therefore known to Sire Pecock, "ever hired Master Furseney?"

"Probably. Master Furseney's place is just along and around the next corner."

"Very good." He didn't tell Dick to wait outside so Dick followed him inside the shop. More broadly fronted to the street than most, with its shutters taken down there was an abundance of south light across the half-dozen desks lined there. The men at work at them did not look up nor the scratching of pens on paper falter as Sire Pecock made his way towards the back, met by Master Hansard coming forward to exchange greetings and head-shaking and regrets over Master Furseney's death, word of it having already spread so far. It gave Sire Pecock chance to ask what he had known and thought about the dead scrivener, and Master Hansard told him readily enough and somewhat at length but it coming down to him having nothing bad to say of Master Furseney except he had been sadly lacking in ambition. "He brought in good work and on time. Very neat-handed and never tried to cheat me on anything. I'm going to miss his usefulness. Though likely his wife will carry on. She's as good at the work as he was and I'll hire her as readily." Master Hansard pursed his lips, considering something. "Maybe I shouldn't fault him for poor ambition either. He bought half a ream of paper off me maybe two weeks back. Poorest stuff I had on hand but, still, that was something he'd not done before. He was maybe starting to build his business after all. Pity then he was brought so short. Damn foreigners." Meaning anyone not of London.

Leaving him to his head-shaking, Sire Pecock went on to Master Furseney's, Dick knowing the way. St Mildred Close was short, dead-ended between other streets, and Master Furseney's shopfront was narrow, shouldered in on either side by larger places. Its sign over the street was merely of a quill pen, somewhat faded, and inside the place was equally modest, with a single, ink-marred desk, a shelf above it with inkpots and other tools of his trade, a long-legged chest for keeping of things along one wall, and nothing else. Like most London houses, there was this room at the front, a room at the back, and stairs to rooms above; and here there were voices in the room at the back and Sire Pecock went that way, paused to lift the chest's lid and look inside, then cleared his throat to warn he was there before going into the kitchen.

Dick followed, braced to face Mistress Furseney's grief and maybe Master Furseney's body again, but it wasn't there and the widow was merely sitting on a joint stool beside a well scoured table, tear-marred but the first shock of her grief seemingly past, leaving her limp and weary. Another woman setting a kettle of water on the small hearth fire and a third was piling some linen towels on a corner of the table. They paused at their tasks and Mistress Furseney raised her head to look at him as Sire Pecock entered. It was the usual moment for some bustle to be made to welcome a priest, from what Dick had always seen in his own home and other places. Instead there was a pause, with stares from the women and no word of greeting before Sire Pecock as if not noticing anything, which Dick very much doubted was the case, went to Mistress Furseney and began to say what could be said about loss and grief. That there were only the two women with her was strange. This was the time for neighbours to flock in. But strange, too, was that the woman tending the kettle was on the only other joint stool and by rights should have given it to Sire Pecock but she didn't; and the other woman, who in the usual way of things should have offered him something to eat or drink, simply went on unfolding and then refolding the cloths while Mistress Furseney merely sat staring into her lap, making no response except, when Sire Pecock paused, she said, still to her lap and dull as the toll of a mourning bell, "He's gone. That's all. He's gone."

At that Sire Pecock sat down on his heels in front of her, took hold of her hands and asked with a gentleness Dick had never heard from him before now, "With him gone, good wife, how will it be with you? Are you able to make your living without him?"

So practical a question found its way through Mistress Furseney's haze of grief. "My living?" She lifted her red-rimmed eyes to him. "Yes, I'm able."

"How?" Sire Pecock pressed.

She shifted restlessly. "How? The work is still there. We did it together. I'll do it alone . . ." – her voice broke a little – ". . . now."

"Have you work presently on hand, to see you through a while?"

"What? No. But something always comes."

"You've money in hand though, to see you through?"

Mistress Furseney straightened a little, her wits stirred awake by his questioning and, laying a hand over the bag-purse hung from her gown's belt, said with an unexpected edge to her voice, "I've money enough for now. Enough to bury him, which is what you're here for, you priests being what you are and never willing to do aught for anyone without payment in hand to you."

"Madge," the woman at the other end of the table said, chiding. Or warning her, Dick suddenly thought, seeing the looks that instantly passed among all three women before Mistress Furseney slumped down to silence again.

But Sire Pecock, who always seemed to see everything, stood up and said as if he had neither heard nor seen anything untoward, "Well, if there's nothing I can do for you now and here, I'll leave you."

To that Mistress Furseney made no answer. It was the woman at the table's other end who said, somewhat stiffly, "Thank you for coming."

"Of course," Sire Pecock said, sketched a sign of the cross in the air towards them and turned to go, then turned back to ask quietly, "Did your husband often keep company with men used to quarrelling and daggers?"

"What?" Mistress Furseney raised her head to frown at him. "No. Of course he didn't. We lived quiet. He never kept company with any such. He never kept tavern-company at all." Her voice strengthened with certainty and indignation. "Ever."

"It was just base mischance he was there and it happened," the woman beside the kettle said. "That's all it was."

"Why was he out this morning?" Sire Pecock asked, still to Mistress Furseney and still quietly.

"To . . ." Mistress Furseney began sharply but stopped, stared at Sire Pecock, then lowered her head again to say dully, ". . . meet someone, he didn't say who, about some work. I think. I don't know."

"Do you want I should start Masses for Master Furseney as soon as may be?" Sire Pecock persisted, to Dick's intense discomfort, who only wanted to be out of there.

Mistress Furseney jerked up her head. "Masses," she said bitterly. "Priest-gobbling. Priest . . ."

"Madge," the same woman said urgently.

Mistress Furseney stopped short, dropped her eyes, and although her breast heaved with swallowed feelings, managed to say, "Thank you for coming, Father," not as if she meant it.

"Of course," Sire Pecock answered mildly, as if hearing nothing amiss. Nor did he seem to hear as he left – although Dick following him did – one of the women mutter behind them, "Can't even wait for a man's body to chill before they come looking for their pence for Masses . . ." and from another one, hurriedly, "Hush."

But outside, standing in the street while Dick shut the door, Sire Pecock asked with a deep-drawn frown between his eyes, "Now what did you make of that, young Richard?"

Dick had been trying to make nothing of it and answered reluctantly, "I've never seen anyone dare that much rudeness to a priest."

Sire Pecock accepted that with a considering nod and, "To what would you ascribe that rudeness? What would you judge is its cause?"

"Grief," Dick tried, but Sire Pecock raised his brows and Dick gave up, admitting, "They didn't want you there. Since I doubt you've done anything yourself to offend them, and guessing . . ." Sire Pecock raised his brows again and Dick changed to, ". . . *Judging* by what they said that it's priests they dislike, not you in particular, they may well be heretics."

He grimaced over the word, it being a vile thing to say of anyone, but Sire Pecock gave a brisk, single nod, one of his stronger signs of high approval and said, "Well reasoned. Things being as they are in this present time, with the rebellion in Oxfordshire and all causing more than a few people – most of them not heretics at all, merely slack of spirit – to show themselves in church again for the sake of protecting themselves against any charge of Lollardy, Mistress Furseney and her friends are rude to a priest who's done them no harm as well as refusing Masses for the soul of a well-mourned husband. Neither such rudeness nor such refusal are sensible things at any time, let alone now. Put that together with other things, such as her husband purchasing a large quantity paper of late, more than could be used up in the while since then even if they had both worked unstopping these two weeks since he is said to have purchased it, which I think we can safely say they have not, sleep and food being unrefusable human needs . . ." As all too usual when caught up in his thoughts, Sire Pecock was running sentences together at too great a speed. ". . . And yet there is no paper in the shop – you did note that as we passed through? – let alone any work in hand according to Mistress Furseney herself, who nonetheless says she has no present worry over money and is likewise certain about what company her husband doesn't keep but says she doesn't know whom he was with this morning, and we are – to use an ever-popular hunting term – on the scent, young Richard, on the scent."

"Of what?" Dick asked, his voice rising with the frustration of having completely lost hold of where Sire Pecock had started.

"Of lies, my boy." Sire Pecock set off along the street at a walk fast enough to keep up with his thoughts, Dick trotting at his side, "Of wrongs and lies. They're laid out in front of us the way a fox's trail lies plain to a hound's nose. It's for us, being men, not hounds, to follow not our noses but our wits. Our wits, young Richard. You scented, so to speak, the start of the trail yourself back at the beginning of it, at the tavern, when you said you couldn't see how Master Furseney could have been part of the fight."

"Well, yes. It doesn't seem so. What else I don't see, though, is how he was stabbed by accident, like?"

"Like by accident. Exactly." Sire Pecock turned in abruptly under the tavern sign of the Goose and Moon, around the corner from St Mildred's Close and a few doors along. "You have it."

Not clear at all what he had, Dick followed him inside. Even so early in the day there were men and a few women with seemingly nothing better to do than share the benches and drink ale or whatever cheap wine was to be had. Their talk dropped away at Sire Pecock's coming in but he raised a cheery hand at them and turned aside to an empty bench near the window, sitting down and nodding at Dick to do the same. Dick would have questioned him then but Master Gregory, the Goose and Moon's keeper, was coming their way with pottery cups, a pitcher of ale, and a smile. Even in the short while he'd been at St Michael Paternoster, Sire Pecock had not sat snug in the College's comforts with his dignity and his learning but had been out and about, talking to folk because, as Dick had once heard him say to Sire Thomas, "How am I to know what they need if I don't know them?"

Sire Thomas had answered to that, "You just have to pray for them, man, not know them," but plainly he knew Master Gregory who poured the two cups of ale for which Sire Pecock asked and then, at Sire Pecock's invitation, poured one for himself and joined them, saying, "You've been to see Mistress Furseney, have you? Old Bess saw you going in."

"A sad business," Sire Pecock said moderately. "She's far gone in grief, it seems."

"Aye. They were a close pair. Never any shouting heard from their place. Good folk."

"Not many women with her just now."

Master Gregory shifted his wide bottom on the bench.

"No. No, they weren't an outgoing pair. Liked well enough but not with many friends, if you see."

"Ah, yes." Sire Pecock nodded. "Sufficient unto each other. That will make it harder for her now."

"My wife is baking a crispcake to take to her later. To help her through these few days she won't feel like cooking. A good many of the women are doing that."

"Aye, my wife is doing that, too," another man said, he and another drifting to the table, ale cups in hand.

Sire Pecock smiled on them and laid coins on the table, saying while Master Gregory poured for everyone, "The Furseneys were good folk, then, but not prospering, I take it?"

"Not so's you'd notice," Master Gregory agreed.

"I don't know about that," one of the men said. "You both heard Harlow, that works for Fouk the tailor, you know, say he saw him coming out of a house over in Lad Lane a few evenings back and asked as he passed him, like you do to be friendly, 'What brings you here?' and Furseney said he was thinking of buying the place."

The other man scoffed. "Harlow told us the house. It's run down enough you'd be better burying your money in a box in the garden than buying it. Not that Furseney had the money to be buying it anyway. I'm betting it was a woman he was there for."

"Now," Master Gregory said, "you mind your talk of the dead. I know the house you mean and if he was there at all, it was for ink. The old woman what lives there makes ink."

"Then why tell Harlow he was thinking to buy the place?"

"Because it was more mannerly than telling Harlow to mind his own business."

Sire Pecock nudged Dick and stood up with a friendly nod at Master Gregory and the two men to show it was need not wish that took him away, and outside in the sunlight again, said, "That went more easily than I'd dare hope. Come along."

Dick didn't ask where but was not surprised when they shortly turned into Lad Lane. The street was one of London's short and narrow ones, front doors crowded near to each other and the upper storeys of the houses overhanging to close out much of the light but the pavement between them cleanly swept and most of the houses well kept, making it easy to choose which of them Sire Pecock sought. Midway along and once as good as its neighbours, there was one with the paint faded on the plaster between the half-timbering, a shutter on an upper window held on by only one hinge and a latch, and the doorstep dirty with old mud though all the others on the street were this-morning scrubbed. Besides that, to add to its ill-seeming, not even the bright day had tempted anyone to open the shutter over the window beside the door more than the merest crack, as they approached, Sire Pecock said in a low voice, "Very likely the woman here will be as close-shut as her house but if we win inside, see all you can of everything while I hold her in talk."

"See what? What am I supposed to see?"

"I don't know," Sire Pecock said and knocked at the door, far too lightly for anyone not close at hand to hear.

But the door was promptly jerked open a crack, a pair of eyes in a head tipped sideways peered out, and a woman's age-thinned voice, sharp with rancour, demanded, "Yes, what do you want?"

As mildly as he had knocked, Sire Pecock said, "Good wife, I'm in need of ink."

The eyes narrowed into a frown. "Why come to me?"

"You've made ink for Master Furseney, haven't you?"

"He talks too much, does William Furseney," the woman muttered, then said, "Best you come in, I suppose."

She drew back and opened the door just grudgingly wide enough to let them into a low, narrow, bare-raftered room that Dick guessed was supposed to be both workplace and shop but was untidy, dim, and dirty, with small sign she did anything there at all. The woman, like her house and business, had seen better days, too. Age came in different ways to people. To her it had come with a humped back and small care for herself, grey hair straggled loose from a headkerchief that probably hadn't been washed since her loose-hanging dress and food-spotted apron had been, and that wasn't lately; but as Sire Pecock, once inside, crossed away from her towards the worktable under the shuttered window, she shuffled after him quickly enough, saying, "What manner of ink and how much are you in mind to have?"

Dick, left behind at the door and supposing this was his chance, slid sideways, trying to be as unnoticeable as possible, towards the room's other doorway until he could see through to the room behind. Somewhat larger than her shop, it seemed to be where she did most of her living because besides a battered cooking pot on the hearth and table, there was a bed with tumbled blankets along one wall and a smell of much use and little cleanliness. The back door stood open to a long, narrow yard, with the remains of a once neatly kept garden, Dick guessed from what he could see of it, high-walled on all sides from its neighbours, and between the two rooms stairs barely wider than his own shoulders went up to the floor above, impossibly steep for a bent-backed old woman managed, which would be why she lived in her kitchen, he supposed.

More than that he didn't dare and sidled back towards the front door, to let Sire Pecock know he had seen all he could. The priest seemed too busy to notice, bent over the table with a quill pen, writing on a scrap of paper and commenting on the ink to the old woman.

"Aye," she answered. "I can make up a batch of that for you in three days' time, if you like."

"That would do well. The price?"

She named a price somewhat more than Dick would have agreed to, but Sire Pecock accepted it without question. It was while he was taking the money from the pouch on his belt that he said, "You've heard about Master Furseney's death, I suppose."

The old woman, her eyes on his purse until then, jerked up her head, staring. "Master Furseney? Dead? How?" she demanded. "When?"

Not noticeably noticing her perturbation, Master Furseney clasped his purse closed. "This morning. Perhaps three hours ago." He held out the coins to her. "He was stabbed in the back in a tavern brawl, they say."

"A brawl?" The old woman's voice scaled up, disbelief warring with alarm in her face. "No."

"I fear I saw him dead myself."

She had forgotten to take the coins. Sire Pecock moved his hand to remind her and she belatedly held her hand out for them, her mind openly elsewhere.

"You'll add your prayers to ours for his soul?" Sire Pecock asked.

"Prayers? I hardly knew him." She shuffled backwards from Sire Pecock. "I sold him ink, that's all. Haven't seen him for weeks. A month or more." She turned towards the door. "I'll pray for him though. I can do that, yes. Thank you for coming. You'll have your ink in good time, sir. Good day."

She wanted them gone and Sire Pecock obliged her, letting himself and Dick be seen out the door with more haste than manners, thanking her as he went and walking away along the street, saying nothing nor Dick either until they had turned the corner and were out of sight of the house. Dick would have said something then but Sire Pecock held up a hand to stop him and called out, "Geva, wait a moment, please you," to a servant woman who had come out of another house as they left the old woman's and gone down the street and around the corner ahead of them. Intent on what he wanted to say, Dick had hardly noticed her but as she turned around he knew her, Mistress Dyer's servant who came with her mistress to St Michael Paternoster every Sunday and feast day.

She, in return, knew Sire Pecock and came back towards him, bobbing a curtsey as they met and smiling a greeting.

"You came out of a house in Lad Lane just now," he said.

"My cousin's." Geva gestured to the laden basket she carried in the crook of her arm. "She does Mistress Dyer's headkerchiefs and I was fetching them. A better starcher you won't find in London."

"Do you take time for talk with her? Because I'd know something about the woman who lives in that unhappy house further along the street."

"Old Mistress Aunsell?" Geva said. "A disgrace to the street she is and has been for years. Even before her husband died she was going strange."

"She lives alone, then?"

"All alone and keeps herself to herself into the bargain."

"No family at all?"

"She's from Oxford, years back, and my cousin has said she used to talk about going back to family there but she never has, worse luck for the street. Some of her kin has come looking for her, though. My cousin says some nephew has been in and out of there off and on the past month."

"She had that from Mistress Aunsell?"

"Not likely. She talks to nobody if she can help it. No, my cousin stopped him in the street one day and asked him and that's what he said. That he was a nephew from Oxford trying to persuade her to go back with him. He hasn't though."

"Early days yet, perhaps," Sire Pecock said and nodded her on her way, waiting until she was away before he turned to Dick and asked, "So? What can you tell me?"

"There's only one plate and cup on the table in the kitchen and that's where she mostly lives, I . . ." He decided not to guess. ". . . think. There's a bed there."

"For this nephew maybe?"

"It's been there and slept in a long time. Longer than a month. Besides, I'd say the stairs are too steep for her, the way she can hardly walk. It's most likely hers."

"Did you note if the stairs looked to be used or not?"

"They were used but not clean," Dick said, pleased with himself. "They looked like the dust had been on them fairly thick but someone had been going up and down them of late so they were clear in the middle but with still the dust still deep in the corners."

"I wonder," Sire Pecock said, considering some distant point along the street, "why a man who could afford to come from Oxford to persuade an aunt to go back with him, wouldn't be able to afford somewhere better to stay than there? But it seems safe to say Master Furseney and this nephew aren't the same and that it wasn't for women Master Furseney went there. Very possibly it was for ink. Hers is surprisingly good."

"Maybe he went to meet the nephew?" Dick suggested. "Maybe we should find out the nephew and ask him."

"Almost undoubtedly, *not* a desirable thing to do," Sire Pecock said firmly and walked onwards again. "We've one thing more to learn and then I think we're finished."

"Finished?" Dick echoed in surprise.

"Finished," Sire Pecock repeated but added nothing more and Dick refused to ask anything, merely kept up with him as they, first, retraced their way until almost back to Master Furseney's house, then swung into another street and along it to the next street's corner, where Sire Pecock paused, looked along it, said, "Yes. That would serve," and turned away.

"What would serve?" Dick demanded, staring over his shoulder as they left. "What did you see?"

"No more than you did. You saw there's an inn along there?"

"The Blue Stag? Yes."

"Can you judge what lies at the far end of its yard?"

Dick reckoned quickly. "Maybe the yard behind Master Furseney's house?"

"Even so."

"I don't see . . ."

"All this morning you have been seeing and hearing. Now you must think, young Richard."

Dick shook his head. He wasn't sure he didn't prefer going to his dinner to thinking just now.

"A suggestion," Sire Pecock said. "Consider Oxford."

"Oxford?" Dick repeated blankly. He gathered his thoughts. "The old woman's nephew is from Oxford."

"So we're told, and since the woman has long been said to be from there, very likely he truly is. Now, what else is there about Oxford?"

At last Dick began to be excited. "The Lollard rebels. That's where the Duke of Gloucester is going. To Oxford against the Lollard rebels." He caught at Sire Pecock's arm, stopping him. "Master Furseney's death is about *that*? About the uprising?"

"I cannot say it certainly," Sire Pecock answered, "but, yes, I think so. We have enough at least to interest the sheriff a little more in Master Furseney's death, I believe."

"We do?"

"There now." Sire Pecock began walking again. "You've gathered your facts, young Richard, right along with me. Now let Reason tell you the sum and meaning of them. I've tried to teach you to reason through. Now do so, please."

Dick tried but trotting at the priest's side and dodging Londoners willing to move aside for a priest but not for a boy made it hard to keep hold all at once on everything there had been today and sort it toward whatever Sire Pecock saw in it. There was Master Furseney, dead in an unlikely way. And his wife and her friends and their unfriendliness. An inkmaker. A man from Oxford. Where the Lollard rebels were. But not all the Lollards. There were Lollards in London, not in open revolt but . . .

"The pamphlets," Dick gasped. "The paper Master Furseney bought. The inkmaker. They've been copying out the pamphlets that've been showing up everywhere!"

"They and some few others, I would reason," Sire Pecock said. "Yes, that's the core of it, I think. Do you perceive the whole of it?"

Going backwards through what they had learned, Dick said eagerly, "The nephew from Oxford is with the rebels and they're hoping for help from Lollards in London. He came and made use of his aunt . . ."

"Willing use, I would say," Sire Pecock put in. "Though if she's wise she'll claim she was ignorant of his purposes."

". . . to find a Lollard who could help him – that being Master Furseney . . ."

"Likewise willing."

". . . who probably knew her because she makes ink. Because he was a scrivener, he could get paper in quantity without rousing suspicion, and if he was a Lollard . . ."

". . . as we think he was."

". . . he'd know other Lollards willing to do all the copying out of the pamphlets in the quantity needed. Where did they do it?" Dick wondered, then answered for himself, "At his house because everything would be there."

"So I suspect," Sire Pecock said, "and thereby lies the usefulness of the inn behind his house, because I doubt that the coming and going of some several people over and over to an unsuccessful scrivener could happen without comment from the neighbours and they needed another way in. People come and go as a matter of course at an inn, to drink and eat if not actually to stay, and these people we are supposing might hope, if careful at it, to go unnoticed. It will be for the sheriff to determine whether there is indeed a way from the inn into the Furseneys' yard and, if there is, how much the innkeeper knows. Now, what of Master Furseney's death itself?"

They were nearly to the sheriff's door but, as understanding struck him, Dick stopped still in the street, at peril of being run over by a pair of schoolboys racing home to their dinner. "The old woman's nephew. Master Furseney was seen coming along the street with another man. Then there was the brawl and he was stabbed in the back, but it wasn't the men fighting who did it. They weren't seen to have their daggers out at all. It was the man with him who did it. In the crowding and excitement, no one saw it. But it was the nephew, wasn't it? I'll bet anything the nephew did it."

"Betting is a perilous pastime, the cost all too often outweighing the gain," Sire Pecock said, "but, yes, I think it was the nephew killed him. Now, why?"

Dick was fairly hopping with excitement. "Because Master Furseney knew both the nephew and the people who did the copying, and if the people who did the copying never knew the nephew, then with Master Furseney dead, there was no link between the nephew and the Lollard pamphlets. Even the old aunt needn't have known for certain what her nephew was up to, only that he needed a scrivener." He sobered suddenly. "What about Mistress Furseney? If she knows about this nephew, he'll want to kill her, too."

"Very possibly she knows next to nothing about him. He may never have come to the Furseneys' and so she may know of him but not how he looks or even his name. To keep everything as secret as possible would be cunning and there is assuredly cunning in all of this. But even if she does know, she's safe enough for now, while the women are with her, and before long, if the sheriff does his work well, he'll have the nephew and she'll be safe."

"Except she's a Lollard," Dick said, not happy at seeing her other peril.

"We only suspect that. We don't know it. For myself, I would judge that presently our good Bishop of London has trouble enough without I raise more trouble over suspicions of heresy just now."

"But the pamphlets . . ."

"If she has sense, she'll deny knowing what her husband was doing. She'll say that if he was doing Lollard business it must have been only for the money."

"But she's a heretic," Dick insisted.

Sire Pecock moved on towards the sheriff's door, saying serenely as he went, "And how much easier it will be for me to reason with her about that if she isn't in prison for it. Haven't you heard me say how better it is to reason a person out of their errors than kill them?"

"You'd have the murderer caught, though."

"Murder," Sire Pecock said grimly, "is not an error. It is sin." And with a firm hand knocked hard at the sheriff's door.

A Moon for Columbus

Edward D. Hoch

*Edward D. Hoch (b. 1930) is almost certainly the most
prolific living writer of short stories, and rapidly becoming
one of the most prolific short story writers ever. That's a
remarkable claim these days when most of the specialist
fiction magazines have long folded. This is short story number
836, and was his last completed story of the millennium
(which ended 31 December 2000, of course), and he reckons
he'll be adding to that total at about twenty stories a year.*

*I just happened to mention to Ed that it would be intriguing
to see a mystery on board Columbus's historical voyage of
discovery, and no sooner had I said it, than Ed obliged.*

On Tuesday, the ninth day of October in the year
1492, the three-ship fleet under the command of
Captain General Christopher Columbus had been at sea for
just over a month, having sailed from the Canary Islands on 8
September. There was talk of mutiny among the crew,
mainly Castilians, who were tired and fearful of being lost
at sea. On that day the Pinzon brothers, captains of the *Pinta*
and the *Niña*, had been rowed across the waters in a moderate wind and come aboard the flagship *Santa Maria*. They
argued that the search for land be abandoned and that they
sail for home on the southerly breeze before it shifted
dangerously. Also in the meeting with Columbus was the
ship's master, its owner Juan de la Cosa. He was second in
command, looking after the safety of the *Santa Maria*.

It was a stormy session in Columbus's cabin, but the Captain General had seen migrating birds flying above the ships. "We are near land!" he insisted. "I feel it in my bones, I see it in the sky! Three more days is all I ask!"

The Pinzon brothers exchanged glances. Martin Alanzo, captain of the *Pinta*, was in his late forties and eldest. His ship was usually in the lead. Vicente Yanez, the youngest of them, commanded the *Niña*, while a middle brother worked with Martin aboard the *Pinta*. It was Vicente who spoke now. "My men are restless. There is mutiny in the air and cockroaches on every deck. My ship is leaking so badly the morning watch can barely pump out the water."

"We all have that trouble. Three days is all I ask. Then we will turn for home." He knew they thought him obsessed with the idea of Japan, and perhaps he was, but he intended to complete this voyage successfully if at all possible.

The brothers returned reluctantly to their smaller caravels and Columbus sighed with relief. He had three days, until the twelfth. A great deal could happen in three days. But by late the following afternoon the easterly winds had picked up alarmingly, reawakening the crew's fears that they might never return home.

"You must speak to them," Paolo Romano advised. He was Columbus's pilot, a sturdy man with a sensible attitude. "Talk of mutiny is never good on any ship."

Columbus reluctantly agreed. A seaman since his youth, he had buried a wife, fathered two sons, one by another woman, been shipwrecked by pirates off the coast of Portugal, sailed north to Iceland, west to the Azores, south to the Gold Coast and east to Cyprus, yet was only forty-one years of age. He was not about to end up with a mutiny on the most challenging voyage of his career. "Assemble the men," he said with a sigh. "I will address them from the poop deck."

There were forty men and boys aboard the *Santa Maria*, and when Columbus stepped out on deck to speak to them, all but Romano, at the ship's wheel, were there awaiting his words. "Turn back!" someone shouted from the rear, but he was heartened to note that none took up the cry.

"We are on a voyage to the Indies," he began. "We are

seeking new routes to old lands, attempting to prove that Japan and China can be reached by sailing west. We are doing the work of the Lord, and the Lord will guide us in our discovery. Already we have seen and heard flocks of birds that tell us land is not far away."

"But what of the wind that blows from the east?" one of the more experienced crewmen asked. "Surely it will hinder our return."

"As you must know, I met on board yesterday with the captains of the *Niña* and the *Pinta*. They agreed to maintain a generally westerly course for three days and to turn back if no land was sighted by that time. I only ask the same from you, just two more days, until the twelfth."

There was more talk back and forth, and perhaps it would have gone on longer but for a providential flight of birds that passed high over the ship in a V formation. The crew members took this as a sign from God that land was truly near. Their leader, a boatswain named Juan Alagar, agreed they would wait two more days. The boatswain, whose duties included everything from stowage of cargo to preventing rats from eating the sails while in port, was highly respected among the others. Though he was younger than some, he was tougher than most.

Later Columbus's page boy, a lad of sixteen named Luis who'd joined them just two days before they sailed from Palos bound for the Canary Islands, brought him supper prepared by his personal steward. "Is it true we are near land?" he asked.

"As true as I can judge," Columbus told him. "If we are, you will be among the first to set foot on it."

The youth's face beamed at the news. The Captain General had first noticed him on the day they sailed, awkwardly taking communion with the rest of the crew at the Church of St George. He seemed to keep to himself rather than mingling with the handful of other youths in the ship's company. Columbus had taken the ship's master, de la Cosa, aside and told him he wanted Luis as his page-boy.

Originally planning to sail from Spain on 3 August, Columbus had delayed a day because of a decree by Ferdi-

nand and Isabella expelling all Jews from the country by 2
August. Columbus did not wish to set sail in the unwanted
company of crowded vessels chartered by the Jews for their
exodus. Once on the open seas the three caravels with a total
of ninety men and boys aboard encountered rough water and
some rudder trouble on the *Pinta*, but still reached the
Canaries in eight days. There Columbus hoped to find a
replacement for the damaged *Pinta*, but finally the rudder
was repaired and the ships began to take on the necessary
supplies. They sailed from the islands on 8 September.

After speaking to his crew, Columbus slept uneasily that
night. He could feel the ship's tossing as the winds increased
to gale force, and he feared what they might see, or not see,
when the sun rose. As he made his way to the deck on the
morning of the eleventh, he was disheartened that no land
had been sighted. It was young Luis who lifted his spirits by
producing a green branch with a little flower attached. "I
plucked it from the sea," the page boy told him. "Surely it is
a sign of land."

"It is indeed!"

And more signs were forthcoming. The other ships hauled
up pieces of driftwood as well, and with each new sighting
the crew's spirits rose. Still, with every man watching the
horizon as the sun set that afternoon, no land was spotted. It
was about five-thirty, though time was kept at sea by a
system of sandglasses which had to be turned each half-hour
by a boy assigned to the chore. If the boy dozed for a few
minutes, a seaman's watch of four hours on duty could be
lengthened. Columbus often wished for a more accurate
system to help with navigation at sea, but he was forced
to put up with it.

As usual at sunset, all hands were summoned on deck and
evening prayers were said. Columbus led them in singing the
traditional *Salve Regina* and then spoke a few hopeful words.
"By this time tomorrow, the good Lord willing, we will sing
his hymn on solid ground."

That night only the boys managed any sleep at all. The
men of the crew, led by Columbus and the ship's master and
the pilot Paolo Romano, remained at their posts, scanning

the night for any flash of light. All that could be seen was the flame in the big iron brazier at the rear of *Pinta*, leading the way as usual. Then, about ten o'clock, there was something else. "Paolo!" Columbus shouted to the pilot. "Did you see it? The light at our rear, like a little flash of fire!"

"You saw the moon," Romano suggested.

"At ten o'clock? The moon does not rise this night until eleven. Surely our sandglasses could not be that far off. Might the *Niña* have been trying to signal us?" Torches of pine pitch were sometimes used to signal between the ships at night. One or two had been lit on their ship earlier, but all was darkness behind them.

"Surely they would have kept signalling," the pilot said.

That was when someone shouted, "A light! Land!"

"Did you see it?" Columbus asked. He recognized Diego Quierdo, a bearded translator skilled in Hebrew and Arabic. If it was truly the mother of all languages as some believed, a knowledge of Arabic could be helpful anywhere, but he had not taken an immediate liking to Diego, a man who advocated a ninth crusade to take back the Holy Land from the Muslims and Jews.

"I saw a light, that was all. Is it land, Captain?"

"I don't know."

For now all was darkness again, except for the *Pinta*'s iron brazier up ahead. Most of the men stayed on deck, scanning the horizon as the moon rose, but after a time Columbus started down to his cabin. He almost tripped over a limp form at the bottom of the steps. Hurrying to get an oil lamp from the cabin, he lit it and gasped at the sight before him.

It was his page-boy, Luis, the side of his head covered with blood. He was dead.

While more lamps were brought in to illuminate the scene, the ship's surgeon, Garcia Gibaro, was summoned to examine the body. "The boy is dead," he pronounced. "The fall down the steps killed him."

Alagar, the boatswain, asked, "Shall I prepare for a burial at sea?"

But Columbus shook his head. "He would want to be

buried on land if possible. Wrap him in sailcloth until we see what tomorrow brings."

He sat brooding in his cabin after that, shocked and unbelieving that a vigorous young man's life could be snuffed out so easily. When his personal steward Pedro brought him something to eat, he pushed it aside. "Are the men still on deck?" he asked.

"Many of them, Captain. They search for land by the light of the moon."

The Captain General sighed. "The land will appear when it is ready."

"You should eat something."

Pedro was tall and slender, a doting servant who had been with Columbus on previous voyages. "Food is for daytime, drink is for night, yet I dare not avail myself of the wine you so graciously provided. Tell me, Pedro, you have known young Luis for two months now, since we sailed from Palos. Was he not a limber lad?"

"He was indeed, sire."

"Then how do we explain his death in such a freakish accident? Any of us could have fallen down those steps with no more than a bruise to show for it."

Pedro shrugged. "The ways of the Lord are strange at times."

When he was alone Columbus pondered the death of this youth he'd barely known. He could hear some of the men returning to their quarters, the exhilaration of the night dampened by Luis's fatal accident. Presently he took up one of the oil lamps and made his way to the main crew quarters. "Where did Luis sleep, Diego?" he asked Quierdo, the translator.

The bearded man motioned toward one of the soft planks that served as beds for the crew. In the rolling and pitching waters, a skilled seaman was able to brace himself well enough to get a little sleep. "Over there, by the bulkhead."

Alagar, the boatswain, who also slept there, shook his head sadly. "I will miss his nighttime mutterings."

"He talked in his sleep?"

"Nothing that anyone could understand. Just the dreams in a strange tongue of a lad far from home."

"Where are his belongings?" Columbus asked.

The boatswain frowned and started to search about as Diego Quierdo joined him. "The youth had few possessions," the translator said. "Nothing anyone would steal."

Yet they were not to be found. Columbus decided they could search better in daylight. In any event there were more important matters at hand. At around two a.m. he returned topside. The waters were calmer now, though a brisk trade wind still blew. The moon, past full, was in the port quarter where it bathed the ships' sails in silver. *Pinta* was still in the lead where it would be first to reach land or, in the words of one old sckeptic, first to sail off the edge of the earth.

Suddenly from the lead ship came the sound of the lombard being fired, the large cannon each ship kept loaded and primed to announce the sighting of land. Already the *Pinta* was shortening her sails to await the flagship. Presently Columbus drew alongside and called out, "Señor Martin Alonso, you have found land!"

Indeed it was true. The lookout on *Pinta*'s forecastle had seen something like a white sandy cliff glowing in the moonlight. Noting it in his journal, Columbus allowed the three ships to drift until dawn in a south-southwest direction. Then they sailed due west along the southern fringe of the island they'd sighted. It seemed too small to be Japan, and he decided it must be an island in the Indies. By the morning's light they turned north. Halfway up the west side of the island they saw a gap in the reefs and a good anchorage, with naked copper-skinned people awaiting them on the beach, and Columbus went ashore with the translator and a party of armed men in the ship's boat, flying the royal standard. The two Pinzon brothers likewise came ashore in boats off the *Niña* and the *Pinta*.

They knelt on the shore to thank God, and Columbus gave the island the name of San Salvador, taking possession of it in the name of the Catholic sovereigns Ferdinand and Isabella. The natives seemed friendly enough, although Quierdo could not translate their words. Both males and females were naked, some with their bodies and faces painted. Columbus presented them with red caps and glass beads that they put around their necks. They seemed to want to give something in return, and after a time returned with some parrots and cotton thread, along with darts for hunting. The darts had fire-hardened wooden points, but a limited range. These handsome young savages knew little of other weapons, and when he showed one his sword the native grasped it by the blade, cutting himself.

"What else do we have to give them?" Columbus asked, and one of the crewmen produced some hawks' bells that greatly intrigued the natives. "Since we surely are in the Indies, I will call these people Indians," he decided.

They investigated the flora and fauna of their landing place. The island was big and mostly level, with green trees and many small bodies of water. Small lizards ran freely. In the trees he could hear woodpeckers at work. Finally, when it was time for return to the ships, Columbus led the men in singing *Salve Regina* as he had promised. He felt that their first day in this new world had gone well. But he had not forgotten the unpleasant task before him. Luis's body still lay wrapped in sailcloth awaiting burial.

Columbus was up at dawn the following morning, Saturday the thirteenth, having barely slept after the excitement of the previous day. By daylight he searched through the crew's quarters but no sign of Luis's meagre belongings could be found. Then he went with the surgeon to examine the body once more before burial. As he uncovered the head for the first time by daylight, Columbus noticed something that had been hidden by the darkness.

"Look here," he said to Gibaro, calling attention to a singed portion of the dead youth's hair, just above the terrible fatal head wound. "What do you make of that?"

The surgeon peered closer. "It seems burnt, and there is a mark of soot here. What could have caused that?"

"Nothing on those steps or below deck. He was hit with something, possibly one of our pine pitch torches." Suddenly he remembered the flash of light he'd seen that night. Not the moon or a signal from the *Niña*, but a torch on board their own ship being quickly swung at its target. "Garcia, my friend, this lad was murdered."

"How is that possible? Who would murder a boy of sixteen? And why?"

"I do not know," Columbus muttered, more to himself than to the surgeon. He began to strip off the dead youth's pants in preparation for burial, then suddenly stopped, pulling them up again. "He will be buried in his clothes, on the beach of San Salvador before we leave."

Before he could organize his thoughts there was a shout from the morning watch on deck. "Boats approaching!"

Columbus hurried on deck and saw a swarm of canoes of all sizes bearing down upon them. Word of their arrival had spread across the island, and the natives paddled back and forth, circling the ships and waving their greeting from craft apparently carved from the trunks of trees. A bit later he went ashore with Gibaro and Quierdo the translator. The surgeon was interested in inspecting the native huts, while Columbus found a quarry of stones that might be suitable for building a church on the island. A native youth showed him the proper method of throwing their hunting darts.

Quierdo proved of no use as an interpreter and Columbus was forced to gather what information he could through signs and gestures. He was anxious to press on to Japan, but decided that San Salvador should be explored more carefully before their departure. On Sunday morning he organized a party made up of crewmen from all three vessels, using their ships' boats to take them to the north end of the island. There they found three more villages. Columbus was reluctant to land because of the reefs, but some natives swam out to greet them with food, urging them to come ashore. They seemed to think these strangely clad Castilians had come from heaven.

"We will take six Indians with us as guides and interpreters," Columbus told his pilot. "Prepare to sail this afternoon."

* * *

Back on board the *Santa Maria*, Alagar the boatswain asked, "What will be done with the body of your page-boy?"

"He will be buried on shore before we sail." He went below to his cabin, removed his sword and stretched out on the bed, thinking of what he had to do.

It was Diego Quierdo, the translator, who found him there that noon when he'd heard the news that six Indians would be travelling with them. "I do not trust those savages, Admiral," he said. Some of the men had taken to calling him that, and it was a title he much preferred. He imagined someday being Admiral of the Indies, Admiral of this land he'd discovered.

Columbus sat up on his narrow bed. "They are peaceful men, Diego. They will not harm us."

"Take them if you wish, and sell them to the first slaver we encounter."

Columbus's eyes hardened. "Would you kill them, good Diego, as you killed my page-boy Luis?"

"I never harmed the lad," the translator replied, turning away.

"You killed him because he was a Jew."

Diego Quierdo turned back toward Columbus, his eyes ablaze. "You are a devil! How could you know of this?"

"When I was undressing him for burial I saw that he had been circumcised, and I remembered the edict ordering all Jews out of Spain the day before we sailed. He passed as a Christian in order to sail with us, but that was why he kept to himself as much as possible."

Quierdo's face was flushed with an anger Columbus had never seen before. "He blasphemed by taking Communion with us!" the translator shouted, and with those words Columbus remembered the boy's awkwardness in accepting the sacrament.

"Only to save his own life. What else could he do under the circumstances?"

Quierdo answered with another question. "How could you have known that I killed him?"

"I know now that the ten o'clock moon I saw was a burst of light when you struck Luis's head with one of the pine torches, yet a few minutes later you claimed to have seen the light too. That would have been impossible. You simply wanted to announce your position far away from the stairs where the lad's body lay. Then there was the matter of his speaking a strange language in his sleep, a language none of the others could understand. But it wouldn't have been strange to you since you know Hebrew. That was what told you he was Jewish, wasn't it? And you could have confirmed it when you saw him naked. After you killed him you threw his belongings into the ocean in fear that they might reveal him as a Jew and provide a motive for the crime."

Diego smiled and drew his sword. "Admiral, forgive me for this."

Columbus's hand closed on one of the native darts. As Diego moved he thrust it into his side.

It had been a shipboard accident, Columbus told his crew. The page-boy Luis and the translator Diego Quierdo were buried in separate graves on the San Salvador beach. Before they sailed away Christopher Columbus paused to say a prayer to the Lord for the soul of this Jewish boy who'd died so far from home.

House of the Moon

Claire Griffen

Claire Griffen is an Australian writer, actress and dramatist. She introduced the character of Don Alessandro Orsini in "Borgia by Blood" in Royal Whodunnits. *Here is a rather more delicate case for the Borgia spy to investigate.*

1502 – the Venetian Rites of Spring. The splendid and solemn ceremony of marrying a city to the sea, Venice made one with the Adriatic. From all the republics and kingdoms came the "wedding guests" in their gaily apparelled hordes. The palazzi fluttered with bunting, and barquess and gondolas festooned with garlands and gold-and-purple regalia crowded the Grand Canal.

"Not a ripple of water to be seen between them," observed the henchman Ugo Beppo.

He stood with his master on the balcony of the *Casa Luna,* named for its façade of Istrian marble. Most of the other guests had gone down to the bridge for a closer view of the regatta. Ugo had persuaded his master to stay behind. In such a jostle, it would be a simple matter for a Borgia enemy to slide a stiletto between the ribs of a Borgia spy.

Ugo, an ex-actor and virtuoso of disguise, was both bodyguard and friend to Don Alessandro Orsini, potentially the most dangerous man in Italy. In the Papal States the flag of the Borgia Bull was flying and Sandro was prince of foxes to the most powerful of that name – Cesare, Duke Valentino, son of the presiding Pope and conqueror of Italy.

And, as a sideline, Don Alessandro Orsini liked to take a hand in murders, both political and domestic.

Ugo had known him since boyhood when he had fished Sandro out of a canal, the victim of a family vendetta, yet there were still moments when he was caught unawares by the exotic, almost barbaric nature of his master's looks. Even in an Italian doublet in his favourite colours of sage and ivory, and with his hair worn in the prevailing fashion of long curling strings, his face with its almond-shaped eyes and olive tints was too Oriental to be Italian and had earned him the nickname *Il Saracen*.

The sunset that gilded the colonnades of the Palace of the Doges gradually faded into twilight. With a little flurry of sound, the evening breeze fluttered the bunting strung along the palazzi. Torches were lit on the watercraft and in the sconces of doorways.

A servant of the *Casa Luna* brought a lighted flambeau out or to the balcony. Ugo was suddenly aware of another presence and a hooded scrutiny beyond the radius of light. He crouched for the stiletto in his boot. Before he could draw it, Sandro's sword was in his hand. Ugo sometimes despaired of his master's carelessness for life, but in a crisis he could react swiftly.

"A thousand pardons for this intrusion," a deep voice came purring out of the darkness, "but I seek the one known as El Saracen."

The intruder stepped into the light. His accent and dress betrayed him as a Turk. Ugo ran an amazed eye over his crimson kaftan and pearl-strung turban and halted warily at the curved dagger thrust through the striped waist-sash.

But Sandro looked only at the face. Bearded, intelligent, cruel with something of the falcon in the hooked nose and piercing glance.

"You would be fortunate to find your quarry in this multitude," he parried.

"My search has led me to the House of the Moon. With so many comings and goings it was easy to gain admittance. I only had to know a name. Don Alessandro Orsini." The Turk made an extravagant flourish. "I am Murad Bey, Grand Vizier to the Sultan Bayezid, Lion of Istanbul."

A cynical smile curved Sandro's mouth. "Surely the fame of Il Saracen hasn't reached the Golden Horn."

"You are too modest, my *cid*. Do you recall Chasimpueg, who came as the Sultan's ambassador to the Vatican in 1493?"

"Vaguely. It was nine years ago."

"The powerful Duke Cesare that we know today was then but a mere Cardinal in the shadow of the Pope. But you were already in the shadow of that shadow. How prescient of you to recognize his potential and he a mere youth.

"There was much talk in Rome of the murder of your wife. The perpetrator had tried to disguise the deed. Your house had all the signs of being looted by revellers during Carnival, but you by astute inquiry and examination of the scene unmasked the murderer, one close to the Vatican."

"One who was said to be the murderer."

"Even so. It was this incident that brought you to the attention of Cardinal Valencia and was a curious tale that clung to the mind of Emissary Chasimpueg. Ah! I see I've opened an old wound." Murad glanced keenly into Sandro's face. "May I be flayed alive if it will appease you."

Sandro shrugged away the fulsome apology. "So the Great Sultan knows something of my history. It's taken him long enough to satisfy his curiosity. Has he no Scheherezade to beguile him with tales?"

"Nothing so trivial as curiosity summons you to the Seraglio. It's an occasion of murder."

The light from the flames flickered over the spy's face, given an illusion of flaring excitement.

"I should have thought murder in the Seraglio was commonplace. From the tales one hears."

"Not this one. The victim was Aysha, the Sultan's kadin, or, as you might say, favourite."

"Isn't murder in the harem equally commonplace? Why does Bayezid require my special expertise when he has an army of halberdiers – and you, his Grand Vizier?"

"He seeks an *impartial* investigation. My galley lies in the lagoon beyond the city. The Great Sultan honours you in sending to escort you his most trusted servant."

"Or assassin," muttered Ugo.

A pearl dangling from the ear of Murad Bey flushed in the torchlight as he turned his head to look at the henchman. Ugo felt the hairs on the back of his neck prickle as the Turk's gaze encountered his.

Sandro was smiling and shaking his head. "I must decline."

Murad sighed. "I must insist. Beyond this curtain are two of those halberdiers, renowned for their strength, who will accept no refusal."

Sandro laughed softly, allowing the point of his sword to rest on the striped sash. "Life is precarious at the best of times. I could make you a candidate for the dissection table, a subject for Leonardo's sketch-book. In plainer speech, I could carve you up, Murad Bey."

The gleam of a gold tooth showed in the Vizier's beard. "My blood would stain this fine terrazzo floor and provoke a diplomatic incident. The Ottoman Empire would make war on Venice to avenge me. On the other hand, I could order my halberdiers to cut you in two. Are you so beloved or invaluable to the Borgia that they'll make either half a cause for war?"

Sandro smiled and sheathed his sword.

"Should you succeed in unmasking the murderer," pursued Murad, "you'll find the Sultan's gratitude beyond expectation."

"And if I fail?"

"Does El Saracen admit that possibility?"

"Is there a body for me to examine?"

"Aysha died a week ago. As is our custom she was interred with all speed."

"No corpse and the site of the murder a week cold. How did she die?"

"There were no visible signs of violence. We leave that for you to discover."

Sandro gave a soft chuckle. "The challenge of a lifetime.

How can I resist?" He rested his hand on his friend's shoulder. "From a wedding to a funeral, Ugo."

"I trust not ours," responded the henchman, gloomily.

"I think we have a few more teeth than the Lion of Istanbul."

In 1453 the Turkish Sultan Mehmet II had conquered the Byzantine capital of Constantinople and renamed it Istanbul. On the isthmus between the Mamara Sea and the Golden Horn he built his Grand Seraglio, Topkapi, the Sublime Port, a jewel in the setting of lush meadows, parks and gardens. Through the Main Gate and under the shadow of the Tower of Judgment, Murad Bey and his captive guest were carried in a litter. Ugo, acutely pessimistic about their ultimate kismet, followed on foot as became the servant of a noble lord. He kept a sharp eye on the halberdiers marching beside the litter and a ready hand on the stiletto in his sheath.

Isolated by the silk curtains, Sandro felt himself being carried through a bewildering labyrinth of corridors, rooms and courtyards and through a maze of sounds and smells, from the music of harps and flutes to the twittering of birds and the snarling and trumpeting of beasts encaged in the Elephant House, from delicate perfumes and foreign foods to the strong musk of African animals.

"Where are we going?" enquired Sandro, mystified.

"To my private *haman*," replied the Grand Vizier.

The *haman* proved to be a luxuriously appointed hall with marble columns and inlaid tiles. Steam from the water which flowed from brass taps into large marble sinks rose in thick clouds to escape through the skylight. From bowls of silver were flung scalding water over the bathers, who sat on stools with pattens on their feet to protect their soles from the heated tiles.

Between deluges of water the skin was vigorously scrubbed with a loofah. Sandro found the experience invigorating rather than pleasurable; his skin shrank in anticipation of the next assault.

"You don't care for Turkish customs," observed Murad.

"I prefer my wooden tub before the fire."

"Aren't you afraid of *ifrits* – evil spirits who thrive in still water?"

Sandro glanced at him curiously, unsure whether or not the comment was serious or flippant. An enthusiastic wielding of the loofah distracted him. He winced and tried to shield a half-healed gash on his chest.

Instantly Murad clapped his hands. "Enough!" He led Sandro into a room furnished with sofas. They were wrapped in bathrobes and brought coffee flavoured with cinnamon and cloves. The air was redolent with the scent of sandalwood.

"I wasn't aware you carried a wound."

"An occupational hazard." Sandro shrugged and experimentally sipped the coffee. It had a strong, cloying flavour and he suspected it was an acquired taste.

"We Turks like to boast of our scars."

"Tell me of that one." Sandro indicated a long blue-grey ridge along the Vizier's left rib-cage.

Murad sat upright on his sofa, his robe falling open while a slave massaged his shoulders. He caressed the scar reminiscently. "That's how I gained my present exalted position. I am one who was born with dung between his toes – of lowly estate. I worked my way up through the Sultan's household, from stable-boy to Chief Falconer. I held that rank when one of the palace slaves – a brute rendered deaf and mute – attempted Bayezid's life when he was visiting the House of Falcons. His former Grand Vizier stood helpless with shock, but I stepped into the path of the blade and saved the Sultan's life. The Grand Vizier was deprived of his post along with his head. Bayezid, you see suspected him of hiring the assassin. Whereas it was I." His eyes glowed with remembered triumph. "These mutilated brutes are useful as assassins since they cannot talk not even under torture. The risk of getting killed myself was one I was prepared to take in return for the Sultan's favour."

"Why do you tell me this?"

"I want there to be no secrets between us. You'll soon learn that the murdered kadin was my own gift to Bayezid. Aysha was unique, a Circassian with hair as pale as moonlight, eyes the light blue of incense smoke, lips shell-pink, skin a pale ivory and a form the envy of *houris*. The Sultan was enchanted with her."

"You did not regret such a gift?"

"The world is full of women. Each month a new moon cuts the sky like a scimitar and blooms like a rose, only to fade and die. Its light is gentler than the sun's but often deceptive, for by its light we cannot read."

"Is that another way of saying that Aysha had secrets?"

"Are you familiar with the Turkish saying *All women are mysteries, even to themselves*?" Sandro nodded. "To understand the nature of harem women one must experience something of the harem itself."

"I imagine rivalry is fierce."

"A deadly ferocity, especially when an odalisque becomes the sultan's favourite and the valid sultana finds herself and her son threatened. If the Sultan prefers the favourite's son to his firstborn, there's a danger of being supplanted. The valid sultana is Roxana, as dark as Aysha was fair, as bitter as Aysha was sweet, as powerful as Aysha was vulnerable. There's no love lost between Prince Rustum and the Sultan, but that's the way of the Sultanate. The Princes scheme against each other with the same jealous fervour as harem women."

"Was Aysha with child?"

"There were rumours."

"But a newborn child could scarcely be a threat to a grown son. What if Bayezid should die this year or the next?"

"There have been infant sultans before."

"But only, I suspect, if the mother has influential friends. Would a Circassian slave-girl have at least one powerful friend?" Sandro allowed his lips to curl in a quizzical smile. "The Grand Vizier and the favourite he procured could well be allies."

Murad showed his gold tooth in a grimace. "But wouldn't *I* have then been the victim?"

A Moroccan slave with a face the colour of the coffee they had just consumed sidled into the room and whispered in Murad Bey's ear.

"It's time for you to dress for your audience with the Sultan."

Ugo was waiting anxiously beside the huge curtained divan in the apartment assigned to Sandro. The spy immediately crossed to the latticed window and cautiously opened one of the casements. The wall opposite was patrolled by halberdiers. In the courtyard below several Arab steeds were tethered and a contingent of janissaries milled about, talking, drinking or tending their weapons.

"I'm being treated to a show of military strength."

"I don't trust that Nabob," muttered Ugo, dourly.

"Murad's busy absolving himself of motive," murmured Sandro, "while throwing one or two other suspects my way."

The furnished garments were appropriately splendid antery and trousers of brilliant green embroidered with gold thread, a silk shirt with a high, jewelled collar and a striped turban of yellow and green to match the waist-sash. There was a jewel cask for his selection, but he wore only the pendant that always hung about his neck – a black pearl. He declined too the embroidered slippers, preferring his own boots of Cordovan leather.

The Great Sultan Bayezid, Lion of Istanbul, Defender of Islam, lord of armies and King of Kings, received him in his audience chamber, a hall with frescoed ceiling and arches, panelled walls and sculptured pillars. Across a large carpet of jewelled colours, sapphire, ruby and topaz, sat the Sultan on a divan of cushions on a raised dais under a silk canopy. Despite the warmth of the room, his long coat of woven thread of gold had a fur collar. From a ruby clasp on his turban rose three peacock feathers that swayed and nodded majestically as he talked.

A man in his late fifties, he had inherited the beak-like nose of his father Mehmet the Conqueror, a nose so long it almost curved over his bearded mouth. He was smoking from a *nargileh*, the bubbles gently gurgling, possibly opium, although the dark, almond-shaped eyes under the artificially shaped brows were alert. He was attended by the *Bostanji*, his personal bodyguard, and one odalisque, heavily veiled, crouching at his feet.

After the presentation and obligatory obseqious obser-vances, the Sultan waved his Vizier away and beckoned Sandro to a recess lower than the surrounding floor in which was a scattering of cushions. Murad Bey bowed low, but as he withdrew Sandro caught a glimpse of his expression. It was a look Ugo would have called *murderous*.

The spy obediently stepped down into the recess and sat cross-legged. At a terse word, the odalisque prostrated herself before Sandro and, to his surprise, spoke in perfect Italian.

"I am Kosem, a humble slave in the household of this mighty lord. Since Italian is my native tongue, I have the honour to translate the words that fall from his mouth."

He could make nothing of her face behind the yashmak. Her body seemed frail within the Turkish costume of rose-pink antery, skirt and trousers and her arms thin within the muslin sleeves of her chemise.

"What is your true Christian name?" he asked, gently.

He felt rather than saw the fearful glance she stole at her master. "I'm no longer Christian, but have embraced the true faith of Islam, the creed of All-Powerful Allah."

Bayezid had been watching this exchange with a cruel amusement. He spoke, his voice oily and insinuating.

"My master wishes to know your age."

"Thirty-one."

"The perfect age for a man. He should be neither older nor younger. Kismet has favoured the Sultan. Since his fair beloved has died young she will preserve her youth like the crescent moon and her *cid* will look neither younger nor older than thirty-one in Paradise. So it is written in the Koran."

Sandro digested this significant piece of information while Bayezid considered his next remark.

"Did you ever meet my renegade brother, Prince Djem, when he was held hostage by the Pope?"

"Several times."

"Did you investigate his murder?"

"He had then passed into the hands of the French," Sandro replied, cautiously, "and I believe the diagnosis was bronchitis."

He did not add that Djem's death had served Bayezid well since he had rid himself of a rebellious brother and absolved himself from further ransom.

"There was another renegade prince in my father's time, Ahmed by name. He escaped and became a hostage of the Doge of Venice. Despite the high esteem in which he was held he died in mysterious circumstances, it was said because of a love affair with a Venetian noblewoman. I have a miniature of this rebel Ahmed. You bear a striking resemblance to him. Why do you think this is?"

Sandro's lids drooped over his almond-shaped eyes. His mouth became steely. "It's usually the fate of hostages to die mysteriously. Tell your master that I've come to Istanbul to discuss quite a different mystery – the death of the kadin."

Sandro could not detect the slightest trace of grief in Bayezid's demeanour. He suspected the Sultan's motive was revenge for the outrage committed against his house.

"Is it true," the slave-girl continued, "that you were discovered in a palace called the House of the Moon? It's a strange omen for Aysha loved the moon more than the sun, she was a creature of the night rather than of the day. She had a whim that the Sultan indulged. On the palace lake he built her a gazebo where she was rowed each night. There within its latticed walls she lay on a divan and watched the moon dance in the dark waters. It was in this gazebo she was found dead."

"Alone? Not even a slave-girl or eunuch in attendance?"

"That was her desire."

Bayezid interrupted with a sharp gabble of words. Kosem prostrated herself so low Sandro saw only the little round hat under the veil. Her voice was muffled.

"I was Aysha's premier slave and with the Kizier Aga, the Chief Eunuch, was the first to find her."

"I understand there were no marks of violence on her body. Was her expression peaceful or stricken?"

Kosem hung her head without reply.

"Did she ever take anything to eat or drink with her?"

"That night she took a ewer of sherbet."

Bayezid waved a languid hand and asked a question which

seemed utterly incongruous to the investigation, as if he had suddenly become bored with it. "He inquires if you wish a companion for the night."

"Since you speak my language, may I choose you?" Sandro seized the opportunity to question the girl away from the intimidating presence of her master.

A tremor ran through Kosem's frail body. "As a novice I lack the skills to please you."

The Sultan gave a throaty chuckle.

"It amuses the Lion of Istanbul that you wish to make speech with a woman."

"When a woman praises my virility I like to hear it in my own language," said Sandro, suavely.

Bayezid chuckled again and closed his eyes. Kosem kissed the hem of his robe and crept away. Sandro realized the interview was at an end.

He was in the doorway when he heard a voice say in Italian. "It would be fascinating to conjecture that you *are* my cousin," but when he glanced back the Sultan was staring into nothingness through a haze of opium.

Sandro found his gloomy henchman waiting in the company of a giant Nubian.

"This is Jevheh Pasha, the Chief Eunuch. I think he wants us to follow him – probably to the execution block. I mislike that huge scimitar in his sash."

"You always take the pessimistic view, my friend," replied Sandro. "He may be leading us to the House of Felicity."

"Not if I value my head and other parts of my person. How did you find the Lion of Istanbul?"

"A jackal rather than a lion."

The Kizier Aga suddenly rounded on Ugo and, in a shrill gabble, indicated he must venture no further.

"This must be the famous Golden Way," observed Sandro, "that leads to the inner sanctum."

Reluctantly, the henchman remained behind while Jevheh Pasha conducted Sandro to a garden walled with cypress and almond trees, fragrant with roses, verbena and jasmine, and dotted with miniature pools of floating water-lilies and exotic fish. In discreet corners stood the black eunuch guards.

Jevheh led Sandro to a stone seat beside a gilded kiosk. Through its latticed walls he could see the silken garments of a woman and hear the low, sinister growl of a large cat. A woman's voice murmured, "It's been so long since he smelled a real man it arouses his killing instinct. Shall I open the door?"

"If it would afford the valid sultana a few moments' diversion I gladly offer myself to be torn apart."

Her laugh was almost as sinister as the cat's snarl. "You're already versed in the idioms of Turkish courtesy. How did you know I was the valid sultana?"

"Some women have a beauty where aura transcends the mere sight of them. May I compliment you on your excellent knowledge of Italian."

"I am Roxana. I speak five languages, embroider with gold thread, and prepare exotic foods and drink – such as this one."

A slave-girl approached with a goblet and ewer. "This was prepared in my own kitchen. *Raki*, made from distilled grapes and flavoured with anise. See how it turns milky white from a dash of water. We call it *Lion's milk* and it's served only to men."

Sandro sipped the *raki* cautiously. It was a potent brew.

"How may I serve you, lady?" he inquired, courteously.

Her laughter rippled through the lattice. "A provocative question in a house of pleasure. Is it true you're the Lion's cousin?"

"Another provocative question. The Sultan feels I can render him an obligement."

"In the matter of the Circassian's murder." He could tell by the rustling of her garments she had risen from her divan. The cat panted eagerly. Roxana pushed open the kiosk door. A leopard sprang out, young, lithe, beautifully marked, pawing the air as it was restrained by a leash. He caught a glimpse of a long, slender arm ringed with bracelets.

"Shah was a gift from my husband. To Aysha he gave a gazelle. The leopard kills the gazelle. Isn't that what the former stable-boy has tried to convince you? He was born with dung between his toes."

"He's made no secret of his humble beginnings."

"Beware his guile. He's a devious, ambitious man. I'm sure he poisoned your coffee with suspicion. But he had his own reasons to be rid of Aysha. Her influence in the Sultan's bed was stronger than Murad's in the throne-room."

"Shouldn't you have more cause for jealousy?"

"If you infer sexual jealousy, couching nights are simply duty, nothing more. I have other pleasures. As for power jealousy, I am the valid sultana, my young lion Rustum will one day be Sultan and then my influence will know no bounds."

"It was rumoured that Aysha was with child."

"Rustum would have killed the child when Bayezid died; it posed no threat. Bayezid himself might have killed it since it could have been fathered by one of some I could name. Murad Bey for one."

"Surely not when she was so fiercely guarded by the palace eunuchs."

"How naïve you are! Not all eunuchs are rendered impotent. Some can please a woman, though they never ejaculate. Many women prefer the love-making of eunuchs since they are expert at arousal and their pleasure is prolonged. Others, if castrated young enough, have regeneration of their male parts and are clever enough to conceal this or else bribe the physician who yearly examines them."

"Did Aysha have such a lover?"

"Why else was she rowed out each night to the gazebo on the lake? If only the moon could tell."

"How do you believe she was murdered?"

"I haven't asked myself that question. To flirt with death is to add spice to the cup of life."

Sandro stood quickly as the sultana followed the leopard out into the open. He had found the slave-girl's cosmetics, visible through her veil, a little outré for his tastes with her whitened skin, kohl-lined eyes and henna nails. Roxana disdained the beauty treatments of the harem for a kind of bizarre beauty of her own devising. Her skin tints were more amber than ivory or alabaster, the transparent veil could not disguise her long, high-cheeked face and extravagantly drawn diagonal brows, her eyes of molten brown and gold-glossed lids. She had a slender, lissom body; every movement held the rhythm of a dance. Her body exuded the mingled scent of cloves and frankincense. She carried in her hand a single white rose.

"Of all the bushes in my garden only one bears a white rose. Aysha tried to take many things from me, but some things are still mine." She caressed the slave-girl.

A young man came striding across the garden. From his splendid dress and his very presence Sandro guessed him to be Prince Rustum.

Roxana confirmed his identity by kissing the hem of his robe and murmuring, "My lion."

The Prince glared at Sandro and addressed his mother in an angry gabble. She answered in honeyed tones and, taking the slave-girl with her, withdrew into the kiosk. Before she closed the door, she swept Sandro a sultry glance.

"You have an outward show all honey and silk, all courtesy and sensitivity, but I think you could kill an enemy in cold blood and not miss the blink of an eye. Let me tell you about my lord and husband. Unwanted wives are sent to the old palace, the House of Tears. Faithless wives are tied in a sack and flung into the sea." She inhaled deeply the perfume of the rose and shut herself from sight.

Prince Rustum was a handsome youth on the verge of manhood, his first moustache darkening his upper lip. Sandro tried to make conversation with him, but he was either too uneducated or too proud to answer. He left the youth to his mother and sought out Ugo.

"I have a task for you, O Master of Disguise and Deceit," he told his lugubrious henchman. "I need someone to infiltrate the harem and listen to the conversation of the women."

"How should I be disguised?" Ugo bridled indignantly. "Not as a eunuch?"

"As a bag-woman, a peddler. Go to the city bazaar, purchase the most splendid of silks and adornments and then present yourself at the Carriage Gate. A bag-woman will be eagerly welcomed and allowed to display her wares."

"But they'll gabble in their own tongue. I know a little of their lingo, but . . ."

"O past-master of mime, where is your skill at reading faces and gestures? The body has a language all its own. Besides, I'm sending in an interpreter, an Italian slave-girl. Use a keen blade when you shave tomorrow."

Ugo groaned. "Why am I always risking my neck for you? And how am I to pay for these splendid adornments?"

"It's time I received an advance on the Sultan's generosity."

Sandro found the Grand Vizier in the House of Falcons. It was the hour of feeding and Murad Bey, with his own hands, fed dissected hares and pigeons to the fearsome birds of prey.

"Behold the ferocity of their beaks and talons. Imagine them tearing apart the flesh of a man foolhardy enough to invade the harem. I admire cruelty. It is the only refinement. What did Roxana say to you?"

"She is both an enigma and a woman of astonishing candour."

"Did she have a theory about Aysha's murder?"

"She said something surprising – that the Circassian had lovers."

"I'm sure she mentioned my name, but not the name of Rustum."

"Was he her lover? Despite the vigilance of the black eunuchs?"

"With bribery, love or lust will find its way. Had they been discovered there would have been no mystery about her death. The Sultan would have publicly cut her throat."

"As you say, the ultimate in refinement."

Murad turned the subject abruptly. "You must dine with me tonight and have the pick of my women."

"I've already asked for the Italian slave-girl."

"Kosem? She was once Roxana's hand-maiden before she was given to Aysha."

"Who watched the gazebo while Aysha lay there gazing at the moon?"

"Jevheh Pasha, who waxes fat on bribes. Who fawns on Rustum, because he'll be the next Sultan."

"It was said she had drunk sherbet that night. Could it have been poisoned?"

"Only half had been consumed. The Mistress of Sherbets was ordered to drink the rest. She survived."

Sandro accepted this pragmatic method of elimination without a blink.

Turkish food was rich, the guests were served with lamb flavoured with saffron, pilav, egg-plant and other vegetables cooked in olive oil, and many sweet desserts predominantly of nuts and honey. They drank *boza*, a drink of fermented barley sprinkled with cinnamon and finished the meal with strong coffee.

To Sandro's surprise there were no knives or spoons. The diners ate with their fingers, a perfected art, and were served with bowls of rose-water and embroidered towels between courses.

When he returned to his own apartment he stumbled across Ugo sleeping in the doorway. Anxiety had at last given way to weariness and he snored lustily. Sandro gave him an exasperated kick in the ribs at which he snuffled, "What's wrong?" before lapsing back into sleep.

The room was dimly lit by an oil-lamp. Sandro threw off his clothes and approached the divan. A shadowy figure materialized from among the curtains.

"My *cid*."

Kosem.

At his first step towards her she shrank back, then seemed to gather her courage and took a timorous step to meet him.

"You've no reason to fear me."

"I'm yours to command," she whispered, submissively.

"It may be possible to bargain for your freedom."

"No!" She surprised him with her vehemence. "I can never go back to Venice; it seems now like a dream that opium brings. I was maid to the wife of the Viceroy of Cyprus. Our ship was attacked by Corsairs. *I* was sold at the slave-market."

Sandro could only guess at the humiliation she had suffered being paraded naked for the eager inspection of prospective buyers.

"I was given into the service of the valid sultana and became Mistress of Robes. Then Aysha saw me at the baths soon after her arrival. She was always jealous of Roxana and when she became kadin she asked for me. The Sultan could deny her nothing."

"Will you now be returned to Roxana?"

"She has another Mistress of Robes."

"Will you let me see your face?"

"No! I'm not beautiful like Aysha. That's why I was put in the women's household."

"I have something to ask of you that requires great courage. Tomorrow my friend Ugo will go into the House of Felicity disguised as a bag-woman."

"No!" She gave a convulsive jerk. "They'll put out his eyes and mutilate him in terrible ways before they kill him."

"He's too clever to let himself get caught. Sit beside him and translate the gossip of the women."

"If he's discovered they'll drown me for being his accomplice."

"In that unlikely event, I'll intercede for you. Promise me, for your mistress's sake."

"For my mistress's sake," she whispered, and fled from him.

She had spoken of opium. He wondered what fevered dreams it brought an exile from life.

Next morning Murad Bey casually mentioned a second tragedy. Selma, the Mistress of Sherbets to the valid sultana, had been found dead. It had been her custom each dawn to sit cross-legged on the terrace wall and gaze out on the Bosphorus and it was assumed she had lost her balance and fallen to the rocks below.

"Yet how many mornings had she sat there and dreamed?" Sandro tried to conjure up an image of a dark-eyed, wistful girl, remembering a far-off land. His image fixed on the odalisque who had served him the *raki*. "I think I've seen this girl. She's the sultana's . . ." He hesitated, delicately.

"Favourite," Murad finished for him. His eyes smouldered. "Ah, that such a woman should be wasted. But it's the fate of harem women."

The terrace was within the harem precincts, but an elderly eunuch disposed to gossip pointed the way. He could not have guessed the agile spy, eluding the watchful gaze of the guards, would scale the walls and find his way there.

The view was breath-taking with the green fields, walnut trees and palms, the two estuaries and the jutting promontory of the Golden Horn, the brilliant blue of the water flecked with fishing-craft and painted galleys.

A flake of white like snow on the terrace floor caught his attention. He bent and picked up the rose petal.

"What have you found?"

Sandro looked up into the smooth black face of Jevheh Pasha. "You speak Italian."

"With the valid sultana so fluent in the tongue I found it advisable to take lessons. I am but a poor novice still."

When he had led Sandro to Roxana's garden the spy had been unaware of his power and prestige. The Kizier Aga was a high-ranking pasha, second only to the Grand Vizier. He was go-between for the mighty, privy to all their secrets and possibly the most feared man in the Ottoman Empire.

"Was Selma holding a white rose when her body was found?"

"Selma was Mistress of Sherbets. It was one of her duties to gather fruit and flowers."

"Even the rare white rose that blooms only in Roxana's garden?"

"Each to their own exquisite taste. I enjoy my sherbet sweetened with honey. The kadin liked her sherbet flavoured with almonds. I noticed when I bent to listen for a breath she had the scent of almonds on her lips."

Sandro studied him intently. "Were her limbs convulsed? Was there froth on her upper lip?"

Jevheh looked uneasy. "The Sultan was coming to view the body . . ."

"So you made her as beautiful as possible for him. What became of the white rose?"

"I don't know. I suppose it could have fallen into the lake. You know, of course, that this place is forbidden to you."

"You'll find me suitably grateful if I am able to pursue this inquiry in my own way."

The eunuch smiled. Another gift of akcha for his capacious purse, Sandro thought, ruefully.

Ugo was agog with the cornucopia of beauty rolled out before his eyes in the inner sanctum of the harem.

"'Twas enough to make a man forswear Heaven in the hope of Paradise. All those voluptuous delights and seductive charms wasted on one man. It's obvious they hunger for diversion. They fell upon my bundle of treasures like wolves on a flock of sheep. As for my disguise, my own master wouldn't have recognized me. My one fear was that the Sultan should visit the harem and choose me for his couching partner."

Sandro snorted derisively. "I'm sure you didn't waste your opportunity to fondle."

"I admit my hands slid over a few delicious curves when I was holding my silks against them. The temptation was too great."

"I'm not interested in your lecherous pursuits, you rogue. What did you learn?"

"The Italian was reluctant to translate, but finally agreed to help. Naturally, the odalisques were enthralled with the murder and eager to gossip. Wasn't there some rumour that Aysha was with child? A lie according to the Mistress of the Bath."

"Mayhap she was anxious to keep the Sultan's enthusiasm alert. Did they speak of lovers?"

"Very cautiously and with many glances over the shoulder. They favoured Rustum and say he swam across the lake each night."

"From under the nose of the Kizier Aga?"

"Ah, he's the one they fear more than the Sultan. But one girl bolder than the rest suggested he was drugged – or bribed. Aysha often made him gifts of confectionery from her kitchen."

Sandro regarded him in silence for several minutes before

he said, abruptly. "I hear all kinds of liaisons and little affairs and jealousies flare up among the odalisques."

"What can one expect when women are imprisoned with no glimpse of the outside world or of other men? They seemed to hold the Italian in the sort of pity and contempt females love to revel in. One of the women tried to caress her and lift her veil, but in a mocking way, and was angrily rejected. It surprised me, master, that she wore a veil even among women."

"What was said of Selma's accident?"

"They seemed more concerned with who would succeed her as Mistress of Sherbets than disturbed by her death."

"The harem hierarchy must be all-consuming." He opened his hand. "What think you of this for a murder weapon?"

"A petal."

"A rose. The white rose that only blooms in Roxana's garden, heavily imbued with a virulent bane that smelled of almonds. *Aysha tried to take many things from me*, Roxana said. She coveted the white rose and it came to her and with it Death. Who brought it? The Kizier Aga, as go-between for Roxana, he who is privy to the secrets of the mighty and waxes fat on his knowledge. Had the Sultan discovered at last her infidelity? Was Murad Bey jealous of her influence? Was it Rustum, fearing betrayal? Or Roxana fearing for Rustum. I've no doubt Rustum was Aysha's lover and that when he swam out to the gazebo Jevheh didn't mistake it for the swooping of a nightbird on the water. No, the rose was placed in Aysha's lap by someone she trusted."

Sandro was glaring at the henchman as if he hated him. His eyes had a burning glitter like a dark exultation. Ugo shivered to the roots of his hair.

"You know who it is, don't you?"

"I want you to carry two notes for me, one to the Kizier Aga and the other to Murad Bey."

With Ugo gone on his errand, Sandro again made his way up to the terrace. The view before him shone with more brilliance in the noonday sun. The dazzle on the water was almost blinding. He shaded his eyes, gazing from the rippling grass and billowing palms out to the Bosphorus where the fishing boats and galleys had been joined by pleasure craft, luxurious barques with metallic strings tied to their prows to leave a sparkling wake.

He sat cross-legged on the wall where he imagined Selma had sat. It was a long wait. He had a sixth sense which had ensured his continued survival, but in a foreign world his nerves felt on the stretch. He was, after all, simply waiting for a murderer to secure his silence.

The soft snicker of slippers was almost imperceptible, but his heightened sense caught it. He swung his legs about at the onrush and stared into the contorted face.

"So yours is the face of the *ifrit*."

She tottered on the brink of falling, her hands outstretched to push him. She had cast aside her veil and her face with its livid scars was revealed.

"You see now why I could never return to Venice. This is the face Aysha gave me when she took me from Roxana, so she would never again want me as her favourite."

"That was what I suspected."

"I loved Roxana as I could never love a man. Do you despise me?"

"I should beware pity. I pitied you, but you had no pity for Selma. I can understand why you took Aysha's life but why Selma's?"

"Because she was Roxana's new favourite. Because she'd been given a white rose. That's why I pushed her from the wall.

"Aysha was shallow enough to believe I could cajole a white rose for her from the Sultana. I stole it. How she gloated when I placed it in her lap before she was rowed to her house of the moon."

"How did you poison it?"

"I've learned many secrets in the seraglio, Il Saracen, secrets that would make your Italian skin crawl. You think you know love, hate, vendetta, you know nothing till you've lived in an harem." Her mutilated face smiled grotesquely. From her sash she drew a rose, a red rose, red as blood. "Will you smell my flower, Il Saracen? Will you savour death?"

Instinctively, he backed away. She scrambled on to the wall. His attention was snatched away by the intrusion of Murad and his halberdiers. When he glanced back, Kosem was inhaling the perfume of the rose.

"Why did she never give *me* a white rose?"

She hovered for an instant and then dropped out of sight below the wall.

"Don Alessandro!" Murad leapt forward with drawn scimitar. "Are you harmed?"

"No, scant thanks to you. If I'd been dreaming like Selma it would have been my body on the rocks below."

"I had to ensure the women were locked away before I could invade the harem." He crossed to the wall and glanced down. Sandro declined to follow his example. "You said in your message she would try to snare you here. How did you know?"

"I also sent a note to Jevheh Pasha, naming Kosem as Aysha's murderer and asking him to meet me here. I suspected he was not well versed enough to understand the written word and would need it translated. Who else but by the Italian slave?"

On the terrace floor lay a petal like a drop of blood. Sandro crushed it under his boot. "You may tell the Lion of Istanbul the puzzle has been solved. Please make the necessary arrangements for my departure . . ."

"The Sultan will cover you with honours . . ."

"I'm not sure I want his honours. He has compounded an unnatural society. This is just one of many tragedies."

In the opulent apartment Don Alessandro Orsini threw off his Turkish trappings and donned his Italian doublet. A slave brought him a purse of money. Sandro made a quick calculation of the coins. "What I might have expected after Jevheh Pasha and Murad Bey have had their cut."

The purse was accompanied by a small gold case and a note written in Italian.

The puzzle of my kadin's death has indeed been solved, but not the puzzle of your identity. I present you with a miniature of the young Ahmed painted by the Italian artist Gentile Bellini, who also painted my father.

"Master, what are you leaving behind?" Ugo stared at the gold case flung carelessly on the divan. "Have you examined it?"

Il Saracen smiled a sweet and melancholy smile. "I prefer to remain a mystery even to myself."

Flibbertigibbet

Paul Finch

Paul Finch (b. 1964) is a journalist and former police officer who has used his knowledge and experience in several stories and scripts for the television series, The Bill. *In the following novella we enter the Elizabethan period, where a serial killer is on the loose.*

AD 1581

The crowd were stunned when Father Campion offered a prayer for the health of the queen; "his queen", as he called her. Even the Lord Mayor, a pompous, self-important little man, who often spoke long and loud at such occasions, was momentarily lost for words.

Was this not Edmund Campion, the infamous Jesuit seditionist? Was he not a scheming subversive, who had abandoned his country for the wiles of Rome, and had only returned here to undermine the Church of England and its most high and noble governor, Queen Elizabeth I?

Abruptly recovering himself, the Mayor rolled up the death-sentence, and laid it across the pommel of his saddle. "In which case," he called out, "do you recant your papist beliefs? Might we take word back to the Queen that at the moment of truth, you returned to the Anglican faith and sought her forgiveness?"

Campion, who'd had difficulty standing since they'd lifted him from his hurdle, made no answer. Instead, he turned painfully to the executioners. "Please . . . do what you must."

The chief executioner, a heavily built man clad entirely in leather, his head shrouded in the customary black hood with eye-slits, nodded, and turned to his red-garbed apprentices. The first one came forward with thongs and bound the priest's hands behind his back; the second looped the noose over Father Campion's head and tightened it into place. Throughout the process, the Mayor leaned forward from his horse, his eyes keen and hawk-like. Too often in the past, executioners and their staff had been bribed by families to end the ordeal swiftly – slipping a knife in here, twisting a neck there; occasionally, during the reign of Mary, they had acted from pity alone, craftily garotting with ligature before lighting the heaped faggots. None of this would be tolerated on a day like this . . . not with Edmund Campion as the object of attention: today's spectacle had to be exemplary.

A moment passed, the chief executioner stoking the brazier in which he heated his tools, then his first apprentice leaped down into the cart, took up the reins and whipped the team away. Instantly, Father Campion was drawn up to the crossbeam of the gallows. There were gasps from the crowd as he swung there, silent but jerking in the frigid December air. He had been a tall man, well made and handsome, with a head of golden hair and laughing eyes. As well as a learned father and fine scholar, he'd also been a caring man. Charismatic in his oratory but patient in the debate, his polite and gentlemanly attitude had won the admiration of many, even those he'd encountered who didn't share his beliefs. Now though . . . now, he was indistinguishable from so many other doomed wretches who had come this way to Tyburn. His lean form, battered and bruised, and through the cruel auspices of the Little Ease, withered almost to bones, was clad only in a filthied, blood-stained shroud. His tortured limbs twitched; his bruised and crudely shaven head turned first a shade of scarlet, then darkened quickly to purple as the rope bit into his neck.

There was an awesome silence in the great square. More

and more people gathered to watch, but still the only sound was the slow and steady creaking of the gibbet.

To one side, behind the line of halberdiers, an elegant gentleman stood watching the affair. He was tall and sleek of appearance, his features smooth and aquiline, and excepting his neat beard and moustache, closely shaven. He wore a goffered ruff at his neck, a blue satin doublet over his lace-edged shirt, and a purple velvet cape to ward off the chill. His padded trunk-hose were the height of fashion, yet were almost concealed beneath thigh-high riding-boots waxed to a gleaming finish. On his head, there sat a tall beaver-hat complete with peacock feather, while at his left hip, a rapier hung in a decorated scabbard. Others of his class were also present, at the rear of the crowd, watching from carriage or horseback, every one decked in his or her festive finest, and clutching smelling-salts for fear they might swoon. Not so this gentleman at the front . . . for all his gorgeous apparel, he had a fearless, steely look, as if determined to see the business through from as close as possible, though by his hard indifference, it was difficult to tell whether he was against the prisoner or for him.

He didn't seem the sort of gentleman to suffer fools lightly, yet he didn't so much as stiffen when a mumbling beggar in ashes and sackcloth came and stood beside him; in truth, of course, the gentleman had already recognized Secretary of State Francis Walsingham, who as ever, was about his business . . . mixing now with the hoi polloi in search of Campion sympathizers.

"Good day, Master Urmston," said the beggar at length. His voice was refined and purring. For all the grime upon his face, up close the Secretary of State's small, demonic eyes and sharply pointed beard were unmistakable.

Urmston sniffed. "Is it a good day, my lord? I wish I could believe that."

"Now now, Robert . . . don't be disloyal."

Urmston didn't look round. His eyes were fixed on the hanging priest. "If loyalty is approving scenes like this, then it's scarcely a desirable state."

The beggar sighed. "This is not what the Queen wants."

"Nevertheless, it's what she has."

"Campion was given every opportunity to recant his views," the beggar replied. "She beseeched him personally during an audience at the Earl of Leicester's house. She *begged* him . . . in her own hand, she held out a royal pardon to cancel all charges, if he would only recant. And even then he refused."

"In which case, we've made him a martyr," said Urmston. "God have mercy on our souls."

The beggar's cool, spy-master eyes slowly narrowed. He glanced sidelong at Urmston. "I trust you're not questioning the supremacy of our Queen and our holy Church of England?"

Urmston wanted to shrug, to say that he didn't care either way . . . but that would have been utter folly, as well as a blatant lie. "Of course not," he finally muttered.

"You've accounted for enough of these scoundrels yourself, Robert."

Urmston didn't wish to be reminded of this. "My lord, my duty is to England and her sovereign. Rebels, traitors and Spanish spies . . . I will gladly dispatch to the scaffold. But to inflict this on some poor monk whose only crime is religious belief . . . in your conscience, you don't find that disgusting?"

Lord Walsingham shook his head. "These men *are* traitors, Robert. There can't be any other way to describe them. They were trained in French seminaries expressly for the purpose of coming here to England and undermining the faith."

"And in response, we wreak a holocaust. I wonder which party history will deem the greater villain?"

Walsingham almost smiled. "I had no idea you felt so strongly."

Urmston nodded. "Why else do you think I've resigned from your service?"

"Ah . . . now that is really the reason I've sought you out."

The beggar was about to speak further, when movement at

the gibbet distracted him. Campion's body was being lowered to the platform. The priest had gone limp, though by
the frantic palpitation of his chest, he still lived . . . which
was greatly to the satisfaction of the Lord Mayor, who was
now able to sit back in his saddle and preen himself.

The two apprentice executioners released the prisoner
from the noose, then hoisted him up between them, and
stripped off his ragged shift, to reveal an emaciated body,
streaked with blood and sweat. Thus naked, he was lain on a
trestle beside the gibbet, and strapped into place at his throat
and feet. The chief executioner came forwards. In one gloved
hand he held a long, slender knife, in the other a vicious-
looking hook; both were glowing hot from the coals. Without
further ado, he set to work with them, slitting the prisoner's
abdomen from his ribs to his groin.

Smoke rose, and a stench of burning flesh tainted the air.
Incredibly it seemed, though the priest tensed and flopped
wildly about in his bonds, he remained silent . . . even
when the disembowelling commenced. At one point, he
tried to raise his head, as if to see what was being done,
though the vision of his own entrails, now being yanked
out from his belly in loop after glistening loop, like coils of
raw sausages, was perhaps too much, and he fainted dead
away; either that, or, mercifully, he died. Either way, the
chief executioner continued with his grim task for several
more moments, depositing a great heap of steaming in-
testines on the floor around the trestle – more, it seemed,
than any man's belly cavity could contain, but at last laying
his hook and knife aside, and reaching for the mighty axe,
with which he might behead and then quarter the wretched
creature.

"Your resignation, yes," said Lord Walsingham, taking up
the conversation where they'd left off. "It's been rejected."

Urmston looked round in astonishment. "What?"

Lord Walsingham shrugged. "You're too valuable an asset
to me. There's no conceivable way I can release you from
your obligations now."

"Obligations!" Urmston almost shouted.

Walsingham only smiled. "My dear Robert, you live the

way you do . . . comfortably, because it pleases Her Majesty to retain you in her private household as Squire of the Royal Body. In return for this lofty honour, you are expected to attend upon her during her public appearances, to doff your cap and bow when she wanders idly past, and occasionally to take a turn around Greenwich Palace to ensure the men-at-arms are awake and the outer gates locked. It is scarcely demanding work."

Urmston felt a tremor of rage pass through him, but also helplessness. He knew exactly what this implied, and more to the point, knew exactly how much, or rather how *little* he could do about it. "With all respect, my lord, this is unfair. You, better than anyone, know the full depth of my service to the Crown."

The beggar shook his head. "You can't have things both ways, Robert. You resign from one office, then I'm afraid you resign from the other also."

Urmston's hand tightened on his sword-hilt. He shook his head with impotent fury. "So be it . . . I still tender my resignation."

Walsingham considered. "I see. Of course, if you really are intent on leaving the State Department, I must instruct my officers to investigate your reasons . . . as thoroughly as they can."

"So now it's a crime in England just to hold an opinion?"

Walsingham's smile became a chuckle. "Of course. That's another of Henry VIII's great legacies to us."

Urmston shook his head. "And this is the land I love?"

"But let's not dwell on the negatives, Robert." Walsingham rubbed his grubby hands against the chill. "Instead, let's discuss how we may use your undoubted skills to our *mutual* benefit." He made to lumber away. "Come with me if you would. There's nothing else to see here."

Urmston glanced again towards the scaffold. Father Campion's head, looking more like a waxen effigy than a fragment of humanity, had been mounted on a spear, a grimace of agony still etched into its dirt-smeared face. One of the apprentice executioners, for the approval of the crowd, was hefting into the air a great square of torso, with an arm and shoulder still affixed to it. It was like something from a butcher's yard, the pallid flesh contrasting sharply with the rich, red innards. Blood dripped steadily from the grisly trophy. At the sight of that, Urmston could only agree; there was nothing else to see there.

A few moments later, they had passed into a small tavern, which had clearly been commandeered for the day. The Secretary of State warmed himself by the crackling hearth, shared a jug of mulled wine with Urmston, then with the aid of a sturdy footman, washed his face and hands in a bowl of rose-scented water, and threw a heavy ermine cloak over his ragged garments. In the tavern courtyard, a royal coach had been drawn up and was awaiting their pleasure. Walsingham dispatched a groom to deliver Urmston's horse back to his home address on Drury Lane, then ushered his unwilling guest into the coach.

"Ride with me, if you would, Robert," he said. "At least as far as King's Street."

A moment passed, then crimson taffeta drapes were closed over the windows, to block out the cold, and with a shout from the driver, the carriage jolted into motion. In the dim, reddish light within, Urmston stared blankly at Walsingham. The scheming nobleman stared back, with a catlike smile. "What do you know of the Southwark Stews, Robert?" he eventually asked.

Urmston shrugged. "Pain, poverty, pestilence . . ."

"There have been six murders there in as many months."

Urmston feigned surprise. "Only six? Things must be improving south of the river."

"Six murders by the same hand," Walsingham added. "And a gruesome, fiendish hand it is."

Fleetingly, the nobleman's poise faltered . . . he frowned, his brow creasing as if something genuinely troubled him, a thing Urmston for one had never seen before.

"I don't understand, my lord."

"Neither does anyone else." Walsingham shook his head. "There's no apparent sense to these murders. The victims are unrelated, they had offended no one . . . they certainly possessed nothing worth stealing."

"In which case, forgive me for asking, but how do we know they're connected?"

The nobleman glanced up and met his agent eye-to-eye. "Because of the mutilations."

"Mutilations?"

The Secretary of State nodded. "Ritualistic mutilations, in fact."

"Tell me more."

The nobleman considered. "Well . . . it's a vile business. The victims have all, so far, been women of low repute . . . whores or serving-wenches. But each one was subjected to a shocking assault. Brutally beaten, then dispatched with knife-blows to the throat. Following death . . ." he paused to swallow his distaste, ". . . at least it is to be *hoped* it was following death, they were gutted like fishes, their inner organs strewn around the murder scene or removed altogether."

Urmston sat back. "Clearly the actions of some lunatic."

"Every known lunatic in the district has already been incarcerated," Walsingham replied. "Yet the atrocities continue."

"And the parish bailiffs . . . what role do they play in this?"

"A rather ineffectual one, it would seem . . . at least, in the opinion of the Privy Council."

Urmston started. *This* did surprise him. "The Privy Council? Since when were they interested in a nonpolitical crime?"

"Since a district of the city which is already a powder-keg of discontent fell under a progressive succession of monthly murder fines."

"Ah." Urmston rubbed his chin. A more familiar story was now starting to unfold.

"Everything which can be done, seems to have been done," Walsingham added. "The Watch has been doubled . . . in fact trebled, all streets and houses have been searched, strangers questioned . . . still nothing arises."

"Except fear."

"Fear and fury. The two go hand-in-hand down South-wark way."

Urmston gave a contemptuous sniff. "Well . . . I don't suppose we can let the lives of a few downtrodden women threaten the stability of the capital."

"With the country torn stem to stern 'twixt Catholic and Protestant, we can ill afford outbreaks of major disorder, Robert . . . especially in London. Mary Stuart waits in the wings. Her supporters need only the slightest excuse."

Urmston nodded. He appreciated the danger of course, but it was enjoyable to see Walsingham discomforted. "So . . . what exactly do you propose?"

The Secretary of State mused for a moment. "Well . . . somewhat to my astonishment, the Privy Council's first response – that a £400 reward be posted – has so far been ignored. I, therefore, propose something more radical; namely, that one man in my employ, needless to say the most efficient of my agents, be brought into this business, presented with all the facts and then commissioned to bring the villain to justice by any means possible."

"And if he fails?" Urmston wondered.

"He mustn't."

"But if he does?"

"He *mustn't!*" Walsingham said again, in a graver tone than his agent had ever heard him use before.

When he returned home that afternoon, Urmston went directly to the solar. It was a smaller, darker room than the parlour, but nevertheless the part of his house he in-habited the most. In here were his shelves of books and maps, his measuring instruments, his ornate globe, his oaken desk laden down with papers and diaries. A good fire was already roaring in the grate, and a moment later, Urmston's manservant, John Kingsley, came in, bringing his master a gown and slippers, and a small repast of bread, cheese and a tankard of beer.

While Urmston ate, he related the events of the morning and the new mission set before him. Kingsley, a middle-aged fellow, with a head of shaggy grey hair, but broad shoulders and ruddy, journeyman's hands, remained taciturn, though even he was mildly surprised by the day's outcome.

"That's a tall order, my lord."

"Isn't it," Urmston replied. "I suppose I should be flattered."

"Has his lordship granted special powers?" the servant wondered.

Urmston nodded, and indicated a small scroll, tied with a ribbon, now lying on his desk. "I requested a warrant to question, search and detain any person I saw fit, in connection with the case . . . and he already had one prepared. Bearing *my* name . . . damn his infernal cheek!"

"At least it should prove a worthy chase, my lord."

"His words too," said Urmston thoughtfully. "For once, we pursue a miscreant whose crimes aren't born of idealism, whose heinous deeds are a concern to us all, whatever our persuasion." Urmston looked round at his servant. "His lordship said that to catch this villain, might even help salve my conscience . . . for all those other poor wretches I've sent to their fate."

Kingsley raised an eyebrow. "He called them 'poor wretches'?"

Urmston gave a bitter chuckle. "Not quite."

"Well, at least he's being truthful in one respect," the servant ventured. "There shouldn't be any sleep lost, if you bring this one to heel."

"*If* doesn't come into it, John. *If* doesn't come into it at all."

This Child alone, and only he,
He hath the world from sin set free.
                    Blest Mary Wanders Through The Thorn

The narrow alleys of Southwark snaked among sordid rookeries of buildings, so filthy, so decayed, so propped against each other that they looked ready to slump into rubble at a moment's notice. The dark and squalid passages between them were more like open sewers than footpaths, rutted, muddy, awash with the contents of chamber pots and infested with rats, which scuttled back and forth careless of kicking or stamping feet. Even on a frosty December morn, when in other stretches of the city, steeples rang the Yuletide solstice, squares teemed with jolly tradesmen and mistletoe bedecked the shop-stalls, where all manor of seasonal delights were arrayed, from dates and figs to hanging rabbits and fat, pink salmon, this dockside quarter was a dismal warren of hopelessness and despair. Little, if anything, was on sale here; drunken cackles were the only sounds of mirth. The swirling smoke of countless coal and wood fires mingled with the mists of the season to bring down curtains of gloom in every court and ginnel. The people who cluttered them, like black phantoms for the most-part, were exclusively of the tattered and lame variety, as dirty and vermin-ridden as the crumbling structures they dwelled in. Everywhere, there was a foetid stench of offal, of rotted straw, of festering human waste.

As Urmston and his servant were conducted through it by officers of the Watch, it struck the spy-catcher that even the most monstrous criminal could move with relative ease in so loathsome a pit as this. There was no one he saw here who wasn't more like an animal than a human, who wasn't gaunt and wolfish, who didn't glare at the intruders through resentful, red-rimmed eyes. Crime was embedded in such a society: wife murdered husband and husband wife; children cheated parents, parents neglected children; neighbour stole from neighbour; women and girls, maybe men and boys too, granted their favours for the minimum price, else otherwise they'd be taken with force; the few coins one might scratch together would doubtless be frittered quickly in the alehouse or apothecary's, anywhere in fact where blissful oblivion, no matter how brief, might be bought and sold.

"This was the scene of the earliest one, my lord," said the first-officer of the Watch, standing back respectfully, torchlight glinting on his helm and breastplate.

Urmston and Kingsley came forward. A heap of cinders lay against the gable wall of a tavern. The indelible bloodstains on a few scraps of rag gave testimony to the tragedy which had occurred there.

"Tell us about it," said Urmston.

"Er . . . a common harlot, she was. Name of . . . Swift, I believe." The first-officer consulted a leather-bound notebook. "That's correct. Abigail Swift. Murdered on the night of July 25th."

Urmston glanced at the fellow, surprised. "That's very informative. You're a credit to your office, serjeant."

The officer was a tall, burly fellow with a broad, ruddy face and a grey tuft of beard. He flushed at the unaccustomed praise, swapping his billhook awkwardly from one hand to the other. "Er . . . thank you, my lord."

The fact that he could write at all was an improvement on most officials of his class.

"You've kept a careful account in each case?" Urmston asked.

"As careful as I could."

Urmston nodded, then snapped his fingers and held out a requiring hand. "I'll take charge of it, if you please."

Rather surprised, the serjeant handed over the book.

When out on the inquiry, the spy-catcher's manner was invariably brusque, even peremptory, though John Kingsley understood the reasons why. As an employer, Robert Urmston was inclined to informal friendliness, while in the privacy of his home life to actual conviviality. But when matters of state were at hand, he would remain disciplined and detached. It helped him, as he said, "maintain an emotion equilibrium essential to the task." Kingsley wasn't entirely sure what this meant, but he had a fairly shrewd idea that it referred to the cold shell from which his master conducted all his secret business; the grief, the fear, the fury his inquiries often inspired, were never allowed to penetrate. Of course, his aloof and fearsomely strict lawyer-father had set standards for this during Urmston's early life, which the younger gent had only aspired to half-heartedly and had never quite achieved. In short, Robert Urmston found it more difficult than his father had to be *continuously* tough and unsympathetic, hence his recent depression and attempted resignation. That didn't mean, however, that he let frivolity or even pleasantry intrude when the game was seriously afoot.

As Kingsley thought on this, his master retained his coolly reserved air, leafing attentively through the serjeant's notebook. The details of the crimes he found there were sketchy, and in a spidery, uneducated hand, but they were more than he'd expected.

"I need as much information as possible," he eventually said. "Do you have a record of all persons known to have consorted with these women on the evenings in question?"

"There are lists back in our barracks," the watchman replied. "Home addresses where possible . . . no one we have spoken to is reported to have been armed at the time or to have borne visible bloodstains."

"They were very bloody murders, I understand?"

"That's correct." The serjeant indicated the heap of rags and cinders. "This particular woman . . . her throat had been cut so savagely that the windpipe was entirely severed. The fiend almost removed her head. He also lifted her clothes and attacked her lower belly . . . I counted at least twenty puncture wounds, the sort made by a sharp but slender blade . . . very deep."

"We were told she'd been disembowelled?" put in Kingsley.

The serjeant shook his head. "Not in this case, sir, though some of the later ones were. This is only an opinion, of course, but these killings . . . well, they seem to have got more ferocious as time has gone on. The last two or three, were . . ." his words faltered, ". . . *bloodbaths*. I've never seen anything like them."

"I have," Urmston replied.

Kingsley looked curiously round. "My lord?"

"Decapitation and disembowelment," his master added. "I witnessed something similar yesterday . . . at Tyburn."

"With all respect, my lord, this is different," the first-officer replied.

"How so?"

"Well . . . this wasn't no clean bit of work, like you might see from an executioner, or even a butcher in his shop. This was done in a frenzy . . . a tearing, a ripping . . . like the culprit had gone berserk." The man shuddered. "Horrible."

Urmston looked at him with interest. " 'Horrible.' Are you qualified to use that word, serjeant?"

The watchman looked puzzled. "My lord?"

"On average, how many murders a week do you see?"

The serjeant shrugged. "Well, this is the Stews, my lord . . . one a week, perhaps. Maybe more."

Urmston considered this. "Then you certainly *are* qualified. Lead on, if you please."

Shuffling in a tight-knit group, the investigators and their escort strolled on, only torchlight casting the way before them. The labyrinthine alleys were almost subterranean in their cloying gloom.

"Tyburn, my lord?" Kingsley whispered. "You think there's a connection there?"

A moment passed, then Urmston shook his head. "Just a thought, nothing more."

But Kingsley wasn't ready to accept this. He knew his master of old; already, he could tell, the razor-sharp mind was in motion, linking clues together, evolving theories. Always in the past, Robert Urmston had shown the uncanny knack for unmasking spies and traitors. For all his personal demons, he seemed to possess a natural-born instinct for detecting the villainous.

Kingsley indicated the first-officer's broad back. "Do you trust this fellow's knowledge, my lord?" he asked quietly.

"I find no reason not to. A man who witnesses one slaying a week, must be deemed more reliable than most when it comes to the basic analysis of murder."

"With respect though, most of the killings he deals with will be assaults during theft . . . or perhaps the results of drunken brawls."

Urmston nodded. "Which proves beyond question that the murders *we* are investigating stand out from the norm. He called them 'horrible' . . . he couldn't suppress a shiver. We have the right man to guide us at this moment in time, though shortly, John, we must dispense with his services."

That surprised and alarmed Kingsley. Even with several armed men, he already felt exposed in this dangerous neighbourhood. "We must?"

"The trappings of authority will only cause the criminal fraternities to close ranks," Urmston replied. "Yet they are the ones we must move among if we hope to progress in our enquiry."

The other five murder sites were much the same as the first . . . grim, lonely little spots in the yards of ruined tenements, in derelict lots or at the deepest points of arched side-alleys. The first-officer of the Watch was as good as his word. In each case, he'd kept some details of the victim, her known movements that evening, and the manner of her assassination. The bodies, of course, had all been removed to pauper's graves, but Urmston still checked off each woman as he examined the scene of her death.

The second victim was Mary Judd; she had been slain on 8 August, throat cut, body stabbed and hacked as if by a madman. Lucy Gibbon had been slaughtered on 24 August . . . over ninety knife-wounds leaving her in a lake of her own blood. Dorothea Jonson had died on 21 September . . . she had been a servant-girl rather than a whore, but her death had marked the first of the disembowelments. Anne Grey had also been eviscerated – virtually torn inside out – and had had her head severed into the bargain; her date with destiny had come on 4 October. The most recent of the victims was Jane Wentworth; she had been killed on 22 November . . . in a fashion which no sane person could imagine. Enclosed in a tanner's shed on a marshy reach of the Thames, just below Neckinger Wharf, which was shunned at night because of the rotted corpses of pirates which hung there, the killer had been able to take his time, and indeed he had, burning articles of the woman's clothing to light his way through the long dark hours. Bound and securely gagged, the victim had been sexually tortured with a variety of crude implements, most of them lifted from the tanner's shelf. A severe and prolonged beating had fractured many of her ribs, so that when the maniac finally cut into her, laying back the flesh in great gory flaps, a variety of soft organs had been easily within reach; one after another of these he had then removed, slicing and dicing them as the fancy took him, all within sight of her doubtless goggling eyes. Nobody could tell when death had finally claimed the poor creature, but the monster had practically emptied her before he'd ceased, slashing off her head with several brutal blows of his knife, and placing it alongside her heart in the glowing embers of the fire, where it had slowly cooked until dawn.

Kingsley listened to these facts with chill horror, though his master remained hard and unemotional.

"Only a devil would do something like this," exclaimed the servant. "Only a devil *could*."

Urmston mused. "If it is a devil, it's a devil in human guise . . . for it needs to move easily in this district without some mob coming in pursuit of it."

"The thing that confuses me most, my lord," the serjeant interrupted, "is what has the villain to gain? These women are penniless strumpets, scarcely worth robbing let alone tormenting to death."

"That is certainly a mystery."

"What, with there being no reason," the watchman added, ". . . well, I think that's what's got the people up in arms." He glanced over his shoulder. "Granted, it seems quiet now, but when the evening comes down and they get some drink inside 'em . . . be a different story then."

Urmston nodded, then pulled on a pair of leather gauntlets. "Despite that, we must proceed from this point alone."

The other watchmen looked round in astonishment. Their officer clearly thought he hadn't heard correctly. "My lord?"

"Serjeant, our duty is to catch this murderer," Urmston explained. "Yours is to catch all those other murderers who infest the borough of Southwark. Please, don't let us delay you any more."

The chief watchman remonstrated with them for several minutes over this, assuring them that any man, no matter whose warrant he carried, would be in danger if he ventured through this district unprotected. Urmston would only point to he and his servant's swords, saying that they already were protected. The fellow then advised them that there was more documentation, lists of suspects and such, which they might wish to peruse. Urmston replied that he would send for it all anon, but that in the meantime, he had questions of his own to ask. Still the serjeant argued, but the only reply he received was a command to secure any further murder scenes he came across, without touching a thing, and in that event, to send for the spy-catcher forthwith.

Shaking their heads in bewilderment, the serjeant and his company strode away into the murk.

Moments later, Urmston and his servant were back-tracking, reviewing the murder scenes again, this time for several minutes in each case. Every foot of the way, Kingsley sensed eyes upon them, sensed ragged scarecrow-figures in dark recesses, sensed thin, hungry faces glowering from the high casements. His gloved hand stayed firmly on his sword-hilt.

"I understand your reasons for this, my lord, but forgive me if I question your judgment," he muttered.

Urmston was barely listening. "All these victims," he said thoughtfully, "with the exception of the last one, were slain quickly. They *must* have been. They were lured away from the main thoroughfares, but never very far . . . and in a district where their screams would easily be heard. What . . . oh, forgive me, yes. Why else did I tell you to wear your dullest clothes today?"

Kingsley acknowledged this. Both men wore heavy black cloaks over dark, functional garments, though the sense of threat was still tangible.

"When we start asking questions, people will know us for what we are," Kingsley warned.

"They'll also know that interfering with officers of the Queen risks a flogging at the cart-arse."

The servant snorted. "Would that was all *we* risked."

Ten minutes later, they spoke to their first potential witness, though it wasn't a satisfactory interview. Close to the scene of the third murder, opposite the door to a noisy tavern called The Black Prince, they encountered a beggar. The laws of vagrancy prohibited beggars from travelling outside their home parish, lest they be deemed vagabonds and be put in the stocks, so it was the norm for such paupers to find a pitch and stick to it. Thanks to the awful ravages of St Anthony's fire, this particular fellow was limbless and thus immobile, which made it doubly possible he had been in this very spot on the evening of Lucy Gibbon's death. However, it was difficult to get any sort of answer from him. Little more than a twisted trunk swathed in tattered bandaging, his face shrivelled and wrinkled like a walnut, he was more a puppet than a real man. He even gave meaningless puppet-like answers, squawks and sniggers, and wild shakes of the head, which served to rattle the metal cup hung round his neck. Urmston put a coin in the cup, but it did no good.

"Flib-a gib . . . flib-a gib," the beggar chuckled.

"Did you see anything at all unusual that night?"

"Flib-a gib . . ."

Urmston glanced at Kingsley, irritated. Then, a harsh voice cut across them.

"You there!"

The investigators turned, to see that a ruffian had emerged from the entry to the tavern. Starkly cast on the red firelight inside, the ruffian seemed to have the build of a bear. His repeatedly scarred face was buried under a dense black beard. His eyes were small but incredibly wicked.

"Are you trying to rob my father?" he demanded. The two men also now saw that he was carrying a heavy, nobbled club. "And him suffering all the curses of hell!"

Kingsley stepped forward, barring the brute's path to his master. "You're mistaken. My lord has just *given* him money."

The ruffian's face broke into a mocking grin. His teeth were yellowed shovel-blades. "Oh . . . *your lord*, is it? Your *lord!* Am I supposed to be frightened by that?"

As always, Urmston remained icily calm. "Tell me, man,

can your father not speak? I've questioned him, but I get no answers."

The ruffian hefted the club to his shoulder. "And who are you to question folk?"

"You oaf!" said Kingsley. "This is Lord Urmston. Squire to Her Majesty's Royal Body."

"He thinks that title will shield him, does he?"

"I need no shield," Urmston replied coolly.

"Ah . . . a braggart too." The ruffian swung his club down. "You'd better listen, Mister Lord Protector of the Royal Tits, or whatever you are! We don't like strangers who go round bragging . . . or asking questions!"

"Even strangers charged with capturing the murderer of these unfortunate women?" Urmston wondered.

The ruffian seemed momentarily surprised. Then his scornful grin returned. "*You two . . . catch the Flibbertigibbet*?" He chortled.

"What did you call it?" Urmston demanded.

"By the looks of you, you couldn't catch the pox in a brothel."

"You said Flibbertigibbet," the spy-catcher replied.

"And if I did?"

"Your father said the same thing."

"Like as not."

"What is it?"

The ruffian gave a sly grin. "Oh . . . a demon. An evil ghost. It comes and goes as it pleases . . . no one can stop it."

"You claim a demon is responsible for these murders?" Kingsley wondered, unnerved.

"Not just any demon. The Flibbertigibbet."

"That's the name you people know it by?"

But now the ruffian was weary with the interview. "Enough questions!" He raised his cudgel again. "Clear out of this district now, if you know what's good for you."

"We have money," Urmston replied.

Abruptly, the man's expression changed. His eyes were suddenly alight with interest.

"We'll pay for information," the spy-catcher added.

"How much?"

"That depends on the information."

The ruffian considered for a moment. All at once, the conversation was more to his liking. "Well . . . my father reckons he's seen it."

"And can you get him to speak?" Urmston asked.

Again, the ruffian considered. He glanced over his shoulder. "Not here . . . you don't go showing your purse round here. Not if you've got any sense."

"Where then?"

"Come with me," the man said. He strode forward, picked his parent up like a sack of meal, and tramped away towards the mouth of the nearest alley. "I know somewhere we won't be disturbed."

The investigators hesitated before following. "Is it far?" Kingsley asked.

"Not far."

Realizing they had no option, they went after him, and a moment later the odd foursome were moving in procession through the drear back-streets, skipping around broken barrels and clutters of rubbish, stepping over pools of slime hardened now to gleaming black ice. It seemed as if they'd passed from the world of men into a world of shadow. The chill there had a knife-like edge to it, yet the air was ripe with the stench of putrefaction. Aside from themselves, nothing moved in the frozen, fathomless gloom.

"I'm not sure I like this, my lord," Kingsley whispered.

Urmston was about to agree, when they emerged from a crooked passage on to a stretch of open ground bisected by a single ditch, along which foul waters trickled. Instantly, it struck the investigators that they weren't alone any more. Several figures lounged against a nearby wall. Another stood on the far side of the ditch, as if waiting for them to cross.

All at once, their guide took himself ahead with hurried strides, laid down the leprous bundle that was his father, and turned sharply. Once again, the hefty cudgel was in his fist.

He laughed harshly. "At 'em, lads! They've more gold than brains, this lot!"

He raised his club and, lunging forward, swiped wildly at Urmston's head. The spy-catcher ducked it smartly, then slammed a punch into the codpiece of the ruffian's hose. With a choking gasp, the brute went down on his haunches. Urmston leaped up and drove a knee into his face, knocking him cold. But the other footpads were now gambolling forward. The first leaped apelike on to Kingsley's back. The servant was in the process of drawing his blade, but was borne down by the bandit's weight. Urmston had his own rapier out in a trice, however, and moved swiftly against the remaining three. As household man to the Queen, it was necessary that he be one of England's finest swordsmen. The first cutpurse had drawn his own blade . . . a tarnished poniard, but in two quick passes, the spy-catcher had disarmed him and run him through at the shoulder. With howls of pain, blood bursting through his clutching fingers, the robber staggered away.

The remaining two, warier now, circled their opponent for a moment. One was armed with a length of chain, the other with a sledge-hammer. The hammer-man was the smaller of the two, but the eyes in his dirt-smudged face were ablaze with madness. Clearly, he was the more dangerous. A second passed before he attacked, swinging the hammer up and over his head, then down with a force that would have shattered an ox's skull. Urmston stepped nimbly to one side, then rushed in, slashing his assailant three times across the ribs, laying open not only the fellow's leather doublet and hessian shirt, but also the flesh beneath, so that white rib-bones glinted in the gory wounds. The man reeled back over the ditch, screaming like a child. Urmston turned quickly to the fellow with the chain. This one had less stomach for the fight. He glanced once at the crimson rapier, and then he was off, scrambling after his wounded compatriots, shouting for them to wait.

Urmston watched them go, breathing hard. Then he heard the smacking impacts of blows. He whirled around, but was relieved to see that Kingsley had finally got on top of his opponent, and though both were now caked in mud, the doughty servant was holding the other down and pounding him body and head with his right fist. It lasted only a moment or two, before the battered footpad lapsed into unconsciousness.

Urmston helped his servant to his feet. "You still throw a solid punch, my friend," he said.

"Surprised myself, my lord," Kingsley panted. "I haven't struck a man since the battle of Solway."

"A timely occasion then, a timely occasion now."

"Are *you* all right, sir?"

"I'll live . . ."

Then, a protracted groan caught their attention. They looked. Beside the stunted shape of the beggar, the first robber was slowly recovering. Urmston strode over to him, and just as the fellow's dull eyes flickered open, placed the sword-tip at his throat. The robber stiffened in alarm. "Wait . . . please!" he gasped.

Urmston put pressure on the weapon, drawing a drop of blood.

The villain's eyes bulged. "Please . . . no!"

"You know why I'm here in Southwark?" the spy-catcher wondered.

"Yes, sir."

"And still you try to waylay me!" He pressed the blade further.

"Please, my lord!" the robber begged. "Please, that hurts . . ."

"Hurts?" Urmston scoffed. "It's only because I've a mind for it, that you're still alive at all!"

"Anything . . . I'll do anything."

"Start by talking. The murders . . . what do you know?"

The robber held up helpless hands. "What does any man know?"

"Perhaps you know *more* than any man?"

"Me?"

Urmston nodded. "You discover I'm here to stop the crimes, and the next thing you attack me!"

"For God's sake, my lord," the man pleaded, "it was thievery. I attacked you to steal . . . you said you had money."

Kingsley appeared by his master's side, dabbing with a

cloth at his bloodied mouth. "That's a risky thing to admit to an officer of the crown," he remarked.

"My life clearly depends on it," the man blabbered.

"Yes it does," Urmston said.

"It's easy for the likes of you to judge," the footpad replied. "You've seen my father . . . his wits are scattered, his limbs wasted. How can I provide for him *and* my family? I look for work, but where can I find anything that pays well enough?"

Urmston curled his lip contemptuously. "You weren't looking for work when you found us."

"I was. The Black Prince *is* my work. I turn out louts and rioters. It's the only thing I know."

"Who are you?" Kingsley asked.

"Cutter, sir . . . Jack Cutter."

"Tell us about the Flibbertigibbet, Cutter," Urmston said. "Tell us everything you know."

"It's only a story . . . a legend."

"Its handiwork is real enough."

Cutter shrugged. "That's true. But those who've seen it have never seen its face. People say there are screams in the night, then a shape running . . . next, a body is found."

"This shape!" Urmston insisted. "Tell me about it!"

"Some say it's tall, others short," the ruffian replied. "One thing we all know . . . it's killed more than these Southwark whores."

Urmston and Kingsley glanced at each other.

"What do you mean?" the servant eventually asked.

"It's been among us for years . . . because Man has been sinning for years."

"But there haven't been any other murders of this sort," Urmston said.

Cutter almost laughed. "How do you know that? You been to other parishes . . . you been north of the river?"

Again, the master and servant glanced at each other, now uneasily. "Have *you* been north of the river?" Urmston asked the ruffian.

"Not lately . . . but word spreads. They say its savagery grows as Man's infamy grows."

A moment passed, then the spy-catcher withdrew his sword. "And what of *you*, Cutter? Do you believe this thing is a monster, or just a man who behaves like one?"

Cutter sat up and mopped the sweat from his brow. "I don't know. But I do know it's a curse on us." His once-threatening eyes now betrayed haunting fear. "It's a curse on us all."

That evening, bathed and scrubbed and seated by candle-light in the solar, Urmston pondered the events of the day. The responsibility of his office had never daunted him; to the spy-catcher's mind, the unmasking of felons was an analytical business, which mainly required common sense and clear, practical thought. If assessed properly, the facts would always speak for themselves . . . the who, the when, the where, the how. The "why", of course, didn't come into it. It couldn't be allowed to, it *mustn't* . . . even in this case, when the villainy was so harrowing, when the object of it was so elusive, so beyond the investigator's extensive experience.

Urmston yanked the bell-cord. Instantly, Kingsley – also now cleansed and refreshed – appeared. "My lord?"

"*You're* a travelled man, John," Urmston said. "Tell me, have you ever heard of anything like this before?"

The servant paused to think, then shook his head. "I know of criminals who've killed repeatedly for a purpose . . . to silence witnesses, or through torture to find out where valuables were hoarded. But never where the killing *itself* was the purpose." He thought about this for a moment. "A rather frightening concept, is it not?"

"Yes," his master agreed. "It is."

"Can I bring you your supper now, my lord?"

Urmston shook his head. "No thank you, John. Bring me paper and some quills. I've several-dozen letters to write."

He met a maiden in a place,
He knelt down afore her face,
He said: "Hail Mary, full of grace!"

                                        Nova! Nova!

Urmston spent the remainder of that week writing to the various bailiffs of London's parishes, and to the JPs and sheriffs of the shires and counties surrounding the city. In all cases, he stated his office, authenticating it with his seal, then explained his business. He was seeking, he said, any information at all regarding the mysterious deaths of women and girls, in the cases of which no persons had thus far been brought to justice. Even so simple a request, he knew, would be beyond the limited abilities of some of those worthy gentlemen, but his hopes were high that at least some records would be made available to him.

He wasn't to be disappointed, for over the next few days, he received a good number of replies. One or two were entirely in the negative, though several bore news of a ghastly but sadly familiar nature. In recent years, in the general London area, a variety of females, it seemed – from aged crones to infant girls – had passed into the next life through the attentions of brutal men. In many cases, as the spy-catcher expected, they were unfortunate wives or faithless mistresses, bludgeoned to death in a fit of rage or drunken madness; quite a few were the victims of robbery, throttled in their beds as intruders searched for goods, or attacked and cut down on some lonely highway. Numerous reports came from the infamous "Thicket" in Burnham, which was far to the west of London, though in all the cases there, there was evidence either of rape or theft, which was nothing new according to the sheriff of that region.

It was not a wasted exercise, however. A number of incidents, particularly and most interestingly, several from the capital's more easterly demesnes, *did* match the profile that Urmston had put to the authorities, and these he made meticulous notes on.

During the previous year, it transpired, two whores had been murdered in Southwark's neighbouring district of Bermondsey . . . several months apart, but both mercilessly savaged with a knife, one of them almost beheaded. North of the river, in the districts of Cheapside and Holborn, there had been similar killings . . . the Holborn victim had been garotted with a piece of rope, but had then been attacked so

fiercely with a heavy blade, that her body was virtually
dismembered. Similar crimes had occurred in the rural
districts to the south. The year before, a harlot had been
butchered close to Lambeth Palace; the year before that, a
farm-girl taken and killed with her own pitchfork, but only
after her abductor had beaten her, then violated her with a
stick. Most telling of all, however, were two murders which
had occurred on the same day – 29 June this very year. Two
tavern-wenches had died only minutes apart, both in the
shadow of St Paul's. One was found in a street to the rear of
the church, her corpse bearing fifty frenzied stabwounds; the
second was discovered in the cellar of a lodging-house.
Apparently, she had willingly gone down there with her
assailant – probably for an assignation – but had promptly
been thrown to the ground, kicked unconscious, then slashed
repeatedly across the throat.

Urmston assessed this data, then took the trouble of
pasting a large map to the left-hand wall in his solar. It
was an impressively detailed diagram, based on the re-
nownedly accurate engraving of the city made by Braun
and Hogenberg. He analyzed the map for a moment, then
consulted his notes and with several pins, each one tied
with a piece of scarlet thread, began to plot out specific
locations. Once he had finished, he stood back . . . and was
stunned.

A moment later, John Kingsley was summoned to the
solar. Without any ado, his master presented the map to him
and asked him what he saw there.

Kingsley mused for a moment. "A pattern of pins, my
lord."

"Each one," Urmston explained, "represents the scene of
a Flibbertigibbet murder."

The servant was taken aback. "Fourteen?"

"The tally has grown, has it not. However, that figure only
refers to slayings in the general geographic vicinity of Southwark . . . and within the last four years. I haven't even begun
to go further afield than that."

"He's been busy," the servant whispered.

. "We *assume* he's been busy," his master corrected him.

"There's no guarantee these crimes are all the work of the same man, but the evidence would suggest they are."

"Either way, it's almost too horrible to be true."

Urmston gave a cynical smile. "No, John . . . things are often too *good* to be true. But nothing is ever too *horrible*. Tell me, does this pattern remind you of anything?"

Kingsley looked closer. The map was basically two separate masses of complex, ink-drawn lines, heavily interwoven and straggling haphazardly along either side of the River Thames, with only the most minuscule and scrawled calligraphy to put name to detail. As far as he could see, the pins were arranged in a simple blotch, concentrated roughly to the map's eastern edge.

"If there's any shape at all, my lord," he said, "a spiral, maybe?" He didn't sound certain.

Urmston shook his head. "Only by a stretch of the imagination. Look again."

Kingsley did, but the answer eluded him. "Well . . ."

"Don't you see concentric rings there? Radiating out from a central point."

The servant narrowed his eyes. "Well, yes . . . I suppose. Good Lord, of course!" All at once he beheld it, saw it exactly for what it was. "It's web-like! A spider's web!"

"My thoughts too," said Urmston. "It's entirely accidental, of course . . . or is it?"

The servant's triumph turned quickly back to bewilderment. "You don't mean to say he's drawing a gigantic web?"

"Not drawing, no. In my opinion, this actually *is* a web . . . of a sort. Of a very sinister sort."

Kingsley shook his head.

"Tell me," his master asked, "where in the web do you generally find the spider?"

Kingsley thought, then indicated the very centre.

"Exactly. This is our murderer's region of conquest. And I don't doubt for one minute that he is able to dominate it the way he does, because he either lives or is employed somewhere here," Urmston pointed with his finger, "in the very middle."

According to the map, one particular building occupied

that spot. Kingsley leaned closer to inspect it. A moment passed, then he took a breath. "I know that place . . . it was formerly the Church of All Hallows."

Urmston was interested. "And now?"

"Well . . . it's a wreck, my lord. It was defaced during the early years of the reform."

"I see."

But Kingsley seemed uncomfortable with the knowledge. "The truth is . . . it's a rather unsettling place. No one goes there, as far as I'm aware."

His master gazed hard at the map. "*We* must go there, John. As soon as we can."

The Church of All Hallows, on the Southwark–Bermondsey border, was a lonely, derelict shell. Though teeming tenements hemmed it in from all sides, it was shunned by the locals, who had heard stories that ever since the place was sacked by the loutish "church-breakers" of Thomas Cromwell, only ghosts walked within its now unhallowed walls.

Urmston and Kingsley entered through the south transept, leading their horses by the reins, the clip-clopping hooves echoing eerily. Once in the main body of the building, the two men paused, awe-stricken. The high, once-multi-coloured windows had all been smashed, and chill December light cross-shafted the cavernous nave, though much of that great chamber still lay in bottomless gloom. Warily, the men proceeded. From the outset, it was evident that the venerable old building had been gutted. All its tapestries had been torn down long ago, its altar and reliquaries pillaged. The only sign of movement in there was vermin: clusters of bats visible among the arched rafters; rats scurrying between the broken pews.

"I'd hate to think our learned Anglican scholars were wrong," Urmston said quietly.

"That kind of talk could cost you your head, my lord," Kingsley replied nervously.

"Rather my head than my soul, John."

They continued to explore, stepping softly, keeping their voices low. At length, they came to the first statue. It stood on a granite plinth by the stairway to the choir, and though its face had been chiselled away and its body bore numerous ugly gashes, the marks of hammers and picks, its double-crown – made from two wreaths, one of roses and one of lillies – identified it as St Cecilia.

"The patron saint of music," Urmston said after a moment. "A lady fair of spirit as well as feature. You must ask yourselves about the men who did this, John . . . and wonder if perhaps they enjoyed their work a little too much."

The servant made no response. As a good Protestant, he had been brought up to oppose idolatry, but in his heart of hearts, like so many others, he now regretted King Henry VIII's savage attacks on Catholic shrines like this, which for so many difficult centuries had symbolized the victory of God over Mammon.

They strode on, and a few yards later came to a second statue. This one too had been vandalized, though by its bare feet and the dove perched on its right hand, it was obviously a representation of St Francis of Assisi. Similar effigies, it seemed, were ranged around the whole interior of the building. The door to the sacristy was guarded by St Bartholomew and St Dominic . . . both of these had had their heads entirely chipped off. To the north side of the altar, a figure of St James was visible, to the south St Matthew and St Lucy . . . in all cases, winter light glittered on their ragged, broken edges. Lucy's head had survived the ordeal, though an immense gash – as if denoting a monstrous sword-stroke – was visible in her delicately carved throat. Such mutilations reminded Kingsley of the many brutal punishments dealt out to real flesh and blood since this great revolution of faith had begun. The servant had been born during the reign of old Henry, a time of nonstop bloodshed and persecution, endless men and women of great name and greater deed, sent to the block; endless men and women of lesser name, to the gallows or, in several truly barbarous circumstances, to the starving-post or boiling-pot. Under Bloody Mary, an era Kingsley remembered even better, the religious tables had been turned, but little else had changed . . . every day it seemed, hurdles bearing torn and twisted bodies had been hauled

through the jeering crowds, their destination Tyburn or
Smithfield depending on the severity of their "crime".
Kingsley couldn't suppress a shudder. How the judge of
judges was viewing all this was anybody's guess.

"Great Heaven," Urmston breathed, interrupting his
servant's reverie.

Kingsley looked up, just in time for his master to hand
over the reins of his horse and walk to the statues ranged
along the church's north wall.

Several seconds passed, as Urmston took the leather notebook from his pouch and consulted it. "St Peter!" he observed aloud, before moving along to the next figure. "St
Paul!"

"My lord?" Kingsley said, approaching from behind.

The spy-catcher wore a suddenly fascinated expression.
His next words, however, were dark and doleful. "My friend
. . . I fear we are hunting an altogether new kind of criminal.
A madman certainly, but a madman who enjoys games."

"Games?"

"Macabre games, John. Puzzles of bone and viscera."

"I don't understand."

Urmston pondered for a moment, as if unwilling to believe
that he'd stumbled on so awful a truth. Eventually, he held
up the book. "You recall that earlier this year, north of the
Thames, two women were killed on the same day?"

Kingsley nodded, still nonplussed.

"Their names were Rowan Marlin and Isabel Stewart,"
Urmston said. "They both died on 29 June." He then
pointed with shaking finger to the two nearest statues.
"The feast day of St Peter and St Paul."

Kingsley looked at the statues, but only shrugged. "Coincidence, my lord."

His master nodded. "So thought I for a second. But look
again." He read further entries from the book, and in each
instance, was able to point to one of the defaced statues.
"Abigail Swift killed on 27 July, the feast day of St James;
Mary Judd killed on 8 August, the feast day of St Dominic;
Lucy Gibbon on 24 August, the feast of St Bartholomew;
Dorothea Johnson on 21 September, St Matthew's day;

Anne Grey on 4 October . . . St Francis of Assisi; the most recent, Jane Wentworth on 22 November . . . St Cecilia. Must I continue?"

The two men gazed dumbly at each other, both thinking the same terrible things: First, that the horror of these murders – these unnamable acts committed in the dead of night, in the decayed depths of the city – could only be only compounded by evidence which suggested the perpetrator was *more* than a ravening beast, which implied that, like them, he was a reasoning, thinking being; secondly, and even more chillingly, that their murderous night-stalker might even be someone of religious persuasion . . . a Catholic fanatic perhaps, a person so scarred by the events of reform that he now fought back in this most depraved manner.

"A monk?" Kingsley ventured. "Or a priest . . . driven out of his mind by our nation's assault on his faith?"

Urmston was unsure. "The fact that, whoever he is, he knows or has at least been in this church, would suggest something like that."

Kingsley glanced uneasily over his shoulder. Their eyes had largely attuned to the dimness, but certain corners were still cloaked in dusty shadow; impenetrable blackness filled apertures between pillars or lurked beyond the doors to tiny side-chapels. For a moment it was easy to imagine some humped, hooded figure lurking there, a blade of wicked steel glinting in the half-light. Kingsley imagined hands that were more like talons, fur-clad and barbed, clenching with insane rage, cowled features that were dark and brutish beyond belief, bloody drool oozing through jagged, yellow teeth . . . more a monster than a man, *the dreaded Flibbertigibbet* . . .

When his master planted a hand on his shoulder, Kingsley physically jumped.

"Oh . . . forgive me, my lord. I . . . I . . ."

"Easy, John," said Urmston, his own face its normal iron mask, unruffled by fear or doubt. "Come along. We've had a bellyful of this place . . . at least for the moment."

They rode back through the arched passage over London Bridge. Normally, the reserve of quality tradesman – silversmiths, furriers, ecclesiastical booksellers and the like – with Christmas in the offing, the tunnel was now thronging with hawkers and coster-folk of every class. Chestnuts cracked, bundled figures laughed and joked, as they huddled around glowing braziers or watched the cockfights. At the very centre of the bridge, a bear on a chain was dancing to reed-pipes, its owner jabbing it with a stick every time it threatened to go down on all fours.

Urmston and his servant saw none of it. They were too enthused by the progress they had made, but also too horrified.

"One thing we can't discount," Urmston said. "The dark pleasure with which the crimes are committed. Whoever our felon is, he commits his atrocities with great relish. What I mean to say is . . . this is not the handiwork of some run-of-the-mill maniac. These women are being killed by someone who not only knows what he is doing, but who obviously enjoys it."

Kingsley agreed. "A staunch and vengeful Catholic, who takes pleasure in extreme cruelty. It almost has the Inquisition written on it."

Urmston glanced round at his servant. "Yes . . . it does."

Neither spoke for a moment . . . they didn't need to. It was only thirteen years since the Spanish Inquisition sentenced the entire population of the Netherlands to death, and thousands were tortured and killed as a result; it was only nine years since the Huguenots of Paris were barbarously massacred . . . in their homes, in the streets . . .

"Of course . . . England is scarcely awash with inquisitors," Urmston said.

"But it was while Mary was queen," Kingsley replied.

Urmston shook his head. "Mary died twenty-three years ago. Besides, most of her torturers fled."

"What if one has returned?"

Urmston considered this. He still had his doubts, but if it transpired that some member of the zealous Catholic queen's merciless clique *was* in London, then he would most certainly want to question the fellow. It would be unthinkable not to.

"There's one way to find out for certain," he said. "Come, John . . . to the Tower."

Condemned we had remained
But he for us hath gained
In paradise afar,
Where joys unending are.

Good Christian Men, Rejoice

They entered through Traitor's Gate, the oarsman a misshapen shadow as he rowed them past one flickering torch after another. The stench, as always down there, was appalling . . . foul water and sewage. Unlike her fierce half-sister, it was not Queen Elizabeth's custom to display fragments of traitors on pikes in this close, half-drowned passage, though one particularly serious exception had been made, and even now – ten years later – the evidence was still on view. Urmston gazed with fascination at it, as they passed. It was top-half of a human skull, the lower portion having long rotted away and dropped into the water. The grisly object hung losided, the hollow eyes still pleading the lost cause of its case.

"John Store," said Urmston quietly.

Kingsley nodded. "Quite appropriate, don't you think, my lord?"

"Alarmingly so," said Urmston.

The trial of John Store, former Chancellor of Oxford, and under Queen Mary an over-eager burner of Protestants, was an unforgettable moment in recent history. Like many of his savage but also cowardly sort, the moment Mary died, Store had fled the country, hoping to find a new position abroad from which he could continue his persecutions. Rather to his surprise, however, a band of English sailors had followed him to Flanders, where they kidnapped him and brought him back. Conviction and death had followed swiftly, though perhaps too swiftly for the countless numbers of his victims whose agony at the stake he had sometimes prolonged, having them raised on spears so the flames could lick at them more slowly, or thrusting burning faggots into their faces as they tried to pray. Store would have made an ideal suspect in the Flibbertigibbet murder-mystery, but as the mouldering evidence attested, *his* reign of terror, at least, was over.

The Constable of the Tower of London, and senior custodian of all prisoners held there, was a portly gentleman of famous family name . . . Reginald Ratcliffe, and he received his guests in one of the oak-panelled state rooms of the central keep, which was now called the White Tower. He was extravagantly clad in scarlet hose, gold satin breeches and a full-skirted doublet of scarlet velvet, trimmed with rich white fur. He sported his chain of office proudly, but was an oddly jovial-looking fellow, with plump cheeks and a neat white beard and moustache. Even so, a pious frown appeared on his face when the business was explained.

"Great Glory!" he exclaimed. "And you think one of those Catholic devils has returned?"

"He might never have left, my lord Constable," Urmston replied.

"Great Glory!" Ratcliffe said again. He nodded, almost to himself. "It would explain everything, of course . . . degenerate Catholic scum. And they have the nerve to call *us* heretics."

"Can you help us?" Urmston wondered.

Ratcliffe nodded. "Certainly . . . it would be an honour to do so. If you would wait here, I'll have some refreshments brought, and then I'll send for the Book."

Urmston nodded, and stood back to wait.

Ratcliffe hurried to the door, where he stopped and shook his head. His rosy cheeks had paled to an ashen hue. "Murder is a dreadful business," he said.

"It is indeed," Urmston replied, glancing through the casement and across the courtyard to the grim stone edifice known as the Bloody Tower.

The moment Ratcliffe left, Kingsley turned to his master. "The Book?"

"They call it that but in actual fact it's several books. The Tower records . . . they tabulate all those unfortunates who have been held here, and, to a lesser extent, those public-spirited officials who've done the holding."

"I suppose it's the best we can hope for."

"It is," Urmston replied.

"At least Lord Ratcliffe seems helpful."

Urmston curled his lip. "Another sycophant, John. No different, I'm sure, from the many Catholic jailers whose names we're now casting suspicion on."

Kingsley made no further conversation. He knew his master's moods well, and detected that this was a dark one, which didn't surprise the servant. For all his service to Lord Walsingham, and despite his outward appearance of iciness, Robert Urmston was inclined towards humanism, though this tended to surface in surly rebelliousness rather than outright sympathy. If anything, the harsh regime under his father, and the intense military training of his youth – imposed on him almost as revenge for his poor schoolwork and subsequent failures in his studies for the bar – had brought this mutinous spirit to the fore, so that patriotic though he was, he regarded the great religious debates with cynicism, and felt that he owed his duty to his country rather than his country's rulers; of course, these environs, the Tower and its impregnable ramparts, were the hard granite shoulders of those rulers . . . little wonder he was ill-at-ease here. In fact, he wandered back and forth in the state room like a caged panther, even ignoring the jug of wine and plate of sweetmeats brought in for them, until at last Ratcliffe returned, weighed down with scrolls and documents.

Hurriedly, Urmston attended the Constable, who laid his various sheets and manuscripts on the table. Kingsley, who despite his master's best efforts, didn't read well, stood back and allowed his superiors to peruse the fading text. Several moments passed – moments of mutters and deep thought. Parchment rustled, dry pages were turned. Then, Ratcliffe pointed something out. "This is a name which might interest you, my lord."

Urmston read it aloud: "Raphael Vesquez, employed here at the Tower from 1553 until 1558. Vesquez . . . a Spaniard?"

Ratcliffe gave a grim smile. "A Spaniard whose activities were infamous."

"They were?"

Ratcliffe nodded. "My lord . . . I think there is someone you should meet."

Five minutes later, he had led them down two winding stairways, then along a narrow passage and into a colder and darker region of the castle. They passed through a barred portal, guarded by a stout yeoman, then down a further flight of steps, this one slippery with moss. The air in these basements was rank; noisome water dripped steadily from the crumbling brick ceilings. Kingsley felt a growing discomfort. From somewhere further below, he imagined he could hear muffled cries for help. He glanced at his master's face, but as usual, not a hint of fear or trepidation was visible.

At length, Ratcliffe bade them wait in a guard-room that was little more than an airless cell. It only had wooden barrels to sit upon, two of which had been arranged with a plank across them, to form a gaming table. The men waited in silence, and listened. There was a loud rattling of chains and a clanking of locks, but only after several minutes did Ratcliffe reappear, now in the company of a much larger man. The Constable wasted no time in presenting him.

"My lord, this is Morgeth, one of the longest-serving jailers here."

Urmston rose to his feet, eyeing the newcomer with interest. Morgeth was taller than any of them by at least a foot, and as broad as a buffalo. His great square head was shaved to the skull, though in contrast, thick stubble covered his huge bottom jaw. The eyes in his face were small and reddish, buried beneath heavy ape-like brows. His barrel body was sheathed in a creaking leather tunic, studded all over with steel points.

Morgeth bowed once, deeply. This was clearly his domain, yet he knew his place.

"Morgeth," Ratcliffe instructed him. "Tell Lord Urmston what you told me."

The jailer nodded. "The one called Vesquez, my lords," he began, in a deep, grating voice. "I remember him."

"You *remember* him?" Urmston asked. "You could only have been a boy in those days?"

Morgeth shrugged. "An apprentice. Else I'd have been chased out with all the rest, my lord . . . when Queen Mary died."

"Tell us about Vesquez," Urmston said.

"A priest, he was, my lord. A Spanish priest . . . but he spoke our tongue. He *had* to, the amount of interrogation he did."

"He carried out interrogations?"

"He was one of the worst . . . especially where the ladies were concerned."

"Just the ladies?" Urmston wondered.

"Far as I remember, my lord. He had 'em up by their thumbs, he had 'em on the rack . . . terrible beast of a man, he was."

"I seem to recall hearing that he would accompany the female prisoners to Smithfield," Ratcliffe put in, "exhorting them to repent every inch of the way. Then he would stand as close as the fire permitted, while they died . . . praying for their souls, it was said, though others reported that he was more interested in gloating over their suffering."

Kingsley was chilled as he listened. In this brooding dungeon, the dark ghosts of former days seemed closer than ever.

"I heard tell," the jailer added, "Father Vesquez used to check the wood before he would permit it to be lit . . . to make sure it was dry. Wouldn't do to have the smoke choke the poor wretches before the flames got to 'em. Once or twice, when families and friends produced their gunpowder bags and what-not . . . he had them arrested. Pain was that man's middle name. And him a priest, an all."

"And what happened to him?" Urmston wondered.

Morgeth shook his head, apparently unsure.

"After Mary died, there're no further references to him in the Book," Ratcliffe replied. "Either as jailer or prisoner."

Urmston mused. "So he went abroad?"

Ratcliffe considered this. "Like John Store, many of the worst offenders who went abroad, were brought back and punished."

"Even those who fled to Spain?"

Now the Constable smiled. "Our relationship with Spain is rocky, to say the least, my lord. But it wasn't always so. At Queen Elizabeth's coronation, Count Feria led the Spanish envoys. A wedding-match with Philip was not out of the question. Several of Mary's criminals were extradited as good-will gestures."

"But not Raphael Vesquez?"

Ratcliffe shook his head.

There was a moment of silence. Kingsley turned to his master. "Sounds like our man, my lord."

But Urmston was pensive. "Vesquez was clearly evil . . . probably deranged. But nothing we've heard here suggests he enjoyed tearing women open."

Ratcliffe gave a chuckle. "Who's to say what he enjoyed in those locked torture chambers? Hideous screams were common-place. And then of course . . . well, all the evidence got burned."

Urmston turned back to Morgeth. "Tell me . . . what did this fellow look like?"

"Cat-like, he was, my lord. Very lean. Had a black beard, long black hair . . . dark eyes, like pools of oil. I hear, at first glance, the ladies thought him very handsome."

"A regular angel of death," Ratcliffe put in, with a thin, cynical smile.

Glad tidings of great joy I bring
To you and all mankind.
        While Shepherds Watched Their Flocks By Night

"A Spanish inquisitor!" Lord Walsingham sat back behind his desk. "How utterly marvellous!"

Urmston stood facing him, one hand on his sword-hilt. "Of course, we can't be certain."

"No, I understand that . . . but well done all the same. I can hardly wait to tell the Queen."

Urmston felt a flutter of panic. "Even with this knowledge, we're no closer to catching him."

The Secretary of State dipped his quill in his ink-pot and began to scratch out various authorizations. "We will be when we increase the reward to £500. I doubt anyone who might be sheltering him could resist such temptation."

It struck Urmston at once that increasing the reward at this stage might lead to all sorts of false accusations. Anyone with tanned skin could find himself dragged into the street.

"I shall also alert George Eliot and his priest-hunters," Walsingham added.

Urmston couldn't resist a snort of disgust. "Much good he'll do us."

Walsingham smiled to himself as he wrote. "Are you an expert in economics as well as criminal investigation, Robert? We may offer a reward, but paying it is another matter. I'd sooner one of my agents made the arrest than some drunken ne'er-do-well in the Stews. That way, it won't cost us a penny."

"It would cost us even less if you cut the entirety of George Eliot's salary."

Walsingham stamped a document with his seal, and quickly began to write out another. "No jealousy, Robert, please. It doesn't matter to me which one of you apprehends the villain, so long as one of you does. Of course, we must try to ensure that he is taken alive. A grand show-trial would be the *coup de grace*."

Urmston made no reply. Here at Richmond Palace, Walsingham's study was only a corridor away from the great hall, where at this very moment the Queen was entertaining the London city bankers to a lavish Christmas feast. Bellows of laughter could be heard; there was a frantic tooting of pipes, a strumming of mandolins.

"This should be a lesson to Catholics everywhere," Walsingham remarked. "Let us hope Vesquez is a Jesuit . . . the knowledge that one of their elite warriors has stooped to such dastardly crimes would be a sickening blow."

"It would certainly make a change from their rising to the heroism of martyrdom," Urmston replied.

The Secretary of State sealed another letter. "You've done well, Robert. Yet again I'm reminded why I tolerate your impudence." He glanced up, his grey eyes suddenly very cool. "But don't push your good fortune too far. In the event of accusations, there's only so much that even I could do to protect someone whose mother was a Catholic."

"Will that be all, my lord?"

"Even someone whose mother then converted . . . at the wise instigation of her husband, of course."

"Will that be all?"

Walsingham went back to his papers. "That'll be all."

For several days, the forces of rumour ran riot in London. With town-criers passing on the news, and posters appearing on every gable wall from Westminster to Lime Hurst, advertising an increased reward for "capture of the detestable prieste of Spayne", the sensation grew swiftly in volume until eventually even Christmas-tide was relegated to secondary chatter. Idle tongues wagged relentlessly, ominous opinions were aired about neighbours and lodgers, all sorts of calumny was cast, while the printing presses ran off hundreds of pamphlets to accompany each new item of morbid gossip. Not satisfied with this, the well-to-do were taken by litter and armed escort, to see for themselves the sordid tangle of streets where the evil deeds were being done. In knee-jerk response, the beggars flocked there too.

But only during daylight hours.

As darkness fell on Southwark, London Bridge creaked beneath wheels, hooves and feet, as a frantic mob made haste to reach safer parishes.

Only Robert Urmston, it seemed, had withdrawn from the scramble. Even a note from the Queen, congratulating him on his identification of the felon, failed to inspire him. He remained in his candle-lit solar, endlessly theorizing, making copious notes, writing and receiving letters. One day, a particular communiqué set him pacing the room like a man in a trance. At length, he summoned Kingsley and bade him sit and listen.

"A cousin of mine," the master began, "who serves with the royal embassy in Paris, has recently returned to England on leave. He has heard about our Flibbertigibbet, and in an attempt to be helpful, has sent me this rather disturbing piece of information." Urmston produced a scroll and unrolled it. "Before I read it, however, tell me honestly . . . is it possible that in naming Raphael Vesquez as our chief suspect, I have been colossally presumptuous?"

"I don't follow, my lord."

"All the evidence pointing to this man is circumstantial. In fact, much of it isn't even that."

Kingsley seemed puzzled. "You can only do your best with the information you have."

Urmston nodded. "I agree absolutely. Now . . . let me tell you what my cousin writes. Eight years ago, it seems, in the Chastenoy region of France, the populace were living in terror. Some ferocious individual was committing senseless attacks. The victims were women and children . . . at least five of them died, their necks broken, their throats torn." Urmston paused for a moment. "Those who survived, only did so through luck . . . to a one, they'd been horribly beaten and mauled and, in the case of the females, indecently assaulted."

Kingsley said nothing, but listened intently.

Urmston continued: "At first, in the level-headed fashion of all Frenchmen, the authorities thought they were searching for a werewolf. But when a suspect was finally apprehended, the most remarkable thing about him was that he was unremarkable. His name was Gilles Garnier. He admitted his crimes, but denied, even under torture, that he killed as a wolf. In reality, it seems, he was a simple vagrant who lived on the outskirts of St Bonnot. He was indistinguishable from the many other vagrants there, in that he was ragged, dirty and ill. He had no great powers of strength, and in fact, his appearance was not even remotely frightening."

"And was he the murderer?" the servant asked.

"Oh yes. He was tried, convicted and subsequently burned to death."

Kingsley considered for a moment. "That's a grim tale, my lord, but if he was burned, how could he be responsible for our . . ."

Urmston shook his head. "I'm not saying *he* is, John! I'm saying that *somebody* is, who may be like him." He tapped the scroll. "There are alarming similarities here. Murders committed apparently for their own sake, a city in terror, everyone convinced that some kind of monster or demon is abroad . . . and yet, at the end of it all, the killer is nobody; an ordinary man who gentlefolk wouldn't even cock a snook at if they passed him in the street."

"But could such an extraordinary thing happen twice?"

Urmston almost laughed. "Of course. If it can happen once, it can happen again and again." He paused for a moment, his brow darkening. "I wonder if this is some new madness of the downtrodden, John. The worm who finally, viciously, turns. The despised nonentity who suddenly realizes there is fame and power in the fear he can inspire."

"It would discount our Spanish inquisitor," Kingsley observed.

Urmston snorted. "I fear our Spanish inquisitor is a figment of our bigoted imagination. Think about it . . . is he not exactly the sort of criminal the English would love to believe is abusing them? A Catholic, a Spaniard!" He shook his head. "The reality is that our killer is of no such consequence . . . he's a carter, a street-sweeper, a vagabond." A worried look came over Urmston. "Is there any chance so anonymous a person can ever be caught?"

At that point, there was a loud knocking at the front door. Kingsley got up and went to answer it, leaving his master alone. A moment later, however, there were excited shouts in the vestibule, and the stammer of urgent voices. Kingsley reappeared, looking flustered in the cheek.

"They've captured him, my lord! Raphael Vesquez! He's been captured!"

"I'm glad," Urmston grunted, sitting at his table. "This is only the third or fourth one captured in the last two days."

"But, my lord . . . I think this may be different. Apparently, he surrendered himself at the Tower." Kingsley was in a visible state of growing excitement. "Under no pressure from anyone, he has confessed to being Vesquez."

Urmston looked slowly up. A thrill of excited uncertainty passed through him.

"Don't you realize what this means, my lord?" Kingsley

said. "Your first theory was right, after all. You've done it
. . . you've smoked him out!"

> All mankind will be redeemed
> Through thy sweet child-bearing,
> And out of torment brought.
>
> *Angelus ad Virginem*

Urmston went immediately to the Tower, but on his arrival
there, his exultation at the capture of Vesquez was tempered
by news that the Spaniard had already been put on the rack.

"How dare you!" he said, as Constable Ratcliffe led him
down the dank stairwells of the White Tower. "I gave no
such orders!"

"We received a missive from Sir Francis Walsingham,"
Ratcliffe replied. "It stated that we were to commence
examination promptly, and to use all methods at our con-
venience."

"Sir Francis Walsingham may no more permit the use of
torture than your man Morgeth!" Urmston retorted. "It
requires a signed warrant from the Privy Council or the
Queen, as a man in your position should be well aware."

"But isn't this villain the Flibbertigibbet? The murderer
of a hundred women!"

"It wouldn't matter if he was Satan himself. The same
rules apply. We don't use torture in criminal inquiries.
English Common Law has no place for it."

"But, I thought in these circumstances . . ."

"You didn't think at all, my lord! That much is plainly
obvious."

A few moments later, they'd passed through the open cell
where Urmston and his servant had been made to wait
previously, descended another subterranean stairway and
entered an icy cold chamber, cut from wet, black stone
and reeking of sweat and offal. Rusted fetters hung on the
greasy walls; trampled, filthy straw formed a decaying carpet. In one corner lay the hideous apparatus . . . a steel
frame, eight feet long and three feet across. Stretched full-
length on it, his wrists and ankles securely manacled to the

pulleys at either end, was a naked man who looked more dead than alive. His limbs were like pipe-stems, his ribs showing clearly through grey, emaciated flesh. If this was the infamous Spaniard, he was no longer the sleek, cat-like creature of legend. His head had been shorn to bristles, and his face, also shaved, was grizzled and brutalized. At present, it was also scarlet in hue and screwed up with agony.

Urmston came warily forward. "This is him?"

Morgeth, who had been administering the torture, glanced up quickly. He hammered a wedge in beside the pulley, to maintain the tension, then stood back. The prisoner could only gasp and cringe. It was plain to see that the chains holding him were already at straining-point. The joints in his arms and legs were fully extended, threatening at any moment to dislocate. As the newcomers looked down at him, fresh sweat broke on the prisoner's brow. A thin trickle of blood seeped from the corner of his mouth.

"You are the Spanish priest, Raphael Vesquez?" Urmston asked.

The prisoner didn't even look up, let alone answer.

"He says that he is being treated unfairly, and that he will speak only to the Queen," Ratcliffe explained.

"The Queen will not see you," Urmston said. "She never comes here. You must talk to me, instead. I am her representative." Still the prisoner held his tongue. "You must speak to me, otherwise this ordeal will continue!"

"You see for yourself how stubborn he is," Ratcliffe put in. "I tell you, my lord, this may look like harsh treatment, but I have seen some Catholic fanatics hold out against it for days."

"My dear Ratcliffe," said Urmston, "he is not here because he is a Catholic, but because he is suspected of murder."

For the first time now, the prisoner glanced up. Fleetingly, there was hope in his glazed, red-rimmed eyes. Ratcliffe also glanced at the spy-catcher, an irritable curl to his lip.

"Murder is the worst crime of all, my lord," he said, "and I take my duty as a punisher of crime very seriously. However, if you wish us to cease applying this device, then we will do so, but you know perfectly well that in a case as serious as this, we would be neglecting our . . ."

"Don't tell me my duty," Urmston replied. "I'm well aware that specific occasions warrant specific methods, but I'd have preferred to leave *this* until the last resort."

"Shall I order him released?"

Urmston considered. Whether he liked it or not, torture *did* have its judicial role, and it seemed doubtful than in so vile a murder-case as this, any lawyer would quibble about its use.

"Not yet," he finally said. "Tell me . . . what were the circumstances of the arrest?"

"He came in voluntarily," Ratcliffe said. "He was wearing a monk's habit at the time. A ragged old thing of sackcloth. He also wore ashes on his head. Repenting, no doubt, for his filthy crimes . . ."

"Yes!" the Spaniard hissed, his grimace of pain suddenly a growl of rage. "*For my crimes!* When I lived and worked here . . . *when I did the things you now do!*"

He might have been Spanish in origin, but he clearly had a good command of English.

"You dog!" the Constable snarled. "You dare liken us to you!"

He signalled to Morgeth, and the jailer knocked out the wedge, re-inserted his crank-handle, and began to turn it. There were agonizing creaks of bone and sinew; Vesquez howled.

"That's enough," Urmston said. "For the moment."

Morgeth glanced round, surprised, his grip slackening.

Urmston turned back to the prisoner. "Talk to me, man . . . don't be a fool!"

"This is against God's law," the Spaniard stammered. "I came here of my own will . . ."

"What do *you* know of God's law?" Ratcliffe sneered.

"I broke it too, many times. It's why I repent . . ."

Ratcliffe glanced at Urmston. "As his penance, he claims to have been living as a mendicant, with no fixed abode."

Morgeth gave a brutish chuckle. "Doesn't sound like the Spanish priests I know."

"Why did you surrender to us?" Urmston asked the prisoner.

"I . . . I hear you are looking for me . . . Raphael Vesquez, the killer of women. I come here to declare my innocence. I have lived in this city twenty-three years, since Queen Mary died . . . never once have I sinned with women. I seek only forgiveness . . ."

"Forgiveness for what? For your crimes under Mary?"

Weakly, the prisoner nodded.

Ratcliffe gave a scornful chuckle. "Would you believe he was wearing a horsehair shirt under his habit?"

Urmston looked round at the Constable. "And that didn't tell you anything?"

Ratcliffe's mirth slowly drained away. "You don't meant to say you believe him?"

Urmston thought again . . . about the terrible suffering of the Protestant martyrs, about how Raphael Vesquez had reputedly revelled in their weeping and wailing, in their shrieks for mercy. He glanced back down at the prisoner . . . granted, this pathetic, wizened *thing* was no longer the smooth and murderous tiger of Tower memory, but did that mean he was any the less a ruthless criminal?

"I don't know what to believe," the spy-catcher admitted.

"Well I do!" Ratcliffe said. He turned to Morgeth and barked: "Rack him! Make him talk!"

The jailer threw all his weight against the crank-handle. The prisoner screamed . . .

Several times that night, the interrogators retired to consider, but at no stage were they able to agree with each other. Urmston wasn't as convinced of the prisoner's innocence as much as he was discomforted by the methods they were using. Ratcliffe continued to call on his own extensive experience, assuring his colleague that even the most heinous felons broke in the end. Each time they went back into the torture chamber, Urmston asked Vesquez, almost begged him, to confess . . . for his own sake if nothing else. He even reminded the Spaniard that the penalty for murder in England was a relatively quick death on the gallows, but the prisoner would only shake his head defiantly and proclaim that he had had nothing to do with the Southwark murders.

It was some time in the very early morning, when the prisoner, exhausted by pain, began to faint . . . not just once, but repeatedly. Each time Morgeth applied a little pressure, he would pass out . . . for progressively longer periods. One glance at his physical state was enough to prove that he wasn't shamming. His limbs were black and blue with bruises, and twisted grotesquely out of shape; at least one of his shoulders had disjointed. In the few moments he spent conscious, he raved deliriously rather than cried out. His nose began to pump out blood and mucus.

The interrogators, weary themselves, finally opted to rest. Ratcliffe ordered that Vesquez be removed from the apparatus and taken back to his cell. Morgeth obeyed, dragging the wretched man by his feet. The prisoner, mercifully unconscious again, slithered out of sight like a sack of shattered crockery. Urmston glanced up at Ratcliffe, now stripped to his shirt-sleeves, his face red as beef and beaded with the sweat of his exertions, and wondered how he could ever have considered that the Constable of the Tower was "jovial-looking". Of course, he ought to have known. No one of a jovial disposition ever became custodian of this cruel place.

Ratcliffe retrieved his jerkin, then, sensing that he was being watched, glanced around.

"I'm surprised, my lord," he said. "For a spy-catcher, you seem markedly squeamish about use of the rack."

Urmston shrugged. "Partly, I am. But mainly I'm doubtful. Any information extracted through torture is likely to be unreliable."

The Constable sighed, as if this was sadly true. "The moral way is often the hardest one to understand."

"The *moral* way?" Urmston replied.

Ratcliffe replaced his cap, and straightened it. "The rules are very simple. If a good man is put to the pains, then God will give him the strength to see it through. If he's a bad man, then he'll crack, and the torture will have served its purpose."

Urmston had to struggle to keep the scorn out of his voice. "And what, I wonder, is the time limit on this distinction? How long, for example, does he have to withstand it to prove himself good? A week, a month . . . six months? Or isn't it simply the case that, if we've a mind to it, we will continue with the torture for however long, until he proves himself bad?"

The Constable smiled to himself. "I didn't invent this system, my lord, I simply impose it. As is my duty." And with that, he turned and left.

Urmston stood there alone, feeling tired and sullied. Dawn was still far away . . . a curtain of frozen blackness hung beyond the tall, arrow-slit window. The spy-catcher didn't doubt that his ride back to Drury Lane would be a cold and lonely one.

"My lord . . . my lord."

Urmston woke slowly from a deep and dreamless slumber, his eyes still gluey with sleep. It took several moments for him to realise that his curtains had been drawn back on a day of pale but intense winter light, and that John Kingsley stood beside the bed, an uncharacteristic urgency about him.

"What . . . what time is it?" the master of the house muttered.

"One o'clock, my lord."

Urmston sat bolt upright. "In the afternoon!"

"You came home very late, my lord. I thought it better to let you sleep."

Urmston kneaded his brow. It ached as the ugly memories of the previous evening came filtering back. "My thanks, John. I . . . needed it."

"My lord," Kingsley replied, ". . . there's been another murder."

Urmston glanced sharply up. "Where?"

"On the riverside, my lord . . . Southwark."

It was the coldest day of the month so far, and despite the gnawing frost, by the time the investigators arrived a large number of people had gathered, thronging along the footpaths and adjoining alleys. They were coster-folk for the most part, porters and fish-sellers, pack-workers, warehousemen. There were so many of them that they crowded right up to the timber wharf, where only the billhooks of the Watch held them back. Even then, a road cleared amid their silent ranks when Urmston arrived. They eyed him expectantly as he passed through.

On the wharf itself, the spy-catcher found the First Officer of the Watch awaiting him. It was the same fellow they had dealt with before. He looked sickly and sallow.

"Over here, my lords," he said, pointing down towards the water's edge. "An old beggar-woman reported it. We haven't touched anything yet . . . as you instructed."

Urmston nodded. "Good fellow."

"I'm afraid it's a ghastly sight."

The two newcomers glanced down. The mud-larks hadn't yet gathered – perhaps it was too cold even for those hardy young scoundrels, though out on the water, a couple of purl-men watched silently from their skiff. The wavelets lapped sluggishly against their hull. Two or three yards from the waterline, perhaps four or five yards from the landing stage itself, what at first looked like a bundle of filthy rags was sunk several inches into the cream-smooth river mud. It *looked* like rags, but on second glance, its pale spread-eagled limbs were visible, as well as its mass of gory hair which thankfully had streaked itself down over a gashed, mutilated face.

A beating was not the cause of death here, however. Even from this distance, it was plain to see that the poor woman had been cut open from groin to throat; a glut of bloody organs now bulged upwards through the long and hideous slit. One or two gulls were already perched beside it, pecking and pulling at the red-pink innards.

Urmston pursed his lips. "God have mercy on whoever did this . . . for I won't." He turned to the serjeant. "Was anyone at all seen near-by?"

"No one, my lord. And there's not a dint in the slime, as you can see . . . no one's even been near her."

Urmston said nothing more for a moment. Beside him, Kingsley's cheeks had paled to a waxen hue. The servant stared at the ravaged carcass with numb shock. He had seen dead bodies numerous times before – in the charnel pit, on the gibbet – many with fingers and noses cropped, or visibly scarred by whip and branding-iron, but the dirt and ferocity of this attack was beyond anything in his experience. Even the battle-wounds he'd witnessed at Solway Moss were as nicks and scratches compared to this. It was as if the woman had been killed by some maddened animal.

The first-officer of the Watch grew agitated. He shifted uneasily from one foot to the other. "Shall I have her removed, my lord?" he eventually asked.

"Not yet," Urmston replied.

"As you can see, it's not a very pleasant . . ."

"Not yet, serjeant!" the spy-catcher said again. "This poor harlot is past caring about the state of her flesh . . . I'm sure that from whichever Purgatory she's watching, she'd much prefer we took all steps necessary to catch her killer . . . as unpleasant as it may be." He glanced sidelong at Kingsley. "It's invaluable that we were informed straight away, John. What we have here is an undisturbed murder scene. There'll be much we can learn from it."

Kingsley looked at his master, surprised. "But isn't it more likely the girl was killed yesterday, and dumped somewhere upstream?"

Urmston almost smiled. "And how would you deduce that?"

The servant pointed down at the unbroken sheet of slime surrounding the woman. "That's a tidal mud-flat, she's lying on. Obviously the ebb-tide left her there."

"Did it?"

"In any case, she *must've* been killed yesterday, else our Spanish friend is innocent."

Urmston considered this, then looked back at the body. "She wasn't killed yesterday, John. She was killed this morning. In the early hours, I would say."

"How can you tell?"

"Look for yourself, she's drenched in blood. Wouldn't prolonged immersion in the river have washed her clean?"

"Not necessarily."

"Then look at the dates," Urmston said. "Yesterday was 12 December. Not, as I'm aware, a holy day."

Kingsley thought about this. "Neither is . . . good grief!" His eyes widened. "Today is 13 December . . . St Lucy's day!"

His master nodded. "And isn't there a statue of St Lucy in the basilica at All Hallows?"

The first-officer of the Watch had been listening to this exchange in silence, and now couldn't resist interrupting. "But, with respect, my lord, if the woman was killed this morning, she must have been dumped here at low tide . . . when the water was out. Yet there isn't a mark in the mud around her. Surely, there'd at least be footprints, drag marks?"

Urmston shook his head. "Not if she was thrown from this wharf."

"Thrown?" The serjeant gazed at him with disbelief. "But she must be twelve feet away?"

"Stranger things have happened," said Urmston.

"Well . . . the timing of this definitely discounts our Spaniard," put in Kingsley.

"So does the fact that the victim was thrown twelve feet," his master added. "Our Spaniard is slightly built and in poor health."

The serjeant was still unable to accept it. "But whoever did this must have prodigious strength! He must be a giant . . . a monster!

"Whoever did this is the Flibbertigibbet," Urmston replied.

At this, consternation began to ripple back through the suddenly restless crowd of onlookers. People started to push and shove, to argue, to hurry away seeking refuge or to spread the terrible word. All around the wharf, the cry went up that the Flibbertigibbet had proved itself demonic; it was no ordinary killer after all . . . it was a ghoul, an ogre. The men of the Watch struggled to keep order; punches were thrown, there was shouting and screaming, arrests were made. Only Urmston remained calm in the midst of the mayhem. Even Kingsley was shaken up, suddenly feeling

PAUL FINCH

nauseous; a tremulous moment passed, then he doubled over
and vomited profusely.

His master viewed the panic-stricken scene with steely
indifference. "Exactly the same thing happened at Chastenoy, I should imagine," he said. "Where they thought it was
the *loup-garrou*."

"But, my lord," Kingsley protested feebly. "This is too
much. Surely, we *are* looking for a fiend. This must be some
sort of judgment on us."

"On us?" Urmston asked. "You mean on mankind in
general?"

"Of course."

"And why would God only punish impoverished whores
like these? Why not dukes and bishops . . . and queens?"

The servant could only shake his head. "But . . . but this
butchery . . ."

"This butchery is the work of Man, John. I told you
before, I've seen its like at Tyburn . . . at Smithfield.
There's nothing here we aren't entirely capable of ourselves."

Still feeling queasy, Kingsley put a hand to his brow.
"Then . . . who? In God's name, who?"

"I should imagine I'll be in a position to tell you that . . .
this afternoon."

The servant glanced up in astonishment. "What?"

"There are several messages I need sending," Urmston
said thoughtfully. "I'd like you, personally, to take one to
Lord Ratcliffe. Have him call out the Yeomen of the Guard
and bring them to the Church of All Hallows in Bermondsey,
at two o'clock this afternoon. Tell him we are about to
unmask the real killer and will need urgent assistance. Tell
him, also, that he must have Raphael Vesquez released and
removed to the Tower infirmary."

"I don't . . . I don't understand . . ."

"Do as I say, John. I'll explain to you anon."

To save us all from Satan's power
When we were gone astray.

God Rest Ye Merry, Gentlemen

The two men rode in silence through a town now muffled by steadily falling snow. Citizens were only fleetingly visible . . . black, crow-like shapes darting here and there against the glaring whiteness, scurrying in and out of doorways, staying no longer than they needed to in the biting chill. However, there was none of the frenzied selling and buying so common in the weeks preceding Christmas; there was no laughter, no misrule, no joyous greetings. London . . . at least this south-eastern corner of it, was a city in fear.

Urmston said nothing, even as the great edifice of All Hallows loomed towards them over the snowy thatchwork roofs. Kingsley regarded it with awe-stricken eyes. He still didn't know what it was his master had learned, but he knew the spy-catcher well enough to take him seriously. The servant held no doubts at all that on this afternoon, the identity of the Flibbertigibbet would be known. For this reason, he carried a dagger as well as his sword, and had donned an old shirt of mail beneath his sheepskin jerkin. He could only hope and pray that the letter he'd delivered to the Tower had reached the Constable promptly, and that as many soldiers as possible would respond.

When they reached the forecourt of the ruined church, they dismounted. Urmston blew on his gloved hands. "You've been very patient with me, John," he said, as they gazed up at the lowering building. Sculpted gargoyles stared back down at them . . . ironic, that these openly diabolic countenances had been allowed to remain while the saints had been defaced. "But all will be revealed. Shall we go inside?"

Urmston led the way, his servant nervously following. Before he went in, Kingsley glanced back. Nothing moved in the narrow ways between the closest tenements . . . all the facing shutters were closed. Doubtless this was to keep out the cold, though it might also have been to shut out this reviled and now-feared relic of the Catholic past.

Inside, the church was criss-crossed with slanting winter light. With every window broken and most of its doors torn from their hinges, there was no discernible change in temperature. The water in the font was lost under a film of ice;

through the various gaps in the roof, snowflakes tumbled down, coating the broken floor-tiles and smashed woodwork.

"The last time I was here, I developed a theory," Urmston said. Echoes of his voice rang back from the high vaults. "The murders, I declared, were related to the statues in this very church."

Kingsley nodded. He glanced at the once-glorious effigies, at the savage marks they bore of axe and mace. Urmston continued to stroll, veering towards the southern wall, where the image of St Lucy stood. Though it had been brutally attacked, the venerable woman was still identifiable for the plate she carried on which a pair of eyes were visible, Lucy being the patron saint of the blind.

"This statue, I think," said the investigator, "is the final proof of it. It was always possible that the coincidence of murders and certain saints' days was an accident of fate. After all, several feast-days have passed on which there were no killings. St Callistus on 14 October, St Martin on 11 November, and most recently, St. Nicholas on 6 December. It occurred to me that I might have drawn a frightfully inaccurate conclusion. However, the murder today disproved that."

"Because Callistus, Martin and Nicholas are not represented here?" Kingsley said. "But Lucy is?"

Urmston nodded. "Exactly. There have only been murders on the feast-days of the saints represented *here*. We therefore know for a fact that our killer has been in this church."

"But, my lord . . . who is he?"

His master held up a cautionary finger. "As a result of what we saw here, we originally found ourselves hunting a Catholic deranged by the events of reform."

"And that led to the arrest and torture of an innocent man," Kingsley exclaimed.

Urmston's brow creased. For a moment, his normally flint-hard eyes expressed regret. "That was my fault . . . I won't forgive myself easily. Nevertheless, the thinking was good. Given the same circumstances, I would probably take the same line again."

"So we still hunt a religious maniac?" Kingsley said.

Urmston nodded. Then his eyes hardened. "But this time no deranged Catholic . . . *this time a deranged Protestant*."

The servant was shocked, and not a little outraged. "My lord . . . the Church of England is now a successful institution. What possible reason could a Protestant have for these atrocities?"

"Perhaps," said a cold, angry voice, "he feels that the atrocities committed by Bloody Mary demanded a firmer reply than those tentative measures taken by Good Queen Bess!"

The two investigators turned slowly. Facing them from the passage to the sacristy stood the Constable of the Tower, Reginald Ratcliffe. He was harnessed for action . . . heavy gauntlets, a thick leather tunic, his sword drawn. Noticeably, however, he was alone. It didn't look as if a single soldier from the Yeomen of the Guard had accompanied him.

"Perhaps," Urmston replied, "he too is a dangerous fanatic."

Ratcliffe smiled thinly: "Perhaps he was raised in an atmosphere where churches were despoiled and saints defaced."

Urmston nodded: "And the next step of course, from desecrating the images of the saints, was desecrating their holy days."

"With a sacrifice in *real* flesh and blood," Ratcliffe added, "as the Roman Mass requires!"

Kingsley could scarcely believe what he was hearing. "You . . . *you*?" he finally stammered.

The Constable of the Tower began to circle them, swishing his rapier. "This servant of yours needs a lesson in manners."

Urmston loosed the strap on his own sword-hilt. "This servant of mine always minds his manners . . . for those who deserve it."

"It's easy for you to be judgmental," Ratcliffe sneered. "What can *you* know . . . a royal courtier, a sycophantic dandy."

Kingsley ripped out his sword and dagger. "Let me ram those words down his gullet . . ."

"Stay calm," Urmston counselled.

"While you were still at your mother's teat, being cooed over and mollycoddled," Ratcliffe scoffed, "I was riding with my father under the warrant of Thomas Cromwell, breaking down church doors, arresting traitorous monks and nuns. While you were learning not to pee in your swaddling, I was learning how to chisel away the faces of saints and angels, how to piss on their slashed and spat-upon portraits . . ."

"You must be proud," said Urmston.

"Oh, I am. Never more so, though, than when I was eighteen . . . when I had to stand and watch as my father burned at the stake under that hell-cat Mary! For the attack he made upon this very church!"

Kingsley snorted in derision. "How can religious war justify these demented murders?"

"Don't look too deeply into it, John," Urmston advised. "The mind of an unholy demon is impossible to fathom."

"You dare call me unholy!" Ratcliffe snapped. "You, who tried to save that Spanish bastard from the rack!"

"Enough talking!" Kingsley said, advancing. "Put up your sword, you're arrested of murder."

The Constable's lip curled. "I don't think so."

"Neither do I," Urmston put in. "John, hold your ground!"

The servant protested. "My lord, it's two to one . . ."

"Hold your ground, I say!" Urmston eyed Ratcliffe warily. "The woman killed this morning was flung twelve feet over the mud-flat. Either by a man of truly gigantic stature . . . which Lord Ratcliffe plainly is not. *Or by two men!*"

"Very clever," said a bass voice to their rear.

The investigators turned, shocked. Despite his bear-like proportions, Morgeth the jailer had stolen up on them almost unawares. He was about ten yards away when they spotted him. He stopped in his tracks, but his sword and dagger were already drawn.

"The partner in crime," said Urmston slowly. "I might have guessed."

It was more of a revelation to Kingsley, whose gaze flickered between Morgeth and the Constable as if he couldn't quite believe it. The idea that one person had embarked on so ghastly a crime-spree was horrible enough, but *two?* . . . that was inconceivable.

"Minds equally damaged by hatred," said Urmston, as though reading his servant's thoughts.

"Not as damaged as you will be!" Ratcliffe retorted. "At them!"

Then, everything seemed to happen at once. The two killers approached from either side, the Constable of the Tower warily, but Morgeth with a charge and a bull-like bellow. Instinctively, Kingsley backed away from him; he might have been a veteran of the last Anglo-Scottish war, but he was neither as young nor as physically powerful as the burly jailer. He raised his weapons defiantly, but in the time it took Morgeth to scramble the ten yards between them, Urmston drew and cocked the firelock pistol he'd been hiding under his cloak, and discharged it over his servant's shoulder. The first thing Kingsley knew, there was a flash of flame and an almighty crash in his right ear . . . then smoke was everywhere and Morgeth reeling backwards, his left shoulder smashed and mangled by a livid, fist-sized wound. The jailer's expression of murderous rage swiftly transmuted to one of disbelieving agony.

Ratcliffe, who hadn't yet joined the fray, seemed stunned. He held his ground for a moment, then with a furious shout, threw himself forward. Urmston cast the empty pistol aside and whipped out his rapier . . . just in time to parry a frenzied blow. The blades flickered like streaks of silver as the two men fenced, though Urmston quickly gained the upper hand, driving his foe back towards the sacristy door. Kingsley, meanwhile, wasn't immediately able to assist his master. The mortally wounded Morgeth was still on his feet, and though his left arm now hung dead and useless, with sheer brute strength, he bullocked his way back into the fight.

Kingsley deflected one wild thrust, and cut the jailer across his neck, but like an enraged animal, Morgeth continued to attack. Indeed, a moment later, his point found Kingsley's chest, but though it punctured the leather and sheepskin, it lacked the force to penetrate the steel mesh below. The servant was then able to smash the blade down with his sword, and drive in with his dagger . . . it plunged to the hilt in Morgeth's stomach. Kingsley twisted it, and yanked it upwards, ripping meat and muscle alike. Boiling blood flowed out over his hand. The jailer's eyes almost started from his burning-red face. The servant released the dagger and backed away. With a gasp and gargle, Morgeth sank down to his knees, then pitched forward on to the flagstones.

Ratcliffe, a skilled swordsman but no match for the trained Urmston, now realized the game was up. Already bearing bloody slashes across his hands, arms and face, he savagely cut and thrust at his opponent, driving him two steps back, then turned and fled through the sacristy door. Urmston took a second to regain his breath, then followed, the puffing, panting Kingsley close at his heels. They hurried along a dark passage, which wound behind the back of the altar, then fed them out into a snow-deep graveyard. Night was falling, but Ratcliffe's trail was clearly visible . . . bright drops of blood interspersed with deep sliding footprints. The fugitive was evidently trying to weave his way through the headstones towards the distant wrought-iron gate. This *appeared* to be his ploy, but Urmston and his servant pursued carefully; at any moment, the madman could leap out and ambush them.

Reginald Ratcliffe, however, Constable of the Tower, Custodian of Royal Prisoners, would not be leaping out at anybody ever again.

The investigators rounded the next corner, and found him lying prostrate in the snow . . . his weapons discarded, a red stain slowly spreading in his fluffy white hair. Over him, lowered an ape-like shadow. Urmston and Kingsley slowed to a halt, at first unsure what this new horror was. The ape-thing rose to full height, shouldered its nobbled club and then came forward, grinning, through the swirling flakes. Immediately, they recognized the thick black beard and wicked little eyes of Jack Cutter, the ruffian of The Black Prince.

"Better late then never," said Urmston.

The footpad gave a surly shrug. "I got your message, but I had to take my father home before I could come."

"Well . . . it was a timely intervention, all the same."

Cutter kicked at the prone body. "So this is the dreaded Flibbertigibbet, eh?"

"One half of him," Urmston replied.

"Doesn't look like much, does he?"

"They never do." Urmston began wiping down his rapier with a piece of rag. "Think you can carry him?"

Cutter snorted. "Not a problem."

"Good. I'd suggest you take him to the Tower, but the Marshalsea Prison is closer. Bind him, carry him there, and present him to the warden with this note." Urmston handed over a letter. "It will fully explain the order of events."

The ruffian took it, but for moment looked uncertain. "You sure there's money in this for me?"

"You're not stupid, Cutter. You know as well as I do, there's a £500 reward."

"And I won't have to split it with you?"

Urmston shook his head. "We're paid officers of the Crown. We don't get rewards."

Kingsley had been listening to this exchange with growing disbelief. Now he felt he had no option but to intervene. "My lord . . . this is intolerable!"

His master gave him a quizzical expression.

"This cut-throat will be a rich man by midnight tonight!" the servant protested.

Urmston considered this, as he watched Cutter grab up the lifeless shape of Ratcliffe and throw it over his brawny shoulder. He nodded. "At least his limbless father will benefit."

"But Cutter's a villain!" Kingsley said. "He doesn't deserve it!"

Urmston smiled to himself. "I know."

Cutter was now making his way through the gravestones towards the gate. Kingsley shook his head in bewilderment. "My lord, why didn't you just summon the Watch . . . have *them* assist us? At least we'd have saved the State Department £500!"

His master thought about this, but then shook his head. "No, this way is better. This way, we get to see Lord Walsingham's face . . . when he has to hand over the purse."

The Vasty Deep

Peter T. Garratt

The Elizabeth period is wonderfully rich in events, characters and settings for mystery stories. In the following story Peter Garratt (b. 1949), by profession a clinical psychologist, reintroduces his investigator, Hamlet Christian, last seen in "Loves Labours, Lost?" in Shakespearean Detectives *(1998) in a mystery that takes us further back in history to the time of Owen Glendower.*

Had either of the documents that were delivered that morning arrived by itself, I would have been hard put to decide what to do about it. As, however, the two disagreeable parchments arrived in quick succession, making a decision was not so difficult.

I had washed and was breaking my fast sparingly with rye bread and apples when the Player Queen arrived as a messenger from the Earl of Derby's men, now sadly renamed the Countess of Derby's men, with the manuscript of a play. The youth had lost his queen's voice completely, and was therefore demoted to sweeping the stage and running errands till he would be ready for men's parts.

I was born a prince, and though necessity had forced me to leave my homeland and seek a precarious living in London as a privileged investigator, until that day it had not occurred to me that I might fall further down the rough steps to the cellars of society, and do the work of a clerk. It is true that many of the English nobility dabble in writing plays, and the note from the Player King invited me to use my erudition to make improvements as I saw fit, but it was clear that my main task was to make a fair copy of the scrawled manuscript, and in particular to make separate copies of the main parts for the actors. It seemed the regular clerk was ill.

The play did not even have a definite title. It was unclear whether it was Henry IV, or Hotspur, or Sir John Fastolfe. I gave the youth an apple as I started to read it. I reached a section which introduced a strange Welsh mystic called Owen Glendower. I knew nothing of him, but was fascinated to learn that he claimed to have power over demons, to be able to learn from them. I had good reason to wonder about supernatural beings, as to whether they told truth, or always served the Master of Lies.

Then another messenger arrived. He was fat and surly, and wore a large black hat and a short, embroidered doublet; like a faded version of the outfit made famous by the Queen of England's father. He said: "Mr Christian? That is, Prince Hamlet Christian?"

"Mr Christian will do." I took his letter, which was brief. It came from the owner of the madhouse where my soul-diseased, treacherous former friends Rosencrantz and Guildenstern had been confined. It stated that his fees were due for the care of these moral lunatics. Though he earnestly wished to continue offering the best possible treatment, and in particular, to stop them reinforcing their delusion (that they were agents of my uncle the King of Denmark) by writing to that corrupt monarch, they had made good progress, and if his fees went unpaid, he would have no compunction about unleashing them onto the community as sturdy beggars.

I considered stalling, but with work in hand, however clerical, decided I had no choice but to offer the keeper's messenger the bulk of my meagre savings, to purchase a little time. Before the oddly dressed fellow left, I put on my antic disposition, and wrote a letter for his master to send to King Claudius Christian, as though I was myself in his care. I wrote that I was now quite recovered from my madness, and had been rewarded by a visitation by the spirit of King Knut, who had informed me that I was to be the next king of both England and Denmark. After reflection, I crossed the last part out, writing instead that Knut's spirit had urged me to ensure the eternal friendship of England and Denmark. I felt that would cause less trouble if the letter was read by Secretary Walsingham, as it undoubtedly would be.

The expense left me with no resources save the tiny purse sent as an advance by the Player King, and no option but to accept his commission as a clerk. I dismissed the Player Queen and spent the morning reading the script. It was a strange piece, a sequel to the tragedy of the deposition of King Richard the Second. However, it was no tragedy, unless the rebel Hotspur was deemed to be the hero, and the fascinating character of Owen Glendower disappeared from the action in the middle.

I took my small purse and went to a shop where much read, corner-turned books could be bought cheaply. I selected a chronicle and repaired to a tavern, where I sat in a window reading and eating a better noon meal than usual. Then I walked down to the bridge and over the river to the Rose Theatre, base of the Derby players.

The Player King was looking harassed. His beard had not been trimmed and I fancied his hair looked thinner. He was pleased that I had agreed to work on the play, but had little time to discuss it. "It's tragical-comical-historical." he said. "The second part will include pastoral scenes, so that will be tragical-comical-pastoral-historical!" He paused and then added: "I have learned that to make a serious play on the deposition of a king, done by an Act of Parliament and not by an assassin's bodkin, appeals little to the groundlings and a lot less to the Court. I have been pressed to write a sequel, showing the consequences of that unrepeatable act, but done differently.

"King Henry IV bent the laws of England beyond the point where many would have said they were broken. He died in his bed, uneasy 'tis true but unpunished." He gave me a cold look, as though to say my own desire for revenge on the King who killed my father must go similarly unrequited. "The whole matter is uneasy, for our beloved Queen traced her line from Henry's branch and not from his victim's. Therefore I will give the clowns their day in the sun, and slide the real matter in gently, like a roll of meat into a baguette."

"What about this Welsh man Owen Glendower? He had a whole nation to avenge. And according to the chronicle, he did it well, and no one knows his fate at all."

"'Tis thought he was defeated and disappeared. Though doubtless the Welsh fancy that he will someday return. Their hills are alive with the shadowy warbands of ancient kings, waiting their moment for ever."

An unpleasant thought struck me. "You don't intend to throw his part to your clowns?"

"I'll be lucky to throw it to anyone, unless you can get the part written for some apprentice to learn. Our clerk and half our senior actors are ill. They gave up wine for Lent, and poisoned their stomachs with foul water."

In the next few days I worked uninterrupted on the play, with no company save the spider I had named Claudius, after my uncle. I had no fresh offers of work, or visitors of any kind, save a message inviting me to dine with Secretary Walsingham. I was uncertain what to make of it. Walsingham's uncle had not been the most famous man in England, but he had been the most powerful and feared, and the nephew had taken over his office and his company of spies.

The work on the play went well, though as the Player King had doubtless half-hoped, I did not have the time to improve it much. I left out some of the coarser scenes of visits to taverns by clowns, and enlarged the conversation between Glendower and Hotspur about demons. I found time to read more about Glendower. His claim, which sounded reasonable to me, was traced to a long line of Welsh princes. In history, his rising had been more successful than that of Hotspur: he gained control of most of the towns and castles of Wales, but eventually lost them again.

The most remarkable aspect of his career was the end of it. For several years he remained alive and in hiding. None of his friends would betray him, even for a reward. No outsider knew exactly when he died, nor where he was buried.

I was much impressed. A man can usually rely on his enemies to be constant, but to find the same consistence in his friends he must be blessed indeed.

I had no choice but to accept Walsingham's offer of dinner, though I could hardly expect him to offer me anything more sustaining than victuals and wine. I knew his queen would not advance me enough money to deal properly with my uncle, and if I was offered any help at all, it would be in exchange for impossible conditions, such as custom-free navigation into the Baltic for English ships.

This was Thomas Walsingham, nephew of the late master of spies. He had kept most of these men in his service, and I knew the Player King was very anxious not to anger him. We dined alone at his London house. His garb lacked the ostentation of many of the wealthy of that city, but was not drab or Puritan. It was sober rather than sombre. He asked me only briefly about Denmark, preferring to talk of the stage. He knew the classic dramas, and the work of the leading playwrights of the day. He asked if I had been to Rome, and was glad to hear I had not.

"Though we can learn, not from the Papists, from the old Romans. From their successes, and their mistakes. They say there's a theatre in Rome so vast it could seat a city, and so well built that if an actor breaks wind on the stage, it can be heard in the back row. That's where the Emperors used to put on plays to impress their policies on the people."

He paused and refilled my glass. "Or, if the censor did not do his job, agitators could put on work to rouse the rabble." Before I could reply, already thinking about Richard II and its comic sequel, he said: "I gather you are acquainted with the Earl of Derby's men?"

"Yes, though I gather the Earl died recently, and their new patron is the Countess Alice." I did not mention that I was now their acting clerk.

"You knew the late Earl?"

"I only met him briefly."

"A very promising young man. It was a tragic loss. Of course, he was Her Majesty's cousin. And there is a matter of succession."

I thought quickly: "The players know well that the Queen is in good health, so discussion of the succession is unnecessary." The Player King had informed me in no uncertain terms that such discussion was banned at Court, though it happened often in taverns.

"That is true, but I spoke of the Derby succession. The Earl was in good health, but died suddenly. His widow is with child, or says she is. She swears she will bear a son, but thus far has only daughters. The next heir, the late Earl's brother William, is kept from his inheritance."

The two discussions of succession were one. The Queen's closest cousin was a Scot, the King of that country, and the tavern-talkers were against him. Now the next cousin had died suddenly in good health, and I of all men knew what that was likely to mean. Both issues lay between an unborn child, and this brother. I admitted to not knowing him.

"William of Derby is not as brilliant as his brother was, but is open to sensible influence. It is hoped he will marry a reliable girl, daughter of the Earl of Oxford. So far, he has not agreed to the match.

"That's where you can help. Of course, I would never dream of asking someone in your exalted position to act as a spy, but it would be appropriate for you to be a diplomat. As a friend of the players, you will be well placed to hear talk about the Countess, as to how likely she is to bear a healthy son. And equally, I have advised William to himself patronize the players, and you will be able to learn if he is under any influence which might be harmful."

Not being a spy, I was offered no payment for this service, though he did inform me that my uncle could be sent "reliable information" that I was still locked up, and that Rosencrantz and Guildenstern had not returned because they were lodging in a house of ill-repute in Southwark, and looking settled into a way of life that suited their depraved natures. As I wanted Claudius to think exactly that, I found myself frugally in Walsingham's debt.

I went back to the rooms I rent over the goldsmith's shop, and stayed up late, working on the play, writing back in the comic scenes I had left out. I saw now there could be no more serious plays about the deposition of monarchs.

The next morning I delivered the text of this comic historical tragedy to the Rose myself. I found the players in an unusually sober mood. Several were absent: the rest were watching with a semblance of respect as the Player King described the theatre to a couple of people I took to be visitors of some importance. Both wore black, and I would have taken the man to be one of the Puritans who were more eager censors of the theatre than even Walsingham could have wished for, save that his black weeds were velvet and studded with jet stones, and his companion was a woman with unbound golden hair, who wore a dress of a similar yellow colour under her dark cape.

Never having learned the disposition of a messenger, I strode up to the Player King, who halted his exposition and said: "Ah, allow me to present my collaborator, the learned Mr Christian, who licks my unformed verses into shape like the whelps of a bear! This is my lord William of Derby, brother of our lamented patron, the late Earl. And Mistress Angharad Atmunt of Lan Bedrock, his protégé."

I know better than to judge by faces, and with William of Derby did not even try. His mouth had a vain and silly smile, but the eyes were less foolish. He looked at me keenly, but I sensed more melancholy than suspicion in his gaze, as though he understood that trust and affection were folly, but still regretted that that was so. As for the mistress, she was easier to assess. She had red lips and rosy cheeks, and an expression of sweetness and innocence which I knew at once to be feigned, as such expressions always are.

"How exciting!" the Earl-who-would-be commented at once. "Dare we hope that your amanuensis has completed your new play, and that we shall soon enjoy a performance?"

"We are not quite ready, my Lord. Due to sickness, we lack players for several parts. The Prince, for instance . . ."

"I could play that part!" The Player Queen had been hiding under the trapdoor in the stage: now he jumped through and declaimed: " 'Hostess, my breakfast, come! Oh, I could wish this tavern were my drum!' "

"That's Fastolfe's line!" I snapped, having burnt my remaining drop of oil the last midnight writing it back in.

"I'll play them both! Didn't I play Queen Margaret, the She-Wolf of France, in the same play as I did the Witch of Orleans? I could play Fastolfe with a few cushions!"

"With one cushion," William of Derby said. "You could play my sister-in-law, Countess Alice!"

He laughed at his own jest, perhaps to show it was one, as no one else made the effort, not even his mistress. The Player King said hastily: "Maybe the boy is ready for the Prince. But we lack anyone to play the great Welsh hero Owen Glendower, this lady's ancestor."

"But you must!" The woman spoke for the first time. Her voice was less blandly pleasant than her face; fiery and exciting, it was like the music for a masque, which displays Dido's lament for Aeneas. She looked at me; disturbingly, she said: "This gentleman knows all the lines, and he has a noble countenance, like one descended from an ancient line of kings. Does he have a part?"

I began to explain that I was no player, lamely, for I was poorer than most of them, and was almost ready to thus lower myself for payment. The Player King shrugged: "He has no part, but knows them all. But that is not enough. We have no one at all who could present a most important character: that is, the daughter of Glendower, she who married King Henry's rival Mortimer. She has to sing a song in Welsh. Our young apprentices are unlicked whelps with singing voices like diseased bats, fit only to play serving-maids. And of course they can't speak Welsh, let alone sing it!"

She looked at the would-be Earl, then at me. "Is the part written? What song do you use?"

I exclaimed: "No one said I had to write a part in Welsh! I don't . . ."

"So the play is not ready, unless you have a someone who can play a lady who speaks and sings in Welsh!!" Angharad Atmunt contrived to look utterly distraught, and her lover William said: "Of course, my dear, no actor's apprentice could sing a Welsh song well enough please those friends of mine who have heard you sing! But 'tis a pity, I had promised them a new play, and it seems they'll have to wait till Countess Alice gives birth to her pillow, which could be a long gesture . . ."

"How about herself!" the Player Queen had been staring at Angharad so fixedly she might have been a Gorgon and have turned him to stone. "If she can sing so well . . ."

The Player King interrupted: "Alas, ladies are not allowed to perform on the stage. Especially Ladies!"

Angharad's face had lit up like that of a Siren sighting a mariner in the distance whom she could lure to his doom, and the Player Queen was emboldened to say: "If I can give you a lady disguised as a man, as I often have, surely she can be a boy dressed as a lady!" He made a coarse gesture, indicating that her lasciviously full figure could be made even less boyish by some artifice. "At least let's hear her sing!"

"Of course you may!" Angharad had let her mask of innocence slip, by grinning at his lewd gesture. Now she said: "Have you an instrument?" The boy produced a little flute, scarcely better than a tin whistle, and she said: "Well, if you perform at my Lord William's house, you'll see I'm used to singing to a much better instrument, a mighty organ, but this'll have to do!" She ran through a list of songs, and it seemed both knew one the Welsh archers had sung on the field of Agincourt. Then he began to play, and she to sing.

I was entranced, though not so much as to forget my unpaid commission from Walsingham. If he wanted the Queen's cousin William to marry a sensible girl of his choice, and this Welsh harlot was William's other option, then he faced a dilemma few men would envy. For the girl had a voice as sweet and chilling as that which the enchantress Viviane had used to ensnare Merlin, as the voice of Morgan the Fay seducing the Knights of the Round Table.

William clearly felt the same way, for he clapped loudly and said: "My dear, no one of the Gaullish race has sung so well since the Lady of the Shallots sang for Sir Lance-a-clot! Now you have your players, Master Will!"

He invited the Player King and I to a meal and a glass of sack in an hour. I was obliged to discuss the arrangements for the play, but my mind was on William himself. I wanted to ask the Player King about him, but I knew it was unlikely that he would give me any useful information that was not required for my own safety. He was a man who spoke freely about distant places, historical times, and imagined persons. But of any important person of Queen Elizabeth's realm, he spoke as little as if the man himself were hiding in earshot behind an arras with a dagger, ready to spring out and avenge his name. As we left the theatre, I therefore questioned him about the woman, Angharad Atmunt:

"Will it cause you problems if she appears on the stage?"

"Probably, but to refuse could cause worse. Every company of players needs a patron of high rank. We were the Earl's men: his succession is unclear, and we dare not offend either the brother or the possible mother of his son."

"You think the Countess is not pregnant with a pillow, and will soon give birth to a son?"

"Hopefully, though so far she has managed only daughters, and none for seven years."

"What about William's Mistress . . . Angharad? Might she be a future Countess?"

"I know very little of her."

I was surprised. "But you knew she was descended from Owen Glendower!"

"I guessed. All Welsh with any pretence at nobility claim descent from Glendower. If you encourage her, she will probably claim to be descended from King Arthur himself!"

As we reached a small house in a relatively quiet street, he explained that the late Earl had left his personal property, including his great town house, to his daughters. William lived quietly and kept few servants. He greeted us in his study, alone, and offered a glass of sack. It seemed he had already partaken of a couple, for he was in a talkative mood. He took us through to his small dining room, showing us a portrait behind his own seat of the first Earl, he who had been king-maker to the first Tudor King, the Queen's grandfather. I realized the Earldom itself was a mighty prize, even if the Queen preferred her Scottish cousin as an heir, and I ventured to ask him why his relatives were trying so hard to block him from his inheritance. He shrugged:

"Block me? I think they fancy I'm a blockhead! A bit of a Nidicock! I don't know why. I have studied my books and read Latin passably well. Even Greek. I follow the plays and know their meanings. I know the play of King Richard's death and why it is not one to be put on again, which is more than my brother ever mastered! That is why I need you to perform this comedy of King Henry and Fastolfe!"

Angharad joined us at that moment. It seemed that while the cook was away she had been supervising the cook's assistant and helping him mix certain Welsh herbs for the recipe she desired. I noted that she was already exceeding her position to undertaken the duties of a wife. William greeted her warmly, bade us be seated, and said Grace in English, after which he said: "What I have never understood, is certain tendentious arguments by which my brother held he could love the Queen, and still flirt with the Pope's religion."

I was about to reply that I had been raised on Luther's arguments when Angharad interrupted: "But he was loyal! When a gang of papists tried to corrupt him, he reported them at once to Master Walsingham!"

She was a good actress, who knew men admire loyalty. I had to admit she was also a superb cook, as well as entertaining company. The meal was mutton with herbs, parsnips, and leeks, taken with a good deal of sack. After this noon meal, which continued until two, I returned to my rooms with the part of Glendower, reluctantly committed to learn it by heart, now I was an acting clerk in every sense.

I sat in my easy chair reading the part for a while, feeling tried from my labours of the previous night . . . the day was warm and I had eaten better and drunk deeper than for some time. I confess I drifted off to sleep. I had a dream, in which it seemed someone from the spirit world was trying to give me an urgent message but then I was woken by a light, but urgent, knocking at the door of my office. I woke suddenly, scarcely aware of where I was, then got to my feet unsteadily, knocking my papers to the floor, and staggered over to open the door.

It was late afternoon. The sun shone through the office window at a steep angle, so that when I saw Mistress Angharad standing in the doorway, with its light catching her golden hair, for a second I could have taken her for a genuinely distressed damsel from one of the old romances, rather than the devious harlot I knew in my heart she was.

She did not look quite so lovely as before, for her eyes were swollen and red with weeping. No doubt she had applied the juice of leeks, or perhaps onions. She rushed into my untidy office without asking leave, and stood there wringing her hands and saying: "Mr Christian! I have heard that as well as an actor and a playwrighter, you are also an investigator, and have solved many famous crimes!"

Of course this was true, for I had unmasked my father's killer, and cleared up some lesser matters after I came to London. She wailed on: "Today after you left us, I was tired from preparing the meal, and went to my own lodgings to rest, and when I arrived, I found the door on a jar, and my belongings had been rifled!"

"What! Have your valuables been purloined?"

She shook her head miserably. "Not my casket of jewels, not that they are valuable, no gold or stones, only some silver rings and brooches, they left them and even the few coins I kept in it. No, they took something far more important! They took my good name!"

I regarded her closely, again sure she wanted something and was feigning. She was affecting to not notice the impoverished state of my dishevelled apartment; indeed, as though by instinct she picked up my papers from the floor, doubtless trying to spy what they concerned, and put them on the desk. I asked her coldly how a maiden could lose her good name without her good body being present at the time.

More tears ran down her cheeks. They made no smudges, and I saw to my amazement that her face was not painted. She said: "My good name was in a lead casket which held the family records, and proved we were all legitimate. These Saxon pigs would not call me noble, for they do not allow the Welsh to hold titles or great estates, unless they forsake their language and even their Welsh names. The Queen herself is a Tudor, and her advisors Cecils, but they call themselves English now. They deny our nobility, and even like to claim our great King Arthur who defeated them so many times, was just a fable of a poet.

"My family have been gentry on the Isle of Anglesey since the time of Owen Glendower, but my mother was from another Isle called Man, which is a holding of the Derby Earls. When my parents died, I became a ward of the last Earl. He treated me well enough, but Countess Alice dislikes me, and has often asked to see a sealed box I have entrusted to me in my casket. It is an obligation never to open it except in the time of direst need, for our family, or for the Queen's family."

"So what does this box contain?"

"I'm not very sure, but I think it is the will of Owen Glendower, and documents proving the legitimacy of my ancestor Lionel Atmunt, that's Lionel ap Edmund. You see, Owen married his daughter to Edmund Mortimer, his English ally. It was given out that all their children had died, but I think one of them, Lionel, survived. By that time the English had again overrun Wales, and the rising had ended, except in the high wild country. Owen took to the hills, and no shepherd was so poor as to surrender him for reward."

She sat at the desk, and after dipping my quill into the inkwell, began sketching, on the back of one of my Glendower speeches, the same man's family tree. This alarmed me, and I found the Royal family tree, which came with the chronicle I had bought. It was convoluted, but one thing was clear: any link to the Mortimers was important, and could be dangerous. I exclaimed: "If I am right, this Edmund, your claimed ancestor, was a descendant of Lionel Duke of Clarence!" That first Lionel was the oldest of King Edward the Third's many sons to have descendants still living; but they were few, and included the Queen, her cousin the Scottish King, and that other cousin, the nidicock William of Derby. All the other lines had been cut off in the savage War of the Roses.

An odd look passed over her face, worried, almost embarrassed. I did not see pride. She said: "It was a junior branch of the Mortimer family. I only want the box that proved I am descended from Owen!"

I wondered if she could be so innocent as to not know her value in the great hidden game that was played in England. She was the pawn that could become Queen: could perhaps make a suitor, King. I said: "How many people know about this?"

"Oh, lots of people know we descend from Owen, but these English care nothing for that. As for the other, that is our secret, mine now, till the sealed box is opened."

"And you have never opened it?"

"No! There's writing on the box . . . but that's a very strange thing! It charges us not to open it unless the Tudors are in danger . . . and our family almost as an afterthought! I wonder why that should be?"

I supposed it meant the box was a fake, made a hundred years after Owen Glendower wrote his will, by which time the Tudors were kings, and any mysterious connection to them an advantage. Still, if that were so, the fake would be less dangerous than the true. I said: "I suppose you want me to look for this box?"

"Oh yes! Oh dear, dear Mr Christian, if you would!" She jumped up and flung her arms around me, a soft yet wild embrace which could have seduced a saint. Saints were less hardened by the rottenness of the world than I had become. I disentangled myself as carefully as I could, putting on the disposition of a tradesman and clearing my throat. She took the hint and said: "Of course, you will need a reward. If you can recover my casket, I will give you all the money and silver the thief left undisturbed in my room!"

I agreed, and suggested we repair at once to her rooms to investigate. She explained that she lodged in a house where nobles paid a small rent for their female wards to live while they looked for honest suitors. The landlady protected them from the other kind of men. Mostly the nobles' wives placed them there, if they did not want these nubile wenches beside their husband's hearths. In Angharad's case, Countess Alice had not wanted her to leave, and her rent was paid by William. "So everything looks proper."

I was reminded with a jolt that women are less to be trusted than anyone, and I had responded to this one's appeal as though I believed every word of it. Still, I had a more compelling commission from Walsingham. If Angharad was a dangerous influence on William, I needed to know what influence she had. What their relationship was.

So I asked.

She said in a stilted voice that William was her protector. She had very little money of her own, the revenue from a mortgaged estate of poor farmers. Officially, she was still the ward of Countess Alice, but William had smuggled her out of the great country house as his brother was dying. "It was terrible. People said awful things about how the Earl came to die. William said it would come out that he had sheltered Papists, and I was best away from there."

"I see. Do any of them know about the sealed box?"

"Countess Alice must know something. She kept asking about it."

"And William?"

"He knows about my casket of papers. I have offered to show him some but he has not yet thought it important to look."

"Not yet!" I thought quickly. "Is it your expectation that William will marry you?"

"I . . . we are not formally betrothed. But . . ." Her eyes

went down and her voice tailed off. I said firmly: "But what?"

"But he has to marry me, if he is the gentleman he seems, the noble he aspires to be!"

I took this to be an admission that she was already a fallen woman, trying to correct her status in a difficult contest with an earl's daughter who had the mighty backing of Walsingham and the Court. She was at least honest about it. Irritatingly, I felt jealous of William.

Luckily, we came then to the house where she lodged. The owner and her servant were out, as were the other lodgers, so no one challenged us as we went up to the room. Less happily, no one could say if anyone had visited or broken in while Angharad was out.

She had but one room, about the size of my own small bedchamber. It was nicely but sparsely furnished. The rug on the floor and that on the bed were alike, embroidered with an odd, swirling pattern like a maze of knots. A small chest of jewels, no bigger than the coffin of a still-born child, had been turned over on the dresser. Silver rings and coins lay scattered about. If any had been taken, more had been left. Angharad started to tidy the room, and I said: "Who could want to steal your family records? Countess Alice?"

"I don't know! I don't know why anyone should want to! I thought they wanted me to marry William!"

"They? Alice and who else wanted you to?"

"Her poor husband who died lately! I heard them talking once, he said: 'She's a silly girl, believes Welsh fables, fit to marry the nidicock!' Not that there'd been talk of marrying between the two of us! And Alice said: 'Perhaps, let's wait and see.'"

So Walsingham thought William's choice of a wife was more important than Alice did . . . or had when her husband was alive. I wondered who might have heard of the Mortimer connection if it was a family secret. She admitted that there might be a few people, but only Welsh-speaking intimates of her parents. She finished refilling the jewel-box, righted it, then said: "Of course, some people will pay more for antique things than you'd think they'd be worth. Why, I used to have another old casket for my jewels, and one of William's friends gave me twice as much for it as I paid for this one."

I spent the evening learning my part, and the next morning I put on the disposition of a collector of antique curios, and did a tour of shops full of old curiosities. I asked in particular for Welsh caskets, but recognized none, Angharad having made a sketch for me. I became an authority on Welsh lead and what was asked for it. Though the prices seemed high to me, I did not think the casket would have fetched more than the silver jewellery the thief had left. I had other troublesome thoughts: though I had lacked time to describe Angharad to Walsingham, he had other spies, many more experienced than I.

It saddened me to spy on Angharad as my uncle's men had spied on me, but that was my destiny now. I sought out the Player King, and took him to a tavern with one of the clowns, who had been born in Wales. After a few cups of sack this man was willing to talk about old Welsh families. He said the Atmunts had been great nobles, as he put it, on Anglesey since the Tudors were even greater nobles there. All had supported Glendower, of course, but when the Tudors took service with King Henry V, the Atmunts remained at home. It was he who told me that one of the Tudors had seduced the King's widow, which might have cost him his head, had his house been less noble. He proclaimed himself a bard, and translated for me many genealogical poems, but knew of no real connection between the Tudors and the Atmunts.

I was sufficiently impressed to ask the Player King why this man could not play Glendower.

"His part is Fastolfe. Why? Would you prefer to learn that one? The first house is tomorrow. Master William's request."

"Ah. Tell me, is his rival patron, the Countess, to see this play?"

"Not yet. She is resting at her country house in the north. One of her stewards was in town recently, to assure Master William that she was well and would soon give birth, but would not risk a journey."

I doubted all that, for William must be a truer nidicock than I suspected, to risk making his pillow talk if he did not believe it. But if Alice was now as concerned as Walsingham with William's marital prospects, perhaps she had asked the steward to obtain the box, in the hope it could be used to stir up some scandal against him.

I hurried off to learn my part, worried that it might not be possible to recover the box of secrets, irritated that I found myself more worried about Angharad's reputation than my reward. I slept badly that night. The wind was high and wailed through the eaves of my lodgings, like a Welsh bard lamenting the fall of a nation, the theft of its secrets.

I hurried to the theatre, confident I knew my part and could put on the disposition of Owen Glendower. I would give some dignity to his struggle to understand the world of spirits, though with an antic flavour, as it was politic to make this a comedy.

When I arrived, Angharad was already there. They were testing her voice from various parts of the stage, fearful a woman's could not fill the theatre. I went into the gallery myself to listen. Oddly, she did not sound clearest from the open apron of the stage, but from the very back, standing in the curtained recess below the balcony. I suppose it acted as a sounding-board, like the box of a stringed instrument.

I was given a rather foolish costume of a large false beard and tin armour, painted with a crest of a red dragon perched on a leek. Luckily, I had brought my own unmistakably real sword.

I had less to complain of than Angharad. They disguised her height by asking her to perform without shoes, the boy-ladies being in buskins, but made no effort to disguise her womanly figure. Instead, she wore a pillow under the back of her skirt, and two cones vast as the Pillars of Hercules in the front of her bodice. She seemed less like herself than a clown's apprentice playing the part of her. She wore a daffodil, which she said was the true symbol of Wales, but did not object to being given an oboe disguised as a leek.

During the first two acts, she played this musical vegetable very skilfully in the musical interludes, from behind the curtain. I was so entranced that I was scarcely repelled by the lascivious way her lips caressed the mouthpiece, when she noticed my eyes on her.

We were only on stage during the third act. I went on first, with a clown who had been promoted to play the doomed rebel hero Hotspur. He gave the character an absurd swagger not written in the lines, for it was no longer possible for rebels to be played as heroes.

At first all went well. The scene was building to the discussion I had inserted on the reliability of spirits. The audience laughed several times at points I had not realized were jokes; but at least they were enjoying themselves. I launched the debate with the line "I can call spirits from the vasty deep." Hotspur was supposed to reply that spirits were not to be trusted, and I that they could sometimes be the shades of those who had been trustworthy in life. Instead, he vouchsafed me a mischievous grin and declaimed: "Why so can I, or so can any man . . . But will the spirits answer!"

This brought a louder laugh than any. Someone in the box opposite me was giving a wild, high-pitched giggle. I saw it was William of Derby. He was laughing so much he was almost collapsing into the lap of a dark-haired young woman who sat next to him, looking rather less amused. I wondered whom this was: then I realized, for on his other side sat Walsingham.

"Hotspur" was milking the laughter. I nearly walked off the stage: instead I gabbled a line at him which had something about the devil in it, and we continued with the original words.

Soon after, Angharad came on to the stage with a lively but very small boy playing Hotspur's wife. I could hear his buskins clumping, and see her bare toes under the skirt. I think she already knew her rival was present: she spoke her lines in Welsh very angrily: I think they were part of a battle poem. Then came the song. Up to then, she had been pacing the stage, her costume attracting numerous base comments: but now she retreated to the place under the balcony. Later I learned that the song she gave was the lament of Morgan over the death of King Arthur. I can only say that the laughter and ribald comments ceased, till there was absolute silence all round the circle of the theatre; only the music and that sad voice, and at the end cheers, the loudest applause of the day.

The scene ended with the boy Lady Hotspur refusing very sensibly to sing the song which was in the lines for him. As soon as we were off the stage, Angharad turned to me and said: "Mr Christian, will you please escort me home!"

"What . . . to Master William's?"

"Of course not . . . did you not see who he was with? She is the daughter of an earl, not a well-liked man, but he will offer a great dowry! How can I compete, having sung bare-foot in a common theatre! Take me to my own lodging!"

Our parts were done and she was shamelessly ripping the cushions from under her clothes in front of the players, who were mostly too busy to take much notice. I took off my beard and armour, lost for words. How could I tell her that no noble in history had ever been persuaded to marry a mistress of a lower class with less dowry than a real harlot, when all I wanted to do was fall on my knees and worship her by kissing her bare feet?

I hurried her out of the theatre and through the streets, then over the bridge to the main part of the city. It was late afternoon and a wind blew off the water. I told her I had heard that Countess Alice's steward had been in town, and she replied that he had visited William a few days earlier, but he was an honest man she trusted, and anyway she though he had left London before the robbery.

I did not accept this. After all, she had trusted William. We were still discussing the matter when we reached her lodging. Without thinking, I followed her in and up the stairs. Before we had reached the top, a voice rasped out from below. "Who's there? Mistress Edmund, is it? Be careful of your reputation!"

She stopped abruptly, so I turned, and saw a woman of about forty, wearing a bonnet and a garishly coloured dress emerge from a room beside the stair. She said angrily: "You, sirrah, you with the sword! Who are you?"

I forgot myself, and forgot I was supposed to be Mr Christian, for I stomped down the stairs and shouted: "I am Hamlet, Hamlet the Dane, and I am this lady's protector, for no one else will do it!"

She stood her ground and said: "I don't care if you're the Great Dane from the Bull Tavern which chases out the drunkards when the landlord wants to get his rest! It's my duty to protect my girls, and I'll not have . . ."

Angharad interrupted: "Mistress Ridley, where have you been? I have not seen you for two whole days and I have been robbed!"

"What! I've only been at my sister's in Richmond! She's poorly, so I took the other girls . . . no use asking you! I told that cook fellow where I'd be."

"What cook fellow!" we both asked.

"Master William's cook. Bold rascal that he was, I saw the girls into the carriage then came back for my bag, found he'd been in and gone right up the stairs to your room. Thank God, you were out. Said he'd been sent to invite you to that nidicock's house, so I said be sure to tell you I . . ."

I asked: "Exactly when did this happen?"

"Two days ago, stroke of noon. I heard the noon clock as he went out, realized I was . . ."

Angharad almost wailed: "Two days ago at noon, I was already with William . . . and you and Master Will the playwrighter. I was cooking, for the cook was . . ."

She pushed past me down the stairs and ran out of the house. I followed. Of course, she was running towards William's place. I caught her up and said: "No cook would have stolen your papers and not your money, if he was stealing on his own behalf."

"No. I suppose he thought me a bastard as well as a pauper, and wanted to know for certain, before he married her money. Me, with the blood of Glendower and Mortimer!"

I said as calmly as I could: "To marry a Mortimer could be dangerous, for a cousin of the Tudors." I told her my theory of the pawn who becomes a queen. "And you have a Queen already."

She stopped abruptly in her tracks. "You're being silly. Me a Queen? No one would believe that."

"People will believe you could be . . . almost anything!" We were nearly at the house. I asked: "Will William be back from the play?"

"I doubt it. Look, it's a couple of hours off sunset. There were two acts to go, and we've been running."

"Will the servants admit you?"

"Possibly, but just in case, I have a key to a side door, which leads directly to William's chamber."

I tried to remind myself that a man's bedchamber key was the sole dowry of the harlot. Instead, I was pleased at how resourceful she was.

There was an alley beside the house, with a gate opened by the same key which then got us into the side door of the house. This led to a dark, narrow flight of stairs. At the top, another locked door led to a bedchamber, large for a small house. There was a four-poster bed sizeable enough for a man with a mistress, more family portraits, but otherwise it was sparsely furnished. There was nothing that could have been the lead box.

She said: "Over there is the door to his study. I wonder if it's locked."

It was, but I was so enraged by the nidicock's treachery that I ran at it with my shoulder and burst it open. Beyond was an airy room facing south. There were shelves of books and a large desk, on which rested a copy of an ancient bust and two lead caskets, both decorated with a knot pattern like that on Angharad's rug.

She gave a little cry and pushed past me. The larger casket was open, and half-filled with documents, mostly in Latin. The smaller was closed, but I could see that the seal had recently been broken. A corner of a document poked out. I said: "Will you read it?"

Without a word, she opened the casket and carefully removed the document. I said: "Is it the will of Owen Glendower?"

"I don't think so. It's in Welsh. Oh, it's a statement, sworn in front of two foreign bishops when he was in exile, by

Meredith Tudor. That's one of the Tudors who were Owen's cousins."

She started to read, translating as she went: "'I Meredith Tudor was once a squire to Henry IV, as my son is to Henry V. I give this statement to two bishops, to be opened in the event of great peril to my family, and also to my cousin Katherine, daughter of Glendower, to use as she sees fit. For Katie was married to Edmund, one of the Mortimers King Henry deprived of succession rights. She bore him three children who all died . . .'' Oh, this is not what I expected."

She steeled herself and read on: "'At the time of her husband's death, she conceived of another child, against her will, by an English knight whose name is black and unworthy to live even in infamy. But the child lived, and she named him Lionel ap Edmund, after her boy who died.

"Now from exile I have written to King Henry, asking protection for my family, and for Owen Glendower, his daughter, and her son, as long as I keep them in hiding, and they make no more wars. I have reminded him of the time when I was his squire, and the fastest rider in his retinue. I reminded him of the great ride I made, to the castle where the former King Richard was held, and the sealed message I took, and how the next day it was given out that King Richard had died. I did not tell him where the other copies of this letter were hidden, but I gave one to Owen's daughter, to use if her father should be taken, or if I should be attacked on returning from exile.'"

"So," I said. "Doubtless that's how Meredith Tudor's son got away with seducing Henry V's widow."

"At least that seducer married his victim!"

I said: "That letter could give you great power."

"What! It makes me illegitimate . . . descendant of . . . of . . ."

I was relieved to see that she did not realize the power of knowing that a Tudor had been accomplice to the murder of King Richard. Such power would be too dangerous.

I got her out of the house as soon as I could. She clutched the lead box as though it were a child. Nevertheless, we were only half-way down the street when William rounded the corner in a carriage, accompanied by Walsingham, but not the dark-haired girl. They pulled up at once and William jumped out. He was looking very angry, but on impulse I put a jovial disposition on and said: "Ho! Master William, you'll be glad to know I've helped your lady recover that casket of records she was so worried about!"

As I had hoped, the villain was dumbfounded by this good news. Walsingham leaned out of the carriage and said: "Anything interesting in those records?"

"I'm not sure. My Welsh isn't good. Do you read Welsh, Master William?"

He shrugged. "Nidicock Welsh. Manx of course."

"I think this record says, this lady's family are all legitimate and respectable, apart from one distant ancestor. Welsh nobility, but not English."

Walsingham invited us all to dine soon, and drove on. William stayed. He looked at Angharad and said: "My dear, why did you leave so suddenly? All London will soon be talking of your marvellous voice!"

She almost screamed at him: "You have stolen my precious . . . my good name! What is to become of me! And you let that . . . puppet-master write your marriage into his play, and you brought your Player Queen to mine!"

He looked genuinely taken aback. "But my dear, if you value the box so much, I'll have one just like it made in solid gold. As soon as Alice gives birth to her pillow and I have my inheritance. As for marriage . . . I never promised it. But you know, in the days of the Greeks, of their great playwrights, a learned man's courtesan had far more freedom and respect than his . . ."

"Courtesan! Mistress you mean! I'd sooner be the pillow's mistress than yours!"

So what did become of her? Luckily, the Player King had observed that her voice carried almost as well from just behind the curtain below the sounding-board balcony. So from then on, the apprentices had to mime some of their songs.

She also sometimes cooks for the players. Sometimes she offers to cook for me. There are times when the night is cold and I sense my father's spirit urging me to avenge, return to Denmark and avenge, whatever the danger. Then I know I have no use for a woman, wife or mistress.

But there are times when I weaken and let her cook. That warms me, and the nights do not seem so cold, nor cold vengeance so tempting.

A Taste for Burning

Marilyn Todd

Marilyn Todd is best known for her audacious series of mysteries set in the early days of the Roman Empire that began with I, Claudia *(1995). For this anthology, however, she wanted to write about someone whom she believes was a distant descendant of Claudia, at a time when it was perilous to be considered a witch.*

The wood wasn't dry enough to burn properly. That meant it would be slow, poor little cow. Martin Pepper took a long swig at his flagon and belched. Look at her. Tied so tight to the stake that the bonds left wheals in her already lacerated young flesh. Only a few straggly strands on her scalp hinted at the lustrous raven black hair which had, until recently, swung with heavy sensuality over her shoulders. The bulk of it had been shorn like a sheep.

She had been lively, then, this Alizon Norton. Kicking, spitting, biting, screeching, with energy enough for six as they dragged her away. She had, alternately, cursed her accusers and protested her innocence to God in a voice loud enough to wake the dead in the graveyard. After two days of dipping, of course, her voice had turned to a rasp. After a week of sleep deprivation, Alizon was barely able to mumble her protests and curses. Although it was only after the floggings that they dried up completely.

Martin upended the flagon, the wine dribbling down his unshaven chin. Where was her precious God now? He wiped his mouth with the back of his hand. Tell me. Where was her God when she she needed him most?

"Burn the witch! Burn the Devil's whore!"

Faces contorted with hatred taunted the whimpering figure. Faces belonging to decent, ordinary folk. Blacksmith Wilkes. Parson Hardwicke. All the good men and women of Sulborough Green who were gathered here today. Carpenters, apprentices, dairymaids, reapers, everyone had turned out for the spectacle and men, women and children chanted in unison.

"Stop!" Martin Pepper staggered into the crowd. "For pity's sake, allow the woman to die with some dignity!"

"It wasn't your cattle she bewitched," shouted someone from the back.

"Nor your child she cursed to be stillborn," spat Bessie Nokes.

"I had no pains in my hip until that bitch came along," someone else piped up.

"And Tom Shaw would not have fallen into his vat of boiling dye," boomed the deep, decisive voice of the blacksmith. One barrel arm was wrapped protectively around a sobbing middle-aged woman. "Jennet here would still be a wife and not be a grieving and penniless widow."

"That's right," snarled the wheelwright. "So piss off, you drunken old sod."

Roughly he pushed Martin away and instantly the rest of the crowd followed his lead, spinning the old man from one to another, their jeers of derision ringing dizzy in his ears. With a final push, Pepper was sent sprawling into the middens. He heard his flagon crack. Saw the last few dregs of his wine soak into the slime beneath him.

"Burn the witch! Burn the witch!"

The stomping of feet and the clapping of hands now accompanied the chant as the mood of the crowd reached fever pitch. Martin did not understand. A few weeks ago they'd never clapped eyes on Alizon Norton. Now they were howling for blood.

"*Burn the witch! Burn the witch!*"

Crawling under an elder tree, the old man covered his ears

with his hands and was almost glad when the order finally came.

"Light the fire, constable."

Martin Pepper noticed the constable's hesitation, his obvious distaste at the task. But the voice of Sir Jeremy Farrell did not brook disobedience. Shuffling backwards under the overhang of the branches, Martin watched as a burning brand was stuffed into the pile of branches and twigs around Alizon Norton. He was right. The wood *was* too green to burn properly. Thick black oily smoke began to swirl upwards, with no breeze to carry it away. The old man blew his nose with his fingers as twigs began to take hold and crackle. He hoped the poor bitch would take with her into the next world not the hatred and bigotry of Sulborough Green, but the beauty and serenity of these rolling Sussex downlands. That her last living moments would capture once again the exquisite song of the warbler in the apple tree, the dance of the river, the scent of the honeysuckle which scrambled over the hedgerows.

As the flames finally began to lick at Alizon Norton's bloodstained shift, Martin Pepper clasped his hands together and prayed for her soul to a God who had deserted them both.

Two weeks later, when calm had descended once more upon the inhabitants of Sulborough Green, when men scythed through fields of barley, oats and rye stripped to the waist in the searing heat of the afternoon sun, and when women and children followed behind with their gleaning baskets, and when the air rang with the sound of Blacksmith Wilkes' hammer, Miller Nokes' grinding wheel and the tap-tap-tap of the carpenter's nails, a flurry of hooves thundered down the main street.

Most of the dwellings, Eleanor noticed, were flimsy constructions of clay and twigs with no chimney and no windows, only a single door serving for both entrance of light and exit of smoke. A crew of thatchers was reroofing one of the better cottages, and a man wheeling beans had set his barrow down to chat to a woman with a babe at her hip. Piglets squealed in a sty.

Outside the Thistle & Crown Eleanor pulled her foaming horse up sharp. There were two inns in the village, on opposite sides of the green, but this was by far the larger and more prosperous of the two. The man she was seeking would be in here, not in the Magpie. Behind her, the other three horsemen of her party reined in. Signalling for them to remain seated, she jumped down and left her exhausted horse in the care of a tall, broad-shouldered ostler who smelled of juniper and fresh hay.

"Lovely day, mistress," the tavern keeper called out.

"Where is he?"

"Who?"

He knew damn well who. Eleanor glanced up the stairs, heard male laughter emanating from a room at the end of the gallery. As she placed her foot on the first wooden step, the tavern keeper laid a warning hand on her arm. The look she shot him would have melted cobblestones and he withdrew his hand as though stung.

"Which of you bastards is Farrell?"

Six men sat around the table.

"It's you, isn't it?" She marched across the panelled chamber, stopping in front of a man in his early forties with steel grey hair and eyes to match.

He leaned back in his seat, taking in the wild tumble of auburn curls, the dark flashing eyes, the dusty, if expensive brocades. "I don't believe I've had the pleasure."

"Nor will you."

The others laughed. Farrell did not. Neither did Eleanor Dearborn.

He rose at last, and bowed. "Allow me to present the other members of the Sulborough Parish Council –"

She glanced at the heavy oak table. Gaming in taverns was illegal, unless, of course, one happens to be the Justice of the Peace responsible for granting the landlord his licence. Underneath the open window, her exhausted horse snorted softly.

Eleanor swept the cards off the table with one furious stroke. "Your puppet councillors don't interest me," she hissed. Coins bounced, spun, rolled into corners, ale from their pewter mugs pooled. "I'm after the man who pulls their strings."

Chairs scraped back in indignation, voices brayed in protest. Farrell silenced the men with his hand. "Your clothes and your jewels are refined," he said coldly, "which is more than can be said for your manners. So let's both of us cut to the chase, shall we? Who are you, and what do you want?"

"What I want, you miserable bastard, is justice."

"I'm a JP," he shrugged. "Reproach goes with the territory. If you have a complaint, I suggest you see my clerk."

"If I have a complaint, I'll see a physician," Eleanor snapped. "What I want from you is an explanation. Namely, why you took it upon yourself to chargrill my sister."

That was on the Monday. By Thursday, Eleanor was no nearer to finding an answer. At least, not a truthful one.

Nor were the lies entirely confined to one side. For a start, since it would not advance her cause any, Eleanor had not given her real name. Sir Geoffrey Dearborn's distinguished reputation would be well-known even in this putrid little downland backwater – as, indeed, would the knowledge that he'd taken a bride thirty years his junior for the specific aim of siring an heir. After seven years in which the cradle rocked only with the weight of the dust, a certain amount of rumour and innuendo would also have filtered through to Sulborough Green. Eleanor's chance of dredging the truth was slim enough as it was. She could not allow it to be scuppered completely.

Sitting in the lee of the church, beside the very pond that had stretched Alizon's lungs to bursting point, she surveyed the village. Being neither on the main route between London and the south coast, or on the road which cut across the saddleback of the Downs, Sulborough Green did not prosper from passing traffic. Indeed, the high street was in such a sad state of repair that the deep ruts in July would turn into rivulets of mud with the first autumn rains.

The parish was too poor to hire itinerant workers. Witness the raggle-taggle, chimneyless huts, whose doors today were flung wide to admit as much light and fresh air as they could, but in winter would be a hotbed of stench and disease. Witness the coarse homespun clothing, the darning, the patching, the rags hanging off the backs of the children. By law, the highway surveyors were only permitted to call out the parishioners six days a year for maintenance work and when they did, local hearts were not in the job. At a time when prices were rising faster than wages and rents were soaring, clogged drainage ditches and overhanging hedgerows came second to putting food on the table.

The graveyard of St Jude's was filling up with men and women literally dropping dead from exhaustion.

Even the church itself had not escaped the run of disaster. When Parson Hardwicke returned from a visit to his bishop in Chichester back in May, it was to find vagrants had stripped St Jude's of every valuable artefact.

Under such vexing circumstances, Eleanor could see why the villagers sought a scapegoat. Times were hard, nothing was sacred, and when a stranger moved in, Alizon would have been viewed with natural suspicion. The viper settling in their midst. A focus on which to direct their anger, their helplessness, their frustration when things went wrong. In short, they had someone to blame for their troubles.

But *burning* . . .?

Eleanor stood up, shook her skirts and stared into the dark depths of the pond where Alizon Norton, bound left hand to right foot and vice-versa, would have sucked in as much breath as she could hold for her repeated ordeals beneath its weed-infested waters. Goose pimples rose on Eleanor's skin. There would have been other tortures, too, to extract the false confession that finally sealed Alizon's guilt. And flogging was one of the better ones.

However, small, albeit isolated signs of prosperity peppered the village, suggesting that at last the land was starting to reward men for their labours. One of the larger houses that she passed was having glass fitted to its windows. Another cottage was in the process of being thatched, and surely that was a physician dismounting with his bag outside the carpenter's? A black foal pranced in the paddock, chickens

484 *MARILYN TODD*

pattered and pecked, and fat bees buzzed lazily round the fragrant wayside roses.

Late afternoon, and Sulborough Green was almost deserted in the throbbing midsummer heat. Eleanor glanced down the lane to the mill, where Bessie Nokes had given birth to a stillborn son, and she shuddered. Was the miller's wife so wild with grief that she did not care whether the confession was genuine? That Alizon would have had her hands tied behind her back and left hanging like that for two, maybe three hours? Perhaps (God forbid) suspended from one of the beams of Bessie's own millhouse?

The stables adjacent to the Thistle & Crown were empty, as Eleanor had timed them to be. The horses were still out to pasture, the groom making the most of the respite with an afternoon romp with the stonemason's pretty plump wife. Inside, dust motes drifted down in the slanting rays of the sun, and from time to time a rat rustled under the straw. Up in the eaves, swallows darted back and forth to feed their ravenous broods, and the air was acid with the stench of the dung heap outside.

"Who are you?" she asked, adjusting her eyes to the gloom.

From the second stall along came a lazy movement and a tall, muscular young man eased himself slowly to his feet. "Me, miss?" His hair was dark, with a glistening shine. "Will Pike."

"So you claim," she replied, "but who are you really?"

"Will Pike," he insisted, spreading his hands. "Ostler."

"You're good with horses, Will Pike, but you're no more an ostler than I am. Your voice is too refined, your hands are too soft, your back is too straight, you have a manner more suited to silk stockings, leather shoes, lace cravats and silver studs. You are every bit a stranger here as my men and myself, and what's more –" Eleanor pointed to his tell-tale blisters "– you're a stranger to manual labour."

"If this is how modern woman is turning out –" "he clasped his hands over his heart in a wildly theatrical gesture "– what hope is there for modern man, when his every secret is probed and exposed?"

Eleanor settled herself down on a bale of hay, drew her knees up to her chin and waited.

"If you insist, my lady," he laughed, resting his shoulder against a timber upright, "then I will gladly tell you the story of a young nobleman who left home to become a travelling troubadour, a poet, musician, teller of tales. And who, to his chagrin, discovered that the price for such an indulgence all too often involves the digging of turnips, the picking of cherries and the minding of horses to keep the wolf from his lute."

There was a count of perhaps thirty. "You were listening," she said. "When I confronted Jeremy Farrell on Monday, you were underneath the window. *Listening*."

"I think you're mistaken."

"I may have my faults, Will Pike, but being wrong isn't one of them. You took my horse when I arrived, so you were aware the poor creature was only one step away from being turned into glue, it was that exhausted from the day's ride. Upstairs, I heard my horse snort beneath the window. Someone calmed him, stroked him, silenced him with kindness and the only thing the groom strokes at that time of day is the thigh of the stonemason's wife."

When he smiled, he revealed a row of even, white teeth. "Perhaps I didn't make myself clear. I meant, you were mistaken in that I might have been listening. My sole concern was for your horse."

"In which case, Will Pike, you would have led him to water. Any more dehydrated and the poor beast was jerky, yet the trough is as far from that upstairs chamber window as a Jew from Christianity." She paused, then said slowly. "I need your help, Will."

"Mine?"

"The villagers talk to you. Me they avoid like a leper, and any whom I do manage to ambush turn mute."

"Conscience," the ostler said. "They're ashamed of what happened, they want to forget it –"

"*Forget* it?" Eleanor couldn't believe what she was hearing. "Alizon Norton was burned alive on their own village green, after being tortured to confess to a crime she didn't commit! Her screams would have carried for quarter of a mile, how can they possibly forget something like that?"

"They can't. That's why there's a hayrick standing where the fire burned the grass, instead of being stacked in the field. Their shame won't permit them to talk about it, not even to one another. They're trying to, but they can't forget. Eleanor, these folk can't look their own parson in the eye, much less their victim's sister."

When the man calling himself Will Pike placed his hands on her shoulders, Eleanor inhaled his heady juniper scent.

"What happened in Sulborough Green is by no means unusual," he said softly. "When mass hysteria takes hold, it invariably ends in a tragedy and I know you find it hard to believe, Eleanor, but these people *are* deeply sorry and they *are* ashamed of what happened."

She shook his hands off her shoulders and turned away.

"Nothing can bring Alizon back," he said, "but the quicker everyone gets on with their lives, the better. Eleanor, I'm not advising forgiveness, but we all have to live with the consequences of our actions. Simply by living in the village, constantly reminded of this terrible deed, will be punishment to last them a lifetime. But you. You mustn't allow yourself to become bitter in the process."

"Oh, no?" she said thickly. "*Convicta et combusta*, Will Pike. That was how it stands in the official record. *Convicta et combusta*, and that bastard Jeremy Farrell is responsible."

"He signed the papers, yes. But before that could happen there was a proper trial by jury –"

"Which he rigged." Eleanor turned round and looked deep into the ostler's chestnut eyes. "You still don't get it, do you, Will Pike?"

"Get what?" he asked, frowning.

"*Jeremy Farrell murdered my sister.*"

"I'm sorry, Eleanor, but the notion is utterly preposterous."

Night had fallen, and they were standing beneath a large beech, its smooth bark reflected white in the moonlight. The rush of the millrace could be heard in the distance, and close at hand an owl hooted.

"You can't murder a woman simply by accusing her of being a witch."

"So you won't help me bring Farrell to justice?"

Will Pike ran a hand over his mouth. "The trouble lies more with the law, I fear, than the man who administered it. So long as there are only four pleas acceptable to the Crown – murder, robbery, arson and rape – everything else falls to the local landowner. Farrell's job as a local JP is more about appeasing peasants and settling grudges than dispensing justice to villains. It's for his constable to nab thieves and lug them off to the Assizes."

"Do you think I'm so stupid as to not understand that?" Eleanor fumed. "That I'm so fired up with anger that I can't be objective? Will Pike, the people of Sulborough Green are living so close to the bread line, they've almost fallen over the edge. Blaming Alizon Norton for their aches and pains, their sick cattle, their stillborn babies is unacceptable, but at least it's partway understandable. Half the scolds and gossips in England have been accused of witchcraft as payback by their local community! The difference is, they weren't roasted like chestnuts."

" '*Thou shalt not suffer a witch to live*'. Exodus. Check with Parson Hardwicke, if you don't believe me. The Bible is left open at that very page in St Jude's."

"Sucking in his thick lips as though he's permanently biting on a sour cherry, how else would you expect that sanctimonious creep to justify his actions? Have you seen him? Striding through the village, his skirts flapping like batwings and a prayer book tight in his hand, you'd think he was the epitome of goodness and love. The hell he is. You watch. Next week, it will be '*Vengeance is mine, sayeth the Lord*' and he'll honestly believe that excuses his conscience. Will, that man has flints for eyes."

"Am I right in concluding that Parson Hardwicke was the prosecuting counsel at the trial?"

"All right, so I'm prejudiced," Eleanor admitted. "But a year in the jailhouse interspersed with the occasional outing to the pillory tends to settle most witchcraft allegations. Alizon Norton was burned at the stake."

"Standard lynch mob behaviour," Will said sadly. "Act first, think later."

"Precisely what Farrell was banking on," she said. "He's in the perfect position to set the ball rolling, then whip up mass hysteria to such a pitch he could rush through the accusations, the confession, the trial, the execution. And another thing. Why didn't he call for the witchfinder?"

A sudden cold gripped her bones. Witchfinder. Witchpricker. Jobber. Brodder. Call him what you will, his task was to prove or disprove allegations of witchcraft. For which purpose he carried a special bodkin with which to probe the woman's flesh to find a place where it didn't bleed. *To discover the mark of the Devil* . . .

"You're shivering Eleanor. What's wrong?"

Will drew her towards him, wrapping his strong arms round her body. In the moonlight, her auburn curls shone like molten metal, and she smelled of chamomile and thyme.

"Nothing," she said, but made no move to disengage herself from his embrace. "It's just the idea of the tortures –"

He placed one finger over her lips. "Try not to think about that."

"Easy for you to say, Will. Did you actually read the list of crimes that Alizon eventually confessed to? It wasn't just the odd sick cow or someone's back pains, by the time those bastards had finished, she'd admitted to everything from night flying to fornicating with the Devil. But that still didn't give them the right to cheer Alizon's screams as living flesh blistered and fell off her bones."

"There *were* grounds for execution," Will pointed out, gently brushing a wayward strand of hair away from her eyes. "Tom Shaw was found headfirst in a vat of his own boiling dye and since no one else was around at the time and since he could not have just toppled in, it was argued that he had been pushed by the Devil. Just one day earlier, the whole village had heard Alizon curse him. It was their natural conclusion."

"Pacts with the Devil! This is nothing but propaganda, Will, put about by the church. An inversion of Christianity designed to feed off elemental human fears and make the people dependent upon the King and the clergy."

"For God's sake, Eleanor," he hissed. "Such talk is heresy and that *is* a burning offence. You know the King's obsession with demonology! He studies the subject, considers himself an authority. For your own safety, keep those views to yourself!"

"The only way I'd be in trouble would be if one of the King's agents happened to be around to report me," she said quietly. There was a beat of perhaps ten. "*Is he?*"

Will Pike stiffened. Licked his lips. "No one can hear you out here," he said tightly. "We're too far from the village, and in any case everyone there is asleep. They need all the rest they can get, before they rise for the fields at dawn."

Eleanor breathed out.

"However, while we're on the subject of executions," he said, looping his thumb in one of her curls, "the Witchcraft Act of 1604 states that it is a 'hanging offence for the devilish act of witchcraft and, by the force of the same, killing or laming their neighbours or harming their cattle.' Unanimously, the jury found Alizon Norton guilty of killing Tom Shaw."

"Then why didn't Farrell have her choke on the gallows?" His earthy, juniper scent prickled her nostrils.

"Guessing," Will said, "I would imagine it was because he didn't want the news to go beyond the parish. Hanging a witch is not as common as people make out. As you said yourself, public humiliation usually suffices, but Farrell was in a difficult position. As far as the jury was concerned, and forgetting this business of incubi, succubi and midnight flights with the Devil, what it boiled down to was that Alizon Norton killed Tom Shaw with sorcery."

"Balls."

In the darkness, Will Pike smiled. "As their landowner as well as their JP, I suspect Farrell found the quickest way to settle the unrest was to give the villagers what they asked for. The life of a stranger. Which is not to say he wanted a reputation for dispensing that kind of justice bandied about. He knew the people would be sick with contrition once it was over. Burning Alizon at the stake almost guaranteed it would be confined to the parish."

"Wrong. Farrell had her burned at the stake *because it was personal*. This is a mean and vicious way to kill someone by anybody's standards, but the worst thing of all is that Alizon's was a murder planned in cold blood. Jeremy Farrell will not get away with it, I assure you. So I'll ask you again, Will Pike. Are you going to help me?"

Another hot, blistering day dawned in the village of Sulborough Green. Blacksmith Wilkes, with his beetle brows and arms like barrels, had stopped to inquire about the health of the carpenter's wife. Inside, no doubt, the stiff-backed physician would be letting blood till the poor woman fainted, while outside his horse whinnied softly and nibbled the grass. The thatchers were making good progress on the new roof next to the Magpie and glass now shone proudly in four of the windows of the house being glazed, the remainder in place by tomorrow. Bessie Nokes, small and slender, was exchanging commiserations with Tom Shaw's widow, Jennet, both women sniffling into kerchiefs with the pain of their losses.

All these things Eleanor observed from the richly embroidered window seat in her chamber at the Thistle & Crown.

Parson Hardwicke, his long, spider's legs eating up the ground as he made his morning rounds. Children playing leap-frog on the green, chasing pigeons, chalking out squares for games of hopscotch. The constable, squat and dour, kicking Martin Pepper the resident drunk who lay spread-eagled under the stocks, snoring. That was the old man who spoke up for Alizon, yet even he would not talk to Eleanor about the execution, clamming up just like the rest, despite the guineas she offered. Getting no response from the drunkard, the constable wasted no further time and moved on.

Now there was an unpopular job, mused Eleanor. Appointed by the local JP, the office was both obligatory and unpaid. It was the constable's role to evict tramps and vagabonds, for which the parish was grateful. But equally it was his duty to report misdemeanours, in other words spy on his own, for which the parish was anything but! Generally, the post rotated annually between the various tradesmen of the parish, but were a particular individual to show aptitude for his duties, in all likelihood he would be reappointed the following Michaelmas. In cases like these, when the annual appointment becomes permanent, power invariably corrupts, especially in tight-knit communities. More than one rural constable had been found in a ditch with the back of his head caved in and the blame laid on vagrants who had never been caught . . .

As the sun began to peep over the soft rolling downs, the first of the harvesters trudged off to their labours, scythes slung over their shoulder, hot loaves of rye in their pack. Bully for them, Eleanor thought, stretching. With a cat-like yawn, she pattered back to her own comfy, four-poster bed.

"What do you think Sir Geoffrey would say if he knew I had bedded his wife?" a sleepy voice asked.

She rolled her eyes. "All right. How did you know who I was?"

"For the simple reason that last year, Ellie, my love, I played at Dearborn Hall. You were so beautiful, with your rich auburn curls, that I composed a ballad in your honour. Milady, of course," he chuckled, "didn't even spare me a glance."

"Perhaps this," she whispered, walking her fingers slowly down his breastbone, lower, lower, lower, "will compensate for milady's omission?"

Was that the best he could come up with, she wondered. Because had "Will Pike" played at Dearborn Hall, milady would have spared him more than a glance. In seven years with that doddery old fart, Geoffrey had not once succeeded in getting it up. A succession of grooms, footmen and handsome troubadours more than compensated, however. And milady would definitely not have let this one slip through the net!

"Do you believe in witchcraft, Will Pike?" she asked later, when they were both lying, panting, on their backs from exertion.

"Convinced of it," he said. "You?"

"Definitely." God, that was good. The best yet. "But Alizon Norton, I assure you, was no witch. Frankly, Will, she wasn't bright enough. So why accuse her of something like that?"

"Why, for that matter, not lure her away from the village and kill her where the crime would have passed unnoticed? She was a stranger, newly arrived in Sulborough Green a matter of weeks previously. No one here would have given a second thought to her leaving suddenly."

Eleanor said nothing. She just lay, staring up at the scarlet curtains above her.

"The idea of Jeremy Farrell killing Alizon through accusations of witchcraft is ridiculous, Ellie." Will rolled on to his side, propping himself up on one elbow and began to trace circles over her breast. "Think about it. Farrell couldn't be sure he could carry it off, and anyway you haven't told me his motive for getting Alizon out of the way."

"I don't know it."

"Ellie!"

"Well, I don't," she said honestly, warming to the arousal of his touch. "Alizon left home at the age of sixteen and I haven't seen much of her since. Can't imagine what brought her to this dreary little backwater!"

"She was a widow, I understand."

"Let's just say my sister wasn't so fortunate in her marriage as I was."

Geoffrey Dearborn's wealth and influence could have secured him a bride among the landed gentry, yet it was the auburn-haired, flashing-eyed daughter of his own tailor that he had plumped for. And Eleanor, young as she was then, had known her worth.

Just as she knew the worth of a handsome, strong-backed lover who was as insatiable as he was considerate. She rolled on top of him and lifted her hips.

"Tipper Norton was a drunk and a bully, a gambler and a liar, and, as it transpired, a footpad as well," she panted. "They hanged him in Chichester, and good riddance."

"Chichester?" Will rasped, writhing with pleasure as her

nails raked his skin. "Wasn't that where Parson Hardwicke was born?"

"That reptile wasn't born, he was hatched," Eleanor gasped, and then gasped again.

"What's the matter?" Will was alarmed by her sudden stiffening. "Did I hurt you?"

By way of answer, Eleanor rolled away. "Goddammit, I should have realized. The bribes!"

Will slumped back on the plump feather mattress and groaned. "So close," he murmured. "So very, very close." He swiped his hands through his hair in frustration. "What bribes?"

"The people of Sulborough Green are dirt poor, yet we have a carpenter who can afford a physician, a house with glazed windows, a new thatch somewhere else, and there's a black foal running around in the paddock. Horses are a luxury in these parts, Will Pike." Eleanor was pulling on her petticoat. "In fact, wasn't it the carpenter who actually saw Alizon copulating with a cloven-hoofed beast in the churchyard at midnight?"

"His wife is very ill."

"Betray a life to spare a life? What kind of morality is that? He lied for money – and I thought those eight pieces of silver came from Jeremy Farrell. Of course, it didn't. Farrell would not have been so obvious, there were other ways he could have enhanced their lives. *It was the priest.*"

Ruefully, he watched her cover her beautiful breasts with blue silk and felt a stab of desire as long russet curls tumbled over them.

"His dingy cassock is frayed and patched and his boots have gaping great holes in the soles. Where on earth would Hardwicke get that kind of money from?"

"Selling his church artefacts and putting the blame on vagabond thieves," she told him. "There was no robbery at all. I'll bet you a guinea to a goose there was no meeting with his bishop in May. That he took the stuff to London to sell it. I told you this killing was planned in advance." Eleanor squealed as warm hands cupped her breasts. "Will Pike, what the devil do you think you're doing?"

"This," he murmured. "And this. And oh yes, this as well." A slip of blue silk wafted to the floor. "Then, when we've finished what we started, I shall come with you to St Jude's and we will tackle Parson Hardwicke together. I'm not letting you walk into danger on your own."

All in all, Eleanor felt that was a pretty good deal.

So much so that she did offer a single squeak of protest when he removed her petticoat. Instead, she used it to tie his hands to the bedpost and revised her opinion of his performance in bed. No, she decided. *This* was the best yet. By a long way.

For a man of the cloth, the parson knew some distinctly unChristian terminology, but in the end he confessed everything. Sensible decision, on the whole.

Because it was either talk – or Eleanor would fire the pistol aimed straight at his stomach.

No one who had met Eleanor Dearborn doubted that she might be bluffing. From the moment she had come blazing into Sulborough Green and bearded Jeremy Farrell in his own council meeting, every man, woman and dog in the parish had her pegged as a force to be reckoned with. They were right.

She gave the churchman a count of five, before a "terrible accident" occurred in which the pistol her dear, sweet husband had given her for protection had accidentally gone off. Poor Parson Hardwicke. Such a good man, as well . . .

"One."

They were standing in the nave of St Jude's. Thick stone walls ensured the church remained refreshingly cool, even in the height of the summer, although it would be perishingly cold inside in the winter. Green glass tinted the windows, adding to the summery feel, beeswax candles lined up like soldiers on parade on the altar and Tull, the church tomcat, lay curled in a ginger ball on Jeremy Farrell's carved pew.

"Two."

While there's life, there's hope, she could see him reason, the sweat breaking out on his brow.

"Three."

Just as she could see that he was weighing up the pros and cons of snatching the pistol from her.

"Four."

"Stop!" There was panic in his voice. "Put it down, put it down."

The snout of the pistol remained level.

"Oh, God." Hardwicke slumped on to the front pew and buried his long, oval head in his hands.

His story was predictably one-sided. How, as a young curate in Chichester, he had been in love with – of all people – his Bishop's niece. And of course the inevitable happened. Jane fell pregnant. But knowing the Bishop would never countenance a marriage between a penniless curate and his niece, Hardwicke suggested the same course of action that the Bishop himself (surely?) would have advised. That Jane paid a visit to a certain surgeon in London, who was known to abort children safely. Jane, unsurprisingly, was horrified. Refused to murder her own child, she said, how dare he even suggest it, and at that point, according to Hardwicke, she stepped backwards and caught her heel in her skirt at the top of the stairs. Frantically he reached out to save her, he said, but it was too late. By the time he reached the bottom, his beloved was dead. Her neck snapped like a hare's.

He panicked, he assured Eleanor.

If he ran, he would not be implicated in any way. If he stayed, his career and his reputation would be in ruins. Jane was dead, he had to consider his own interests, he whined.

"And that was when I first met Alizon Norton," he said mournfully.

Alizon had been a servant in the house, and whereas he believed everyone was out, Alizon had been confined to bed with a megrum. When the argument broke out, she got up to listen. She had seen everything, too. Including the young curate's crucifix clutched in Jane's stiffening hand . . .

"By Alizon's reasoning," Hardwicke said, "this was proof positive that I had murdered the girl. Alizon threatened to go to the Bishop, tell him about Jane's condition, the row over abortion, and that I had deliberately pushed my darling down the stairs. It was an accident, of course, but the way Alizon told it, it looked bad."

It *was* bad, Eleanor thought. Jane would not have reached out to clutch at her lover had she been tipping backwards. Her hands would have been outstretched to cushion her fall. Instead, she clutched at whatever she could to save her own life.

Hardwicke gulped at the unwavering pistol.

"She blackmailed me," he said. "Not money. I had none. But her husband was a criminal of the vilest order. Alizon demanded I gave him an alibi from time to time, to save his neck from the gallows."

A year later, promotion brought him here, to Sulborough Green. Three more years passed. Life settled into its rhythm.

"Naturally, during one of my visits to the Bishop, I heard that Tipper Norton had finally got what he deserved. At last, the nightmare was over. I was free of that bitch's stranglehold on my life. Or so I thought."

He could not believe his eyes, he said, when she turned up in the village in May.

"'Hello, parson,' she said. Just like that. Calm as anything." Hardwicke wiped his ashen face with his hand and Tull, the church tomcat, turned around in Jeremy Farrell's pew in his sleep. "With just two words, my world crumbled," he said thickly.

"She wanted money, I suppose?"

Money was the reason she married Tipper Norton. She imagined his thieving would keep her in luxury, when the reality was he gambled and drank away his ill-gotten gains, usually before it had gone fifty yards from his victims' purses.

"She knew about the chalices and the cross inlaid with jewels. 'Sell them,' she demanded. 'Then I swear you can have your crucifix back.' As if she meant to keep her promise, the blackmailing cow."

"You could have sent her on her way. After all this time, there was no proof, only her word against yours."

"The damage was already done. At the time, there was

some concern raised about bruising on Jane's body. Whether the Bishop believed me or Alizon, I would have been tainted with suspicion. That would have ended my prospects. They would have stripped me of even this wretched parish. I would have been *ruined*."

So he decided to kill her instead. In a way that left him totally blameless.

Witchcraft is a basic human fear. Shape-shifters, blood-suckers, unnatural lusts. It was easy. Hardwicke sold the artefacts in London, making up some cock-and-bull story about thieves breaking in while he'd been visiting his Bishop in Chichester and spinning another tale to Alizon about how payment had been deferred temporarily. Then he set about bribing the more vulnerable and needy villagers. Like the carpenter, whose wife might live with the ministrations of an expensive physician – but who would have gone straight to her coffin otherwise. Alizon Norton is a witch, he would whisper. We all know she cursed Bessie Nokes's baby and I personally have listened to her satanic chants, seen her consort with the devil. She must stand trial for witchcraft – but (and there is always a but) it would add strength to the church in its fight against evil if others had witnessed her wickedness. If anyone else could add weight to the case, then naturally the church would reward their bravery and courage in stepping forward.

When prices were outstripping wages, the temptation was too great to resist. The witch was denounced. Selling the idea to Jeremy Farrell had been easy, too, he explained. He simply reported the mood of the villagers, so that by the time Farrell saw for himself the crowds jeering and screaming outside the place where Alizon was under arrest, he needed no further convincing. JPs are no less removed from the terrors of Satanism than anyone else.

"Why kill Tom Shaw?" Eleanor asked.

"Expedience," he shrugged. "He'd made a pass at Alizon the day before – pawing at her in the alley behind the Magpie – and the world and his wife heard what she called him. Next day, I asked him to show me how he boiled his dyes . . . and tipped him in. He died instantly."

Of course, none of the villagers saw anything out of the ordinary. Who notices a priest on his rounds? He is as much a part of the scenery as the cows and the pigs and chickens –

"What I can't understand is why Alizon didn't denounce you straight away," Eleanor said. "From the minute she was arrested?"

A small, smug smile twitched at his mouth. "That was the clever part," the cleric said. "She, too, believed it was the village rising up against her, and I did nothing to dispel her fears. Instead, I told her, be patient, I would speak to Farrell on her behalf. I might despise her, I said, for blackmailing me, but it was my duty to God to see justice served, regardless of personal feelings."

In fact, he did nothing. And by the time of her trial, Alizon Norton was incoherent. He could stand up and prosecute without repercussions.

"What are you going to do now?" he asked, lifting his flinty eyes to Eleanor Dearborn's. "Denounce me? The word of a rambling, grief-stricken sister against that of a respected clergyman?"

"Ah." Eleanor smiled radiantly at the parson. "It is possible that I may have misled people on that particular matter. Alizon was not actually my sister. In fact, we weren't even related."

"What?" His jaw dropped. "Then . . ."

"Why am I here?" Her smile broadened. "Let's call it a vested interest, shall we?"

Eight months ago, Alizon had come to her for training. She had heard there was money to be made in the business of potions and charms and incantations, and Alizon, bless her, was a hard girl when it came to the readies. Eleanor quickly put her straight, though. Witchcraft, she told her, was no means to get rich.

At least not directly. Not unless you use your powers to hook yourself a rich husband.

And besides. As she had quite rightly told Will (or whatever his name was), Alizon was not bright enough to pick up the trade. You had to have a proper bent for that line of work. A vocation.

"There are some of us, you see, who don't approve of our sisters being hanged willynilly, much less burned. It troubles us."

Hardwicke clenched at his stomach. "God in heaven," he breathed.

"He may well be," Eleanor acknowledged. "But we don't believe in him any more than we believe in the Devil. What we practise is the art of healing and the promotion of well-being – interspersed, of course, with redressing what I can only describe as the occasional *imbalance*."

His face was white, and streaming with sweat. "My God," he muttered. "What are you going to do to me?"

"Nothing," she said, putting the pistol back in her soft velvet bag. "It's already done. The ale that you had with your breakfast. Tasted a little strange, did it not? Bitter?"

Gargling in the back of his throat, the parson clawed at his stomach.

"Don't bother to see me out," she trilled, as he slumped on to the floor, starting Tull, the church tomcat. "And if there is a Devil, do give him my regards, won't you?"

As she closed the door, the draught blew the pages of the Bible from Exodus to some obscure reference in Leviticus.

Up in her bedchamber in the Thistle & Crown, Eleanor packed away the last of her clothes. Outside the window, four horses snickered irritably. The ostler was not there to soothe them and the groom was too busy nursing his bruises to bother. The groom couldn't understand it. The stonemason *never* left his workplace until dark. For that matter, the stonemason was equally bemused. He had just bidden a cheerful "good day" to the redheaded stranger, when he was gripped by this sudden urge to go home.

"This will get me fired, you know. Dereliction of duty."

Eleanor leaned across the bed and checked the knots of her petticoats binding Will Pike's hands to the post. "You'll survive," she said, running her hands lightly over his naked, muscular body.

Across the green, windows were glazed, roofs thatched, Bessie Nokes's grief was lessened and would be lessened further next time, when she gave birth to bouncing twin sons. Although that would not be for another eleven months yet. She must have time to grieve properly before rejoicing in her new pregnancy.

"Suppose there had been any danger?"

"Well, there wasn't," she said soothingly. "I told you, the parson wasn't at home and I decided that you were probably right, after all. Forgive and forget, and let go."

"Hm." His patrician nose wrinkled. "There's something decidedly fishy about all this."

"Apart from your name?" she laughed. "Will *Pike*, indeed!"

She leaned over and kissed him with genuine regret. Pity. She liked men with wit, intelligence, courtesy and compassion.

"I shall miss you," he said, his dark curls shining in the rays of the sun as his hands strained at the knots. "Perhaps, God willing, our paths will cross again in the future."

"I doubt that, Will Pike." She inhaled one last breath of his juniper scent to carry home with her to Winchester. "But if it's any consolation, I shall miss you, too."

She had known from the outset that he was King James's man, although she had taken him for a common spy. Except he, too, had come to investigate the unauthorized execution.

Eleanor knew this because – in his pack – she had found a small, sharp, pointed bodkin . . .